IN THE SHADOW OF VICTORY

SHADOW SERIES BOOK 4

J.E. LEAK

ISBN 978-1-955294-07-2 (eBook Edition)
ISBN 978-1-955294-08-9 (Paperback Edition)
Library of Congress Control Number: 2023923246
Edited by Pam Greer

Published by Certifiably Creative LLC
Ocala, Florida
press@certifiablycreative.com

First Printing December 2023

For my wife.

SENSITIVE CONTENT

This novel contains instances of PTSD and violent wartime experiences. While it is not the central theme of the story, it is woven into the tapestry of the characters' lives, and I am mindful that for many, such forewarning is appreciated.

CHAPTER ONE

January 1944: Paris, France

Kathryn tried not to flinch as two German soldiers approached.

They adjusted the rifles slung casually over their shoulders and eyed her up and down before positioning themselves beside her on the busy Montmartre street corner. She tightened her grip on the leather folio in her arms, then forced herself to relax. Even if they looked through her folio, they wouldn't find the troop movements hidden in invisible ink on the sheet music.

Unless someone betrayed her.

Her heart hammered in her chest, as she feared rough hands would grab her by the elbows at any moment. "You're coming with us," they would demand sternly, and without hesitation, she would throw herself into oncoming traffic rather than suffer their incarceration again.

Breathe.

Raising her chin, she swallowed her fear and reminded herself they were interested in her because she was beautiful, not because she was an OSS agent on her way to meet a resistance contact in a city swarming with Nazis.

She crossed Boulevard de Clichy as if she hadn't a care in the world and breathed a sigh of relief when the soldiers didn't follow. Turning down a cobblestone street, she headed to a music store run by an older woman she'd known in the resistance before leaving the city early in the occupation.

A small brass bell tinkled as she opened the door, and she was met with a rush of air smelling of old wood, musty paper, and tobacco smoke. Kathryn's heart rate picked up again. The smell of tobacco, instead of the herbal substitute she knew her friend smoked, probably meant Germans had been here.

"Claudette?" Kathryn called out into the empty storefront. No answer. Her instincts told her to get out of there fast, but the tuning pluck of a stringed instrument drew her to the back room. She pushed aside the curtain at the doorway and found Claudette sitting at a workbench with a small tuning fork pressed between her lips and a violin tucked beneath her chin. She drew the bow in a smooth legato stroke across the D string, then fine-tuned it until the note rang true.

"Perfect," Kathryn said.

Claudette looked up. "Ah, you made it." She rose and greeted her with *la bise*, then offered her a drag from the hand-rolled cigarette burning in the ashtray.

Kathryn declined. "Where did you get tobacco?"

"Payment from a German for restringing this masterpiece." She picked up the instrument with care. "He had the audacity to brag that it once belonged to the Conservatoire Orchestra's first violin."

"Morton Bloch?"

Claudette nodded grimly. "He was taken away last year. Bastards."

Kathryn clenched her jaw in sadness and fury. Morton was Jewish, and gay. He didn't stand a chance, and now some German was staying in his beautiful apartment and pawing his prized violin. And there was Claudette, servicing the instrument and marveling at its tone, seemingly oblivious to what it represented.

Claudette settled the violin beneath her chin again. "I can feel your disdain all the way over here, my dear. If I don't cater to the Germans, I don't have a store, and if I don't have a store …" She dashed a scale over the freshly tuned string and launched into Massenet's "Méditation" from *Thaïs*.

She was right. No store meant no cover for their resistance activities. Kathryn brought her anger under control. This was survival in an occupied city.

"I know. You scared me when you didn't answer. I thought the Germans had taken you."

Claudette set down the violin and fluttered her lashes innocently. "Why would they want me?"

Kathryn chuckled without much humor and pulled the marked sheet music from her folio. Claudette was her first contact when she returned to Paris, the one person she trusted and who shared her deep hatred of the Nazis. Claudette had been happy to see her but was wary and questioned her motives. "I'm here to finish what I started," was all Kathryn had to say. Claudette knew of Juliette's betrayal and all that came after and had declared anyone foolish enough to come back for more worthy of her trust.

"Did you have any trouble?" Claudette asked, handing her another binder of sheet music to pass along.

"No trouble."

Kathryn had been posing as a private voice tutor, which enabled her to meet up with resistance members behind closed doors all over the city. The seemingly innocent sheet music she carried was the perfect transfer device, and unless someone suspected her of something and wanted to cause trouble, she could pass a typical on-the-spot search and papers check. It didn't stop her from being paranoid though.

"You sure?" Claudette asked. "You look a little pale."

"Bit of a stressful morning. I'm fine."

Claudette nodded, but Kathryn sensed she didn't believe her.

"Don't worry, darling. You're doing well. Did Jean tell you we got that family out last week?"

"No, he didn't. I'm so glad."

"You did that."

Kathryn had been frequenting music halls and cabarets, eavesdropping on conversations, and noting unusual behavior in case the information might be useful. "I just kept my eyes and ears open and scribbled a few notes."

Claudette laughed. "Oh, yes, ho hum, just saving lives. You haven't changed. Go on, get out of here. I'll see you next week unless something comes up beforehand."

Before stepping out of the store, Kathryn looked both ways for soldiers or questionable characters. The street was empty except for a woman heading toward the bustling boulevard while fussing with the colorful scarf on her head. She pulled the scarf away and wrapped it around her neck, flipping beautiful shoulder length blonde hair from under her collar. Kathryn's breath caught.

Jenny.

It wasn't her. It couldn't be, but Kathryn hurried after her anyway. The woman crossed the boulevard with the same quick skip step Jenny had when she was trying to hurry but not run. Kathryn reached the boulevard only to get caught on the wrong side of the road by a line of traffic.

It took everything in her not to call out. She kept telling herself it wasn't her. Jenny was safe at home. Kathryn had given up everything, including Jenny's love, to make sure of it. But her heart was beating for her again, aching for her, and all the longing and grief she'd suppressed was clawing at her, propelling her blindly forward. Damn logic and truth. When she reached the other side of the boulevard, she saw the woman heading for the Metro. She raced after her, but the woman stopped, picked a stone from her wooden soled shoe, and continued on. Kathryn got a good look at her face. It wasn't Jenny. Of course it wasn't.

A crushing pain squeezed Kathryn's heart. It was like she'd lost her all over again. She grasped a lamppost for support, fearing she'd collapse on the street. How many times would she have to tell herself Jenny was gone forever? Her life was here now, with her assignment—Dr. Thierry Bouchaule. The sooner she gave herself over to that the better. She couldn't afford these ridiculous fantasies, where Jenny was going to magically show up and somehow all would be forgiven. No. She steeled her emotions and straightened, closing off her stupid heart again.

Tonight, she would be on Bouchaule's arm playing the doting American girlfriend of the lead doctor in the Nazis' biological weapons program.

This was her job, and she was damn good at it.

Kathryn gripped the edge of the art nouveau vanity in the bedroom she shared with Bouchaule and closed her eyes. The unsettling encounter with the soldiers that morning still clung to her, and it made her impending introduction to Bouchaule's social and professional world unexpectedly fraught with insecurity.

She prided herself on her composure, even if inwardly she was less than confident, but no amount of internal dialog calmed her as she prepared for Bouchaule's welcome home dinner party, to be held at an associate's grandiose estate in the Faubourg Saint-Germain. She blamed it on the upper echelon German military presence she'd been warned would be in attendance, something she promised herself she wouldn't let get to her even before they stepped foot in Paris. But with the city in chains, the swarms of soldiers, and the stench of oppression, it all made her keenly aware of her precarious position and the consequences of failure. Should she get caught, death would be a welcome friend, not a punishment, but she feared it would not come easily.

Since returning to Paris, an overwhelming sense of foreboding had stalked her, as if her story had already been written and she was merely biding her time until her inevitable tragic end. She'd had many fleeting moments of panic questioning her sanity coming back into the lion's den, but her fate was tied to this place. It was where she belonged and could do the most good. She wouldn't survive another round with the Nazis—mentally or physically—so she would just have to make sure that didn't happen.

She blew out her trepidation and picked up a lipstick with a shaky hand. *Breathe.* Whatever was going to happen wasn't going to happen tonight.

Bouchaule watched her in the mirror from his dressing room and she smiled, trying to feign nonchalance.

"Nervous, darling?" he asked, coming up from behind as he negotiated a gold cufflink into its hole.

"A little." There was no point in lying. Even if she hadn't been so obviously unsettled, she found it harder and harder to conceal her thoughts and moods from him. He had acquired the mutual skill of seeing right through her, never more so than when she put on an indifferent facade, a sure sign that she was concealing something.

He kissed her bare shoulder. "Don't worry. You look beautiful."

Kathryn smiled at his reflection. "I'm not nervous about that." She finished applying the color and capped her lipstick, becoming serious. "I just don't want to make any mistakes."

He offered his hand, which Kathryn took as she stood. "There are no mistakes to be made," he said. "They know who you are and why we are together, and when they see you tonight, there will be no doubt it is all the truth."

Bouchaule had dared not lie to his associates about her presence or her situation. Both were too easy to check. He'd explained that she was an American, wronged by her government to entrap him, and that scared for her safety, she'd fled with him, willing to help the project if she could. He emphasized they were lovers—not as a boast but as a warning.

Once at the party, introductions went smoothly, and everyone appeared convinced she was on their side. That bought her cautious approval but not blind acceptance. She felt like der Führer's girlfriend: respect was feigned but not necessarily heartfelt. They all were outwardly gracious, but she felt the questioning glances at her back as she moved through the room on Bouchaule's arm.

He put his hand over hers. "Are you all right, darling?"

"Yes. Fine." It wasn't true yet, but she no longer felt nauseated, as she had when they'd first arrived.

Bouchaule seemed satisfied with the evening and right at home with French socialites and German officers alike. Kathryn fed off his confidence and eventually found her center.

Dinner was obscenely extravagant, with an array of gourmet foods and expensive French wine and champagne. It mocked the struggle of average citizens trying to feed themselves and their families. Food rationing had become an exercise in party line oppression, as there was no longer enough food to ration. The black market thrived despite severe consequences for its use, and the rural farmer became the city's lifeline. In Bouchaule's circle, such hardships were absent, and Kathryn swallowed her disgust, along with her dinner, trying not to draw attention to herself.

Her plan to lay low didn't last long. After dessert, Bouchaule suggested she sing while he accompanied her on the piano. Singing after a meal wasn't great for vocals, but the curious crowd urged her on. She chose "Parlez-Moi d'Amour" because it was one that she and Bouchaule had performed together before, albeit not in public.

One night, the sound of him playing the piano in their salon drew her downstairs. Her folio of secretly marked sheet music was open beside him on the bench, with this song on the piano's music desk. He smiled brightly when he saw her but must not have recognized the shocked look on her face.

He'd held out his hand. "Come, darling. Sing for me. I love this song."

She'd hidden her resistance activity from him, sticking with the lie that she spent her days giving private voice lessons, and since the sheet music looked perfectly normal, she'd not bothered concealing her folio.

He glanced at it as she approached. "Sorry, I didn't think you'd mind."

"Of course not," she had said, and leaned on the piano to serenade him.

All eyes were on her now, but she didn't see smiling faces anticipating her performance; she saw a uniformed sea of black and silver SS collar tabs. Stark and chilling.

A nauseating combination of decadence and terror descended, and panic threatened to paralyze her. She wished she hadn't eaten. Her throat constricted, and she reached for a glass of water, struggling to hold it steady as she brought it to her lips.

What the hell was wrong with her? This was what she'd wanted from the beginning. To get back to the fight. To pay her debt. She couldn't falter now. She'd defied the Office of Strategic Services to be here, and even the pall of dread wouldn't make her regret it.

Something was rotten in her government, something she couldn't do anything about, but she had saved Jenny and put her father's biological weapon research out of the reach of those who would misuse it, especially his axis counterpart—the man beside her playing the introduction to a love song. No matter what happened to her here, she would never regret that.

Breathe. This was your plan.

She steadied herself on the grand piano's polished lid. The subtle vibration of the notes took her hand like a harmonic caress, reminding her that music was her sanctuary. She would not let them take it from her. Inexplicably, she heard Jenny's voice in her head. *Fuck them.*

A sneer threatened to curl her lip, but she turned it into a smile for the audience. The root of her defiance was her strength, and though the first line of the song was forced, she grew bolder as she went on, until her voice flowed easily, with no hint of trepidation. She closed her eyes and let the words and the sentiment of the song soothe her. Everything fell away until a familiar tendril of warmth broke through her newly hardened heart. Jenny, finding her way in. *Fuck.* Why now?

She opened her eyes, breaking the spell and banishing her from her thoughts. When the song ended, the room was just a room full of people again, with no one person more unsettling to her than another.

Even those who had seemed wary of her at first were applauding and smiling now.

Bouchaule embraced her and kissed her cheek. "You've charmed them all," he whispered, and apparently, she had.

They mingled through the crowd and were having an interesting conversation with an older couple about the pitiful state of France's vineyards, now that copper sulfate wasn't available to stave off diseases that attacked the vines, when Kathryn sensed Bouchaule stiffen beside her.

"Gestapo," he whispered, as a well-dressed man approached.

The older couple quickly departed.

Kathryn's defenses went up. Just the word conjured up sinister men in the shadows exacting a horrific agenda with little provocation or morals.

Bouchaule dipped his head in greeting. "Herr Vogel."

Kathryn recognized the name as that of Bouchaule's overseer. Vogel didn't seem menacing at first glance. He seemed sophisticated in his dark blue double-breasted suit. If not for the swastika pinned on his lapel, one would think him a friendly businessman.

"Monsieur Bouchaule," he said.

Vogel turned to her. "And you must be Miss Hammond," he said in English, saturated with a guttural German accent. "Albrecht Vogel. I've heard so much about you. I must tell you, my English is only slightly worse than my French, and both are appalling. My apologies." He snapped a quick bow of his blond head, accented by what seemed a reflexive click of his heels, as if a string connected them.

Kathryn smiled politely. "My German is most certainly worse than your English, but I'm fluent in French if you prefer." It was the first time she'd spoken English since she returned to Paris, and in this setting, it made her uncomfortable.

"How kind of you," he said in acceptable French, though his inability to liberate his thick German tongue crushed its lyrical beauty. "Thank you for the song. Your performance was exceptional. Nostalgic. It reminds me of the good old days, as you Americans say."

Kathryn found his obvious pandering reminiscent of the occupation's early days, when the Germans tried soothing the worried minds of the conquered through displays of gentlemanly conduct. That had given way to boorish nationalism when the beleaguered Parisians became an annoyance to them by using up precious resources. His attitude irritated her, and she did her best to mask it behind a pleasant smile. "Were you in Paris during the good old days?"

"I lived here for several years in my youth."

"Then what's happening here now must break your heart too."

Bouchaule tightened his grasp on her waist as a warning.

Vogel didn't seem offended. "It does."

Kathryn lifted her glass. "Then we must make the best of it. To Paris of old. May she return soon."

"And better than ever."

Vogel drank. She did not. His crooked grin in reply had *you'll pay for that* all over it.

"I would like to hear you sing again," he said.

Here we go. Kathryn imagined a private setting, where a song would only be the beginning. Payment for her obstinance, she supposed. Before she could reply, Bouchaule exhaled what she swore was a low growl. Kathryn sensed Vogel wanted to laugh out loud at the both of them, but he drowned it behind another sip of champagne.

"My favorite nightclub needs a new singer. The job is yours."

That was unexpected, but the decision was easy. She didn't want to disrupt her resistance work with Claudette, and Bouchaule certainly didn't want her anywhere near Vogel. "I'm flattered, but I'm sure there are plenty of French singers who would be more suitable."

"I promise you, a job awaits," he said with a glare that surely meant *or else* for the club owner.

"I'll think about it," she said courteously.

Vogel took her hand and squeezed her fingers uncomfortably hard. "No need to think."

Bouchaule took Kathryn's elbow. "She'd be delighted."

Quiet manipulation—that was the way of it—and by Bouchaule's reaction, Vogel would present it that way only once.

He removed a small notepad from his jacket pocket and scribbled something on it. "Report to the *Propagandastaffel*." He tore off the note and offered it to her.

Bouchaule snatched the paper from his hand. "If you think this entitles you to anything other than the pleasure of her voice at that club, you are mistaken."

Vogel carefully took the note back from Bouchaule, as if he were a petulant child, and offered it to Kathryn again.

"Report to the *Propagandastaffel*. Give this to Dieter. It will ensure you are processed quickly. I look forward to the pleasure of your talents at L'Heure Bleue."

All performers had to have their material vetted by the Nazis before they were allowed to perform, and despite Bouchaule's connections, she would be no different, only fast-tracked because of Vogel's influence.

L'Heure Blue was in the 9th arrondissement but only a fifteen-minute walk to Claudette's shop in Montmartre. Maybe this would work out after all.

"Stay away from him," Bouchaule urged quietly as soon as Vogel was out of earshot. "I've tended to more than one of his charity cases. He is neither a gentleman nor kind without reason."

Kathryn tried to calm him by lending her confidence, as he had for her earlier. "I can take care of men like—"

Bouchaule grabbed her forearm. "He has no soul and no conscience!"

Kathryn jerked from his grasp. "Thierry—" She quickly glanced around, as his outburst drew attention.

He composed himself, taking her hand gently. "I'm sorry, darling. Please, just … stay away from him."

Kathryn nodded with a worried eye on him. She'd never seen Bouchaule undone by a particular person before. Situations, yes, but Vogel made him anxious, which troubled her. She caught the man watching them from across the room and could tell he delighted in their discomfort.

Bouchaule had a healthy respect for the Nazis and their unconscionable treachery, which was understandable given his history with them, but they never discussed Vogel's offer again.

The next week, Kathryn gathered her players, jumped through the required bureaucratic hoops, and as promised, a job was waiting at the club.

CHAPTER TWO

Fortune often flourishes at the expense of the oppressed, and Vogel's perception of a good deed did not go unpunished.

Kathryn stepped into the narrow passage behind L'Heure Bleue and wrapped her cashmere scarf around her neck against the frigid air. Her first night performing had gone exceptionally well. The club catered to the German occupiers, and though it was filled with soldiers and officers, the fear she expected never materialized. She was relieved not to falter in the face of every German soldier she encountered. All she saw were tables filled with loose-lipped marks primed to spill information. She didn't push that angle tonight, but she hadn't lost her touch. She was the most popular girl in the room in no time.

Fish in a barrel, she thought to herself with a grin as she pulled on her gloves and walked toward the street to catch the last Metro for the night.

She hadn't gone fifty feet before a knife-wielding man pressed a thick forearm to her chest, planting her roughly against the window-less limestone facade of the building. The cold knife blade against the soft underside of her jaw made sure she'd stay there. Or so the man thought.

"Not a sound, you Nazi whore!"

Another man tapped a short length of pipe into his gloved hand, as if a knife at her throat wasn't enough persuasion. A few yards away, a nervous young woman played lookout. She turned her head, and a flash of blonde hair against the light at the end of the passage way made Kathryn's heart skip a beat, but she quickly recognized the woman as the singer she'd replaced at the club. She'd been sitting at a table in the back staring daggers at her all night.

"You're making a mistake," Kathryn said, trying not to move her jaw any further into the blade.

"You made the mistake, bitch," the man said as he pressed the blade in.

Kathryn closed her eyes and took in a slow breath as she slid her left heel to the wall at her back. "Look, I don't want you to get hurt, so how about you back away slowly and put that away."

The man leaned in with a scowl. "It is you—"

Before he could finish his sentence, she kneed him in the groin and twisted him around by his wrist until he faced his stunned friends, with his arm bent behind his back and the knife now at his throat.

The move was instinctual, but Kathryn was not trained to take hostages. She was trained to kill an attacker without a second thought.

The man foolishly struggled, and Kathryn was glad she had the wherewithal to turn the blade out, not quite trusting her muscle memory to follow her head's instructions for mercy. "I'd stop moving if I were you. I'm out of practice and in no mood to be considerate."

"Please!" The woman stepped forward with her arms outstretched. "Don't hurt him."

Kathryn looked to the man with the pipe. "How's it going to be?"

The pipe clanked to the ground and rolled into the gutter.

"As I said," Kathryn addressed her captive, "you're making a mistake. Now, I'm going to let go of your arm, and you're not going to do anything stupid, right?" She pressed the dull edge of the knife deeper into his neck for insurance.

He smartly agreed.

For Kathryn, forgiveness came easily for the three in the alley. They were not her enemy, just frustrated and desperate. The young singer she replaced had probably just lost the only income her family had. She was an attractive young woman, and there was no doubt where her desperation would lead if left unresolved. As a compromise for taking her job, Kathryn promised to leave the woman her paycheck at the corner café every payday.

"Why would you do that?" the man under the knife asked skeptically.

"Because I don't need the money. I just need to work in that club. Do you understand?"

It didn't take long for the three to get the picture. With Kathryn's defensive skills and the way she cozied up to the German officers all night, plying them with drinks and compliments, her intentions were suddenly obvious. They were all remorseful, and the two standing away moved in with apologetic concern.

"Forgive me," her attacker said.

Kathryn slowly let him go, and sure she was no longer a target, handed him his knife. The woman offered a handkerchief from her purse, holding it out like a delinquent child returning a stolen item.

Kathryn pressed it against the underside of her bleeding jaw. "Is there someone I can get in touch with?"

She could tell the three knew exactly what she was asking, but they hesitated, caution rendering them mute behind their furtive glances.

Kathryn understood. The men were obviously underground, dodging the deportation of young Frenchmen to Germany for forced labor under the *Service du Travail Obligatoire* policy. That they risked discovery to right a wrong for the young woman spoke volumes about their desperate situation.

"Leave word at the café if you can help me," Kathryn said, accepting their silence without judgment.

It was a dangerous game, disseminating information to the resistance. The Gestapo had made it far too easy for neighbor to inform upon neighbor, and the overflowing letters to their Avenue Foch headquarters were a shameful testament to the hate and distrust germinating among the populace in the harsh occupied environment. It would be a long time before she trusted an unknown contact, but if she'd interrupted a network's flow of information because of her job at the club, she'd give them a chance to reestablish it. Eventually, she would have to get word to the OSS about her whereabouts and current activities, but so far, Claudette hadn't had any word from the feelers she put out.

When Kathryn arrived home at the standalone two-story red brick townhouse she shared with Bouchaule in the 16th arrondissement, she couldn't hide the blood and the mark on the underside of her jaw. As expected, Bouchaule was livid. He tended to her superficial wound in tense silence and then picked up the phone.

"What are you doing?" Kathryn asked.

"I'm calling that bastard Vogel, who insisted you work in that club, and I'm demanding increased petrol rations to cover your new driver. You will be accompanied at all times from now on. I don't want you on the streets alone. I was mad to have left you on your own for this long."

"Thierry—"

"No argument, Kathryn!"

"Thierry," Kathryn said again, this time in a reasonable tone as she curled her fingers around his on the handset. "The Germans let you keep your car because you are a doctor, but I wouldn't push it. And flaunting an endless supply of petrol will not endear me to the locals."

"I don't care about *them*. I care about keeping you safe." He resumed dialing. "I know you can take care of yourself, but these are not common street thugs."

"You're right, they're not thugs at all. They're just regular people tired of being pushed around."

"So they push around innocent people?"

"Typically."

Kathryn had noted a distinct shift in attitude since she was last in the city at the beginning of the occupation. Those left to endure the German invasion had gone from a cautious compliance born of fear, hatred, and uncertainty, to a tired conformity honed by years of oppression-induced tolerance. Most citizens just wanted it all to be over—for some, whomever the victor—while others remained ever vigilant for any chance to foil their captors.

Bouchaule snorted derisively and shook his head. "Unacceptable. Such outrageous behavior needs to be punished."

"Well, not tonight. Come on"—she eased his hand from the handset and replaced it on the receiver—"let's go to bed. It's been a long day."

He exhaled his anger. "You are far too forgiving."

It was the last they spoke of the incident. Having gotten an earful from Bouchaule the next day, Vogel sent his personal driver to escort her to and from the club from then on.

For weeks she visited the café on payday. She suffered the ersatz coffee—toasted barley mixed with chicory—and waited for a sign about a contact. The only unusual thing was the constant appearance of a nervous little man, too small in the shoulders for his heavy coat and two inches too tall for his worn corduroy pants. He was there every day, sometimes already waiting, sometimes arriving shortly after, casting furtive glances her way until she would return one, and then he would turn his attention anywhere but on her. He was not a good spy, if that's what he was. Too odd, too conspicuous. Perhaps he was the newest member of a resistance cell, one being tested for skill or loyalty, or merely the most expendable, should she happen to be the enemy. Maybe he was just admiring her. Whatever his story, experience told her to stay away from him. They usually just played eye tag until one day, he sidled up beside her as she stood at the counter with her coffee.

"Cigarette?"

She looked in the dented brass case in his shaking hand and smiled at the home-rolled smokes. In lieu of cigarette paper, he had used the delicate tissue pages of a Bible. She eyed him warily. Typically, women didn't smoke in public. A local would have known that. She thought for a moment that there was a message to be found in the text, so she indulged his offer. He let her choose the cigarette and then lit it for her, smiling at her grimace when she inhaled and found it contained dried corn silk instead of tobacco.

"Sorry."

"No need," she assured him.

He didn't start a conversation or ask questions. He didn't slip her a secret note or make any other gestures that appeared covert. He merely smoked his cigarette in silence, content to share her space, and then left.

The man behind the counter smiled at Kathryn's confused expression as she watched the nervous man exit the café in the reflection of the mirror on the back wall.

"You've made a friend," he teased.

"Apparently. You know him?"

"Showed up when you did. Been here ever since."

She snuffed out her cigarette in the ashtray. "What do you make of that?"

"I think you should watch your back. The walls have eyes."

He didn't need to tell her that, and she knew the odd man's contact with her would ensure that no one would dare approach her there. From that day on, she had the paycheck delivered by courier, and she never returned.

When another contact with the resistance came, it was through the most unexpected source.

Kathryn heard a disturbance coming from the downstairs kitchen, and knowing Bouchaule's housekeeper, Annalise, had gone for the evening, she tiptoed quietly across the tile floor to investigate. From the shadows of the pantry, she saw Bouchaule with a woman he had let in through the back door. Her clothes were of fine quality, but worn, and spoke of a wealth no longer enjoyed. She was in trouble, and her despair was palpable as she pleaded her case.

"I told you, I can't," Bouchaule said in an urgent whisper. "I can give you medical supplies. It's the best I can do."

"He'll die, Thierry!"

The way the woman gripped his arm and said his name, Kathryn sensed there may have been something between them once, and the woman's situation was one that clearly moved him. He cupped her cheek and paused, as if considering his options, but in the end, the woman did not dissuade him.

"Marie, I can't. If I'm caught … well, you know I just can't."

The woman fell to her knees in tears, obviously at her wits' end. "Please. You're his only hope."

Kathryn had seen enough heartbreaking desperation since her return to Paris, and tired of being helpless, she could no longer stand by. She stepped into the light. "Can I help?"

The woman scrambled to her feet and wiped her eyes, letting Bouchaule handle the explanation.

"It's nothing, darling," he said, turning to intercept her. "Go back upstairs."

Kathryn dismissed Bouchaule's lie and approached, noticing the dried blood that caked the woman's hands and extended up her wrists and on the inside of her sleeves, staining the old newspapers sewn into the lining of her coat for added warmth.

"She needs your help, Thierry."

He took Kathryn by the arm and led her away. "This is none of your concern."

Kathryn jerked free. "I'm not blind, nor am I to be handled. Someone is badly hurt and obviously needs your help."

"I can't," he said in a terse whisper.

"Why? Because he's with the resistance?"

Bouchaule clamped his jaw shut.

Kathryn turned to the woman. "Where is he?"

"Not far. A place at the west end of the park."

"Kathryn—"

"Thierry, listen"—Kathryn glanced at her watch and took his hands

—"we'll get dressed and go to the theater. We'll go in together, and once the lights go down, you slip out the back. Help her friend and be back before the lights go up. We'll leave together, and no one will know."

Bouchaule tilted his head in exasperation.

The theater was conveniently located at the other end of the park, which Kathryn knew made it possible, but any such plan was a risky one.

"Please," the desperate woman said.

Bouchaule obviously couldn't resist the hope of one set of eyes and the scrutiny of the other, because he finally gave in. "I'll give you my bag," he said to the woman. "Have someone meet me at the back door of the theater."

"Thank you!" She hugged him.

Bouchaule returned her embrace and then excused himself to retrieve his medical kit.

The woman hugged Kathryn. "Thank you."

"He'll do what he can."

"He always does," the woman replied cryptically.

Bouchaule helping the resistance was an unexpected surprise, but Kathryn learned he had been passing medical supplies throughout the occupation via Annalise. He was careful never to get personally involved with the people he helped, and he vowed to denounce his housemaid as a thief should she get caught by the authorities with supplies.

"I'll not cover for her, no matter how dear she is to me," he said on the way to the theater.

His answer was cold and matter-of-fact, automatic, so as not to tax his moral compass, she imagined.

"Would you cover for me?" Kathryn asked.

Bouchaule was silent, but she could see the unthinkable darken his brow. He swallowed and raised his chin defiantly. "No, I wouldn't."

Kathryn smiled, which he must have mistaken for disdain.

"I'm sorry if that upsets you, but my work is—"

Kathryn took his hand before she had to hear again how disposable she was in the almighty shadow of his work. She assured him she truly wasn't upset. There were no romantic gestures where the Nazis were concerned, and she expected nothing less than the answer she received. Whether Bouchaule would remain true to his conviction, should push come to shove, remained to be seen, but it was one question she never wanted answered.

Kathryn was right about Bouchaule's relationship with the desperate woman at their back door that night. They had been lovers many years ago, but that was long over.

"She's a communist," he said, as if that gave her two heads and a well-deserved boot to the curb.

The man she pleaded for so passionately was her husband, wounded in a raid on the train yard. Bouchaule was able to slip away from the theater and return unseen, as planned. The man lost his leg, but not his life, and the incident forced Kathryn and Bouchaule to peel away another layer of their carefully crafted facades.

As they undressed from their evening out, Kathryn could see from Bouchaule's brusque movements that he was angry about her interference.

"Thierry—"

"Don't you ever do that again." He untied his tie and yanked it from his neck. "That was none of your business. You endangered both of us. That is the last time you meddle in things you know nothing about."

Kathryn threw her long gloves onto the bed, flashing a little anger herself. "You forget, I lived here before. I was here when the Germans rolled in, and I was here after, when we did what we could to make things difficult for them. As long as I am here, and as long as they are here, I will do what I can, when I can, to make things difficult for them. If that means helping the resistance, I will."

"That is not why I brought you here," he shouted. "I brought you here to keep you safe, and as long as we go along with them, you will be. I forbid you to get involved with these people."

Kathryn could barely contain a disparaging laugh as she took off her earrings. "First of all, you don't forbid me to do anything. I'm not your property. Second of all, no one is safe here. Kowtow to the Nazis all you like, but you live and breathe at their pleasure, so don't fool yourself that you curry favor because you *go along*. They're using you as much as you're using them, and you know it."

Bouchaule stalked closer. "I have arranged my affairs carefully and specifically to ensure the continuation of my work, no matter how distasteful you find my methods, and I *will not* have that jeopardized by your bleeding heart. You *will* do as I say."

His French machismo was the hammer blow that broke the chain restraining a restless tiger, and Kathryn couldn't wait to get away from the stench of it and all it represented. She yanked her wrap from her shoulders and threw it at his chest on her way to her dressing room. "Go to hell, Thierry. At least I still have a heart."

"I won't lose you too, Kathryn!" he shouted at her back, emotion breaking in his voice.

The guilt over the deaths of his sister and brother-in-law was never far from his thoughts or actions, Kathryn realized, and she, of all people, appreciated the validity of his fear and how it can taint every move you make. Understanding unfolded into forgiveness, and she stopped walking, letting the tension dissipate before turning around. When she turned, the hopelessness she saw in him surprised her. Bouchaule's broad shoulders slumped weakly, and her wrap dangled sadly from his hands, as if she'd already gone and it was all he had left of her.

She took him in her arms. "I'm not going anywhere."

"I won't lose you too," he repeated, burying his face in her shoulder. "Everything can change in an instant."

She looked him in the eyes and saw how vulnerable he was. There was no hiding the pain he'd seen or the impending defeat he felt now. She comforted him as best she could, but she had a job to do too. "I'm not going to blow up trains, but I will keep my eyes and ears open and pass along what I can. It's the least I can do, and I mean the *least* I can do."

He shook his head. "You don't know, Kathryn ... if you're caught—"

Kathryn reflexively looked away, her own fears interrupting their reconciliation. It was only a split-second lapse, but Bouchaule caught it and forced her to look at him with a hand on her chin. Concern now creased his brow, as if he realized there was more to her insistence than moral obligation.

"Why did you leave Paris?"

Kathryn stepped away, unprepared to deal with that aspect of her life. "It just became too much for me," she lied. "Germans everywhere—"

Bouchaule was instantly at her side, seeking her face. "What did they do to you?"

"Nothing."

She turned away. He brought her back to him.

"Kathryn."

Her past shoved her from behind, daring her to tell the truth. "Nothing!"

She could tell by the doubting tilt of Bouchaule's head that he didn't believe her.

"Nothing to me," she said quietly.

He closed his eyes. "Tell me."

Her demons crossed their arms, waiting with great interest for her response.

"They killed my friends because I wouldn't talk. Then I was rescued." She paused, finding the truth an ally for a change. "I had a breakdown. I went home."

Her demons exchanged raised brows, impressed.

Bouchaule stared at her, as if seeing her for the first time, and then gently took her in his arms. "I shouldn't have brought you here. What a fool I was."

Kathryn resisted his comfort, standing stiffly in his arms until her past slithered back into its dark corners.

"This is your home, Thierry. Your work is here. Now it is my home again, and I will defend it whenever and wherever I can. Understood?"

He answered with a curt nod.

Their relationship changed that night. They had gone from guarded companions to respected partners. Bouchaule understood Kathryn's angst at every moment spent in the presence of his German associates, and when such an occasion was to be endured, he was never without a reassuring hand on her back or a loving look from across the room. They became the couple to envy, as wives nudged husbands at their romantic example, hoping they'd follow suit.

Bouchaule's focused attention and the effect it had on her startled her. She had been admired before, had people in love with her, but to have this man, who she was so sure was above the complete surrender of his heart, look at her with such intense devotion, jostled her from her dispassionate perch and forced her to admit she had found a new affection for him as well. He was more than she thought. Better.

She was returning one such affectionate glance at yet another dinner party when an older society woman standing beside her placed her hand on her arm and said, "It's so beautiful to see love flourish in these horrid times." She then leaned in and whispered, "Enjoy it before the Nazis outlaw that too."

Kathryn smiled cynically in agreement—the notion was a distinct possibility—and watched the woman walk away to greet a Nazi officer with an extended hand and a well-practiced smile that reminded her everything about the evening was a charade. Every Frenchman in the room despised every German in the room, and they all cloaked their animosity with polite chatter and insincere gestures of civility.

Kathryn shook her head. Amid all the posturing, a stranger thinks she sees love. Kathryn dismissed the woman's observation with an amused chuckle. She wasn't in love. She'd been in love with Jenny and had any clichéd notions of romantic love displaced by the complete physical and mental surrender of her being to the care and longing of another. No, she knew what love was, and she couldn't imagine surrendering so utterly to a man as preoccupied as Bouchaule, nor he to her. He was more like a pleasant surprise on a blind date. They were two people thrown together with cautious expectations, finding not only their feet on common ground, but that they were two halves of the same broken whole.

They were fighting on the same side—against the Nazis. Kathryn had kept an eye out for any hint of a lie or deception from Bouchaule regarding his work and had found none. He was who he proclaimed to be and more. How well he played the game of perception for his audience. She looked around the room. How well they all played it.

While the average citizen scraped and groveled to carve out their meager existence, this room full of people shifted and swayed with the prevailing wind, their moral pendulums swinging only so far as their disparate goals would allow. What was important to them? Saving the world? France? Paris? Their lives? Their home? Their fortune? Their honor? Their pride?

She wondered what she was trying to save. She had all but deserted the OSS and, by association, her country, to save Jenny's life. Saving the woman she loved was the only decent thing she'd ever done, and while it cost her everything, she'd do it again. That was the highest arc of her moral pendulum. Everywhere she looked, there was injustice and brutality begging for action. Yet here she stood in a fine dress, sipping French champagne with the enemy and its cowardly sheep.

She felt ashamed, distracted by the trappings of her surroundings and blinded by her own myopic goals. She was no better than Bouchaule and no less guilty of collaboration by association than anyone around her. The difference was, she could do something, anything other than playing house with the doctor, pretending the little bits of gossip heard or coerced from the German patrons at the nightclub and passed through Claudette to her contacts absolved her of a greater effort to disrupt the occupation and aid its victims.

She felt a hand on her back as Bouchaule arrived, his brow knit in concern.

"You don't look well."

She swallowed her self-disgust and handed him her champagne. "I feel a little sick."

He supported her gently by the elbow and looked around, settling on the stairwell leading to the upper floors. "Here, we'll find you a place to lie down."

"No. I need to get out of here." She scanned the room with disdain. "Away from *this*." She wrapped the entire occupation in the word. "I just want to go home."

Bouchaule glanced at the associates he'd left, and Kathryn understood he had important business still to conduct.

"It's all right," she said. "You stay."

"Nonsense, I won't hear of it. I'll get our coats."

She held on to his sleeve as he tried to pull away. "Honestly, Thierry, I'll be fine. I just need some air, and … I think I'd like to be alone for a while."

He eyed her with hurt added to his concern. She kissed him and gave him a hug. "I'll be okay. I just …" She was at a loss to explain. Now was not the time for rash decisions. She needed a plan and a clear head.

Bouchaule cupped her cheek and acknowledged her discomfort with a regretful smile. He arranged for a *fiacre* to take her home, with terse instructions to the horse-drawn carriage driver for her safe delivery straight to their door.

Two hours later, Kathryn arrived home only to have the front door yanked from her grasp by Bouchaule as soon as her key was out of the lock.

"Where have you been?" he said as he flung the door open. "I've been frantic." He peered past Kathryn's shoulder to the curb. "Where is your cab?"

"I dismissed him."

"When I find that man, I'm going to beat him senseless. *To the door, I said!*"

Kathryn put a calming hand on his chest. "It's all right, Thierry."

"It's not! It's after curfew. What if—" He stopped and took in the sight of her in only her long-sleeved evening gown. "Where's your coat?"

"I lost it."

Bouchaule narrowed his eyes. "You gave it away, didn't you?"

She didn't answer.

He shook his head and led her to the warm fireplace in the living room and began rubbing her cold hands.

"That was foolish, darling. Not only will you catch your death, that person will probably get mugged for it or arrested for stealing it."

Kathryn closed her eyes and bowed her head. She couldn't pass the shivering woman on the street in her woefully ineffective spring overcoat as she gathered twigs to burn for warmth, so she had shed her coat and placed the warm fur-lined virgin wool garment around the woman's shoulders. She got spit on and cursed at for her troubles. The woman let the coat fall to the ground and kicked it to Kathryn's feet.

"Collaborationist swine," the woman had said with disdain.

Kathryn picked up the coat and held it out to her. "Take it. Survive to hate me another day."

The woman had stared at her as she struggled with her decision. *Life? Honor? Pride?*

Her gaze darted to the dark recesses of the lampless street for any witnesses to her impending hypocrisy. Seeing no one, she took the coat and ran, leaving a trail of discarded twigs in her wake.

Kathryn had straightened and wiped the woman's spittle from her cheek, satisfied with her punishment for the evening.

Bouchaule tried to comfort her. "I know it's hard, darling."

"I can't just watch anymore, Thierry. I've got to do something."

"You're giving that girl your paycheck."

"I wouldn't need to give her my paycheck if she still had a job."

"That's Vogel's fault, not yours."

Kathryn shrugged it off—not the point at all.

"You saved that man," he said. "Marie's husband."

Kathryn shook her head. "*You* saved that man."

"But I wouldn't have if not for you."

Kathryn smiled. "I saw your face when you looked at Marie. In the end, you would have helped him on your own."

"No, I wouldn't have. I did that for you. Because I couldn't stand that look in your eyes … the disappointment in me."

Kathryn demurred, touched by his sincerity but sure it wasn't true. "I don't think I have that power over you."

He became very still, and Kathryn was struck again by the intensity of his stare. In the end, he just kissed her hand. "We do what we can, when we can, darling."

"And sometimes we don't do enough."

Bouchaule sat back without responding.

Kathryn knew he didn't have the answers, but she wasn't sure he even understood why she was upset.

"You have your work, Thierry. That's your goal. Your life, every move you make, revolves around the continuation of your work. What do I have?"

He smiled. "You have me."

She knew he was trying to deflect his inability to resolve her dilemma with humor, but he obviously underestimated the depth of her discontent. He was so consumed by his goal. How could he understand what it was like to live without one? She would have to find a way to live with the limitations of her situation, or change her situation. One thing was for certain; it would be the last time she would complain to Bouchaule about it. If knowing her history with the Nazis didn't make him sympathetic to her restlessness, he wasn't worth the effort of trying to explain it. She would just file away his insensitivity and formulate some plan to deal with her moral obligation on her own.

"I'm sorry. I'm just feeling a little helpless tonight."

"What are you going to do about it?"

She knew what he wanted to hear, and she lacked the strength at that moment to fight against it. "What I can, when I can," she said dejectedly, parroting his party line.

"Within reason," he reminded her.

She fought back a disgusted sneer and forced a polite smile. "Of course." She got up to go upstairs, but he held on to her hand.

"You're upset."

"I'm tired."

He rose and brought her into his arms. "Forgive me, darling."

She braced for his condescending platitudes—wanting nothing to do with them, or him, at that moment—and prayed she could keep still as he sealed his apology with soft kisses down the side of her neck. He straightened and smiled, as if he'd made everything better, and then stood back and became serious, like a parent about to scold a child.

"When you agreed to come to Paris—"

She pulled away from him, not willing to hear an unsympathetic tale about how she'd made her bed and now must lie in it. "Trust me when I say you do not want to finish that sentence." She walked away. "I'm going to bed."

"Kathryn!" She stopped with one foot on the stairs and a hand on the ornamental metal railing. He came to her side and began again, this time softly, sympathetically. "When you agreed to come to Paris, I admit I was hesitant, but once here, you handled everything so grace-fully. Your strength makes me forget what you've been through some-times, and I'm sorry for that. I can be a self-absorbed man, as you know."

He said it with a self-deprecating smile, which made Kathryn more receptive to his apology. She turned to face him and leaned against the wrought iron balustrade, her hands behind her back.

Bouchaule held out his hand, and after a contemplative pause, she took it.

"Your strength humbles me, Kathryn. More than you know." He shook his head. "I know loving me alone is not enough to make your suffering here bearable or worthwhile."

Kathryn opened her mouth to protest, but Bouchaule silenced her with a raised hand. "Just as loving you is not enough to make me leave this place."

Bouchaule didn't try to present any illusions, which Kathryn found refreshing. She knew he could do his work anywhere in the world, take them both out of harm's way, but the Germans were footing the bill, so he stayed in Paris.

I have my work," he went on, "and every day I appease my anger and can suffer the rest by knowing I'm denying the Germans their precious weapon, but you … what have you got to appease the anger, fear, and frustration you must feel here? I've been no help, I know."

"Thierry—"

"Come with me."

He led her to the coat closet under the stairwell and opened it.

"Where are we going?"

"Not far." He dug into his pocket, producing a set of keys, and pushed their ample supply of coats to one side, exposing a locked door.

Kathryn was beyond being surprised by secret rooms and hidden doors and had actually begun to expect them, though she was surprised Bouchaule disclosed his willingly.

He unlocked the door and turned on a light, revealing stairs descending into the basement.

Kathryn was wary. "What's down there?"

"The truth."

Kathryn would never understand this man. After the paranoia surrounding Forrester, Bouchaule was the complete opposite, and he had so much more to hide. She couldn't figure out his angle.

"Why are you doing this?"

"Because I'm afraid that left to your own devices, you'll join those hoodlums and blow up trains."

She put her hand on his arm, demanding a serious answer. "Why are you doing this?"

He paused, piercing her with his intense stare again. "Because I want you to understand what has cost us both so much."

Kathryn took Bouchaule's extended hand and lifted the hem of her long gown as she negotiated the steps down into the basement. The walls were made of irregular shaped blocks of limestone, held in place by lime plaster, reminding her of the tunnel to the lab under Jenny's house. But unlike the damp, musty concrete and brick tunnel to the lab, this basement was dry and cool, with no decerning smell.

The lab was very much like the other two she'd encountered since her assignment began, first Daniel Ryan's and then Bouchaule's at the estate, but this was much smaller in scale.

Bouchaule was making the most of his limited space. A variety of microscopes stood at attention on one side of the room, and jars of mystery objects floating in what she assumed was formaldehyde lorded over them on the shelves above. Lab animals in cages resided on the other side of the room, and inside a separate glass partition were a few pieces of equipment and more small animals, isolated, she assumed, because of the hazardous nature of his study.

She wandered past the bookshelves and filing cabinets and then watched with interest the frantic mice and rats in their cages react to their unwanted guests. She couldn't help but sympathize. When she got to the bored fat rabbits she joked, "We could have them for dinner," alluding to the shortage of meat in the city.

"Who says we haven't?" Bouchaule replied seriously and then laughed at her stricken look.

Kathryn straightened and smiled as she nonchalantly took in the rest of his workspace. Everything was meticulously kept except for his desk, which was cluttered with papers, folders, open books, and behind it, stacks and stacks of files, just like in his lab at the estate. It sobered her.

"Dead?"

He nodded regretfully.

She hadn't questioned the origin of the files back in the States, but seeing the voluminous pattern repeated here, in a place where human life held so little value to the occupiers, she had a horrifying thought.

"Who are these people, Thierry? Where do they come from? How do they get sick?"

Bouchaule hesitated, and Kathryn took issue with it.

"I thought I was here for the truth?"

He agreed, casually slipping his hands in his pockets. "They're prisoners."

Kathryn stared at him. There was something about the way he said prisoners. "Refugees?"

"Undesirables."

"Jews?"

"Some," he said unapologetically.

She searched his face for any trace of disgust or remorse and found none. She remembered Colonel Holmes shoving a laboratory prospectus in her face and pointing to Bouchaule as the head of the department that turned out the dead patients.

Ghosts of those dead filled the room, reprising their horrific deaths, lest they be forgotten or ignored. They were neither. The sickening memory of Johnson writhing in pain and terror as he suffocated in his own blood beside her was multiplied by each folder neatly stacked against the wall—orderly murder, with Bouchaule standing before it like a jaded executioner.

Any charm she'd ever seen in him fell away in the face of his indifference. She wanted him to say something, anything, to silence the choir of accusations rising in her.

"Please tell me you had nothing to do with their deaths."

"On the contrary," he said coldly. "I killed them."

A chill ran down her spine as the dark arms of betrayal enveloped her like a cold sarcophagus. She froze, trying desperately to comprehend the monster he'd suddenly become to her.

The ghosts chanted their guilty verdict as they pressed in, tearing at her ill-conceived notion of Bouchaule as a good man. Even her demons stepped aside, unexpectedly bested by the extent of the evil presented to them.

She wanted to scream, "It isn't true! It isn't true!" Only then did she realize how much of herself she'd emotionally invested in him. The truth physically hurt now that he was unmasked. What a fool she was. She believed him, believed *in* him. She had dropped her guard only to find that her anointed savior was the devil in disguise. It was Juliette all over again, only more devastating, because she was wise to the game this time and was taken in spite of it.

He moved toward her, and she could only think he had murderous intentions. Why else would he confess such a thing? She moved away from him, step for step, circling the center aisle lab table, trying to make her way to the steps to escape.

"They are dead before I kill them," he explained nonsensically, reaching out like a criminal trying to convince the police they have the wrong man. "It's for the best."

Kathryn couldn't breathe. She had to get away from Bouchaule and his sick Nazi ideology and out from under the strangulation of her appalling lack of judgment.

Bouchaule stood between her and the stairway, poised to counteract her next move, but she didn't care. If he wanted to kill her, he would have his hands full, because hand to hand with him, she liked her chances. She darted for the stairs, adrenaline fueling her flight.

"Listen to me—" he pleaded as he reached for her.

Kathryn easily brushed off his halfhearted effort, nearly stumbling on the first step, expecting more resistance from him.

"I offer you the truth and you run from it like a coward!"

Kathryn stopped halfway up the stairs and turned, ready to tell him exactly what she thought of his "truth." Rage replaced any fear she'd had when she saw him standing there at the bottom of the stairs, propped up by his anger like he was the slighted one. An unrestrained urge to kill him herself filled her, and all she could think of was revenge for the innocent dead.

"You want to talk of helplessness?" Bouchaule continued angrily. He grabbed a file from the desk behind him and held up a man's identity card photo. "I watched this man die today. Three hours he suffered! And this woman!" He held up her photo, and then another. "And this child! She was ten! *Ten!*"

Bouchaule went on shouting about patients brought to him after the Nazis had infected them in their pursuit of the perfect viral weapon. The path to their goal was littered with the bodies from the files until they had honed the virus to its lethal pinnacle, celebrating when the child died in less than an hour of being infected.

"I could do nothing for them but watch as Vogel and his madmen put on their demonstration. These people—" He pointed to the stacks against the wall. "They are the lucky ones. After Vogel has his way with them, they are sent to me to study. I ease them quickly into death to end their suffering, and they are thankful for it." He threw the files he'd been waving at her in the general direction of his desk, missing badly as they spun to the floor. "Who are you to judge me? Go, and take your righteous indignation with you!"

Kathryn stood in stunned silence. *"Vogel has no soul and no conscience,"* Bouchaule had said. The people in the camps were his rats in cages, and Bouchaule did what he could to clean up the mess handed to him. The horror of it stripped away any rage or disappointment she had toward him, and she sat on the stairs, momentarily felled by the wave of truth crushing her swirling emotions.

Bouchaule ran his hands roughly through his hair and kicked at the papers littering the floor. He sat on the corner of his oak desk, his head bowed, with his clenched hands propping himself up on the top of his thighs.

Kathryn stared at the picture of the young girl on the floor next to Bouchaule's shoe. She reminded her of Stephanie, and she couldn't imagine witnessing her suffering, or the suffering of the others, or the invasion of her country, or the heartbreak of watching loved ones ripped from their homes and loving arms to become fodder for the evils men do. She covered her eyes with her hand to hide her tears. Bouchaule's world was more horrific than she could have imagined, and the image of the immaculately coiffed doctor in his pristine white lab coat shuttling from one microscope station to another, far removed from the source of his study, was shattered by the knowledge of his brutal reality. Who was she to judge, indeed?

"Adele was one of the first victims brought to me," he began quietly.

Kathryn looked up in shock. His beloved sister.

"They thought if I knew something, surely I'd save her, and I would have." He closed his eyes tightly, his emotional struggle for composure obvious. "But I couldn't, you see."

Pain gripped Kathryn's chest as if the tragedy was hers too. "Oh, Thierry…"

He explained that he was tasked with finding the vaccine solution. They held his sister until they felt he was dragging his feet purposely and then used her in the vilest way to draw out the truth from him. When they found he still had no vaccine, they began sending others.

"She begged me to end her suffering. So I did." Bouchaule paused until his raw emotions were under control. "And that's what I do for them." He looked at the files against the wall. "I can't save them, Kathryn. I can't save any of them, but I won't let them die for nothing. I must do what I can, learn what I can, but without the reservoir, a merciful death is all I can give them."

Kathryn closed her eyes. There was no reservoir because of her. Bouchaule's hands were tied, and she provided the rope. She couldn't trust him, but what if his work could have saved these people? Or the poor souls who come after?

Her regret was fleeting when she remembered the treacherous game Bouchaule played against his sadistic wardens. No matter how hard he tried to hide a vaccine, it could be discovered, and then all her fears would be realized when the already actualized weapon was released upon the world.

Well-versed in the insufferable weight of helpless guilt, and now even more aware they carried the same stone, she regretted she could not ease Bouchaule's burden.

"I'm so sorry, Thierry."

He pushed off from his desk. "I don't want your pity. That's not why I brought you down here."

"Then why did you?"

Bouchaule climbed the stairs and sat on the step below her feet, with his back against the wall.

"I want you to understand why I stay here. A decent man would take you far away from this place were he able. I am able, yet I stay. If you want to think it is because I don't love you enough, you would be mistaken. If you want to think it is because the Germans fund my work, then I admit that is part of it, but more than that"—he looked at the stacks of files—"they are my countrymen. I can't just desert them."

Kathryn reflexively looked away. She had deserted her countrymen without a thought, and Bouchaule, whom she had thought so selfish, shamed her with his loyalty.

"This scene is repeated every day," he said. "I know you think me cold and unfeeling, but I have no tears left for them." He stared blindly into the room. "I sometimes feel I have no soul at all."

As Kathryn studied his anguished demeanor, a dark kinship welled up in her. Her own battered soul welcomed his into the fold. She lightly combed her fingers through his disheveled hair, and he turned to her with a crooked smile, conveying equal parts gratitude and regret.

"I do love you," he said, his eyes confirming his words. "You lift my heart from this terrible place ... remind me there is good in this world, beauty to be had beyond this madness."

Kathryn couldn't imagine he found anything beautiful or good in her soul, but she recognized the need to reach for any light in the darkness, and she accepted her role as that in his life.

"You once offered me freedom, Kathryn, and I so want to be free ... with you, at least." He glanced toward the lab. "This I needed you to know, and whatever happens because of it ..."

When she didn't respond, he relaxed his back into the wall and dropped his disappointed gaze to his clasped hands.

"You may go if you like. I can get you an exit visa, and I know people who will get you anywhere you want to go in the world, and they will make sure you're safe."

Kathryn was still processing Bouchaule's unbearable situation when she heard his offer to let her go. It took her a moment to comprehend the idea of it. She had never felt closer to him than at that moment. His vulnerability wrapped itself around hers, making her stronger—making them both stronger, she hoped.

"I'm not going anywhere, Thierry, and it's not pity, believe me."

Bouchaule looked deeply into her eyes. "No, it isn't, is it?"

Kathryn pressed her lips into a determined smile, seeing the strength she felt reflected back to her. Slowly but steadily, it seemed, they were always moving toward each other, dragging themselves through the rubble of their broken lives for the chance to be understood and accepted by one of their own. The relief of each of those moments, where they accepted their flaws without judgment or guilt, healed another wound and pushed them without fear toward the next, knowing comfort would be found there too.

"We're better together," she said, hoping the statement would warm the icy chill of their confrontation.

He nodded. "I'm sorry I called you a coward."

"I'm sorry I thought you were a murderous Nazi bastard."

Bouchaule looked at her sideways and almost grinned until the reality of the insufferable situation permeated the space between them. They were like bugs in amber, unable to free themselves from the stifling grasp of the Nazis and unable to absolve themselves of their guilt.

"They won't win this war," Bouchaule finally said into the contemplative silence. "Good will always triumph over evil."

Kathryn slowly cut her eyes to him, perplexed, as always, by his many faces.

"Man is inherently good," he explained, as if it were common knowledge.

"I hope you're right," is all she could say, surrounded by overwhelming evidence to the contrary.

Bouchaule searched her doubtful face and smiled before turning away. A slight chuckle escaped as he stared at his shoes.

"What could possibly be funny at this moment?" Kathryn asked.

He ducked his head, and Kathryn swore he was blushing.

"What?"

He looked up at her. "How are you feeling?"

She paused, confused by his change in direction. "Fine?"

He smiled again but seemed disappointed in her answer.

"What is it?"

"When you said you were ill at the party … I thought you might be pregnant."

"Oh, good Lord," Kathryn blurted out, as the mere mention of it straightened her back in protest. "No. I promise you I am not."

Bouchaule knitted his brow, and his amusement quickly fell away. "Would it be so bad?"

Kathryn stared at him in disbelief. "This is hardly the situation I'd want to bring a child into."

"A child is hope, a chance to get it right, create a better world."

She was caught off guard and tried to stall as she wrapped her head around the unexpected twist in the conversation. "Why, Thierry, I had no idea you were such a philosopher."

"You're making fun of me."

"No." She took his hand, reacting to the hurt in his eyes. "You just … well, honestly, it's the furthest thing from my mind."

"Will you think about it?"

"You're serious?"

"I hadn't thought about it before, but when it became a possibility …" He squeezed her hand and let his hopeful eyes finish the sentence. He smiled at her shell-shocked expression. "Sorry, the idea of it … well … it swept me away."

Kathryn squeezed his hand back, relieved he'd come to his senses. "There'll be time enough for that later."

He nodded offhandedly, as if to say *it was worth a try*.

For Kathryn, the shock of the suggestion melted into contemplation as they sat in silence on the stairs. Motherhood had never been something she longed for. The thought of a little being relying on her, of all people, for their very existence, bordered on the absurd.

Her maternal instinct went only so far as a fleeting plan to use a pregnancy to trap Bouchaule in the desperate days of their separation, and even then, she'd given no real thought to the consequences of that plan nine months later. The more she thought about the idea, the more ridiculous it became.

She glanced at Bouchaule, staring aimlessly into his lab, and imagined him as a rough and tumble boy, with a sailboat under his arm and worms in his pockets as he kicked stones in the road on his way home from the park. It made her heart smile and ache at the same time for the innocence lost. She imagined him with a son, a little man with her dark hair and his infectious smile. Bouchaule no longer seemed a self-absorbed man consumed and tortured by his work but, rather, a proud father doting on his child, teaching them everything he knows as he orchestrates his plan to make a better world. She was struck by her power to give him that joy, but more than that, by the unexpected urge to want to.

She closed her eyes and wondered what was happening to her. She wasn't mother material, but she couldn't stop playing out the idea of it once it had been set in motion. *When it became a possibility ...*

She thought of Clay with Stephanie and the joy the mere mention of her name brought to him. Her own experience with the girl had taken her by delightful surprise, and she missed her terribly. She longed for her innocence, her unconditional love, and her youthful honesty. A child was a chance to get it right, to start over, to make a better world.

A tear stained her cheek when she imagined herself worthy of such a chance. What was an absurd notion only moments ago had suddenly filled her with the shining hope only a new life can promise. She understood Bouchaule's excitement and sense of euphoria about it, but now was definitely not the time, and she was glad, because it would give her a chance to come to her senses.

She opened her eyes to find Bouchaule staring at her, and he did not appear at all surprised by her tears. "Overwhelming when you really think about it, isn't it?"

She could only nod as she wiped the tear from her cheek.

"Someday," he said with an understanding smile as he stood and helped her to her feet.

CHAPTER THREE

Kathryn noticed Bouchaule had become more relaxed around her as the weeks went by. It was as if they had struck the final set on their carefully staged play and there was no longer a need to step around the furniture serving as props for someone else's melodrama.

He continued to be up front about his work, often having her in his lab for company as he waded through menial tasks, like checking and rechecking data and experiments. Kathryn had free rein there, and he often explained procedures and theories as running commentaries while he worked, and he appeared delighted with her interest. It allowed her to monitor his work with the virus, a tedious exercise with very little return. It seemed she had stalled his progress by denying him Jenny, and he was confounded as to why Donnelly's remaining group hadn't contacted him regarding their prize and its application to the project.

He complained often about the lack of contact, leading Kathryn to commiserate while internally dismissing her responsibility in the matter. It all seemed so long ago, and it hardly mattered anymore, since she couldn't do anything about Jenny's whereabouts even if she wanted to, which she didn't.

Kathryn's life with Bouchaule had taken on an odd domesticity about it that both surprised and comforted her. She was no longer restless, and she had gotten a message to the SOE via a group known to Claudette to help English flyers escape. She basically informed them things were status quo and to please pass that along to the OSS, along with a request for a contact in the city. They replied days later with a short but sweet *KBO, will advise.*

So, keep buggering on she would, but she hadn't heard anything more since the initial exchange. Communications were often difficult to arrange and even harder to sustain due to all the justified paranoia about, so she really wasn't concerned with the silence. Perhaps they'd written her off as a bad investment, and that, too, would be fine. She had her bits of information she dropped into Claudette's pool of contacts, and she had a close eye on Bouchaule for anything untoward. In the meantime, they went on with their lives doing what they could, when they could.

Vogel still loomed ominously in the background, and Kathryn could always tell when the man had another of his "demonstrations" for his superiors. Bouchaule no longer hid bad days like that, and Kathryn comforted him when he needed it.

He didn't need comfort on the occasion of Vogel's fiftieth birthday. Bouchaule was obliged to attend with Kathryn in tow, but they had become highly skilled at the art of avoidance. He and Kathryn moved about Vogel's vast estate—one procured from a wealthy Jewish doctor who had long since disappeared—in a well-choreographed circle, with Vogel always at the opposite end.

The crowds at these functions had changed of late. There were those who retained their wealth, usually by collaborating with the Nazis, and those pretending to retain their wealth, hoping to entice a German to reside in their home. For them, it was only at these parties that an abundance of food and heat existed. For some, it would be the only occasion outside a theater or movie house where they could remove their winter coat.

With coal constantly diverted to buildings with German interests, there wasn't enough left for the legitimate rations of the average citizen, but if one's household included an important German, it would be blessed with an abundance of the prized resource.

Bouchaule was considered an honorary German by those standards, and they were never without coal for heat or electricity or food. Now that he no longer felt the need to impress Kathryn with the illusion of an unaffected home front, and at her insistence, they lived modestly, perhaps too modestly, according to Annalise, who was instructed to distribute the excess food to the less fortunate. The "excess" she claimed was already less than what the average person required to be healthy, but Bouchaule insisted she take what she and her husband needed and to use her discretion with the rest. Her discretion always included enough for the household, but the bulk of their meals came from social occasions.

This evening was truly social, and although most of his colleagues were in attendance, they didn't discuss business. Kathryn and Bouchaule were relaxed in each other's arms as they swayed and stepped to a slow orchestra of mellow swing.

Kathryn opened her eyes to see someone staring at them from a few feet away. He was impeccably dressed—a collaborator's wardrobe, to be sure—and striking, with his chiseled good looks. To her surprise, he stared at Bouchaule and offered only disdainful glances at her.

Kathryn maneuvered Bouchaule to look. "Who is that?"

Bouchaule quickly maneuvered his back to the man. "No one. Pray he doesn't come over here."

"But who—"

"Pray," he whispered, as he attempted to dance them out of the man's general vicinity.

It wasn't a frantic request, so she knew he wasn't dangerous, but she found it curious that Bouchaule was doing his best to move away from him like a magnet from its opposite pole.

The song ended and Bouchaule took her hand. One more to add to their avoidance chart. They'd lost sight of the man in the mingling crowd, but as soon as Bouchaule uttered, "That was close," the man appeared in front of them.

"Why, aren't you a beautiful couple," he said with more than a tinge of resentment. "I don't think we've been formally introduced. How rude of you, Bouchaule." He presented his hand to Kathryn as if she should kiss it, and at the last moment, slid it into hers and brought it to his lips, stopping just shy of kissing it. "Enchanted, Miss ..." He turned to Bouchaule with Kathryn's hand still poised at his lips. "It is Miss, isn't it? What are you waiting for, Bouchaule? Surely you aren't going to let her get away?"

Kathryn plucked her hand away. "I assure you, there is no danger of that, Mr.?"

"Georges Delcourt," he said with a dismissive dip of his head, seemingly annoyed she was speaking.

Kathryn glanced at Bouchaule, wondering if she should be impressed, but he was indifferent as he slid his hands into his pockets and looked decidedly bored.

Delcourt stared at him expectantly until he got his introduction.

"Georges, Kathryn Hammond," Bouchaule finally said.

"There"—Georges put his hand on Bouchaule's shoulder—"that wasn't so hard, was it?" He didn't remove his hand as he addressed Kathryn. "I am delighted to finally meet you. The rumors of your beauty are not unfounded." He turned again to Bouchaule, massaging his shoulder like a nesting feline. "I'm very jealous."

With that, he walked away, leaving the point of the man's scene a mystery to Kathryn. Bouchaule shuddered and grabbed the nearest glass of champagne he could find. Kathryn smiled when she realized Delcourt was not jealous of Bouchaule but of her.

"Well, then," she said with a raised brow. "I'll bet that's an interesting story."

"One that includes a blackout at work, an inappropriate hand on my backside, and a broken nose. The broken nose was not mine. If he wasn't an expert in his field, he would have been gone long ago, and as soon as I find a suitable replacement, he will be, I assure you." Bouchaule swallowed his glass of champagne with one gulp. "Don't you dare leave me alone with him ... ever."

"I don't know, darling," Kathryn said with a wicked grin, eyeing the attractive man up and down. "I find the thought strangely erotic."

Bouchaule was not amused.

Kathryn laughed, and after a quick glance around to make sure no one was paying particular attention to them, she led him around a corner and erased his discontent with a slow, probing kiss.

Bouchaule licked his lips as she pulled away. "How erotic?"

A master of the smoldering invitation, Kathryn needed no words. Bouchaule deposited his empty glass on the side bar next to him in the hall and took her roughly in his arms, kissing her urgently, as if to purge the foul specter of Delcourt's hand upon him.

Kathryn let the kiss go on until it had reached the point of no return and then led him into the nearest room, where it continued until Bouchaule realized where they were and stopped abruptly, as if the walls were watching them.

"This is Vogel's office."

Kathryn was well aware, and she would use her seduction to distract him while she memorized the layout of the office and eyed it for anything useful.

"Even better," she said. She eased a strap of her dress from her shoulder, revealing the soft white porcelain skin of one breast and then the other.

Bouchaule's trepidation didn't last long in the face of her strip-tease, and he led her to the comfortable large leather couch against the wall. She resisted with another mischievous grin and indicated with a tilt of her head that she preferred to defile Vogel's large mahogany desk instead. Her wicked side had its desired effect, and Bouchaule changed direction.

There was a purpose to Kathryn's debauchery as she leaned, facing forward, over the desk. She took in the three neatly stacked folders on the blotter beside her and then lifted her eyes to the shelves beyond. The folders were labeled in German, while the works on the shelf were in French. She doubted the books belonged to Vogel.

They helped themselves to the liquor cabinet while they gathered themselves, and then Kathryn retreated to the bathroom to properly put herself together. When she returned to Bouchaule's side in the main room, his companions greeted her with polite nods and inquisitive stares. In the midst of an incredibly boring tale from one of them, Kathryn squeezed Bouchaule's arm and subtly pantomimed the loss of her purse, which she had purposely left behind in Vogel's office. She excused herself from the group, and Bouchaule distracted them with a discussion about a very fine example of Flemish art hanging on the wall behind them to divert the wandering gazes that usually accompanied Kathryn's departure.

She slipped into Vogel's office, retrieved the miniature camera from the purse she left on the mantle, and picked the lock on the large side drawer of his desk. The drawer opened easily, and she photographed the contents of the briefcase she found inside. The files on the desk belonged to three wanted resistance fighters, so she took photos of them too, hoping someone would recognize them and warn them they'd been targeted. She had just returned the briefcase and locked the drawer when a floorboard squeaked on the other side of the door. Grabbing her purse, she shoved the camera back into its hiding place and scurried before the large, ornately carved gold gilded mirror over the fireplace, where she pretended to arrange her hair.

Vogel didn't say anything as he entered the room, and Kathryn knew from experience that he would wait for her to hang herself with excuses. She knew the game though, so she treated him like any other man, despite what she knew about him and Bouchaule's fervent warning.

"Hello," she said calmly. "I seem to have taken a wrong turn on the way to the ladies', but any mirror will do in a pinch, hm?" She smiled sweetly. Success was all in the attitude. "I don't think I've had the chance to personally wish you a happy birthday this evening. Lovely party."

She intended to casually exit the room, but he intercepted her and took her arm. It wasn't the rough grasp she expected but a slow enveloping of her biceps, as his hand slid up from her inner elbow and settled there like a warm glove.

"This is my office," he said accusingly in perfect French.

Her heart pounded. "Is it?" She glanced around as if taking it in for the first time. "Why, that explains the exquisite taste in furnishings. I love that rug." She raised an impressed brow at the Persian silk Kashan beneath her feet.

He wasn't buying it at all.

"It smells of sex in here." He pulled her close and inhaled her scent. "Or is that you?" He rubbed his cheek against hers and exhaled a pleasurable moan in her ear. "No. It must be the room. You smell delightful."

She tried to pull away but couldn't. His grasp was still gentle but rigid, like a cat not ready to crush the bird between its teeth. Fear rose in her as the cruelty in his voice replaced his casual demeanor when he whispered all the dirty things he'd like to do to her, none of which involved pleasure for her. She could have used the defensive techniques she knew to get away from him physically, but he wasn't a thug in an alley; he was Bouchaule's overseer and someone to access and use if she could.

She took the disgusting comments he breathed down her neck and shook the eerie sensation of a dark alley in turn of the century London with Vogel like Jack the Ripper, priming his victim for the slaughter.

"You could have just asked me for whatever it is you're looking for," he said, sliding his other hand around her waist.

Kathryn found it hard to breathe, as the paralyzing chill of Vogel's inherent evil seeped into her very core. "I don't know what you're talking about," she managed evenly.

He smiled and held out his hand. "Camera."

"Really, you're mistaken. Let go of—"

He grabbed her purse and made quick work of the false bottom, producing the subminiature Minox camera with a smirk.

Kathryn backed away, casting a furtive glance at the tall French doors leading to the balcony behind her, her only means of escape. It was déjà vu all over again, but this time she had no gun or L-pill to do what she must. The room was on the second floor though, and if she was lucky, diving headfirst over the ornate stone balcony beyond the doors at her back would do the trick.

"You know," Vogel began pleasantly, eyeing the camera in his hand, "this was manufactured in my hometown. Now spies around the world are using it against us." He extended the camera to its full size with a gentle pull and held it up between his fingers like a sparkling diamond to the sun. "Ironic, isn't it?" A press into the device's back with his thumbnail and another gentle pull revealed the small film magazine.

"I haven't done anything," Kathryn lied before he could get the cassette free from its snug compartment and have solid evidence against her.

"I don't care." He smiled and snapped the camera shut without removing the film. "The people who need the information you seek already have it. I gave it to them. I just needed to make sure you are who I think you are."

Her brow knitted in confusion as he put the camera back in her purse and handed it back to her.

"And who do you think I am?"

"Kathryn Hammond, agent for the OSS, briefly of the burgeoning SOE, and before that, making trouble for us here in general."

Her breathing stopped while her heart pounded wildly. She was done for and on the verge of panic. How could he know all that? "You're mistaken." She scanned the desk for anything she could use as a weapon to keep the man at bay.

He moved toward her. "I also know *other* things about you, Miss Hammond. Perhaps we could … come to an arrangement." He smiled. "No pun intended."

She had no intention of playing that game with Vogel now. He was a ruthless murderer whose policy was to kill enemy agents on sight. Any sexual favors she allowed him would merely be a prelude to her execution. She eyed a letter opener as she backed up, in case he tried to stop her from leaping from the balcony, but as she rounded the corner of the mahogany desk, she saw something better: a gun holstered to the inner side panel of the desk. She shoved the heavy wooden chair aside. The revolver was in her hand in an instant and pointed at Vogel.

He smiled, not concerned at all by her threat. "Kill me, and you'll never get out of here alive."

"I don't intend to," she said calmly, putting the gun to her temple.

Vogel sneered at her. "Kill yourself, and I will make sure life becomes very difficult for Mr. Bouchaule."

She pulled the hammer back with her thumb, undeterred.

He stepped forward, with malevolence in his eyes. "I think you underestimate my definition of difficult."

She stepped back, calling his bluff. Her time had come. "I think you overestimate my capacity to care about anyone but myself."

She pulled the trigger and heard an anticlimactic *clack* as the hammer fell on an empty chamber. She panicked, sure history was repeating itself. Vogel lunged for her, but the desk between them kept her out of his reach. She quickly raised the gun against the man's aggression and glanced at the remaining chambers, relieved to find they all had rounds.

As adrenaline coursed through her body, a memory from her childhood surfaced among her frantic thoughts: the vivid memory of her father leaving the first chamber of his revolver empty in case of an accidental discharge. Vogel must have done the same, to give himself a chance should the gun, hidden to protect him, fall into the wrong hands. He knew his enemy would have to pull off two shots to do any damage, and he could afford to be unconcerned by the first, but with the threat of death very real now, he was serious.

"Please, no, Miss Hammond!" he shouted before she could pull the trigger again. He held out his hands as if to steady a fragile vase on a jostled pedestal.

She raised the gun to her head again.

"Please, no!" he repeated urgently, as if saving her life was infinitely more important than saving his own. He was speaking perfect English now. "I won't hurt you. I'm not here to hurt you. I'm here to help you." He was creeping closer, working his way around the desk as he spoke.

"Stay where you are!" She pointed the gun at him again and backed up toward the balcony as an alternative death plan in case the gun failed her. She thought briefly of taking Vogel to the grave with her, but the fear of Bouchaule being implicated in his death and the virus program falling into more diabolical hands kept her focused on the inevitable. Vogel took another step closer, and she pressed the gun to her temple again, pulling back the hammer. "I'll do it, I swear to God. I'm not going back there again."

She didn't know why she was hesitating. He was a liar, and she wasn't going to walk out of there a free woman. Her life wasn't flashing before her eyes, only the satisfaction that she had saved Jenny and derailed the virus weapon.

"I'm your contact," Vogel explained calmly. "You requested a contact, and here I am."

Kathryn nearly laughed out loud as she continued to step back onto the balcony after unlocking the door at her back. His lie was absurd. She knew he was a Nazi through and through. Besides the horrors he inflicted on the poor unfortunates he passed on to Bouchaule, she knew for a fact he had presided over the public execution of four suspected resistance members only the day before. There would be no reprieve for her. She couldn't tell whether it was the cold winter wind chilling her bones or death extending its welcoming grasp.

"You're insane if you think I would believe you're working for the OSS. I know what you do."

"SOE, actually," he said matter-of-factly, "and one does what one must to preserve a legend."

Preserving a legend—the spy world term for a false identity—was one thing, but wholesale slaughter was another.

"You're a monster."

"Perhaps, but it would be a shame to lose you over a misunderstanding. Please, come inside and put the gun down."

"Misunderstanding? That's rich. Why should I trust you?"

Vogel pointed at his desk, asking permission to approach.

Kathryn nodded but backed up even further, getting a better angle on that balcony.

He pulled a slip of paper from under the desk blotter and slid it to the corner closest to Kathryn before backing up to the far side of the room to make her more comfortable about retrieving it. "You'll be under the jurisdiction of the SOE now. Holmes specifically. I believe you are familiar with him. Your OSS handler has been assigned to the Pacific Theatre."

She eyed the note and then him, as the chance he might be telling the truth overpowered the pull of death. "What does it say?"

Vogel settled his hands behind his back. "I don't know. It's a private message in code for you. For all I know, it says shoot the bastard before you without delay."

It was tempting, as Kathryn pointed the gun in his direction again and inched toward the desk. She snatched up the note and saw it contained a small square of text. It wasn't a long message, but there was no key. She cut her gaze to Vogel, sensing a trick and Nazis behind the drapery, ready to pounce, now that she'd entered the room again.

"The key is the rhyme you chose for your first mission," he said.

Her first mission was for the SOE. Only they would have access to that information, though she doubted things like keys were archived. She searched her memory and skeptically applied it to the code. *Trust him,* it spelled out. *Holmes.* The message and the man before her were incongruous. Her instincts told her it was all wrong, but the proof was in the proper execution of the code. *Trust* and *Holmes* in the same sentence made her teeth hurt, but Vogel had apparently known about her for some time, and she was still alive.

She tried to piece together a timeline. "Was the odd little man in the café yours?"

Vogel smiled. "We had to make sure you didn't get involved with the wrong people."

It was an obvious dig at the communists and fascists peppering the resistance groups. "You took your sweet time getting in touch with me."

"We had to make sure you were still with us."

"And where else would I be?"

The man smiled again. "Dr. Bouchaule is a very attractive man, persuasive … I know. You are a very attractive couple. If I didn't know better, I'd say you were in love."

Kathryn was ready with a counter to his accusation. "He is also a very smart man, intuitive in a way I've never encountered. He is not easily fooled. One does what one must to maintain their cover, as you said."

Vogel raised his brow. "Well done then. I commend you, but hardly a chore, hm?"

Kathryn didn't trust him, especially with a stamp of approval from Holmes. Vogel ignored her disdain and poured them both a drink, which she refused.

"We want you to take your camera and photograph what you can of Dr. Bouchaule's work."

"What makes you think I have access to his work? Why don't you do it? You're his boss. Who has more access than you?"

"We think the good doctor is perhaps not being completely honest with us."

"Us the Germans or us the English?"

"It is the same."

Kathryn eyed him skeptically, to which he laughed.

"If he is not honest with the Germans, I cannot, in turn, be honest with the English. You see?"

"No, I don't see. How am I supposed to get information that even you can't access?"

"He has a lab in the cellar beneath your home."

She pretended to be surprised.

"Get in there, learn what you can. Pass what you learn to my driver in a sealed envelope. He will see that I get it."

The mousey driver who delivered her to and from the club every night didn't seem like the high intrigue sort. "He's in on your little double-cross?"

Vogel chuckled. "Of course not. He will probably think we're having an affair."

Kathryn was instantly put off by the idea.

"That's all right, isn't it, Miss Hammond? Perfectly understandable, don't you think?"

There wasn't much for her to say. His arrogance spoke for itself. "Of course."

She warily relaxed her defensive position and set the gun on the desk within easy reach, just in case. She found Vogel hard to accept as an ally, but she was alive, and friend or foe, as long as he thought she could give him what he wanted, she would remain alive.

"Who are you?"

Vogel smiled and moved uncomfortably closer, setting the drinks on the desk beside her hip. "Who do you want me to be? The despicable German?" He affected the accent as he said it. "The proper Brit? The proud Frenchman? The easy-going American?" Every accent was perfect, and Vogel became even more frightening than before, able to insert himself into anyone's game and have his intentions remain transparent.

"Come now, Miss Hammond," he said with a cajoling smile. "No need for hostilities." He ran the back of his fingers lightly up her arm as he leaned into her. "We're on the same side."

Before she could spit out "I sincerely doubt it," Bouchaule burst into the room. "I warned you to stay away from her!"

He lunged at Vogel and decked him with a single blow, backed by all his weight. He grabbed the revolver and trained it on the man. "I warned you!" His hand shook with rage.

"Thierry, no!" Kathryn shouted, pulling on his arm.

"Wait outside, Kathryn," he said, struggling against her.

"Thierry—"

"Please!" He shed her hands from him. "Outside."

"He's not worth it."

"Please. I know what I'm doing."

Kathryn complied with a final glance at the man sprawled on the floor. Vogel rubbed his jaw and laughed at Bouchaule's machismo.

Kathryn waited just outside the door, glad no one had noticed the drama unfolding inside. She heard the rumble of loud voices but then nothing. She didn't trust Vogel, despite the coded message supposedly assuring her of his alliance. When he first revealed himself, she thought his despicable behavior was part of his cover—the stereotypical heinous Nazi, instantly revolting—but, clearly, it was his true nature, whatever incarnation he was affecting. He could be betraying her to Bouchaule right now, playing both sides just because he could. She looked at the oblivious crowd and thought of running. It might be her last chance to get away.

She didn't have a chance to form a coherent plan as the door flung open and Bouchaule emerged, holding his hand. A quick glance into the office as she turned to follow revealed Vogel, alive and well, smiling as he raised a drink in her direction.

She liberated a towel and some ice from the bar as Bouchaule continued on his way out, and she joined him in the car, where he silently accepted the cold compress for his swollen knuckles. It reminded her of their first meeting, where he had done the same for her cheek, but the concern and kindness of their first meeting was absent now. He didn't ask what happened or even if she was all right, and she feared whatever spell he'd been living under with her had broken. She missed the easy connection they'd found and could only imagine what Vogel had said to destroy it.

Bouchaule was acting so strangely that she didn't know what tack to take, so she let him plot the course and remained silent for the trip through the deserted streets of the city.

If Bouchaule knew about her, he would feel betrayed and would have no choice but to kill her. It was the only scenario she could think of that would elicit such a cold reception after everything they'd been through to finally trust each other.

They moved like strangers through their home until they reached the bedroom. Bouchaule sat on the bed and stared at the floor, and sensing he had something to say at last, Kathryn dutifully sat beside him, waiting to hear her fate.

"You accused me once of playing a game," he said. His eyes swept over her face and narrowed accusingly, as if searching for the proof of her duplicity. She remained silent. He looked away and stared at his swollen knuckles. "I have always had questions about you … your devotion, your motives." He cut his eyes back to her. "Knowing what it was like here … why would you agree to come back?" He returned his gaze to his hand. "I wanted to believe what you claimed, that it was out of love for me, that you couldn't bear the separation." He looked at her again, helplessness seeping into his tired glare. "That is how it is for me."

Kathryn remained silent, afraid any hint of emotion would be a potential misstep in the minefield of Bouchaule's ambiguous ramble.

"But it just never quite rang true," he went on with a regretful tilt of his head. "Vogel told me something about you tonight. Something I didn't think you capable of. But now I see you so clearly, and I am sure of you." Bouchaule paused, taking in Kathryn's face as if he'd never made a more important decision. "For this last hour, I've been struggling with what to do about it."

Kathryn held her silence, formulating a defense against Vogel's obvious betrayal.

Bouchaule stood, and Kathryn tensed, bracing herself for a violent strike across the face, for starters. She had murder in mind when she thought herself duped by him; she couldn't imagine the rage he felt at having his heart betrayed and his precious work threatened.

Bouchaule suddenly dropped to one knee and took her hand. "Kathryn, will you marry me?"

CHAPTER FOUR

*J*enny paced nervously across the wooden floor of a deserted farmhouse located in the rolling hills just outside of a village near Dijon, France. It was her first field mission, the one she'd been working toward since the day she walked into Colonel Holmes's office seven months ago.

She had become the colonel's favorite person after her appearance with her father's books and the revelation of the newly discovered lab at her home. She had left Kathryn out of her tale of discovery, saying she found the bookcase door in the study ajar when she returned home from her upstate visit with Bernie. The body on the floor of the study had conveniently disappeared by the time agents arrived to investigate, and Jenny couldn't even venture a guess as to whose lackey he was.

Holmes had kept her under wraps after she'd appeared at his office that day—not exactly under, but out of sight until the risk to her safety was determined.

She had moved out of OSS jurisdiction via an Inter-Allied cooperation agreement and never saw Colonel Forsythe or another OSS representative again. Holmes became her singular contact, and he came alone when they met. There were no office meetings with secretaries or aides and no reunions with family or friends. Instead, she'd spent long, solitary hours in a very well-appointed hotel suite, where she pieced together her veiled past and came to terms with the actions of those who had shaped her life.

She'd longed to speak to Kathryn again, to tell her she understood why she broke things off and that she didn't really hate her. The words were said in anger, fueled by shock, and she'd regretted them as soon as they left her mouth. She didn't want to think about where Kathryn was now. When Jenny had asked her where she was going just before they parted, she had said, *"Back to the fight. Where I belong."* The words haunted her, and she'd tried every day to put them out of her mind.

After a few weeks, Holmes had said he had an overseas mission suited only to her, and he presented papers for her to join the SOE. She'd accepted the assignment but not the transfer, finding the change of allegiance akin to desertion. Fair enough, Holmes had conceded, and she was whisked away to Toronto under the perfunctory umbrella of the OSS, where she'd immersed herself in the science and technical intricacies of training for her new assignment and tried to earn the grace she'd been given by those who had loved and protected her.

As she'd secretly poured through the decoded documents and transcribed her father's journal in the days following their disclosure, her future had become clear to her, and it would not include a new identity or living her life in obscurity. She had felt humbled to the point of insignificance by what she'd discovered in her father's papers. It felt abstract, a vivid dream about someone else. It had to be. It was the only way she could bear the price paid by her loved ones.

She had yet to do anything to merit the sacrifices made on her behalf—her father's life, Kathryn's future, their love. Maybe she never could, but she would never stop pushing toward that end. She finally had a reason for throwing herself in harm's way. It was the type of dedication Kathryn was looking for when she'd asked *"Why do you want to do this?"* at the beginning of her training.

Once she had answers and a plan, only the government could give her the means to fulfill her destiny. She'd turned to Holmes, who she realized was brought in specifically for her case.

She'd been told the Chicago syndicate, the key player in her case since the death of Marcus Forrester, had crumbled with the death of their leader, Colin Donnelly. Plans and documents so carefully hidden were easily discovered, and the doctors and scientists who were under Donnelly's iron fist gladly offered their cooperation. The government had welcomed them with open arms and guaranteed their continued loyalty by holding a death sentence for treason in a time of war over their heads.

Thanks to Colonel Holmes, Jenny had learned exactly who her enemy was and spent the next seven months north of the border, at the University of Toronto, under the tutelage of some of the brightest minds in the field, devouring every bit of technical knowledge available about the application of the new field of electron microscopy to her father's work. On her own time, she had absorbed all the theoretical knowledge she could about cytology and histology, hoping the knowledge of cell and tissue structure would not only help her understand her unique physiology but also allow her to convincingly bluff her way to the man who had taken everything from her.

"Find this man and you'll find Kathryn Hammond," Holmes had said. It didn't take much imagination to know what he meant. The man was Kathryn's assignment, and then everything made sense. Kathryn had pushed her away purposefully, using Marcella as the perfect knife to cut the cord between them. Jenny would deal with her anger over the deception later, but for now, she could kill two birds with one stone. With the help of their contact in the city, she would position herself in the lab in Paris, mine all the information to be had, and then she would take her revenge on the man who killed her father. This would also free Kathryn from her self-imposed prison.

Jenny considered it a public service, not murder. She would eradicate the bastard, and Kathryn would be allowed to choose her own path in life for a change. No matter what had happened in the last seven months since they parted, Jenny knew they belonged together, and in the end, nothing would keep them apart.

She settled against the wall in the dark farmhouse, with no regret about her decisions, and visualized the triumphant moment her mission would be complete—with the death of a monster named Thierry Bouchaule.

CHAPTER FIVE

athryn slipped the envelope of notes she'd copied from Bouchaule's lab journal to Vogel's driver, just as she had done for months since her run-in with the double agent in his study. Double agent was a loose description of Albrecht Vogel. Despite the offered proof to the contrary, her gut told her he was rotten to the core.

She was almost certain he had told Bouchaule she was an agent. To prove her loyalty in the event she was right, she informed Bouchaule of Vogel's little scheme to spy on him. Bouchaule thought it typical German skullduggery and reacted with an amused sniff. He gave her an appreciative kiss on the cheek for her devotion, as if he expected nothing less, and then laid out a plan to give Vogel new but useless information that led to a scientific dead end.

Even if Vogel was on the up and up, there was nothing to report to her superiors, so she didn't consider her duplicity detrimental to the cause. Bouchaule's research was stalled—nothing had changed in that regard—and she could at least take comfort in the fact that her plan to keep the virus in check and Jenny safe had succeeded.

As the winter of 1944 dragged on, life in Paris had grown harder. Food had become more difficult to come by. Even the black market, once merely an alternative, had turned into a necessity after new, unrealistic rationing rules had made it too expensive for those who needed it most.

Care packages from the country were intercepted by the Germans, and despite their oppressive dominance, even they were feeling the pinch of a city on the verge of starvation. Spring brought little relief, as the Germans funneled the bulk of resources to their military to counter the Russian surge in the East, and by early summer, the Allied landings at Normandy did little to curtail the hardships.

The Germans stepped up the fight against the resistance, and the resistance, in turn, pushed back. With the help of Allied weapons drops and agents to train them in their use, the strengthening rebel Maquis groups in the hills grew as fast as they could arm themselves. There was a general unrest in Paris, an anxious buzz, like the impatient squirming during the last mile of a long journey home. The people were growing bolder, starting protests and skirmishes in the streets against the soldiers, but they often paid with their lives. Their anger and sparse weapons were no match for the occupying forces still very much in control.

Kathryn sensed the anxiety more and more every day and found the impending changes unnerving, but Bouchaule seemed oblivious, going on with their routine as if whatever happened would happen to someone else and not to them. All that changed one day in late July.

Kathryn came home to find Bouchaule in his basement lab, frantically packing up boxes of files and burning others.

"What are you doing?" she asked.

"We have to leave."

"Leave? Why?"

He stopped what he was doing and looked up. "Have you not heard? The Allies have broken through the hedgerows in the West."

She was speechless. Finally, progress. She tried not to show her relief and pride.

"This war will be over soon," he said as he continued his task. "There's nothing to stop that now. The city will fall quickly. We can't be here." He looked up. "Do you understand?"

She blinked for a moment. He was talking like a German, like the city back in French hands was a threat to their safety.

"Do you understand?" he repeated impatiently.

She nodded. The citizens would view her as a collaborator. No matter what she had done for the resistance in the past, or what Bouchaule had done for them, they would be considered collaborators to an angry mob that wouldn't listen or remember the details.

"I want you out of here tonight," Bouchaule said, as he tossed more papers into the furnace.

It was all happening too fast. "Thierry, wait—"

"Tonight!"

She stared at him, her heart racing as she tried to take it all in. "And you?"

Before he could answer, Annalise opened the door at the top of the stairs.

"Thierry! Gestapo!"

They both looked at each other wide-eyed, momentarily paralyzed by the word.

"Stay here. I'll be back."

"Thierry—"

"I'll be back."

Kathryn stared in disbelief at the disarray around her. She sifted through some papers on his desk, picked one up, and sat numbly in his chair as she heard him lock the door behind him.

He returned, calmer than when he left, and she thought he must be the only man in the world calmed by a visit from the Gestapo. It was a work-related delivery, he assured her, and nothing to worry about. He put the large envelope he'd just received into his briefcase and led her upstairs to tell her the plan and help her pack a small suitcase.

The time had come for them to part, and Kathryn waited anxiously in the foyer as Bouchaule gave instructions to his driver.

"Make sure she gets safely on that train. It's going to be a madhouse down there."

"Of course," his driver replied.

Kathryn lifted her chin as Bouchaule approached, finding her emotions hard to place and even harder to disguise after what she'd found on his desk.

He took her hands, which she couldn't stop from trembling. "It's going to be fine, darling. I promise. I'll be right behind you in a few days."

"Then let me stay, Thierry. What's a few days?"

"The tide outside is turning. I know you feel it, and I will not risk your safety just to have a few days. Besides, I will be so busy tying up my affairs, we'd hardly have a moment. Please"—he stroked her cheek —"I'll be right behind you."

Kathryn exhaled and closed her eyes as her skin crawled at his touch.

"Think of it as a holiday," Bouchaule said with a smile, trying to put her at ease. "The countryside is beautiful. I've been assured the Maquisards have the area secured, and you can relax—"

"What a ridiculous thing to say," Kathryn said. It was no less dangerous in the countryside, *especially* in the countryside, places so remote as to be the lawless Wild West.

Bouchaule's anxiety about their separation finally surfaced when he took her in his arms and held her tightly, burying his face in her hair.

"We're stronger together than we are apart," he reminded her. "I won't rest until I am with you again."

She forced a smile to reassure him and played her part to perfection. "I can take care of myself."

Bouchaule held her tighter. "If I had the slightest doubt about that, I would not let you out of my sight."

His driver held up his wrist and pointed at his watch. Bouchaule nodded and reluctantly released his hold.

Kathryn backed off and shook her head. "I have a bad feeling about leaving you here."

"Darling—"

"Don't you stay in this city one moment longer than you have to," she warned with all the sincerity she could muster. "Do you hear me?"

"I'll be right behind you. Three days at the most."

Kathryn placed her hands on Bouchaule's chest and found his heart racing. She searched his eyes, eyes that at times reflected so much and at times so very little. Today they reflected fear, uncertainty, and love.

Kathryn's kiss held a mix of emotions, but mostly anger, which he mistook as desperation. It would be their last, thank goodness, and she lamented that it took her so long to see what was right in front of her.

CHAPTER SIX

As predicted, the train station was a madhouse. People were rushing everywhere, like rats leaving a sinking ship. But these rats differed from the pack that left during the exodus before the occupation. These were well-off collaborationist rats. Some looked over their shoulders, haunted by shame. Others feared reprisals by those who had endured the hardships of the occupation without the comfort of wealth or status to secure them a bearable existence. And still, others walked with their heads held high, like they were above the mayhem beneath their arrogant chins.

It was easy to offer the concerned farewell wave to Bouchaule's driver as the train pulled out of the station. It wasn't an act. From the moment she saw the communiqué about the arrival of the reservoir—which meant Jenny—among the scattered papers to be burned on Bouchaule's desk in the lab, she knew the life she'd built in Paris was over. She had to remain calm and pretend she didn't see the rest of the papers surrounding it. For the next few hours, she'd have to hold on to the lies she'd been living with and savor the sanity the delusion afforded her. Then she would succumb to the truth, which would devour her once and for all.

Kathryn didn't have time to plan anything or pack accordingly or even sort out her emotions about how and why her perfect scheme to protect Jenny had gone awry. As usual, she was running, but instead of running from something, she was running toward something. She had to get to Jenny's appointed position before dawn the next day, warn her, and this time, keep her out of harm's way for good. It was the only thing of value she had left to offer.

She made the connections to Dijon, and after trading her fine clothes, food, and much sought after toiletries and makeup from her suitcase for a practical pair of trousers, blouse, light jacket, and a bicycle, she eventually arrived at her destination, exhausted and barely in time.

She crouched in the brush, which overlooked an open field nestled between dry-stacked lime rock walls, and took a well-needed break after spending the night climbing through defunct vineyards and small deserted farms pocked by recent Allied bombings. From her vantage point on the hill above, she could see the deserted farmhouse by the dim light of the first hint of dawn. She exhaled a curse at whoever chose the isolated building. It was the lone structure in the middle of nothing but open fields, with no protection for someone arriving or running away.

She stared for a few moments, considering her approach, but her harried journey soon caught up with her, and her gaze drifted aimlessly into the distance. She was nearly there, but the intensity that had driven her so relentlessly to this point abandoned her, and she deflated, all energy gone. The lack of sleep was washing over her like a warm blanket, and she sat back on her heels, momentarily giving in to fatigue. She scrubbed her face with her hand to pull herself out of it. When she focused again, she saw, to the left and below, a lone figure on a bicycle pedaling up to the deserted farmhouse and then entering, carrying a small case. This was definitely the place, and unless another reservoir had been found, that would be Jenny, smack dab in the middle of the last place on earth she should be.

Kathryn took a steadying breath, as adrenaline straightened her spine. Just as she was about to start a determined but conservative descent to the farmhouse, a distant rumble came from above and behind. She turned to see the twinkle of muted headlights threading their way down the road from the hill looming at her back.

She hadn't run into any German patrols all night, so when she glimpsed the distinct shape of a *Kübelwagen* staff car followed by a three-ton troop transport teeming with soldiers, she knew it wasn't by chance that they were heading her way.

She had made it this far unnoticed, protected by the darkness of night, but the only way to reach Jenny before the Germans was to cross the open field, while the vehicles took the long, winding road down. She would be exposed, but maybe the night would hold on for just a little while longer and shelter her mad dash.

All fatigue was forgotten when she bolted from her cover, and she was miraculously across the field and just hopping the last fence at the farmhouse gate before the Germans noticed her and started shouting. They were close now and barreling down the drive. She begged her spent body for a burst of energy that would carry her the last ten yards before the soldier manning the MG42 machine gun mounted on the bucket car could cut her down in a rain of bullets.

There was no time for a warning or for identifying herself. Jenny would have heard the commotion by now and braced herself against the far wall for action. Kathryn knew Jenny's training taught her to shoot low, then high, when defending a room, but they'd had many "discussions" disagreeing over various procedures, and she couldn't remember if that was one of them. Not willing to come this far just to be gunned down by her own, she picked up a large rock just before landing on the porch and tossed it at the door a split second before hurling herself backwards through the large front window like a pole-vaulter clearing the bar.

Jenny was eager to get on with her mission. The eerie silence around her was a jarring contrast to the constant drone of the Lysander's engine that had buzzed in her brain on the flight over the channel in the early morning hours. She was thankful she was part of an agent exchange and could land in France, rather than leap into the dark void beneath the belly of a plane and drift helplessly to the earth at the mercy of the wind and the ability of the pilots to dump her at precisely the right moment to hit her target on the ground.

She was one of the lucky ones, and she had exhaled in relief when the signal torches on the ground came into view. A man had helped her from the plane, and she had shed her oversized jumpsuit, resisting the urge to throw up after the bumpy field landing. With her blonde hair tucked up under a dark beret, she looked more like a French boy than a girl, but she would blend right in wearing slacks and a blouse accented with a light scarf around her neck.

After handshakes and well-wishes all around, she bicycled toward a meeting with a French resistance group that was waiting for the compact communications radio she carried in her small leather suitcase.

She had found the farmhouse without incident, but now, the waiting was killing her.

Everything that had led to this moment swirled in her head and flooded her with memories, starting with her father's death. The unexpected barrage of emotions churned on until thoughts of Kathryn rose to the surface and overwhelmed her senses. Lust. Love. Pain. Forgiveness.

Jenny breathed deeply and tried focusing on the job at hand, but everything she had learned in mission training was melding together until she couldn't pull out any one detail and say for certain she had it right. Falling apart now wasn't an option. "Settle down, Jenny. Think," her father used to say when she was a child and got worked up.

She missed her father, something she fought hard against while she was studying for her assignment. The science came easily to her—it always had—and it was more out of rebellion than dislike for the field that she had turned her back on it. She regretted that decision now. So many questions would forever remain unanswered. As the key to his work, they could have worked side by side, sharing ideas as they grew closer. She closed her eyes against the tragedy of it. Why was she feeling this now, of all times?

Needing a distraction, she crouched to the floor, turned on her flashlight, and opened the radio case to make sure everything was in working order. What she found left her wide-eyed and ready to panic. Inside was a cardboard facsimile of a radio, and inside that, a small sack of sand for weight.

"What the—?"

Holmes had betrayed her. He was her only contact after she got to London, where they finalized her mission preparation. His aide, Brian, was so sincere when he handed over the radio case and shook her hand for luck before she boarded the plane. She didn't even have time to process the betrayal, or her panic, when the rumble of approaching vehicles and shouting Germans spurred her into action. She turned off the light and reached for her gun. The back window was the only escape route, but a loud thud at the front door startled her before she could move.

Never fire at anything you can't see, she'd been taught since she first held a gun, but those rules no longer applied. She slid to the floor, with her back against the wall, and reacted with four shots in rapid succession, spraying the door from floor to ceiling in a precise line, right up the middle.

A large dark object crashed through the front window to the left and drew her fire there. Four more shots rang out, and her Colt automatic was empty. The object landed at her feet, and now obvious that it was a person, she was about to pummel them with the butt of her gun when, out of the darkness, a familiar voice said, "Low to high. Good girl."

"*Kathryn?*"

"We have to go!"

Her state of shock notwithstanding, Jenny wasn't about to disagree.

Kathryn ducked out the back window, close on Jenny's heels, and ran through the abandoned muddy fields, dodging bomb craters, leaping drainage ditches, and hopping over stone walls on the way to a stand of tall trees, where they would spoil the pursuit of the soldiers' vehicles. Foot soldiers were giving chase, and Kathryn was glad she and Jenny were running downhill, because she would never make it otherwise.

Jenny stayed in pace with her, despite her shorter strides, and it was not by intention that Jenny was slightly ahead. Kathryn had nothing left, her legs numbly churning on pure adrenaline, and as they reached the edge of the tree stand, she looked back at the five pursuing soldiers gaining on them and knew they would never outrun them. She could see the vehicles in the distance weaving their way through the maze of farms, and there weren't enough rounds between them, even if Jenny had an extra magazine to take them all down. By the time they reached the trees, the elevated terrain had done her in. She couldn't run any longer, and their only chance—Jenny's only chance—was to keep the Germans occupied while she got away.

When Kathryn gave up her flight, she didn't call out to Jenny. That was an invitation to a protest and a guarantee that Jenny would be by her side when she was captured or killed. She let her run on alone and leaned against a tree to steady her aim. Despite the support, she was unable to control her shaking limbs and labored breathing, and two shots missed badly. The soldiers stopped running and dropped to the ground, raising their rifles like snipers in the grass.

"Kathryn!" she heard, predictably. Kathryn grimaced. If Jenny came back for her now, the soldiers would have them.

"Go, Jenny!"

Shots rang out from all sides, as partisans appeared from behind the trees, firing at the Germans. The gunfire startled Kathryn, and what began as a flinch turned into an involuntary collapse, as her body gave in to exhaustion and the relief that someone else had taken up her cause.

She was grabbed by the collar and found herself peering into Jenny's very determined green eyes.

"Come on!"

"I can't."

Jenny tucked her gun into the back of her waistband and dropped to her knees, searching her up and down with worried hands. "Are you hit?"

Kathryn shook her head, still gasping for air.

With renewed determination, Jenny curled two fists into her shirt, stood over her, yanked her close, and annunciated each word precisely when she said, "I am *not* going to leave you here, so we die together right now, or you get off your ass and we run! Now, *come on!*"

Kathryn knew she meant what she said, and she offered what help she could as Jenny hoisted her to her feet and pulled her deeper into the tree stand.

A young Frenchman waved them forward, and they followed him out of the trees and into the outskirts of what had once been a small picturesque village. The buildings were bombed out shells now, with only memories and stubborn defiance holding up their crumbling walls.

Kathryn found some untapped strength in the renewed hope that they might actually get out of the situation alive. Sporadic gunfire echoed in the distance as she glanced over her shoulder before entering the nearest doorway. There was no trace of the German vehicles or soldiers on the road behind them.

The man led them into a cellar that housed rows and rows of empty wine racks. The skeletal sentinels stood tall under gently arched ceilings that seemed to go on forever. They hurried past the forlorn reminders of a once flourishing industry and emerged at the top of a tight stairway into what used to be a store. She couldn't tell what kind exactly. The interior was in shambles and had been picked clean of its goods. The windows were blown out, and the door was missing, but the roof was still intact, which was a rarity if the surrounding buildings were any indication.

The Frenchman instructed them to stay put. His friends had a truck, and they would come by shortly and take them to safety. He warned that if the Germans were pursuing them, the truck would slow down, but it wouldn't stop, so they would have to run for it. He looked at Kathryn specifically, suspecting her capacity for physical exertion was at its limit. She nodded she'd be fine, knowing Jenny would toss her in bodily if necessary.

The man started to leave, but Kathryn grabbed his arm and said in French, "They cannot take her. Do you understand?"

Jenny stepped between them. "They cannot take *us*."

The Frenchman smiled and bridged the two women with a hand on each shoulder. "We'll get you both out of here. Be ready."

Kathryn nodded as she watched him run out the door. The last of her adrenaline went with him and she bent over, supporting herself with her hands on her knees.

Jenny put her hand on her back. "Are you all right?"

Kathryn shrugged out from under her concern and stepped away. "Out of shape."

Jenny stared at her in disbelief. "What was that, a brush-off?"

Kathryn's carefully crafted world had fallen apart, and now that they were out of the hunt for a few minutes, grim reality was quickly replacing the panicked fear that had propelled her at breakneck speed through the French countryside. Anger was welling up in her, and she paced in frustrated silence, trying to funnel her volatile emotions into some semblance of civility.

Jenny had no such restraint. "Wait, are you angry at *me*?"

"What are you doing here, Jenny? I sent you away to keep you safe."

"What did you expect me to do, Kathryn? You dropped the key to everything in my lap and just walked away. Here, Jenny, deceive your government, skip off into the sunset and have a happy life? I am an OSS agent. I swore an oath to my country. I can't just drop off the face of the earth and pretend none of this happened. We're at war. It's my duty to fight until I'm dead or we've won. I don't know what makes you so special that you think you're above it all. You took the same oath."

"I was trying to save your life! Maybe millions of lives by keeping that project hidden."

"That wasn't your decision to make."

Kathryn laughed humorlessly into the air. Jenny's response was so typical. "Well, look around. I'd say it was the right decision, and I'd make it again." Jenny's lack of vision and eternal naiveté was nothing new, but how blind could she possibly be? "Don't you realize that chip on your shoulder has made everything your father and I did to protect you worth nothing? When will you learn to think past your first impulse?"

"I've thought plenty, Kathryn. I've learned my lesson well, and you're the one who taught it to me. You let your personal feelings distract you from the big picture. I don't have that luxury, and I won't make that mistake."

Kathryn resisted the urge to point out that Jenny's high and mighty detachment was missing back there in the trees when she refused to go on without her. "So, this situation is my fault?"

"Don't be juvenile," Jenny said. "You want to see a chip on the shoulder? Look in the mirror. We could die here today, and I don't really give a shit whose fault it is. We both did what we felt we had to do, and here we are. I'm sorry your little plan has gone off the rails, but my life of late hasn't exactly been the bed of roses I planned either."

Kathryn returned Jenny's stare. The animosity between them was ridiculous. Jenny's accusation had merit, and Kathryn acknowledged it. She blew out a tense breath and wiped the sweat from her brow with the back of her hand. "I know."

She wanted to scream from the deepest pit of her soul that she hadn't prevented this from happening, but she also ached to hold Jenny in her arms. Tears welled in her eyes, and she didn't know if it was horror or joy at seeing her again.

Jenny read her like she always did, and in an instant, they melted into a desperate embrace. Kathryn lost herself in the intoxicating comfort of the only place she called home.

Kathryn never wanted to let go. "I'm so sorry. This is my worst nightmare, and I thought I'd licked it."

Jenny tightened her hold.

"I know what you were trying to do, and bless you for it, but this is bigger than you and me. It always has been. I know you're scared. I am too. But did you really think I would just do nothing when I learned the truth?"

Kathryn closed her eyes in defeat, admitting Jenny's reaction was only a small consideration in her plan. Realistically, she knew Jenny would do something, but she never thought she'd wind up here of her own volition. Fearing her legs might give out, Kathryn gave Jenny a final squeeze and then sat on the nearest pile of rubble, which was a partially demolished wall of stone and plaster.

"I just wanted you safe. As for the big picture ... without you, they have nothing, and now—" Her voice trailed off.

Jenny sat beside her. "I'm not afraid to die if I have to, Kat."

Kathryn cut a worried look at her. The thought of her death was a kick in the gut that sent a renewed wave of panic through her. Jenny was steady, with no hint of fear to leave this world. Kathryn didn't know this woman. Whatever had happened to her in the seven months they were apart had hardened her. She held determination and resignation with equal regard and was prepared for either. Jenny had become stronger, and she had grown weaker. Resignation had beaten down any determination left in her, and she felt hollow, void of anything good or right, and incapable, based on her history, of telling the difference.

"You're not going to die, Jenny," she said wearily. "You're too important to them. You notice they weren't shooting at us, just pursuing. They want you alive, and if they take you—" She shook her head, still dumbfounded that after everything, it had still come down to them running for their lives. "You have no idea what's going on over here."

"I know exactly what's going on over here, and I assure you, I'll kill myself before I'll let them make me a part of it."

Kathryn watched Jenny reflexively fondle what could only be a lethal L-pill sewn into the seam of her sleeve's cuff. Their eyes met again, and love, thought long lost, welcomed her.

Jenny tenderly took Kathryn's hand and then eyed the automatic Walther P.38 clutched in her other. "If it comes to it, you can have my L-pill if you'd rather. I don't mind the bullet. I promise they're not going to get me alive, and I won't let them take you again either … if that's all right."

Jenny was definitely stronger than she ever was, and Kathryn marveled at her resolve. She couldn't imagine watching her bite down on the rubber-coated glass capsule and seeing the cyanide exact its gruesome toll. If Jenny were to die, she would gladly follow, feeling that her utterly useless life would be complete. She tightened her grip on the German pistol that Bouchaule had given her and knew it would serve her well if it came to that.

"I don't think that will be a problem this time, but thank you for the backup plan."

Jenny nodded.

Kathryn couldn't help the sense of dread settling around them in the silence. They were sitting ducks in the center of the storm, waiting for the inevitable next wave of hell to break loose. She looked at Jenny and wondered what possessed her to expose herself like she had.

"If you know how vital you are to the big picture, why would you put yourself in this position?"

"Only I know the information in my father's documents. I'm the only person who can carry out this mission."

Kathryn shook her head in self-recrimination. Jenny was here because she gave her those papers. "I should have burned it all."

Jenny squeezed her hand. "We're going to win this fight because you protected my father's work."

"But I couldn't protect you."

Jenny pursed her lips and tilted her head with an expression that said *you're being ridiculous*. "I have to do this. We have to know how far things have progressed here."

"I've already reported that. Why would they send someone else?"

Jenny looked at her strangely. "Kat, no one has heard from you since you disappeared. You're considered a rogue agent."

"What?"

"You've had plenty of time to set up communications, at least get a message through. What else were we to think?"

Kathryn was stunned for a moment, having sent reports to Vogel nearly every week and through Claudette's friends before that, but with her initial instincts about Vogel confirmed and her doubts about Holmes reiterated, she wasn't surprised by the betrayal. She was, however, surprised by Jenny siding with the agency. She dropped her hand and leaned away to look into her eyes.

"And what did *you* think?"

Jenny dropped her gaze. "That's part of what I'm here to find out."

Kathryn couldn't believe it, not from Jenny. "You think I'm with *them*?"

Thinking Kathryn was anything but loyal seemed irrational in the shadow of her incredulous glare, but Holmes had done a good job convincing Jenny that Kathryn had given up the good fight for the bad.

"We've not had contact with Miss Hammond for many months," Holmes had said grimly as he detailed the added incentive for her mission. "This usually means the agent is dead or has gone over to the other side. Delcourt has reported her alive and well and with Bouchaule in Paris, so we are left with the ugly alternative."

"She wouldn't do that."

"We should hope not, but Miss Hammond has been through some trying times. Sometimes they believe their legend. Sometimes, to survive, they get lost in their cover and cannot help themselves."

Jenny didn't like Holmes's suggestion, but she had to admit, if she'd been through even a fraction of what Kathryn had been through in her life, she would have lost her mind ages ago. Kathryn was a survivor, and there was no telling what that entailed behind enemy lines.

"She knows too much, Miss Ryan. Do you understand?"

Jenny blinked in disbelief, as his implication washed over her with the violent revulsion of the absurd solution that it was.

"She trusts you," Holmes went on.

The picture was clear, and Jenny didn't like it.

"We have located her whereabouts, and among your other duties, we need you to get close to her, analyze the situation, and act accordingly."

"Accordingly?"

"Accordingly." His eyes pinned her with all the weight an execution carries. "Will you have a problem with that, Miss Ryan?"

She didn't dare refuse for fear they might send someone who would actually eliminate her.

"No, sir. No problem at all," she had assured him with practiced indifference.

She would infiltrate Bouchaule's Paris lab, take over for their failed agent, Georges Delcourt, and thanks to her technical training with the temperamental new electron microscope, she would become an indispensable part of the research team. She alone knew the direction of her father's work, and only she could judge the danger posed by the enemy's advances. If Kathryn was moving in those circles, she'd find her.

The sun slowly burned through the early morning mist, bathing the bombed out storefront with the first rays of dawn. As the light struck Kathryn's face, Jenny was shocked by the first clear glimpse of her since the day they parted in her father's lab. She was thin, terribly thin, something she noticed during their embrace. Her once glowing complexion was pale and sickly opaque, and her skin was like wet rice paper, clinging to her angular frame. Her eyes were tired and dull and full of hurt, waiting for an answer.

Kathryn couldn't believe Jenny had nothing to say for herself. Instead, Jenny just stared at her with a helpless look that registered somewhere between *I had no choice* and *I had to be sure*.

"Jesus, Jenny." Kathryn stood abruptly and stepped away. After all they'd been through, after everything she'd done, Jenny doubted her loyalty. She felt like a fool, her sacrifice folly, like a teenager with a crush on the popular girl who would never like her back.

She turned, ready to address Jenny's lack of faith in her, when a bullet ricocheted off the stone doorjamb and embedded itself in the plaster wall just past her shoulder. Both women hit the deck and quickly crawled for the safety of the thick stone wall beneath the missing front window. A smattering of gunshots rang out in the distance, but then ceased, giving way to the dull drone of an approaching vehicle.

"So much for not shooting at us," Kathryn complained. She got into position to stick her head up and assess the situation, but Jenny grabbed her by the shirt and pulled her back down.

"Of course I don't believe them," she said. "I'm here partly because I was afraid they'd send someone who doesn't know you like I do. No matter what it looks like to them, Kat, I *know* you. I know you would never turn."

Kathryn realized Holmes had used the notion to ensure Jenny's cooperation. She looked into pleading green eyes and fell into the love and desperation she found there. Clutching Jenny's hand buried in the front of her shirt, she kissed her. Hard. And then took a breath. "I'll apologize for that later."

Jenny's gaze dropped from her eyes to her lips. "Don't bother."

The ensuing kiss released months of pent-up longing and grief. All the things she'd banished from her heart came flooding back when Jenny's fingers tangled themselves in the hair at the nape of her neck and deepened their kiss. Healing and forgiveness poured into her soul, and the heady rush of emotions pulled her far away from the dust and destruction around them. Jenny's insistent moan into her mouth was a heavenly sound she never thought she'd hear again. Her head swam with memories of their lovemaking—the weight of Jenny's breasts in her hands, her lips on the soft flesh of Jenny's inner thigh, the taste of her, and her rapturous cry when she came in her mouth.

God, she'd thrown it all away for nothing. Fate had played its hand, and the enemy was upon them. She wanted to sob at the tragic irony of it all.

She took a breath and pressed her forehead against Jenny's, grateful they had each other, despite the circumstances. A tear fell as she closed her eyes. Whatever happened next, she would never forget this moment of solace. "Thank you."

Another smattering of gunshots caused them to duck again, and hurried footsteps joined the ever-increasing rumble of a truck grinding through its gears as someone shouted, "Now! Now! Here they come! Run!"

Jenny pulled Kathryn to her feet and quickly peered down the street before pressing their backs to the wall beside the doorless entry. The man who had helped them ran toward them at full speed, with the promised escape vehicle gaining at his rear. "Come on!" he urged, as the truck pulled up beside him and matched his pace. He hopped into the open bed, where two companions pulled him up, and then leaned over the side, motioning them over.

The truck was almost to their doorway when Jenny darted from the safety of the store, her fist still clinging possessively to Kathryn's shirt, making sure they weren't separated. No more gunshots rang out, but she could see a group of German soldiers pursuing on foot, with their own truck about to barrel past them.

They ran toward the partisan's outstretched hands and tossed their guns into the jostling bed as they easily made the leap onto the back of the truck and into waiting arms. Jenny was in first and made a reassuring glance to her left to see two strong arms hauling Kathryn in. The third man, clinging to the front of the truck bed, reached around the large tank of the wood gasifier fueling the vehicle and banged on the roof. "Go, go, go!"

The truck lurched forward and simultaneously hit a mortar crater, throwing everyone off balance, and suddenly, strong arms were useless, as Kathryn and her anchor flew toward the open air at the back end of the truck.

"No!" Jenny screamed as she lunged for the pair. She grabbed the man's ankle, and the other Frenchmen had a secure grasp on the man's waistband, but she could only watch helplessly as Kathryn slipped from his grasp and hit the ground hard, her body awkwardly tumbling backwards, head over heels onto the cobblestone street like a discarded rag doll, before finally rolling to a face down stop.

Jenny froze only for a second. She had a promise to keep. Kathryn's P.38 was within easy reach, so she tried to crawl forward to retrieve the gun, but a well-meaning Frenchman who thought she might leap from the truck to save Kathryn held her tightly at the waist. She had no such intention and quickly landed a hard elbow to his chest, freeing herself. They were moving quickly out of range. The Germans were closing in on Kathryn fast, and every second counted. Without thought or hesitation, she trained the gun on Kathryn's motionless form, but the uneven road and motion of the truck reduced her marksmanship skills to dumb luck. She held her breath and tapped out tracking shots aimed at Kathryn's head. After a heavy first pull, the trigger was light and crisp, and six shots of the expected eight rang out in quick succession. Each shot was closer to its ultimate goal, but the sixth, the killing blow, coincided with a jarring thud as the truck hit another pothole.

The pistol's slide blew back in surrender, having spent its ordinance, but Jenny kept pressing the immobile trigger as if it would magically produce more chances for a shot to find its mark. She was knocked off balance and didn't see the final shot strike, so she didn't know if she'd done the job. A swarm of German soldiers capturing their prize obscured her last glimpse of Kathryn, and then the truck careened around a corner, throwing her into her well-meaning Frenchman again.

The pursuing German truck soon appeared around the corner, and Jenny stared blindly at the explosion that took it off their heels. Its burning hulk blocked the narrow street against the remaining pursuers, and they were in the clear, but too late for Kathryn.

There was no celebration of their escape as they bumped down the road, and the Frenchman who had Kathryn jolted from his grasp stared at her mutely.

"Did I hit her?" Jenny asked, barely able to speak the words.

They had no answers for her, only condolences and what looked like newfound respect. She wanted neither. She stared at the empty P.38 clutched in her shaking hand. Her fingers had a white-knuckled grasp around the German pistol's art déco bakelite grip, as if letting it go would solidify its failure. Her failure.

Kathryn's last words, delivered with a trembling voice, drowned out everything around her. *"Thank you."*

For what? For getting her killed? For getting her tortured and then killed?

She closed her eyes and tasted Kathryn on her lips. Her heart raced as her misstep consumed her. She would never see her again, taste her again, hold her again.

She should have leaped from the truck and made sure Kathryn wasn't taken. She promised. It would have cost them both their lives, but she should have done it. Kathryn would have. She never would have left her like a wounded dog in the street to be eaten alive by the hungry wolves. Never.

CHAPTER SEVEN

Jenny loved guns. She loved the weight of them, the intricate mechanisms that shaped their form and function, the sound they made as the slide eased back and released with a forceful clack to load a round into the chamber, the raw power of the recoil after the trigger pull, and the graceful dance of the spent casing as it twirled in the air and landed with a *tink* at her feet. What she loved most about guns was the satisfaction of a well-placed shot. She prided herself on it. But in one horrible moment, pride and skill became useless, and now she stared at the elegant P.38 in her hand with hatred, the instrument no longer something she admired.

It was easier to hate the gun than herself. She'd run that gauntlet already and found herself struggling to live with what she had done. She tried to convince herself she'd done the right thing by honoring the big picture, but it wasn't working. The scene played over and over in her head, and she mentally cringed at the moment she raised the pistol, so sure of her proficiency and so full of her cursed principals that she didn't even consider leaping to Kathryn's side to fight for their freedom or die trying. It was something she would regret until her last breath.

Now, she sat alone with her anguish outside her rescuers' hideout, nestled deep in the hills. The sun had just fallen below the tree line, and darkness seeped through the dense woods with long, shadowy fingers, ready to drag her down into its depths of despair. She would go without a struggle.

It seemed they had driven for hours to get to safety. It wasn't so far, really, as the crow flies, but the dirt road twisted and turned as they made the lumbering climb up the mountain and time and distance blurred into a hollow silence. Jenny was too numb to speak; the others weren't sure what to say.

She had tried not to imagine what was happening to Kathryn if she was still alive, and she prayed and loathed at the same time the possibility that she might have killed her outright.

The truck had finally stopped, and one of her somber companions helped her down from the bed. A group came out of a small well-kept cottage to greet them. The leader, an elderly Frenchwoman who wore the whole of the occupation on her tired face, had asked about the others—the ones who blew up the pursuing truck—and assured they were holding their positions, turned her attention toward her.

"Why have you brought her here?"

Jenny's well-meaning Frenchman had led the older woman a few steps away. The rest of the group followed, and Jenny had watched as they turned their backs to her and listened to her story told in a hushed whisper. They all looked her way when he had finished, their faces wearing a mixture of compassion, pity, admiration, and indifference, as if to say, *Welcome to the fight. Now you're one of us.*

The weight of their stares had shattered any rationalization she'd made to keep her sanity, and reality came crashing down on her. She couldn't breathe. One way or the other, she'd murdered the woman who meant everything to her. It was inconceivable. She tried to tell herself she'd done everything right.

She'd worked so hard to become detached, to be a good agent. Always focus on the mission and remain indifferent. Personal attachments and desires only led to the same mistakes her father had made.

The same mistakes Kathryn had made. She had succeeded where they had failed. When she saw Kathryn again, she had the resolve to do what needed to be done. When the action started, she did what she'd been trained to do without hesitation. She put the mission above everything and survived to see it through. Even Kathryn had instructed her to do that. *"Don't ever go back, people,"* she had said after their failed mission simulation. *"Do not needlessly sacrifice yourself to a losing cause."*

Kathryn was the losing cause this time, and she was justified in leaving her to the Germans. It was the right thing to do. Jenny buried her face in her hands. The thought of what she'd done tore at her, and she wished she was still that impetuous girl who questioned every-thing and followed her heart above her head. Leaving Kathryn defenseless to the enemy wasn't right. It was cowardly.

All her high and mighty talk of putting personal feelings aside for the "big picture" was bullshit, and Kathryn was the one who knew what was important. Kathryn had saved the one she loved *and* kept her out of the hands of those threatening mass destruction. What had she done? Nothing but selfishly live another day under the threat of capture, ensuring the next misstep would make every sacrifice made by others on her behalf worthless.

Even if she completed her mission, learned all Bouchaule's dirty little secrets, and killed him, what then? What could she do with that information? Who could she trust? For all her noble posturing, it was all about personal satisfaction—revenge—and it had cost Kathryn her life.

"When will you learn to think?" Kathryn had shouted. The words echoed in her head, and Jenny broke down. Her heart ached with grief, and she was sure she would die from guilt. Her legs gave out, and she crumbled to her knees and promptly threw up. The elderly woman came forward to help her, but the rest walked away, well aware of what was to come.

Retching gave way to sobbing, and she became hysterical, unable to bear her decision. "I have to go back!" she begged the woman. "I've made a terrible mistake. I have to go back!" She scrambled to her feet and accosted anyone within reach. "I have to help her. Where would they take her? Tell me! Please!"

The group was sympathetic, but there was nothing they could do. There were no answers for her, only the unforgiving burden of the unknown truth.

"Your friend is probably dead," the old woman had said bluntly. "They're no longer interested in prisoners."

The hopelessness in the woman's weary eyes told Jenny she'd known too much death, and from her grim confidence, she had seen this scene repeated too many times, with tragic results.

Unfortunately, she was wrong about Kathryn's captors. Her immediate death would have been horrible but merciful. What was truly tearing up her soul was the more likely scenario.

"They want me, and they'll torture her until they find me."

The Frenchwoman raised her chin slightly, realizing the stakes were higher than she thought. Jenny wasn't just another freedom fighter, she was a target, and that made them one too.

"What is your plan?"

Jenny could see a defensive wall going up, and she understood completely. Every moment she stayed put her new friends at greater risk.

She stood and wiped her face on her sleeve. Bouchaule was still out there, and she still had something he wanted. Now, more than ever, she had a mission to complete. "I need to get to Paris. If you could just point me in the right direction, I'll—"

The woman had put her hand on her shoulder. "Stay till morning. We'll make sure you have what you need and help as best we can."

Jenny almost broke into tears at her generosity. They were perfect strangers, but united by their common fight, they were sisters. "Thank you." Those words again.

The woman offered a half-smile. "Come inside and eat."

It was the last thing she wanted to think about. "I don't think I can."

"It's not often you find a decent meal. Come inside."

Jenny knew it would be an insult to refuse, but she wasn't sure she could hold it down, which would be an even bigger insult. The Frenchwoman understood but was not without wisdom learned the hard way.

"Would your friend forgive you for leaving her behind?"

Jenny didn't even need to think about it. "She wanted me to live, no matter the cost."

"Then live. Forgive yourself. You did what you could."

"It's not enough."

"Sometimes it's all you get."

Evening crept in until the long shadows surrendered to the night. Jenny sat beside a felled tree, lost in the numbing shock of grief. An owl unleashed a hollow screech nearby, startling her into awareness. Another screech followed, the cry trailing off into a gentle warble to await a reply. The dark forest threw back silence, and the bird didn't ask again. Jenny heard the whisper of its flapping wings as it took flight to seek companionship elsewhere, and she envied its graceful escape. There would be none for her. She would never see Kathryn again and may never know what became of her. She had to come to terms with that.

The Frenchwoman's words, "You did what you could," felt more like an accusation than a comfort. There were so many things she could have done, starting with following Dominic's carefully plotted path to her new life. Instead, she said tearful goodbyes to her aunt and uncle at The Grotto and embarked on what she thought was the perfect plan to honor the sacrifices made on her behalf and bring down the bastard that made them necessary.

If only she had stayed stateside, Kathryn would be in Paris with her assignment. She might be miserable, but at least she would be alive.

Jenny had exhausted herself with what ifs and self-recrimination, and in her isolation, she realized that no matter what she could have done, before she came overseas or after, there was nothing to be done now. Kathryn was out of her reach.

Life had played out, and now she must live with the consequences. She would have to move on, but she would never forgive herself. She thought of Kathryn, not what was happening to her now—that was too unbearable to imagine—but the strong woman she knew back home, carrying her guilt effortlessly. Kathryn faced every day with her sanity intact. Her guilt gave her purpose. Somehow, it conjured up strength and courage from the dark shroud of shame and self-loathing that it thrived on, and Jenny was only now beginning to comprehend the labored mechanics of such an existence.

She closed her eyes and took stock of her life, but it was pointless. She no longer recognized herself. Her past was irrelevant, and her future was all that mattered, but each step forward was a struggle. She had lost something integral to her being, and she couldn't help remembering Smitty's words about Kathryn: *"You should have known her before."*

Jenny cried again, this time gentle tears for the woman she never knew—tears she had denied herself when Smitty told her Kathryn's story, and tears for herself, for the woman she would never be again.

She thought of Smitty and the panic he must have felt when he learned they had taken Kathryn the first time and then his desperate mad scurry for a plan to rescue her. She imagined she would do the same if she could. It would save her from having to face her guilt.

Sounds of heavy ceramic dishes clanking against each other came from the cottage behind her. Jenny couldn't say she'd reached a truce with her anguish, but she was stubborn enough to put one foot in front of the other and begin the long journey back to the rest of her life.

She pushed herself up from the ground, brushed off the pine needles and self-pity, and joined the group in the cottage. They welcomed her with gentle smiles and made a place for her at the long wooden table, where a young woman brought her a piece of bread, a glass of wine, and a bowl of stew. The elderly woman who had come to her aid sat at the head of the table and tipped her glass in Jenny's direction before she drank. Her eyes were warm and welcoming now, proving she still had a rewarding glow for anyone brave enough to pick themselves up and carry on.

Jenny drank first, hoping to distance herself from reality, just for a little while. She looked around the table at her new friends and cleared her throat.

"I don't think I thanked you properly for helping us today."

Her well-meaning Frenchman, sitting across from her, shrugged. "You were running from them, and you were loyal to your friend. That's good enough for us."

Jenny nodded, as the sting of her failure momentarily stole her speech. She took another gulp of wine and began an apology into her food bowl for falling apart on them. "I'm sorry about before ... I just—"

She looked up to meet their eyes and stopped mid-apology. Stern stares, like she had just insulted their respective mothers, made her feel foolish for mentioning it. She clamped her mouth shut, and they went back to their conversations. The man next to her refilled her glass. She grinned a *thanks* but focused on her food, not willing to give up lucidity completely.

She had just finished mopping up her bowl with the last bit of bread when everyone went on high alert at the sound of an approaching vehicle. They all grabbed their guns, and the elderly woman stood with her hand out, ready to lead Jenny out of sight.

"It's Pascal!" someone yelled from just outside the door. "He's on a German motorbike! He's alone."

The young man burst into the room, and amid a cacophony of questions excitedly said, "We got them! Just the six of us! We got them all!"

The group crowded around him, pressing for details. One young woman grasped the tall, gangly youth by the shoulders.

"Your brother?"

He smiled and grasped her arms as he gleefully retold the valiant fight and how they had triumphed unscathed.

Jenny stepped forward. "There was a woman—"

"Yes! We have her. She is hurt, but—"

"Take me!"

"That's why I'm here," the boy said. He told the group that the others would meet them at the usual place and then led Jenny to the motorbike, motioning to the sidecar as he threw his leg over the bike.

"How badly is she hurt?" Jenny asked as she climbed in.

"Scrapes, bruises, pretty nasty knock on the head, but she's awake and aware."

That was all Jenny needed to hear. She held on tight as the boy sped back down the twisting mountain road toward the town.

Neither noticed the two cars creeping out of the woods after they had passed or the headlights peeking out from behind the canvas blackout shades when they winked on, illuminating the swirling dust of the path to the hideout.

Jenny was almost giddy with relief as she closed her eyes against the assault of road dirt and random insects drawn to the muted headlight of the motorcycle. She didn't care. She'd been given a reprieve. She wasn't a religious person, but at that moment, God was on the receiving end of a never-ending stream of thanks, and she was seriously considering rethinking the matter of an almighty being.

What would she say to Kathryn when she saw her? Would Kathryn be angry that she had shot at her? Suddenly, she was praising the gorgeous little P.38 and its measly eight-cartridge magazine and blessing the pothole that had pulled her off her mark. She had to laugh at the reversal of fortune. What just an hour ago was her soul-crushing regret was now her saving grace. *Everything happens for a reason*, she couldn't help thinking.

Their destination was not what Jenny expected. They didn't return to the town but instead went to a remote, sprawling building. It was an abandoned factory of some sort, the only structure standing in an area bombed into oblivion. The motorcycle weaved and dodged craters and rubble as they sped past the twisted wreckage of concrete walls cradled in the mangled fingers of reinforcing iron bars. One end of the vast rectangular building had collapsed, but the other, save the broken windows, stood strong and proud.

The boy pulled up alongside two heavy steel doors and dismounted. "This is it."

Jenny climbed out of the sidecar and corralled her windblown hair into a ponytail. "What is this place?"

"Used to be an armament factory," Pascal said. He took a flashlight from a saddlebag and led Jenny to the entrance.

Jenny noticed he proceeded without hesitation or fear. He seemed excited, like a child showing off his special hiding place to the neighborhood girl he liked. His enthusiasm was infectious, and for the first time in a long time, Jenny felt everything was going to be okay.

The boy haphazardly swept his light down the long, empty corridors as he recounted how the building had been abandoned for years after the company built a larger factory closer to town. The Germans had stolen whatever remained when they invaded, and the Allied bombs took care of the rest. No one had any interest in the abandoned shell, and it made a perfect hiding place.

Pascal moved along at a fast pace, and Jenny sensed him feeding off her impatience. They hadn't gone far into the building, but every moment spent in anticipation seemed like an eternity.

"There," he called out, pointing as they turned a corner.

A fan of light seeped out from under a closed door, bathing the dirty concrete floor in a dramatic halo that washed all it touched clean. Jenny sprinted the final yards past the rows of closed doors until she came to the room and flung open the door, squinting against the sudden burst of light.

Kathryn lay on her side in the middle of the small room, her arms pinned unnaturally to her sides by restraints pulling her biceps behind her back and rope tying her wrists together in front. A small island of blood grew on the floor beneath her split lower lip. She'd been beaten, and her hollow gaze seemed disoriented.

"Kathryn!"

Kathryn blinked twice, her bloodshot eyes growing round with recognition. "Run!" she croaked out in French, her voice hoarse and strained before absorbing a boot to the ribs from an SS soldier stepping out of the shadows with a smirk on his face and an MP40 submachine gun resting in his hands.

Jenny suffered a paralyzing split second of utter defeat. *Don't ever go back, people* kept playing in her head. Jenny had run into a trap doing just that. She was not leaving again. Kathryn would hate her for it, but she'd tried doing the right thing and found it too hard to live with. They were going to die together, but Pascal was not part of their death pact. He could still escape, and he had to warn the others.

From the opposite direction, the unmistakable grind of nailed boots on concrete got closer. Reaching behind her back for her gun, she turned and ordered Pascal to run. He was standing calmly in the middle of the corridor with his revolver raised at her face.

"I'm so sorry," he said. His once youthful eyes were now years older, reflecting the somber consequences of his actions in the half-shrug of his apology. "They have my brother and my friends."

CHAPTER EIGHT

Kathryn repeated her order to run, and feeling a boot at her back, rolled backwards, taking the soldier standing behind her off his feet. She craned her head around to the door, hoping Jenny had taken advantage of the distraction, but she was still standing in the doorway, staring down the hallway she'd just come up, with her hand frozen on the gun tucked into the back of her waistband.

Before she could yell again, a soldier had Jenny from behind. He took her gun and wrestled her into the room. They were followed by a young man pointing a revolver at Jenny, demanding his reward.

"My friends ... now!"

Kathryn released an anguished breath as despair stole the last of her strength. She would have cried if she had any emotion left. Her physical death would be redundant, because she was dead inside already, having failed at the most important task in her life.

She watched with apathy the scene before her. She could not blame the boy, whom Jenny had obviously trusted. He had clung to the hope that the Germans would keep their end of the bargain. They wouldn't, of course. He would be dead in moments.

"Put down the gun and I'll give you your friends," a seated *SS-*

Hauptsturmführer said in adequate French from his comfortable position at the back of the room. He lazily pushed back from the edge of a wooden table with his raised boot as he balanced his chair back on two legs.

The boy's gaze darted to the four Germans present until he settled on the only one in motion, the soldier Kathryn had knocked down, now scrambling to his feet.

"How do I know you'll set us free?" the boy asked warily of the man in charge.

The SS officer smiled and dropped his foot, letting the chair fall forward with a crisp clack on the concrete floor. He was a thin, middle-aged man of average height, with a strong jaw and platinum hair, in the cut of Heinrich Himmler. He stood, chest thrust forward, and snapped his open *feldgrau* tunic over his hips.

"Look around you, boy." He gestured to the armed soldiers. "If I wanted you dead, we wouldn't be having this conversation." He walked closer and crossed his arms. "I am a man of honor. I promised if you brought me the girl, I would set you free."

"And my friends," the boy reminded him.

"And your friends." He nodded. "You need only put down the gun."

The boy took stock of his limited options, slowly set the gun on the floor in front of him, and kicked it over to the officer, who picked it up and handed it to the nearest soldier.

"Now, that wasn't so hard." He motioned to the guard. "Show this young man to his friends."

The soldier brought the boy to the door across the hall and opened the door for him. He turned on the light with a quick mash to the switch beside the entry, and there the boy's friends were, all five of them, hanging by their necks from the water pipes above, bodies battered and bloody. The boy collapsed to his knees before them with a whimper, and the soldier nonchalantly put a bullet in the back of his head before turning off the light and closing the door.

"There." The SS officer turned with a smile. "Now he is free too. I am a man of my word."

. . .

Jenny struggled against the wide leather strap pulling her biceps tightly behind her back. She twisted in pain as her back and shoulder muscles began to spasm from the unnatural position. They'd bound her wrists in front, forcing her arms to her sides until she resembled a Tyrannosaurus Rex. She kept pulling against the strap restraining her arms, as much to relieve her muscles as to test her access to the cyanide pill sewn into her sleeve. She couldn't even touch her hands together let alone reach her cuff.

She had no intention of leaving Kathryn to suffer while she took the easy way out anyway, so she concentrated on what she could do to get them out of there.

Kathryn lay on the floor, tied in the same way, her wrists bloody from hours of restraint. Her body convulsed involuntarily as her cramped muscles sought relief. Every periodic tremor forced moans from her, while her semiconscious gaze remained fixed on the vacant corner of the small concrete room.

Jenny hadn't had time to feel terrified before, but now it was all she could do to hold herself together. She needed to be strong, needed a plan, but as the officer approached, hands behind his back in contemplation, all she could think of was begging for mercy ... for both of them.

From Kathryn's condition, Jenny could see this man knew no mercy, and as he slowly circled her, she tried desperately to remember her training. *Chapter Thirteen: Interrogation. Welcome to hell, you've been captured.* It was all she could remember of the lesson. That and Branson in the back of the room telling everyone they were royally fucked. She now knew why Kathryn had insisted the recruits memorize their manuals until the information was second nature. When in the situation, all thought is replaced by panic and fear. Only instinct remains, hopefully honed by training. She closed her eyes. *Do something! Reason with them. Threaten them.* She was valuable, after all.

The officer looked her up and down with a leer and a smirk, and Jenny decided he was a caricature. He was the archetypal evil German, with a peaked service hat propped perfectly on his head, riding breeches, knee boots, and a riding crop tucked under his arm like he seriously rode in there on a horse. All he was missing was a monocle and a long-stemmed cigarette holder.

"You are a very important person, my dear," he began.

She wanted to raise her chin and say, "That's right, you fucker. So you'd better let us go!" But she held her tongue.

"Someone went to a great deal of trouble to bring you here," he continued in his maddeningly condescending tone. "Why is that?"

He continued to speak in French, so Jenny assumed he either didn't speak English or didn't know they were Americans and, therefore, hadn't a clue about who they were or what was going on.

She snuck a look at Kathryn, knowing the officer wouldn't be asking if he could have gotten something out of her. Jenny knew if she cracked now, it would make Kathryn's suffering worth nothing, and she'd already done that once, so she boldly pursed her lips and remained silent, earning an approving nod from Kathryn.

"Don't look at her!" the officer said as he grabbed her chin and jerked it violently to his face with his leather-gloved hand. It smelled of blood, cigarettes, and sweat, and when he spoke, his breath smelled of liquor and rotting teeth.

Jenny nearly gagged as the stench of him filled her nostrils and lingered in the back of her throat like an odiferous eddy with nowhere to go.

"Answer me!" he said as he removed the riding crop from under his arm and raised it above his head to strike.

She sneered in defiance, trying to be brave, but she knew her trembling body gave her away.

"Harm a hair on her head and your boss will kill you," Kathryn warned convincingly, considering her condition.

"Shut up, you!" He flicked his head toward the nearest soldier, who dutifully kicked Kathryn in the gut.

Kathryn folded around the force of the soldier's boot, and blood and spittle flew violently from her mouth, forming a viscous red ribbon between her grimacing lips and the floor.

"Leave her alone!" Jenny couldn't help shouting.

The officer yanked her closer and pierced her with his cold gray eyes. "Or what?"

Jenny didn't dare antagonize him.

He smirked. "That's what I thought. You won't be so brave in a moment." He pushed her chin aside and made his way over to where Kathryn lay sputtering in pain on the floor. "You went out of your way to return for this woman," he said to Jenny as he undid the flap on the dark leather hard-shell holster cradling his Luger. "You must care for her very much."

Jenny could see his next move clearly, and a wave of anguish weakened her knees as she experienced firsthand what Kathryn must have felt as they slaughtered her friends in front of her while she clung to her silence.

The officer drew his weapon and nonchalantly aimed it at Kathryn's head. "Tell me what I want to know or I'll kill her."

No! I'll tell you everything! Jenny wanted to scream as panic gripped her. She suppressed the urge, but the effort to remain silent felt like hands closing around her throat as she struggled to feign indifference. She couldn't breathe for fear she'd break, and when she felt the truth about to force its way out, she sought Kathryn's eyes to beg forgiveness for her weakness. Relief stared back at her and a frightening lack of anything else. Kathryn mouthed "It's okay" behind the officer's back, and Jenny turned her head away, on the verge of sobbing at the resignation in her eyes.

Once you give up hope, you're as good as dead, Kathryn had taught her. She had seen Kathryn give up in the forest and again now, but she wasn't ready to let her go. She would never accept absolution for Kathryn's execution, and damn her for thinking she possibly could. Anger turned her horror and fear into renewed purpose, and she found her nerve.

The officer, thinking she'd turned away to avoid witnessing the execution, extended his free hand in her direction, as if to magically coax her chin forward. "No, no," he said in a sweet tone, pure spider to the fly. "You must watch."

Jenny gathered herself, prepared to fight for both of them. She looked him directly in the eyes with a furrowed brow, as if he were crazy, and offered Kathryn a silent apology, in case her plan backfired.

"Look at her," she said in a deceptively steady voice. "I think you'd be doing her a favor." She held her breath, hoping the reverse psychology worked.

The officer's eyes narrowed. He relaxed the arm pointing the gun and then slowly holstered his weapon. "Well, well," he said, sizing up the pair, "two clever women. Whatever shall I do?"

"You can go to hell," Kathryn said.

Jenny's eyes snapped to Kathryn, and she wanted to tell her to shut the fuck up. She was goading the man into killing her! She quickly paid the price, as the officer sniffed derisively, and like a soccer player executing a corner kick, swiped at the back of her head with the instep of his boot. Kathryn's head snapped violently forward, knocking her out cold.

Jenny winced but didn't cry out this time. She hadn't thought past getting them both through the next moment alive, but seeing Kathryn helpless and unconscious, she considered for the first time the horrors that could befall her at the hands of the soulless man before her. Letting Kathryn take the bullet may have been the merciful thing, but Jenny couldn't let her die, not when this was all her fault.

The officer instructed the soldier on guard to put Kathryn into the adjoining room. The brute of a man picked her up roughly by the shoulders and dragged her toward the wooden table and chair set up there. He propped her up in the chair like a marionette with no operator and let her head fall listlessly onto the table with a thud, eliciting only a slight moan of consciousness.

The officer leaned malevolently close to Jenny. "I want you to know that every sound you hear coming out of that room is because of you."

Jenny tried hard not to react, but her insides were burning, screaming, all bravery diffused. The urge to beg for mercy was stronger than ever.

The man smiled. "This is your last chance to put a stop to this."

Her jaw tightened as she tried to remain stoic. Guilt shredded her soul until she was nothing but a fragile shell, with obstinance the only thing keeping her from collapsing. She glared at him without seeing, trying to think of anything other than what was about to happen to Kathryn. The officer turned with an *as you wish* smirk and joined Kathryn in the next room.

He stood at the head of the table, facing the door. "Cut her free and wake her up."

The soldier cut the bloody restraints from Kathryn's wrists and then unbuckled the strap that pinned her arms behind her back. As her limp body melted against the table, he cracked open a small glass ampule containing smelling salts and waved it under her nose until she flinched with a snort and a cough. Finally released from her contorted state, she moaned in relief and nearly fell out of her chair as she tried to regain the use of her arms. She was quickly jerked back into place with a violent tug on the back of her shirt collar.

"Spread her hand on the table," the officer instructed.

The soldier twisted Kathryn's right arm behind her back to a yelp of protest and held her left wrist firmly to the table. When she wouldn't unclench her fist to expose her fingers, he let go of the wrist and in one swift movement, removed his heavy metal helmet and smashed it down on her hand. She cried out and couldn't resist when the soldier spread her fingers and leaned on her wrist again. The officer made sure Jenny was watching when he held up his riding crop and separated the handle from the shaft to reveal a long stiletto blade.

Kathryn, now fully aware, stared in horror at the blade and then at her fingers. She started hyperventilating. "No, no, no, no," she begged.

Jenny's heart hammered in her chest. She couldn't breathe. *He wouldn't dare,* she wanted to believe, but she knew he would. "No!" she screamed, pulling against the two soldiers holding her back. A slamming door was the reply.

Jenny shouted and struggled to get free until a chilling shriek—sharp, drawn from the depths involuntarily, and then abruptly cut off—silenced her. Another cry, deeper, reactionary, but more controlled, echoed off the stone walls, and then a sob, and then nothing.

· · ·

With her face pressed into the wooden tabletop and unable to fight against the large man bearing down on her, Kathryn tensed for the impact of the blade across her fingers when, suddenly, the officer's face was next to hers, smiling.

"It doesn't have to be like this," he said sweetly. "Tell me what I want to know—"

"And you promise to set me free?" she ground out. It should have been sarcastic, but there was too much hope in it to pull it off.

The officer chuckled. "No, I'm afraid I won't do that. You want it too much. You can thank your friend for that tip, and her betrayal will be complete when she tells me what I want to know."

"Go to hell."

He chuckled again and then considered her thoughtfully. "Your devotion to your friend impresses me even more than hers to you. I may not be able to harm her, but you, I'm afraid, will suffer horribly, and it will all be for nothing. She will break." He paused as he glanced toward the constant barrage of desperate cries coming from the other side of the door.

Jenny's screams of protest were mixed with mournful apologies and angry curses, but Kathryn noticed at no time did she utter, *Stop! I'll tell you what you want to know!* Not Jenny. She was strong. She understood the stakes, and she would not break.

"Get on with it, fucker," Kathryn said.

The officer straightened, his face a diabolical mix of delight and hatred. "With pleasure."

Sweat trickled down the small of Jenny's back in the stifling heat of the damp, windowless room as she tilted her head back, attempting to relieve the burning pain between her shoulder blades and escape the stench permeating the room. A putrid combination of mildew, body odor, and urine, the latter coming from a bucket in the corner used by one of the soldiers before they left, was overwhelming.

She felt lightheaded and sick and slid down the wall at her back when her weakened knees refused to support her any longer. She had struggled and screamed herself hoarse before the eerie silence from the room beyond gave even her guards pause. They exchanged questioning looks, and then left her to her hysterics. The show next door was apparently over. Jenny crumpled on her heels, dreading the next sound to come from behind the closed door across the room.

Since the first initial screams and some shuffling violence after, she'd heard little but the officer shouting, "Cry out!" first in German, as his temper got the better of him, and then in French, in case Kathryn didn't understand.

Kathryn was taking it all in silence. Whether it was to spare her the horrific sounds of her torture or an "up yours" to her captors, hoping to make them furious enough to put her out of her misery, Jenny didn't know, but they were definitely hurting her. She could hear the blows and then Kathryn's stifled whimpers between pained, rapid breaths, as she valiantly tried to suppress the sounds of her suffering.

"If you are captured, don't be a smart ass, and don't be obstinate," Jenny had been taught by the very person breaking those rules. *"It will only bring more pain."*

"Cry out!" in French echoed off the concrete walls again, followed by a hard crack and what sounded like a body hitting the floor along with the clatter of a tipped chair. Then silence.

Jenny held her breath, now praying for a sound from Kathryn. Surely, they hadn't killed her. The longer the silence, the more panicked she became. "Please, please, please," she whispered, hoping there was a God, and then the low rumble of men's voices seeped from under the door. She cocked her head in their direction, trying to decipher what they were saying.

They were speaking in German and were disagreeing, but she couldn't make out what they were saying. Finally, *"Idiot!"* rang out clearly and what sounded like the heavy wooden table skidding across the floor. The silence resumed.

Had they killed her by accident? She knew they had a better

chance of coercion with two prisoners, so they wouldn't have killed her so quickly on purpose.

Before the notion that Kathryn was dead could really unhinge her, the officer stepped out of the room, followed by the brute of a soldier, his fist bathed in Kathryn's blood. Jenny tried to see around them, but they blocked her view before shutting the door.

She struggled to her feet, damned if she would kneel before the Nazi bastards. "What have you done?" she demanded, as the other soldiers entered the room from the hall. "Is she alive?"

"Of course she's alive."

"I don't believe you!"

The officer nodded at the soldier, who opened the door and approached the balled up heap on the floor. He yanked Kathryn's head up by the hair, eliciting a pained groan, and then extracted another when he callously let go and her head hit the floor. He seemed quite pleased with himself as he closed the door and took his place at the officer's side.

Jenny couldn't contain her rage and lunged at the men. "Bastards!"

One of the guards grabbed her sharply by the strap holding her arms behind her back, and the pain brought her to her knees, much to the delight of the SS man, who leaned over and said, "Just the way I like my women, bound and on their knees."

Training be damned, Jenny couldn't help herself. She spat in the man's face. He responded with a hard slap across hers.

"*Hauptsturmführer!*" a male voice boomed from the open doorway. The officer snapped to attention, as did the soldiers, including the one restraining Jenny.

She fell forward, letting her shoulder take the brunt of the impact with the concrete floor.

"Get out!" the newcomer shouted in German. The lower-ranked soldiers knew this meant them, and the officer remained at attention as the three of them filed out into the hallway.

To Jenny's surprise, the newcomer commanding such respect wore a neatly pressed beige linen suit and not a uniform. He stood toe to toe with the SS officer, with his back to Jenny, as outrage rolled off his tense shoulders to his clenched fists. She thought for sure a knockout blow was forthcoming.

"You and your men are dismissed," the man said angrily instead. "I'll take over from here."

Jenny was vaguely aware of a soldier he'd brought with him, dutifully stationed just inside the door, his helmet shadowing his eyes like a wary turtle in its shell and submachine gun at the ready.

The officer was not impressed. "My orders are to accompany you to your destination."

"That won't be necessary."

"I'm afraid I must insist."

The man in the linen suit leaned menacingly forward. "You take orders from me, and I say—"

The officer raised a defiant chin and pointed at Jenny. "This package is property of the Reich, and until it is processed and officially released to you, I shall uphold the interests of the Führer."

The two men stared at each other with obvious disdain.

"Very well," the newcomer finally said calmly. "Dismiss your men. You'll ride with me."

As soon as the officer left the room, the man in the suit turned to her with some urgency. Jenny had to do a double take to make sure she had it right. Bending down to cut her free was the man she had come to kill: Dr. Thierry Bouchaule.

"I am so sorry," he whispered quickly in French-accented English before the officer came back. "It was not supposed to be like this."

Jenny nearly wept in relief as he set her arms and wrists free.

"Are you hurt?" Bouchaule asked as he examined her slapped face and looked into her eyes. "I am so sorry," he said again.

Jenny was struck by his sincerity, but then realized, of course he was sincere … she was his missing link. She glanced at the doorway, judging her ability to disarm the doctor's guard and use his automatic weapon to mow down everyone in sight.

Bouchaule must have taken her glance as concern for the *Hauptsturmführer's* return.

"Do not worry about him," he said as he helped her to the chair. "We will be rid of him soon enough."

The doctor was nothing like she expected. His genuine concern was disconcerting in the wake of what she'd witnessed from the Nazis. He was fussing over her like a wounded baby bird, and he straightened with a protective hand on her shoulder when the officer returned. Jenny didn't know what his game was, but she had a definite sense of us against them.

"Is that wise?" the officer asked in German when he saw Jenny rubbing her freed wrists.

"She's not going anywhere," Bouchaule replied in French instead of German.

Jenny cut a look at him. He spoke perfect German, so she figured he was trying to make things difficult for the Nazi, who spoke acceptable but not stellar French, or trying to perpetuate the assumption she was a French girl by including her in the conversation.

"She came here for me," Bouchaule went on. "To kill me, because she thinks I am responsible for her father's death."

Jenny barely contained her shock as she watched everything she'd tried so hard to conceal thrown casually before her enemy like dice on a craps table. Her mark had been waiting for her all along. Her mission was a failure before she even began, and since Holmes was her only contact, she laid the betrayal squarely at his feet. He was a traitor, his motives unknown to her. Kathryn had been right all along. She was always right.

The officer was skeptical. "I hardly think all this trouble is about a simple case of revenge."

"Revenge is rarely simple." Bouchaule looked at Jenny expectantly. "Is it?"

Jenny was too lost in her failure to speak. All the work she had done, all the training, the secrecy, the sacrifices of the people who loved her—all of it for nothing. Kathryn knew it was all over the moment she saw her again, and Jenny now understood her despondency.

She closed her eyes just as Bouchaule gently took her elbow. "Come."

Jenny yanked her arm free. Kathryn was her only concern now. She didn't know what kind of relationship the doctor had with Kathryn or where it had left off, but she would not leave without her, and knowing her importance to Bouchaule, Jenny felt she had infinite leverage with the man.

"You want me? You take her too."

Bouchaule's face instantly clouded, and he cut questioning eyes to the officer, who made his way to the closed door and opened it.

Kathryn was still in a heap on the floor. Bouchaule approached her with caution at first, as if not believing his eyes, but then he proceeded with purpose. Jenny rushed to be with her too, but the officer grabbed her as she tried to push by him.

"Let go of me!" she shouted as he grabbed her already bruised biceps, sure Bouchaule would come to her aid.

He did not. He kneeled beside Kathryn instead and gently guided her blood-soaked hair from her battered face. The bruises, blood, and swelling had made a mockery of her former beauty, and he appeared to hardly recognize her. He took a moment to gather himself and looked to the ceiling, as if he were praying for control. "Did you do this to my beautiful wife?" he shouted.

There was a silent beat of complete astonishment before Jenny and the officer both said, "*Wife?*"

The officer recovered first, finding the need to defend his actions against a clearly enraged husband. "Your *wife*," he said the word with disdain, "is an enemy of the Reich, and I shall address *your* association with her to *Obergruppenführer* Oberg when we return to the city."

Bouchaule didn't seem concerned by the threat of running afoul of "the butcher of Paris," as *SS-Obergruppenführer* Karl Oberg was known to the French, and went on examining Kathryn.

It was all so surreal, and Jenny was having a hard time grasping the fact that Bouchaule was Kathryn's—even the word stuck in her thought process like a new addition to her vocabulary—husband. This is how far Kathryn had gone to protect her. This is how far she'd gone to keep this man away from her.

Jenny snapped herself out of it. This was no time for guilt. She had to use Kathryn's sacrifice to their advantage. It was obvious the doctor was furious at what the Germans had done to her and obvious he cared for her very much.

He was speaking softly to her as he rolled her carefully onto her back. Jenny couldn't hear if Kathryn was answering, but she saw her wince in pain when she was moved. Her bloody hand was wrapped into the bottom of her soiled white shirt. Her eyes were open, and from experience, Jenny knew Kathryn's intense gaze would render words moot. Whatever their relationship, he would surely help her.

Despite Jenny's hatred of Bouchaule, he was her only ally now against their captors and Kathryn's only hope for survival. She let their tender scene go on uninterrupted, trusting in Kathryn's ability to handle the man.

In the meantime, the officer had muscled her back to the chair, while Bouchaule's soldier loomed in Kathryn's doorway like a bored spectator awaiting his orders.

Bouchaule finally stood, had a few more quiet words with Kathryn, and wiped his hands on a handkerchief he'd taken from his pocket. He turned and stared at Jenny with an indecipherable expression.

She had a bad feeling about it and decided she'd help him with his next move. "You have to get her to a hospital."

"I'll do better than that," he said, and addressed the soldier before him. "Kill her. Bring the body to me."

CHAPTER NINE

*P*rotests were the furthest thing from Jenny's mind after the doctor issued his execution order. The moment Bouchaule said "kill her," she knew she had to act quickly. She burst out of her chair and threw her body, shoulder first, into the midriff of the officer. He absorbed her blow like a punching bag and hardly moved. While he regained his composure, Jenny reached for the Lugar on his far hip. The confounded holster foiled her plan, and once again, the officer had her arms twisted behind her back in a knot of pain.

"Take her to my car," Bouchaule said calmly, as if Jenny's outburst was a mere annoyance.

As the soldiers dragged her away kicking and screaming, Jenny assured everyone within earshot that they were "fucking dead men!"

The last thing she saw of the scene was Bouchaule's soldier releasing the bolt handle from the safety notch on his MP40 submachine gun and Kathryn reaching out for Bouchaule as he walked away. Once in the hallway, Jenny screamed even louder, dreading the horrific explosion of weapon fire that would signal the end of Kathryn's life.

The door to her torture room opened, and in Kathryn's mind, she curled up like an abused dog terrified of its master. In reality, she couldn't move. Constant pain emanated from every part of her body. Her impaled hand throbbed in time with her rapid heartbeat, and it hurt to breathe, to moan, even to blink. The kindest blow was the one that struck her hard on the side of the head, sending her to the floor in a heap of unconsciousness.

She had a vague recollection of someone holding her head up by her hair, but then everything went black again. Time had no meaning. She didn't know how long she'd been out since then, but the slow creak of the hinge on the heavy metal door sent a jolt of adrenaline through her like the sudden ring of a telephone in the early hours of the morning.

For a moment, she was disoriented, but the pain drew her back to reality. Panic seized her when she realized the beating would begin again. Her lungs forced out excruciating huffs of air against her will. "N-n-no more," she gasped. She couldn't take it. Not again.

She'd done her best. She'd taken every blow with stubborn indifference, but that angry defiance was gone. Fear gripped her now. What if she broke before they killed her?

She tried desperately to find a place to hide in her mind, but nowhere was safe.

Someone stood over her. Jenny's protests echoed off the concrete walls in the background. She braced for the inevitable kick in the gut, but it didn't come. Nothing came. Someone kneeled beside her. They were going for her head again. What this time? A fist? A club? A boot? Someone touched her face. The touch was gentle, and if she didn't know better, kind. Wasn't that the game though? Wait for her to relax, then resume the blows?

"Did you do this to my beautiful wife?" a familiar voice bellowed, the volume causing her to flinch.

Kathryn looked up and saw Bouchaule with tears in his eyes, hovering over her. He gently turned her onto her back. Her panicked breathing evened out, and she wanted to sob in relief, but the searing pain in her side from what she was sure was a broken rib or two left her wincing in agony.

"What have you done?" Bouchaule whispered as he guided hair matted with blood from her eyes. His concern quickly gave way to consternation. "You knew how important she was to my work. Why would you do this to me?"

Kathryn wasn't sure what would happen between them now, but she held the line just a little longer. "You're not the man I hoped you were."

Consternation melted away and a wry smile pulled at Bouchaule's lips. "And you are exactly the woman I knew you were."

Kathryn didn't believe that. They had both given pieces of themselves they never intended to relinquish.

"You were a bad agent, Kathryn," Bouchaule went on. "You always have been. You should have gone to your superiors from the beginning with the information you gathered. It would have made things so much easier."

Confirmation of a mole in the agency and Bouchaule's knowledge of her agent status was of little consolation to Kathryn now. Her break with protocol had made things more difficult for Bouchaule, and for that she was pleased. Her game forced him to be patient, and despite his scolding, she had a feeling he didn't regret that as much as he should.

"My job was not to make things easy for you, Thierry."

"I am the good guy, Kathryn. I thought you understood."

If it didn't hurt so much, Kathryn would have laughed in his face. "I saw the papers you threw into the furnace." She nearly burned her hand retrieving them. "*You* requested those prisoners for experiments, not Vogel."

He shook his head, not in denial but in disappointment. "How can you be so naïve? They were going to the camps to die anyway. Like I told you, I gave their deaths meaning. The research gathered from their—"

"God, you make me sick," Kathryn interrupted with an unsteady voice as she turned her head away. She made herself sick. Her skin crawled with the memory of their last goodbye, when she struggled to hide what she had just discovered in his cellar lab. What should have been utter revulsion at his touch was an unsettling mixture of regret, horror, and loathing at herself for allowing Bouchaule to lull her into a twisted, symbiotic charade she foolishly accepted as something of value.

She had closed her eyes to things right in front of her. If she had looked closer with more objective eyes, she would have seen it. But she hadn't. She didn't want to. She'd found a place where she felt she belonged—no, deserved—and had made her home there without reservation. How fucking pathetic.

Appalled by who she'd become, she couldn't wait for Bouchaule to take her life now. Finally, there would be no more running, no more hiding, and no more pretending her base character wasn't inherently and irrevocably flawed. No love in the world could change that.

Bouchaule stood and looked down at his wife with disgust as he yanked a handkerchief from his pocket and snapped it open. Who was she to judge him?

"So high and mighty," he said. "Look at you now."

He turned, and in a symbolic gesture, wiped any trace of the woman's blood from his hands. The sight of Jenny Ryan in the next room interrupted his emotional cleaving. He'd spent his entire professional career looking for the key to his work, and now he had her. The hatred in Kathryn's eyes had stung, but he absorbed it quickly. She was just another sacrifice in a long line of sacrifices, all made worth it for this very special day. He tucked her existence away in his pocket along with his bloody handkerchief.

"You have to get her to a hospital," Jenny Ryan said.

The suggestion occurred to him briefly before Kathryn all but spat in his face, but in the end, there was only one thing to do with his traitorous spouse, and this time, he would go through with it.

He had consigned her to death once before, in a scene he orchestrated with Colin Donnelly in the lab at the estate. She had survived exposure to the virus once—a victim of her own government's scheming—and he had prepared a mutated strain of the same virus to test the limits of her body's resistance.

When Jenny Ryan disappeared, he had to work with what he had, and quickly. If Kathryn died from the test, she was of no use to him anyway, but if she lived, his work could move forward. He certainly couldn't have her think he infected her as part of an experiment—the game would be over—so Donnelly played the heavy and he played the victim. The only stipulation he'd given Donnelly was that Kathryn not suffer. The man kept his word and injected her with a sedative before unleashing the virus.

A strange thing happened when the first needle went into her arm. He felt panic at her loss. He wasn't pretending when he struggled against Donnelly's thugs and begged for her life. He wasn't ready to lose her. Not yet. Not like that. When Bertrand showed up at the lab's door, shot by Donnelly's men, he knew Donnelly had betrayed him, and suddenly, Kathryn's life meant more to him than ever.

Donnelly's death by Bertrand's hand was not unplanned; it merely came sooner than expected. Concern for Kathryn's condition had eclipsed any thought about the fallout. She didn't die immediately, which was a good sign, but it was touch and go as her body fought to devour the new strain of virus.

He had destroyed anything of value in the lab that he could not take with him, and he had two thousand miles on the way to Martinique to figure out what the hell this woman had done to him. Torn between guilt at what he had done to her and the promise of what her survival meant to his work, he vacillated between setting her free and continuing their game. The conflict confounded him.

He remembered the tinge of sadness he'd experienced when he saw her for what he thought was the last time in the cemetery at Forrester's funeral. It was nothing more than the regret of losing a good lay, he told himself. Then, when he experienced rage as he stood over her hospital bed and saw what her government had done to her trying to draw out someone with the vaccine, he told himself it was anger because he hadn't thought of it first. That illusion didn't last long. When the vaccine never appeared, he realized they had used her to draw him back. Her condition was his fault, and when he saw her burned flesh and watched as she struggled for every breath, it physically pained him. She had gotten under his skin, and he liked the company.

He could go on and on, lost in sentiment, but he shook his head of his memories. There was no place for them now. She had betrayed him. He could never trust her, and more than that, he had the reservoir now. He didn't need her any longer.

"Kill her. Bring the body to me."

The Ryan woman was hysterical, as expected, and he regretted she would probably hold Kathryn's death against him, making cooperation difficult to attain. He would deal with it later.

"Take her to my car."

He'd taken a step toward the door when he felt a hand grasp the cuff of his trousers and heard Kathryn call his name. She sounded pitiful. Weak. He despised both coming from her, yet he had an overwhelming urge to turn around. Anger over her betrayal had given him the strength to turn away and order her death but not without a thought to what might have been.

He had come so close to believing in her. Leaving the communiqués about Jenny Ryan on his desk where she would find them was his final test. If she passed, he would give himself to her fully and never doubt her again. He should have seen her failure coming. It was Kathryn's unusual interest in Jenny that initially caught his attention and ultimately led to the breakthrough he'd been looking for.

The first hint Jenny was the reservoir came from her own government's assumption that the young woman had access to a vaccine developed by her father that would save Kathryn when they put her life in danger. It was a eureka moment when he realized Daniel Ryan had the perfect hiding place for the reservoir in his daughter. Bouchaule kicked himself for not thinking of it before.

When Jenny Ryan disappeared on the verge of his acquisition, he thought Kathryn may have had something to do with it, but Bertrand found her exactly where she said she'd be that night, and he put his suspicions on hold. She never did anything to make him doubt her again—she played the game brilliantly—and his heart sank when he saw her on the floor of the interrogation room. He would dispose of her and then wipe the memory of their life together and her brutal end from his mind. He would fill every waking hour with his work.

When Kathryn said his name, he stopped, knowing full well he should just go. She had a way with him … a way to get what she wanted. She was clever and persuasive, and the last thing he wanted to do was look into her beautiful eyes as she pleaded for her life, because he would give it to her.

She called his name again, this time softly, pleading intimately. He felt it to his core, and he didn't want to walk away. Of all the times he thought her disposable, all the times he wanted to part ways when she no longer served a purpose to his work, he could never bring himself to do it. He loved being with her. For all their games, and there were many, he loved her. They were so alike, it was uncanny, and now, forced to really ponder her death, he didn't want to be without her.

He raised his chin, starting their game anew, and looked forward to her next move. What approach would she take to save her life? Their relationship had gotten better every time it had seemingly reached an end, and he smiled when he thought of the challenge overcoming her betrayal would bring.

He feigned annoyance as he turned—Kathryn was always at her best when she thought she was losing—and as he feared, the love and desperation in her eyes drew him in. It weakened his resolve, and her battered state finally wounded him. He wanted to take her in his arms and give himself to her once and for all, prove he would do only great things with his work, and he would, but first she had to play her scene, work for her reward.

"Please," she begged softly. "Please don't hurt her."

He stared in confusion as her mindset proved wholly incongruent to his. Her thoughts were only for the girl. She wasn't even going to try to save what they had. It all became so clear to him, in the vilest way. It had all been about the girl. He felt like dry tinder soaked in gasoline, and the revelation struck him like a match at his heel. She not only betrayed his work but his heart as well. Rage swelled in him as he realized what a fool he'd been. Hatred strangled any notions of love or sentiment, and he glowered down at her, his temper barely restrained.

"If only you had been that devoted to me."

"If only you hadn't been a murderous Nazi bastard."

He kicked her hand from his trouser cuff and addressed the guard. "Don't let her suffer." He turned to her for the last time. "My gift to you. Because I loved you."

CHAPTER TEN

An echoing burst of automatic gunfire accompanied Bouchaule's appearance in the hallway. Jenny stopped breathing. She went limp in her captor's arms at the sound of spent casings tinkling against the concrete floor. She no longer loved that sound. In an instant, everything that ever mattered in her life was taken from her.

Bouchaule carried her to the car, where he put her in the back seat and slid in beside her. Before closing the door, he instructed the Nazi officer to retrieve Kathryn's body, and then sent the truck carrying a half dozen remaining German soldiers on its way.

Upon hearing *body*, Jenny's surroundings came into sharp focus. It was still dark, but early morning lit the top of the tree line. She was alone in the car with Bouchaule, who seemed as lost as she did. She wasn't restrained, and all the other soldiers had gone. Bouchaule didn't have a gun that she was aware of, but she had no urge to try to overpower him or even a thought to escape. She was torn between killing Bouchaule and killing herself. Anger and an overwhelming thirst for revenge made her decision for her. If it was the last thing she ever did, he would pay with his life.

"I admired your father very much," Bouchaule began reflectively into the silence of the car's interior. "He was a brilliant man. His death was a great tragedy."

Jenny gritted her teeth, infuriated that he dare speak of her father. "Then why did you hire LaPaglia to kill him?"

The subtle bow of Bouchaule's head confirmed that Colonel Holmes was telling the truth when he claimed LaPaglia was working for Bouchaule and not Forrester when he ran down her father. At first, she didn't understand why Bouchaule would hire a Forrester lackey to do his dirty work, but then it all became clear.

"You wanted Forrester to take the fall for my father's death. Then he would have been out of your way."

"And yet, it seems the only person who thought Forrester was guilty was you."

His ensuing grin could have been condescending, but the shake of his head when he said it telegraphed disappointment that his plan didn't work.

"So, you killed all those people on Forrester's plane just to get to him and disappear?"

He raised his brow as if to say, *wouldn't you?*

She shook her head. "You're a heartless bastard."

"Despite what you may think, your father's death pained me deeply, but he had to be stopped, you see. He was selling our project to the Nazis."

Jenny snapped her head in his direction. "He was protecting it from the Nazis and men like you!"

Shock registered in Bouchaule's eyes, but he fell back into his calm demeanor as he accepted her words as the truth. "Then his death is indeed a tragedy."

Jenny was about to lunge for his throat when a slamming exterior door drew their attention.

Bouchaule flicked on the interior lights and watched his accompanying soldier approach with Kathryn's body slung over his right shoulder and his arm wrapped tightly around the back of her knees. When the soldier arrived, Bouchaule rolled down the window and fondled a tendril of dark hair blowing in the gentle breeze.

Bile rose in Jenny's throat as she choked on the dread and despair. The upper half of Kathryn's body hung limply down the soldier's back, and Jenny couldn't tear her eyes from the white shirt now stained red and riddled with holes. Bouchaule rolled up the window and shut off the light. The weight of Kathryn's body rocked the car as the soldier tossed her into the trunk with a thud. The slamming lid intensified the anguish of Kathryn's eternal silence, and Jenny swore she would add murderer to her resume very soon, because Bouchaule would not get away with taking Kathryn away from her too.

Bouchaule leaned on the door's armrest and brought his knuckles to his lips. He tried to focus on all the things he could now learn of Kathryn's altered physiology and how the Ryan girl's blood could affect others, but as he imagined himself holding the scalpel over Kathryn's bare chest to cut her open, the thought made him sick.

"I think I'm going to regret that for the rest of my life," he said of her death.

Jenny looked at him with seething hatred. "Then you won't regret it for long."

Bouchaule ignored her, lost in his thoughts.

The soldier got into the driver's seat and started the car. Jenny glanced toward the building when the *Hauptsturmführer* didn't show up.

"I told you we'd be rid of him soon enough," Bouchaule said, still preoccupied.

He was thinking of how much he would miss Kathryn. She was beautiful, of course, but more than that, he would miss her cunning and the depth of the shadow life she lived, just beyond his reach. He admired the skill in which she kept it all in balance—until she didn't.

He would never forget Vogel's birthday party, when the man had caught Kathryn snooping around his office. Afraid of falling into Nazi hands again, she had put a gun to her head and pulled the trigger. He thought her smarter than that—stronger, a survivor who would do anything to live another day. He saw her differently after that. She was more fragile than he ever expected, someone who needed to be cared for, and he had the irresistible urge to take up the cause.

He had asked her to marry him that night, and he meant it, shaken by the fact he nearly lost her and confident that she needed his strength to make her whole. She was a puzzle with an endless well of pieces. When he found a new one, he knew precisely where it fit, because their puzzle was the same. They were better together, she had told him, and he agreed. He closed his eyes for a moment and couldn't help but regret all he'd lost in her.

"She couldn't have children. Did you know that?" he asked, and then chuckled at Jenny's astonished look. "Of course you didn't."

A routine gynecological visit for a new pessary had revealed that scarring from an ill-fitted one from many years ago had left her unable to conceive.

"She was devastated … as was I," he said. He realized he was letting his grief show—a weakness—and added a cold, "An opportunity lost," to preserve his hubris.

Jenny was speechless, not only that they had discussed children, but, if she understood the implication, that he would use his own child as part of some research experiment.

"I hope you will not have such difficulties," Bouchaule said dispassionately. "I am curious to see if your gift is passed on to your offspring."

Jenny raised her brow. "If you think for one minute that I'm going to—"

Bouchaule laughed. "I don't need your cooperation."

They rode on in silence from that point. Jenny didn't even want to know what he meant. She fondled the L-pill still tucked into her shirt sleeve cuff and wondered if she'd have the strength to carry on after she killed Bouchaule. Could she live with what she'd done to Kathryn, who had paid the ultimate price for loving her?

The car slowed to a halt, as a cow in the middle of the road, too skinny to even be worth the hide on its back, appeared in the muted headlights.

"Move that animal," Bouchaule barked to the driver in German. "If you can't move it, kill it."

The soldier nodded his helmeted head and removed a pistol from his holster. Before Jenny knew what was happening, a Luger appeared over the front seat aimed at Bouchaule. His door flew open, and two men dragged him out of the car. A third man knocked him out with the butt of his rifle before Bouchaule could say a word.

All Jenny saw was the barrel of the pistol. If she didn't do something quickly, she was next.

CHAPTER ELEVEN

Move! Move! Move! Jenny thought, as the soldier shifted his position to get a better angle on her. This was her chance to get away. She fumbled for the door handle and fell out of the car when the door gave way. She tried to get up quickly, but the soldier was on her before she could tell which end was up. He was shouting at her and was all arms, but Jenny got an elbow to his face before he really got a good grip on her.

The soldier yelped, "Shit!" and let her go as the pot helmet tumbled from his head of close-cropped blond hair. He brought his hand to his face to make sure he still had his eye.

"Damn, Jenny!" he spat.

Jenny was on her feet and halfway to the woods when she skidded to a halt and realized the man was shouting in English and had just said her name. She turned and blinked in disbelief. Everything about the German soldier illuminated by the dimmed headlights was shocking. It couldn't be.

"Cal?"

The imposter she'd known as Calvin Richards was steepling his fingers around his nose in case it was broken. "Christ, you pack a wallop."

His hair was blond now, with the sides shaved halfway up, leaving a wide patch of wavy curls to fill out the top of his head. He no longer sported a southern accent. In fact, she heard no accent at all.

Recovering from her shock, she didn't know whether to hug him or punch him in the face.

"Please tell me she's still alive."

He headed for the car's trunk. "She's alive, but we've got to hurry."

Jenny ran to his side.

She didn't know if he was friend or foe, but he was helping her save Kathryn, and that earned him her trust for the moment. She offered a wary glance toward the dark road behind them.

"What happened to the SS goon?"

"Whose shirt do you think she's wearing?" He released the trunk catch and handed her the officer's Luger. "Here. We might need this."

He let her have a weapon. That earned him another notch in the friend column. She tucked the pistol in the back of her waistband and leaned into the trunk. Movement in the woods caught her attention, as four men emerged from the forest. She quickly drew the gun.

"No!" Cal said, forcing her weapon down with a hand to her forearm. "It's okay. They're with us."

Us. Jenny took his word for it and secured the gun as she turned her attention back to Kathryn.

"Kat—" She eased her onto her back. Jenny couldn't see very well, but she could feel something wasn't right. Kathryn's skin felt like cooling wax, all its resiliency gone, and the smell of urine told her Kathryn's bladder had released its contents—all signs of death. "A light?"

Cal pulled a lighter from his pocket and leaned in with it after igniting it with a quick one-handed swipe across his hip.

The bloody shirt was so convincing, Jenny couldn't resist checking it for bullet holes. She lifted the large cotton shirt and replaced it, appalled by the bruises she saw but relieved to find no corresponding holes in her body. She felt for a pulse at Kathryn's bloody wrist and noticed she had all her fingers but that her bruised and swollen hand had been run through by the Nazi's stiletto blade.

"Something's wrong with her."

Cal handed her the flickering lighter and felt for Kathryn's pulse, first at her wrist and then at her neck, leaning closer, as if that would make the faint fluttering stronger. He took back the lighter and checked her pupils, which had a nearly imperceptible reaction. She wouldn't have passed a thorough exam by Bouchaule, but the appearance of death was sufficient.

"She's okay," he said. "I gave her something to slow everything down a bit."

Jenny looked at him as if he'd just performed the disappearing dove trick and handed her back a crushed bird, proclaiming the trick a success.

"She'll be fine." He pulled a small black case from his uniform pocket and removed a syringe and a small vial.

Jenny cursed under her breath. She knew exactly what that was. He had injected Kathryn with a concoction known around the agency as the Kiss of Death because it made the victim appear dead. Rumor had it the cocktail contained a mixture of drugs and a paralyzing neurotoxin extracted from snake venom. She didn't know if that was true, but she did know only to use it as a last resort, and if you use it, you'd better have the antidote ready. The injection's success rate in the field was not a good one. Several agents died because the second injection wasn't administered in time, and the ones who did survive wished they hadn't for the first few days. It had a one hundred percent success rate in the lab, or so the agency claimed. Theoretically, as long as the second shot was administered in time, Kathryn would survive, and the drugs used to pave the way for the neurotoxin would wear off in their own time.

"You're sure?" Jenny asked, more as a warning than a question.

He arched an *of course I am* brow and injected the contents of the second vial into her arm. He placed the empty vial and syringe back into the case and handed it to her to hold while he lifted Kathryn gently from the trunk. He laid her across the back seat, where Jenny slid in after her. She put the case in her pocket and drew the gun from her waistband, in case the scene was not as it appeared. She eyed the other men with suspicion.

A flash and an echoing gunshot from the woods where they had dragged Bouchaule drew her attention. She tightened her grip on the gun, ready for anything.

A man came running toward Cal from the spot, carrying a small sack. "It's done," he said when he arrived.

Cal shook his hand. "I'll tell them."

"Tell who? What's happening? Is he dead?" Jenny asked.

"We're going to get you out of here. Consider your father avenged." He pulled civilian clothes from the sack and shed the German uniform.

"The plane?" he called to the man moving the cow.

"On schedule. You must hurry."

It was a short but bumpy ride to the airfield, and Jenny was glad that Kathryn was out for the duration. She had a million questions for the man behind the wheel as they rode in the back seat of Bouchaule's car. He was supposed to be dead.

"What's your name?" she called over the low growl of tires on the rough road.

"You can just call me Cal and leave it at that."

She didn't like that answer, but she understood it. He was like them. Questions would just lead to lies or dead ends. She thought of Bernie and his love for the good-natured southern boy who stole his heart. She would never tell him the truth. One more lie between them. She brought Cal into Bernie's life, and his betrayal infuriated her.

She glared at him in the rearview mirror. When his eyes flicked to hers, she couldn't contain her rage.

"He loved you, and you broke his heart."

Cal looked away and then looked at her again. "I loved him too. Maybe you can tell him that one day."

Jenny swore there were tears in his eyes.

She wouldn't give him the chance to hurt Bernie twice. "Not fucking likely."

He glanced at her one more time, but Bernie wasn't mentioned again.

She shook off thoughts of her part in Bernie's misery and the future of their friendship. There would be time enough for that later. For now, her concern was Kathryn.

She cradled her head in her lap, watching for any hint the antidote was working. She couldn't help but recall a similar scene when they first met, only in reverse, as Kathryn cradled her head in her lap and Smitty drove them to the hospital after the accident. It all happened then, she realized. That night, they were bound forever by love and blood.

Through their respective injuries, she had infected Kathryn with whatever inherent properties made her blood worth killing and dying for. That's why Kathryn survived the incident at the center when Johnson had died from his exposure. That's why Bouchaule returned and pursued her afterwards. The miraculous return of her voice was no miracle after all, and Kathryn must have discovered why. That's why she sacrificed everything to protect her.

Jenny's heart swelled with the memory of their love, and she thought it might break for the suffering Kathryn had endured on behalf of it. *"When did you fall in love with me?"* she once asked Kathryn. *"When you took my hand in the car after the accident,"* she had replied. *"I felt like everything was going to be okay ... as long as you didn't let go."*

A tear fell as Jenny gently took her hand. "I'll never let you go, baby," she whispered, holding her tightly in the dark. There was no response, and she felt any hope buoyed by memories of their love drifting away like a balloon from a distracted child's hand. She never should have let her go that last day at the house. They should have gone under together, fought as a team, anything other than going it alone. How could she have been so careless with something so precious? She saw it in Kathryn's eyes when they parted. Her resolve was faltering. One word, an extended hand, a pleading look, and she would have crumbled. She wanted to crumble, Jenny could tell, but instead, she walked away, and Jenny let her. She couldn't even remember why, just that it was the biggest mistake of her life.

She pressed Kathryn's hand to her cheek. "It's going to be okay now. I promise. I'm not letting go, see?" She rubbed her cold hand. "I'm not letting go." Kathryn's stillness frightened her. Please, Kat," she said as more tears fell. "Please don't leave me."

A sob escaped at the thought of life without her. Cal glanced at her in the rearview mirror again.

"Everything all right back there?"

She nodded, getting a hold of herself. Kathryn would be fine. *They* would be fine. There was no room for negative thoughts. She tried to turn off her brain, to moderate effect, and was glad when they arrived at the plane so she could focus on getting the hell out of France and safely to England.

Cal came around to her side of the car and held Kathryn's head and shoulders as Jenny slipped out from under her. Kathryn's condition hadn't improved, and Jenny turned to him for answers.

"How long until that stuff wears off?"

"I don't know."

Jenny didn't press him about it. There was nothing to do now but wait.

The Lockheed Hudson's engines were already fired up, which meant the crew was preparing to leave without them. Evidently, they were late, and they weren't the only escapees whose lives were at risk. Their passage was a fortunate courtesy, not the reason the flight existed. She grabbed Bouchaule's briefcase from the car and followed Cal, who was cradling Kathryn in his arms, to the plane. A man leaped from the cabin and raced toward them in a wounded sprint. Jenny swore it was—

"Smitty!

He came to a skidding halt with a hand on her shoulder and ran beside her. "Are you okay?"

He only glanced at Cal and didn't register who he was or who he was carrying.

Jenny clutched his hand. "I'm fine. It's Kathryn…"

Smitty's eyes widened and followed her head tilt to the body in Cal's arms. His knees buckled and he nearly stumbled at the sight of the bloody shirt.

"Christ, no." He ran to Kathryn's side.

A Royal Air Force sergeant hopped out of the cabin and urged them on with frantic arm motions. When Cal and Smitty tried to pass Kathryn to two men waiting inside with their arms extended, the airman took one look at the pale, bloody heap in Cal's arms and stopped them with a raised hand. "Hold on, now. This isn't a hearse."

"She's not dead," Smitty countered dismissively, shouldering past him.

"Hold on!" the airman shouted again as he grabbed Smitty's shoulder and tried to spin him around. "I know dead when I see—"

Before Smitty could unload his balled up fist, Jenny forced Bouchaule's heavy leather briefcase into the airman's chest and pinned him against the circular bulls-eye of the RAF insignia on the plane's fuselage. "She's not dead!"

The men inside the plane pulling Kathryn in paused, but after Jenny's ferocious rebuke silenced the sergeant, they continued easing her gently into the plane and onto a makeshift bed of blankets that another man spread on the floor.

"She's not dead," Jenny reiterated to the sergeant as she backed off, "and she's not going to die."

The airman didn't protest further. Jenny acknowledged his wise decision with a curt nod of her head.

"After you," the sergeant said with an outstretched arm.

Cal stayed on the ground.

"You coming?" the airmen shouted over the revving Wright engines.

Cal shook his head and backed away.

Jenny lunged for the door. "Wait! Cal!" She saw a completed mission in his eyes and knew she would never see him again. "Thank you."

He tipped an imaginary hat to her and jogged away.

CHAPTER TWELVE

*J*enny counted three downed English airmen lucky enough to find a way back home on their flight, plus the pilot and copilot, the latter the sergeant who had greeted them at the door.

They all looked like they'd been through the ringer, and after helping the newcomers aboard, no one paid particular attention to them in the back.

After they were in the air, she caught Smitty up on Kathryn's injuries. He nodded grimly, glad it didn't involve bullet holes, and covered Kathryn with a blanket, tucking it tenderly under her chin. Jenny wet a handkerchief with water from a borrowed canteen and attempted to clean Kathryn's battered, bloody face.

The sergeant made his way back to them and sheepishly offered a first aid kit, for what it was worth.

"You should drink some, Miss," he said, pointing at the canteen, his voice just carrying over the din of the engines.

Jenny capped the water and took the offered kit with a shaky hand. Any bravado she'd mustered during their ordeal was gone.

"Thanks," she said, and then explained to his skeptical look that the bloody shirt wasn't Kathryn's.

He seemed to understand her optimistic outlook better and handed Smitty an L-shaped flashlight, which he took with an appreciative nod.

"Sorry about before," the sergeant said to both of them.

Jenny apologized for her outburst, but Smitty ignored him as he turned on the flashlight to give her a better look at what she was doing. She soaked a piece of gauze with antiseptic, bravely attempting to play nurse, but her first really good look at Kathryn's face nearly made her retch, and she had to look away. The woman before her bore very little resemblance to the Kathryn she knew. Uneven swelling and discolored skin distorted her features beneath the blood and grime. It was surreal, like a reflection in a fun house hall of mirrors, and Jenny wished it just as easily forgotten. She had purposely avoided looking too closely before, but now, having seen the extent of the damage, it hit her with the force of a physical blow, and she couldn't stop her reaction.

She trembled uncontrollably, as everything caught up with her. Smitty took the first aid items from her hands.

"I'll do it, honey," he said, his hands trembling too.

The sergeant offered to hold the light, and Jenny backed off, wedging herself between the equipment rack and the metal bench seat installed along the fuselage wall. She pulled her knees to her chest, hoping to control her trembling, but it had little effect. Her insides felt like they were collapsing in on themselves, and between that and the heaving motion of the flight, she was trying desperately not to throw up.

Smitty reached out for her hand, which she took. He squeezed it. "She's going to be okay."

Jenny nearly sobbed at the hope and determination in Smitty's eyes. He returned to his task with a tenderness that took her by surprise. It wasn't a secret that he was in love with Kathryn, but she never realized how much of his life revolved around hers. Seeing him tend to her … it made perfect sense now. They'd already been through something horribly traumatic together, and having someone near who shared your history and understood your pain and your triumphs over it must be comforting. His tie to her was more than just love and comfort. He was a disciple worshiping his goddess, and the devotion he felt toward her shone through every gentle caress. He whispered to Kathryn as he worked, winced on her behalf at the seeping wounds on her lip and face, and when he was done, he guided her hair into some semblance of order, as if to restore some dignity to the woman who had been stripped bare of it.

Jenny felt a pang of sadness for him, because she knew that no matter how much Kathryn loved him in return, she would always hold him at arm's length because she couldn't give him the love he wanted.

Tears welled up in Smitty's eyes when he eased Kathryn's swollen, bruised hand from beneath the blanket and cleaned the blood from around her impaled palm. When his tears spilled over, Jenny's followed suit. She imagined his emotions ran the same gamut as hers, but while she couldn't corral hers, he cut his off with a sniff and an annoyed swipe at the moisture staining his face.

He tore open a packet of sulfa powder from the first aid kit, sprinkled it on Kathryn's open wounds, and covered them with bandages. Visible signs of breathing had returned, so he took her pulse at her wrist and then her neck.

He nodded and lifted his eyes to her. "Better."

Jenny didn't dare move to check for herself. Her tensed muscles had locked her into an emotional iron maiden, and to loosen her arms from around her knees would unleash a barrage of feelings she wasn't sure she could handle in her present state.

Smitty asked if she was all right, and she nodded, but his lingering gaze told her he knew she was barely keeping it together. He offered a tight-lipped smile that said *hang in there*. He nodded to the sergeant, who shut off the flashlight and returned to the copilot's seat.

Nothing else could be done for Kathryn, and exhaustion finally won out. Jenny rested her head against the equipment rack and closed her eyes for a few wits' gathering moments.

When she opened her eyes, it was hours later, and the unfiltered light of the new day was filling the cabin of the plane. They were approaching the small RAF airfield in Tempsford, England, the SOE's disembarkation point for supplies and agents bound for occupied Europe. A quick check of her companions found Kathryn still out, with Smitty, whose fingers were intertwined with hers, keeping vigil beside her.

Once the sergeant shouldered open the cabin door and everyone disembarked, a hectic rush of personnel assaulted them. The plane had its ground crew to look after it, and each recovered airman had a representative to meet him. Their group had no less than five heading toward them with determination. There were two British army officers, a major and a colonel; two American men in plainclothes, whose nationality was betrayed by their longer suit jackets; and a British woman dressed in the khaki battledress uniform of Queen Alexandra's Imperial Military Nursing Service.

The nurse hustled ahead of the others, checking with the airmen as she passed. Assured they needed no assistance, she headed for Kathryn on the stretcher, borne by two orderlies.

"Are you injured?" she asked Jenny when she arrived.

"No, I'm fine," Jenny said, happy to give way to a professional.

She was a tall redheaded woman, with earthy good looks and a soothing voice that cut through the roaring din of the airfield like a friend whispering in her ear. Her presence calmed Jenny, and for a moment, she had the feeling everything was going to be fine.

The nurse gave Kathryn the once over and signaled the orderlies. "Get her to the ambulance."

"Stop!" shouted the British colonel, catching up with the group. "They come with us."

"Not so fast," the Americans said.

Jenny straightened her spine. She'd hidden Bouchaule's briefcase under the blanket on Kathryn's stretcher, and she didn't want anyone in this group to get a hold of it. She was about to raise a stink when the nurse took care of it for her.

"Go," the nurse told the orderlies, and held up her hand before the men could protest. "That patient isn't going anywhere but to hospital … sir," she added.

"And I'm going where she's going," Jenny said.

"Ditto," said Smitty.

"You've got no say in this matter," the colonel said to Jenny and Smitty. "And you neither, Sister."

It would have sounded like inappropriate slang from the British colonel, but Jenny could see from the insignia on the epaulets just above the QAIMNS badge that the nurse was indeed a QA Sister, whose rank was captain.

The colonel only now seemed to notice how badly Kathryn was injured and he acquiesced. "Fine, but they come with us."

"Bullshit. I'm going with her," Smitty said. The Americans restrained him when he tried to follow the orderlies, and he struggled against their grasp. "No!"

Jenny tried to calm him. "Smitty—"

"I'm not letting it happen again, Jenny! I'm not letting her out of my sight!"

All movement around them ceased, and Jenny stared at him, worried by his outburst. She knew he was talking about the incident at the center and how they took Kathryn away from them without a word, but it seemed irrational now. Smitty was on edge, and it was clear their ordeal was taking its toll on him too.

QA Sister Vivienne Barclay could see the desperation in the man's eyes and sensed from the blonde's reaction it was well-founded. Whatever was going on, she only had one concern. She put a protective hand on her patient's shoulder.

"With all due respect, gentlemen, my duty is to see this woman gets medical attention. It's apparent these two will not leave her side, and I assure you, this patient's not going anywhere but to hospital, so you know where to find us. Go!"

The orderlies obeyed.

Vivienne stared at the officers, daring them to override her order again.

The four men glanced at each other. They must have judged the lack of cooperation they'd get if they forced the two to go with them, because they stepped aside without another word.

"Thanks for that," the blonde woman said once they were in the ambulance and on their way.

Vivienne smiled curtly, barely looking up as she made a more thorough examination of the woman on the stretcher. "There are things that are important and things that are important."

The blonde nodded, and Vivienne watched her slide a briefcase from under the blanket at the patient's feet and set it beside her without comment. Whatever skullduggery was going on was none of her business. She had one job: take care of the wounded.

"What happened here?"

"Nazis," came the reply in unison.

"Mm," she said, unable to mask the air of unfortunate familiarity. She noticed bruises around the wrists of the haggard blonde and took a moment to assess her.

"Sure you're all right?"

The woman nodded and gazed at her like she had all the answers and everything was going to be fine now. She knew the look and the need for hope, even if things were dire. All she could do was exude calm and confidence until they had answers. "Nice field dressings."

The blonde pointed to her companion. "Frank Nightingale over there."

"Well done, Frank."

"John." The man held out his hand. "John Smith.

Vivienne looked at him with a wry smile. The cloak and dagger atmosphere prompted her to think it was a bad assumed name. "Sister Vivienne Barclay." She took his offered hand. "Nice job, John."

"Jenny," the blonde said, getting in on the introductions. "This is Kathryn. Oh, here …" She opened a small black case that contained two glass syringes and two empty vials and handed it to her. "Do you know what this is?"

Vivienne looked at it in disbelief before quickly composing herself, trying not to let her concern show. "Yes, I do." She'd seen two corpses and one man who might never wake up because of it.

Jenny seemed unaware of the drug's shortcomings and nodded confidently. "The second vial was administered well within the time required for a complete recovery."

Vivienne nodded without expression as she zipped the case shut and put it in her pocket. Her patient's chances just dropped precipitously.

CHAPTER THIRTEEN

It was a twenty-minute ride to the hospital, but to Jenny, it seemed like an eternity. Kathryn needed a doctor, and fast. The ambulance rumbled past a massive brick gatehouse and pulled up before a two-story manor house on a large estate in Bedfordshire, which was now a hospital, with its interiors and out buildings divided into wards for patients.

As she and Smitty sat outside the examining room waiting for word on Kathryn's condition, Jenny leaned her head against the wall and stared at the ceiling. Ornate crown molding peeked out from behind walls erected to make the ward partitions, and she wondered if its beauty would ever see the light of day again.

Jenny received a cable that said the OSS was sending someone, and she was glad, because she wasn't sure she trusted the SOE, considering they had given her the phony radio and practically handed her over to the Nazis. She had stowed the briefcase in a safe place and would assess who she could trust later. Only Kathryn mattered to her now.

She closed her eyes against the trauma of the last twenty-four hours and tried desperately to shut it all out.

Smitty rose from his chair and started pacing. Again. He was going crazy waiting for answers. She was too, but impatient pacing wouldn't make things move any faster. He needed a distraction.

"How did you wind up on that plane, Smitty?"

"The SOE pulled me down from Milton Hall and put me in a holding pattern twenty miles from here."

Jenny assumed they brought him to Gaynes Hall. That's where they put her up before her ill-fated mission.

"Two SOE bigwigs blew in there this morning with Colonel Holmes in tow," Smitty continued. "Said, 'be ready to rescue an American agent whose identity was compromised.' He let me know it was you."

"Fucking Holmes. If I ever see that son of a bitch again, I'm going to deck him."

"It was his aide, Brian, who betrayed you. Big fan of the Nazis, apparently. Was spilling secrets to them all along. Took cyanide when they came to arrest him."

"No," Jenny drew out in disbelief. "And Holmes?"

"Cleared."

Jenny shook her head. "He's no angel."

Smitty raised his brow and sat beside her. "None of us are."

Truer words, Jenny had to admit.

"Based on the scene at the airfield, I fear you're going to get very popular shortly."

"I know."

Whatever the agencies were going to throw at her, she was ready. She wasn't the naïve rule follower any more. Kathryn sacrificed everything to give her control over her life, and she wouldn't relinquish it ever again.

Smitty's irritation only got worse the longer they waited. He guarded the entrance to the examining room like a sentry, and Jenny just let him go on asking rhetorical questions instead of answering.

"Why didn't they send *me* to investigate what happened to Kathryn if they thought she was compromised? Why didn't I know she was in France?"

He paused at the door and peered intently through the small square window.

Jenny went to his side, hoping there was news from inside, but instead saw Sister Barclay give the doctor the black case with the syringes. He raised his brow, followed by what looked like an exasperated shake of his head.

"Did you see that?" Smitty said to her. "That look? Did you see it? Christ." He put his hands on top of his head. "I should have been there. I never would have put that shit in her veins."

Jenny tried to reason with him, but he was inconsolable as he paced and escalated his venting.

"Smitty!" She shook him by the shoulders as a last resort before slapping his face. "Pull it together. You've got to be strong now, do you hear me? If you lose it, I'm going to lose it, and she needs us." She shook him again. "She needs us."

That he understood. "Okay."

He still looked frazzled, so Jenny gave him an extra squeeze to calm him. She knew he was concerned about the injection. She was too, but there was nothing they could do about it now.

"We did what we had to do to get her out of there, and now we just have to trust that these people will do what it takes to pull her through."

He nodded and wrapped his arm around her shoulder for support. He scrubbed his face with his hand and apologized.

She patted his chest. No apology necessary. They had come a long way, the two of them, and it was only fitting that their love for Kathryn had finally brought them together instead of putting them at odds.

Sister Barclay disappeared through the doorway on the far side of the room, and minutes later, approached from the far end of the busy hallway with her arms full of towels and neatly folded clothes. Before they could even ask, she said, "I have nothing new to report. There's been no change in her condition. In a few moments, they will move her upstairs for some radiographs, and barring any major surprises, we'll move her to a room. These are for you." She handed Jenny a towel and a few items of clothing and directed her down the hall to the baths.

Before Smitty could unleash the full force of his concern, Sister Barclay had her hand on his forearm. "X-ray is a little backed up, so deep breaths, relax, and we'll let you know if anything changes."

Smitty stared at her as she walked down the hallway.

"If she thinks I'm going to be cajoled into dropping my guard—"

Jenny put a hand on his chest. "Deep breath, Smitty … deep breath. They're doing all they can for her."

Smitty hovered outside the X-ray room—protests by her and the staff be damned. Jenny left him to it while she headed for a much needed bath.

The staff moved Kathryn to a building away from the main hospital, into what they were told had once been the coach house of the estate. It had few rooms, and all were small but private. Jenny sensed they were being isolated, but she didn't know why.

Kathryn had a corner room on the second floor that overlooked a field beyond the estate's property that housed an army camp. Jenny stood at the arched window and watched the soldiers march to and fro in the distance while Smitty sat at Kathryn's bedside in an uncomfortable metal chair, waiting for word from the doctor.

An intravenous drip ran through a thick red tube into Kathryn's right forearm, and two loose wraps of gauze, one at her elbow and one across her upturned palm, held her arm to an arm board, making her look like a crucified sinner. Now bathed and her wounds properly treated, the bruises bloomed against her pale complexion like stark islands of deep purple inside blotches of an angry red shoreline, marring the left side of her face, from forehead to jawline. Lacerations of varying degrees checkered the right side of her face, and her bottom lip was deeply split, almost down to her chin. Blood still tried to seep from the neat row of stitches. Jenny couldn't look at her without tearing up, so she just stared out the window and tried to take her mind off the events of the previous day and her part in Kathryn's condition.

The door opened with a creak, and Smitty and Jenny both turned in anticipation, but it was just Sister Barclay, now in her gray ward dress and white apron.

"The doctor will be here soon," she said, setting a tray down on the adjustable rolling table beside the bed. "Excuse me, Mr. Smith," she said politely, prompting Smitty to abdicate his chair and drag it out of the way.

She wasn't always as polite with Smitty. The day before, he had drawn her ire and a pair of orderlies to escort him out of the building when he became unruly when they tried to keep him from Kathryn's room. Jenny couldn't blame Sister Barclay. She couldn't know their history or understand Smitty's unreasonable behavior.

Jenny had calmed him and then led Sister Barclay a few steps away.

"It would be better for everyone if you just let him in. He needs to be with her. You won't keep him out."

Sister Barclay looked past her shoulder at Smitty. "I see."

Jenny wasn't sure she did. She probably thought them lovers, but that would do. The nurse issued stern instructions that he do as he was told or she would bar him from the premises. Smitty had nodded with an apology and straightened his shirt as the orderlies let him go. He had been a model citizen since, and Sister Barclay had been her usual professional self.

They hadn't heard from the doctor yet, and the adage *no news is good news* was having the opposite effect on all of them.

Vivienne tried to ignore John hovering over her shoulder as if he was suspicious of every move she made. Jenny Ryan was the exact opposite, looking anywhere but at the patient as she tended to her. Today, she ventured closer.

"Can you tell us anything?"

"Sorry, no."

"Surely, you must know something?" John asked too aggressively for her lousy mood.

Vivienne clutched the small jar of penicillin powder the Americans had provided tightly in her fist. "No, Mr. Smith, I do not."

She surprised herself with her voracious reply. What she did know wasn't particularly good news, and it wasn't her place to deliver it. She felt sorry for the lot of them, John Smith in particular, because he was already overwrought. Jenny was taking it all in stride, but she, too, would be tested when the prognosis amplified the helpless feeling that was already beginning to wear her down. As for the patient, there was nothing medically they could do other than maintenance and hoping they could stave off infection. The sooner the woman woke up the better, but with consciousness came pain, and in her physical condition, it would be considerable. The doctor didn't hold out much hope of that happening, though, especially after news of the injections. "Why don't they just hand them a gun with a round in the chamber," he had said bitterly, based on his experience with the concoction.

Vivienne didn't know why she had taken such a personal interest in the trio. She saw patients all the time, and in much worse condition than this one. She'd seen death, hopeless situations, and plenty of soldiers carted off to coma wards, never to wake again. This woman was probably another one of them, but she felt it to her core this time. After four years of working in Casualty Clearing Stations in war-torn Europe and dealing with all its tragedies as a matter of course, this case got to her.

She was used to working swiftly with doctors, orderlies, and other QA Sisters in the field. They focused on injuries. There was no time to think beyond the moment. No time to ponder their patient's future or past, or to think of their families and what they would go through when their loved one came home a shell of their former selves—if they came home at all.

This time was different. She saw this patient through the eyes of those who loved her, and it made her feel for all of them. She would never say she didn't care for her other patients, but she certainly didn't feel like this. She'd formed a callus over those feelings out of necessity, and now she was suddenly vulnerable. It made her angry—at them, at the war, at herself.

She was sick of war, having seen too much of it, and she was thinking she should have taken that ten days' leave instead of working through it while waiting for her promotion to major and her next post.

John mumbled an apology, prompted by a dirty look from Jenny. Vivienne ran a calming hand down her starched white nurse's apron and accepted it after offering one of her own.

She went about mixing the penicillin powder with the sterile saline solution and started a slow drip injection just as the doctor arrived. The doctor made a superficial check of the patient while she went to the other side of the bed and took scheduled vitals.

The doctor was noncommittal about the prognosis. He ran down Kathryn's injuries dispassionately, like one would a shopping list: lacerations and bruising to the face and midsection, several fractured ribs with no complications—meaning no damage to the surrounding organs or internal bleeding—and an impaled hand with tendon damage. "I've got a colleague from Grimsby stopping by in a day or so, on his way to London, who will be very interested in that hand."

He quickly scanned Kathryn's chart for the latest readings. "Her respiration and blood pressure are back to normal, so the drugs are out of her system—"

"So why isn't she waking up?" John asked, a little panicked.

The doctor looked up. "And you are?"

"This is John Smith. They came in together," Vivienne said. She knew that would satisfy the doctor and that she needn't say more.

"She's had severe trauma to the head, Mr. Smith." The doctor looked at Jenny. "You said she'd been knocked unconscious several times."

Jenny nodded solemnly.

The doctor confirmed a concussion, but then pursed his lips. "Well, that and the injections—" His voice trailed off, and Vivienne knew he was deciding how blunt to be about the side effects. Brain damage and permanent coma were not only a possibility but very likely. His answer was curt and to the point. "It's just not a good combination. We've done all we can do, I'm afraid. It's up to her now."

"That's fine then," John said. "No one is a stronger fighter." He turned to Jenny, Vivienne assumed for confirmation, but she had turned her back to them and was staring out the window again.

John was in denial. The doctor left him to it and nodded before excusing himself. Vivienne adjusted Kathryn's pillows, picked up her tray, and left the room without a word.

Smitty approached Jenny from behind and placed his hands on her shoulders.

"Did you hear that? It's up to her, and you know what that means."

Jenny bowed her head. Smitty's optimism was breaking her heart.

"What?" he said.

"I'm not so sure she wants to wake up."

"What are you talking about? Of course she wants to wake up. After everything she's done for you, you think she's going to give up now, when you're home free?"

That was the last thing she needed to hear. He could see it was all her fault too. Jenny turned to face him. "You didn't see her, Smitty. She was done."

"If I had some ape beating the shit outta me with no hope of escape, I'd be done too!"

"No, before that, before they captured us. We were running, beating them out, and she just ... gave up ... like she wanted them to catch her."

"That's crazy, Jenny."

She would have thought so too if she hadn't seen it with her own eyes. "Something happened to her over there, Smitty."

True to form, Smitty refused to believe Kathryn didn't want to come back to them.

"You're tired, Jenny. Why don't you get some rest and I'll take the first watch."

Jenny went to Kathryn's bedside and her heart clenched. Every bruise and cut was a painful reminder that Kathryn was there because of her. Despair threatened to overwhelm her, but it was selfish, and she pushed it aside. She needed to have faith in Kathryn. Smitty was right. She was a fighter, and she would come back to them. She had to.

Jenny kissed her forehead. "I love you." She turned to Smitty. "I'll be back in a few hours."

He settled into the chair beside Kathryn and gently arranged a stray lock of her dark hair on her pillow. "Okay. Rest well."

She didn't have time to rest. She had something more important to do.

As the door slowly closed behind her, she heard Smitty talking to Kathryn.

"I know you're not a quitter, honey. Fight, damn you, fight!"

CHAPTER FOURTEEN

$\mathcal{V}$ivienne stood just outside the doorway of Kathryn's room and watched John Smith pace. He went to the window and leaned on the sill, bowing his head against the beautiful day outside. His thoughts were on his friend, Vivienne had no doubt. She was in surgery after the hand specialist from Grimsby determined her injury was perfect for his latest study in tendon repair.

John had protested, thought it too soon with all the other physical injuries Kathryn had, but the visiting doctor impatiently informed him that if he wanted her to have any chance at using that hand again, the sooner they repaired it the better.

He and Jenny had sought her opinion with their questioning eyes, but she remained stoically neutral. The doctor, dusting off his bedside manner, assured the worried pair that it would be fine. They would use a nerve block instead of general anesthesia so that sedation wouldn't affect her current condition. The swelling in the hand had gone down. There was no sign of infection, nor was it likely, thanks to the prophylactic penicillin regimen, and now, really, was the best chance she had for a reasonable recovery of mobility in the hand.

When asked to define "reasonable," the doctor was more cautious in his enthusiasm. A severed tendon was a challenge, but he assured them his technique had a very high success rate and that Kathryn was a perfect candidate. Jenny deferred to his expertise, but John bristled at his assurances. Vivienne understood his reticence. After three days, Kathryn was still unconscious. It was taking a toll on everyone—including her.

After they'd taken Kathryn down to surgery, Jenny had asked John if he wanted to get some air. She was clearly going stir crazy and had to get out of there. He had declined, and Vivienne, at the end of her shift, had left shortly after Jenny, leaving him alone to contemplate what she knew was his worst nightmare: What if Kathryn never woke up?

The image of John torturing himself in that dingy little room all by himself wouldn't leave Vivienne alone. She didn't know his history with Kathryn Hammond, but she recognized guilt and regret from personal experience, and it drew her to the man's misery. She was a healer, after all. Surely, she could help.

She cleared her throat before entering the room and set the small cloth sack she was carrying by its wooden handles onto the rolling table beside the bed.

"Are they through?" John asked anxiously.

The fear in his eyes made her heart hurt, and she wondered when her heart decided to care again.

"No, they had to prep her, and then the surgery will take at least an hour."

He stared at her as if he'd never seen her before.

"I thought you might be hungry," she said. "Care to have a picnic?" She tilted her head in the direction of the garden outside the window.

"No, I'd rather wait here."

Vivienne smiled and pulled two sandwiches wrapped in wax paper from the sack. "Thought you'd say that." She poured two cups of water from the pitcher beside the bed, lamenting that it wasn't tea, and handed him a napkin.

He still stared at her in confusion. He swept his eyes up to her hair, which made her self-conscious, and she thought he was looking at the starched white nurse's veil that only the day before she had overheard him dub "the flying dinner napkin."

"We've got to eat," she said defensively. "Don't make anything of it."

"Of course not," he said, like the thought never occurred to him. "Thank you, this is grand."

He pulled the two chairs in the room together and warily took a sandwich from her.

"I guess you think I'm a little nutty."

Vivienne looked at his kind, worried face and admired him for his loyalty. "Why? Because you care deeply for someone? We should all be so lucky."

"You don't have anyone?"

"No."

"Sorry, that was none of my business."

"I'll tell you when you step over that line, Mr. Smith."

John smiled. "I'm sure you will."

It was the first broad smile she'd seen from him, and he wore it well.

"Got any booze in that bag?" he asked, leaning toward it.

"No, sorry."

They ate in silence for a few awkward minutes until he wiped his mouth and set down his sandwich. "I guess they think she's going to be okay if they're bothering to fix her hand."

In truth, Vivienne got the sense the operation was more a needed statistic to prove a medical point than an expectation of recovery. The doctor on staff didn't think much of the woman's chances of coming back to them, and the doctor from Grimsby was so focused on the hand and honing his techniques that one could hardly consider his interest an indication of the patient's bright future. She couldn't really begrudge the doctor his focus—it was what made him so good, she imagined—but having developed a secondhand fondness for the patient through the devotion of her friends, his enthusiasm came off as cold, and it bothered her. She was glad John hadn't picked up on it, and she certainly wasn't going to start that fire.

"We all want her to be okay," she replied professionally, "and everyone's doing their best towards that end."

He nodded and returned to his sandwich.

"Wait until you meet her," he said, beaming with pride. "She's a singer. Did Jenny tell you? A damn good one too."

Vivienne smiled politely. The more time she spent with the man, the worse she felt for him and the more intrigued she became by the woman he thought was *all that*.

"I look forward to it."

CHAPTER FIFTEEN

*J*enny walked into Kathryn's room just as a young staff
nurse exited with a towel-covered basin, which meant
the sponge bath that ended Smitty's watch was done. She
watched Sister Barclay change Kathryn's dressings with a gentle efficiency she appreciated and admired. It had been two days since the
hand surgery, which had gone very well, they'd been told, but
Kathryn's overall condition hadn't changed.

"Evening," Jenny said. She went to Kathryn's bedside and tenderly
touched her shoulder in a silent hello.

"Good evening," Sister Barclay said, cutting the gauze bandage
from around Kathryn's wrist and discarding it into a square
enamel pan.

"Any change?"

Sister Barclay shook her head as she finished what she was doing
and then came around to Jenny's side.

Jenny surveyed the freshly uncovered wound, noting the skin had
begun to heal over the lacerations where the restraints had cut into
her flesh. "The wrists look better."

"Yes, healing quite well. They'll stay uncovered now."

An angled splint supported Kathryn's repaired hand, elevating it to reduce swelling. The splint started mid-forearm and continued to her fingers, leaving the back of the hand and injured wrist exposed and bent, as if cradling an infant. Sister Barclay carefully cut the loose-fitting bandage from around the hand, exposing the site of the surgery.

Jenny winced at the stitched incision along the back of Kathryn's hand. What the doctor had called a pull-out button, secured by a twist of fine stainless steel wire, sat atop a compressed pad of cotton behind the knuckle of the ring finger. The pull-out suture exited her skin further down, near her wrist. All this so the doctor could remove the sutures after the wound had healed without going in again. The concept was easier to swallow than the reality, but she had to admit, it was a clever solution.

"It looks odd, but it's really a first-rate job," Sister Barclay assured her.

"Oh, I'm sure," Jenny said, as she backed off to let her finish applying a new bandage. Jenny liked the Sister, who had gone out of her way to make sure they understood everything that was going on. She was always encouraging but never without reason, so when Smitty beamed with renewed optimism, she felt hopeful too.

"Smitty tells me you think she may wake up soon."

Sister Barclay raised her brow in surprise. "What I said was that we are all doing our best towards that end."

Jenny exhaled a disappointed huff at Smitty's twisted interpretation. "I thought that sounded a little definitive, considering."

"He's um ..."

Jenny grinned. "I know."

"That's not to say it won't happen soon," the Sister clarified. "That's just not what I said."

"It's okay." Jenny would have asked for her honest opinion, but she knew Sister Barclay would give it to her and it wouldn't be something she wanted to hear.

Silence fell like a dark pall between them, and Jenny sensed from the straightening posture beside her the moment Sister Barclay's professional optimism kicked in.

"She is doing well. Her body is healing, her vitals are good … it's just going to take time."

Jenny didn't buy the sunny forecast. Kathryn could be "doing well" for a long time and never wake up, but she appreciated the attempt to make her feel better.

"You're very kind."

It took only one beat to know she'd said the wrong thing.

"I don't say things to be kind. What I said is true. She has a good chance. Her recovery is just going to take time."

Jenny raised her hand in apology. "I'm sorry. I just need her to wake up. Everything will be fine when she wakes up."

A heavy silence filled the room again, and she eyed Sister Barclay until the woman spoke her mind.

"Forgive me for stating the obvious, but when your friend wakes, she's got a long road before her, and I don't just mean physically."

That truth weighed heavily in the back of Jenny's mind, but she'd purposely pushed it there in favor of one step at a time. First, Kathryn had to wake up. Then they would deal with her recovery. "I know."

"I mean to say," Sister Barclay went on, "this sort of thing changes a person."

"I know."

Jenny was well aware of how Kathryn's first encounter with the Germans had affected her. She would never forget witnessing her breakdown at The Grotto or stories about youthful, carefree days told by Tommy Wallace and the gang. Smitty's recollection of their younger years painted a vivid contrast to the serious, haunted woman she came to know and love. She felt cheated not to have known her before, but what drew them together was borne out of the ashes of her former life, and had they met years earlier, maybe the outcome would have been different.

She and Kathryn were bound as never before now, and what came next would be harder than she wanted to imagine. They both had wounds to heal, physical and emotional, but they would do it together and emerge stronger than ever. She would make sure of it. Jenny already felt stronger and more grown up than she ever had. No one would see her as the *innocent kid* ever again. She was one of them now. The damaged. The days of never quite being one of the gang because she couldn't comprehend the intricacies of a life tainted by the extreme were over.

Sister Barclay still had the look of someone who, despite her best efforts, felt she hadn't quite made herself clear.

Jenny tenderly ran her hand down Kathryn's badly bruised biceps and let the Sister know she knew the score. "This is her second round with the Nazis."

Sister Barclay's eyes snapped up to Jenny's and her chin slowly lifted on an inhale.

"Bloody hell," she muttered under her breath, as her gaze dropped to her patient in empathetic reverence.

From the Sister's warnings and her stricken look, she seemed to know a lot about broken lives, and Jenny could only imagine the horrors she'd seen as a nurse during the war.

"Do you see a lot of this sort of thing?" she asked quietly.

"Not really. Once caught, they rarely make it home. You were both very lucky."

Jenny saw a hollowness in her eyes that spoke of experience.

"Did you lose someone?"

The Sister paused briefly and busied herself packing up her bandage caddy. "I lost my man at Dunkirk."

"I'm so sorry," Jenny said. "And I'm sorry for asking."

The Sister straightened and banished any sadness with the action. "Seems so long ago now. We only married because of the war. Life is short and all that, you know." She smiled fondly. "He was a lovely man. A dear friend. I miss him."

"Sorry," Jenny said again, for lack of anything else that would help.

The Sister's response was typically British: a curt smile, a lift of the chin, and on you go. She dropped her gaze to Kathryn. "This is your lady then?"

The question took Jenny by surprise, but she obviously wasn't fooling anyone. "Yes."

Technically, they weren't together, but everything that had kept them apart was over now. As soon as Kathryn woke up, they would put everything behind them and move on together.

The Sister nodded as if she'd heard her thoughts.

"Why *my* lady and not Mr. Smith's?" Jenny asked out of curiosity, noting he was just as attentive, if not more so.

Sister Barclay smiled. "He has the devotion part down, but you've got a way about you when you're with her. John's approach is different. That of someone clinging to something they can't have."

Jenny raised a brow at her honesty. "He's a good man. They grew up together."

"Ah." The Sister said it in a way that made Jenny wonder if she had experienced something similar. They both paused as they considered what was to come. Jenny quickly shoved the overwhelming prospect in its place, but Sister Barclay wouldn't let her push it too far away.

"When she returns to you, you must be patient with her."

Jenny would have the patience of a saint, if only Kathryn would wake up.

They stared at Kathryn until Sister Barclay finally gathered the last of her supplies and said, "Well, my shift is done. I've brought you a new book." She pointed to the bedside table. "You've read the other twice to your friend, and I fear she's growing tired of it."

Jenny chuckled and thanked her.

"You're welcome. And Jenny? Call me Vivienne. Unless there's someone else about … then, you know, professionalism and all that."

Jenny smiled. "Thank you, Vivienne. For everything you've done."

The expected curt nod was her answer.

She felt like they were friends now. And friends always tell the truth, even when it's painful. "Do you think she'll wake up?"

"I don't know. But I wish for it with all my heart."

Vivienne's words broke something in her, and the tears that she'd been holding in for days streamed down her face. Maybe it was the stress, or that she had to leave Kathryn's side that started the waterworks, but Vivienne was ready with a handkerchief, which Jenny took with a grateful nod.

"I've got to go away for a few days," Jenny said.

"The brass hats?"

"Yes."

She'd put it off as long as possible. She took a note from her pocket and held it out. "When she wakes up, I know Smitty will tell her I'm all right, but if I'm not around, she may need a little convincing. Could you give her this, tell her I love her, and I'll see her in a day or so. Would you do that for me?"

Vivienne took the note. "Of course."

"And one more thing. Don't tell Smitty until after I'm gone. He won't like it."

Jenny moved to Kathryn's side when Vivienne left the room. She would have crawled in beside her if she wasn't afraid of hurting her in the narrow bed. She moved as close as she could and put her head on the pillow so she could whisper in her ear.

"I'm here, honey. I love you." She paused a beat, as emotion overwhelmed her. "Please wake up."

There was no response, and tears flowed again. She remembered the hopelessness in Kathryn's eyes when they were in the forest. If only Kathryn could see the future she saw.

"This war will be over soon, you know. We're going to put all this cloak and dagger shit behind us, and we're going to be disgustingly happy together for the rest of our lives." She imagined Kathryn's lips curling into a smile. She'd give anything to see that smile again. But not a muscle twitched in Kathryn's bruised and battered stone mask.

Jenny closed her eyes, fighting back a sob. "Please, Kat. Please wake up."

She covered her mouth and stood before a sob escaped. She didn't want to leave Kathryn's side—not until she woke up and knew she would be okay—but she had orders and had to go. She wiped her eyes and paced at Kathryn's bedside with her hands on her hips, trying to talk herself into leaving.

"Fuck," she muttered in frustration. The sooner she left the sooner she would return. She kissed Kathryn's forehead and squeezed her shoulder. "Duty calls, honey. I'll be back in a few days, and I want to see those baby blues, okay? I love you."

After another kiss, she quickly left the room before she changed her mind.

Vivienne answered John's inquiry about Jenny's whereabouts casually, but Jenny's warning that "He won't like it" was an understatement. He was livid when he found out Jenny had gone, and her absence threw him into a panic.

Vivienne tried reasoning with him, but evidently, he didn't trust anyone, British or American, so he took his worry and frustration out on her.

"A few days?" he snapped. "A few *days*? What were you thinking, letting her go like that? You should have come to me immediately!"

Vivienne simply would not put up with that, no matter how badly she felt for the man. "I don't know where you got the notion I was her keeper, or yours, for that matter. I've got one job. which, if you'll excuse me, I'll do, and I'll thank you to keep your personal drama to yourself." She pushed past him on the way to the penicillin injection she'd prepared.

"If something happens to her—"

"If something happens to her what?" Vivienne snapped back as she spun on her heel. "You'll blame me? Pull yourself together, Mr. Smith, or get out of this room."

She turned back to her patient, soaked a cotton ball with antiseptic for the spot of the injection, and after an irritated swipe, jabbed the needle into the thick muscle of Kathryn's upper arm a little more roughly than she intended.

"You have no idea what we've been through," John said from behind her.

Vivienne held up her hand, silencing him. She thought she saw Kathryn wince when the needle went in. "Kathryn?" she said firmly.

John scrambled to the other side of the bed and took Kathryn's hand. "Kat?" He leaned in close and held her hand to his heart. "Kat? I'm here, honey, can you hear me? Kat?"

When Kathryn didn't respond, Vivienne couldn't bear the pleading desperation in John's eyes when he looked to her, so she focused on Kathryn's eyes instead and checked her pupils.

"Kathryn?" she repeated loudly, trying to pull her from her deep sleep. There was no reaction. She squeezed her trapezius muscle hard enough to elicit one. "Kathryn?"

John stared intently at his friend, willing her to react. "Come on, honey," he whispered.

They both stared with concentrated anticipation for some sign of consciousness but got nothing in return. Vivienne straightened dejectedly. It must have been a random muscle twitch. John looked at her, shattered hope welling in his eyes, and she felt his pain and disappointment to her core. His personal drama had become hers. It wasn't supposed to be that way. It was totally unprofessional, but she couldn't help it. She cared about all of them.

John brought Kathryn's hand to his bowed forehead, and Vivienne reached across the bed and rested her hand on his shoulder. "I'm sorry, John." For everything.

He leaned his head into her forearm, and she naturally cupped his cheek when he lifted his head.

"I'm sorry for flying off at you," he said.

Vivienne withdrew her hand, the gesture feeling intimate instead of comforting.

"Jenny asked me not to say anything until she'd gone."

John shook his head. "Figures."

They both stared blindly at Kathryn for a few silent moments, and then, gathering her professional detachment, Vivienne began methodically packing up her tray.

John suddenly squeezed Kathryn's hand. "Kat?"

They both saw her wince in pain. It wasn't a random twitch. It was a definite wince, and then another, and then a moan, and then her eyes fluttered open.

CHAPTER SIXTEEN

Kathryn grimaced through her liminal haze as a blanket of pain greeted her return to consciousness. The term *everything hurts* took on new meaning, as every breath felt like a sharp knife twisted in her side, and each movement sent an unyielding urge to cry out. Her wounded hand throbbed and itched, and she had a blinding headache that made her brain feel like a pillow stuffed into a bass drum, while her heart relentlessly kicked its rhythm against her skull. She found it hard to keep her eyes open, and she wished briefly to be unconscious again.

She could hear Smitty assuring her she was all right, and slowly she began remembering the circumstances that led her to her current state. She remembered lying on the concrete floor of the small room in the abandoned factory, Bouchaule ordering her death, and the clack of a machine gun bolt releasing as Jenny's anguished protests echoed in the background. A hail of bullets fell around her, a body crumbled to the ground, and in the silence that followed, she wondered why she wasn't dead. She found the answer in familiar eyes, out of place in a German uniform.

Cal was kneeling beside her, and she thought maybe she was dead after all. He assured her he was going to get her out of there, and her second thought was that Jenny had a chance. Cal had asked if she could play a convincing corpse, but she hadn't the ability to pretend anything in her condition.

He'd held up the black case containing the drug that would simulate her death, and she knew what it was. Based on its reputation, it was the last thing she wanted to wake up from. But she remembered thinking that if fate was kind to her, she wouldn't have to worry about waking up. She only had to be sure of one thing. "Don't bother if you don't plan to save her too," she had said.

"That's the plan," he'd promised.

The memory, accompanied by the incessant pounding in her head, forced her eyes open, and Smitty read her desperate look of concern instantly.

"She's fine. She's safe."

His casual confidence alarmed her. He didn't know Bouchaule. "Nowhere is safe. He won't stop. Not now. He—"

"He's dead," Smitty interrupted. "Bouchaule is dead."

Kathryn stopped breathing. Bouchaule was dead.

"It's over, honey."

She was vaguely aware of someone else in the room drifting from one side of the bed to the other like a lost ghost, but her eyes fixed blindly on the ceiling as she tried to wrap her head around the news. The pain and the pounding in her ears faded into the background, and she closed her eyes as the tension drained away. Her head sank deeper into the pillow, and she just wanted to fall into a void of nothingness and drift away. She was still for so long that Smitty must have thought she'd slipped back into unconsciousness.

"Kat?"

"Still here."

"Okay." He rubbed her hand.

Bouchaule was dead. She felt nothing … no sorrow from whatever piece of herself she'd surrendered to him, no satisfaction from the agent in her, no sense of relief that it was all over.

Jenny was safe—that was good—but again, emotion deserted her. She felt no joy for Jenny's freedom, no ache in her absence, no anticipation of her return. It should have terrified her. Why wasn't she terrified? She felt like a stranger in her own body, a collection of dispassionate memories poured into a broken shell. God, her head hurt.

Soon there was a doctor shining a blasted light into her eyes that felt like a hot poker searing into her brain.

"Are you in pain?" he asked stupidly, even as she winced with every breath. "How do you feel?"

"Yes, and like hell," she replied.

"We'll get you something for that." He motioned to the blurry gray ghost in the background, who then disappeared from the room.

An avalanche of questions ensued. She knew her name, who Smitty was, who the prime minister of England was, who her president was, and the date as it related to her last conscious moment, the week prior.

The doctor straightened with a self-satisfying but slightly bewildered look and pronounced her progress nothing short of a miracle.

The gray ghost reappeared at the bedside, and now in focus, Kathryn could see she was an attractive redheaded nurse, handing the doctor a syringe on a tray. He injected the contents into her arm, and the relief was instantaneous, as her pain eased from intense to moderate.

"Thank you," she moaned.

The doctor put his hand on her shoulder. "That should help. I know it hurts, but do try to breathe deeply. When you become mobile, we'll wrap your ribs, which may aid in managing the pain as you move about, but for now, just rest and breathe as best you can. We can't have you getting pneumonia now." He smiled that clinical phony smile doctors must develop in medical school and beckoned the nurse to accompany him.

Vivienne followed the doctor into the hall. "When you go to the main building," he began when they cleared the room, "tell the admin office to notify Colonel Jeffries the woman is awake."

The woman—Vivienne bristled at his detached reference—had a name and certainly wasn't ready to be grilled for information by impatient military brass. "Perhaps we should give her a few days to get her bearings, Doctor."

He looked at her as if she'd suggested he cheat on his final exam. "I was told to notify them as soon as she regained consciousness, and that is what we shall do, Sister Barclay." He handed Kathryn's chart to her with a glare and walked away.

"Yes, sir," she said coldly to his back as he disappeared down the hallway. When the hell did she start questioning authority?

"Look," Jenny said again as she leaned into the wooden table in the small room serving as a temporary office by the visiting brass, "I got on the plane, I slid the briefcase under the equipment rack to get it out of the way, and that's the last I saw of it." She was in a hotel room somewhere between the hospital and London. Driven there by a pair of tight-lipped Americans, she didn't pay attention to the route, and she'd already forgotten the name of the village.

A British colonel leaned in, mirroring her frustration. "You mean to tell me you spent months training for a mission, you go over there, we get you back, and you conveniently *forget* the one breadcrumb salvaged from your failed assignment on the plane?"

What began as a debriefing had turned into an interrogation, and it had been going on like that for hours. The Americans—the OSS representatives supposedly there to support her—had absolutely nothing to say and were silent observers. The British were indignant about the situation, treating her as if she'd orchestrated the whole thing on her own with an eye toward failure, in order to keep the prize for herself or whomever she was working for.

She tried to get someone, anyone, to explain imposter Cal's involvement to her, but all she received were blank stares, as if she were crazy. Invoking Colonel Holmes's name made them visibly uncomfortable and even more irate.

"Colonel Holmes hadn't the means or the authority for such an operation, and you would do well to cooperate with us."

Jenny recognized the veil of deniability settling over Colonel Holmes's activities. It was an obvious case of *do what it takes to get the job done, but if it goes badly, we never heard of you.* They had hung him out to dry, and she was the last bit of dirty laundry.

"Gentlemen, you seem to forget, I was captured by the Germans." She held up her wrists, still stained by a fading palette of pale blue and yellow bruises. "Do you think I planned that?"

The British major crossed his arms. "According to your story, you practically gave yourself up to them."

Jenny's temper barely stayed in check. "I went back to save my fellow agent."

"Is that what your OSS training taught you to do?" the colonel asked coolly, pissing in the SOE corner.

Jenny glanced at the Americans for help, but they just raised their brows in anticipation of her answer. She took a settling breath. Losing her temper wouldn't help; it was probably what they wanted. They wanted her to repeat the same story over and over, lose her temper, and slip up. Good plan, except that she was telling the truth. Mostly.

"I've told you all I can, and I've told you the truth. As for the briefcase, if you want to say it was not my shining moment to leave it behind, then fine. I was physically and mentally wrung out, as I'm sure you can understand, and worried about my fellow agent. I remembered about the case on our way to the hospital and sent word back to the airfield about it. I didn't hear anymore about it, so I just assumed you'd retrieved it."

"The airfield received no message," the major said accusingly.

"Then it's still under the equipment rack. Just go get it."

The colonel sat back in his chair. "We lost that plane and her crew two nights ago."

The news stung. Jenny pictured the young copilot who had helped them and ached for the crew and their families. "I'm terribly sorry to hear that."

The colonel glared at her, realizing he'd gotten all there was to get. "So you're saying all was lost? It was all for nothing?"

Jenny glanced from the irritated British to the indifferent Americans, sitting quietly with their arms crossed, the picture of humble defeat.

She raised her chin. "That seems to be the case, sir. I'm sorry."

The British major uncrossed his arms and exhaled. "We still have the Hammond woman. She's got to have something useful."

"If we can trust her," the colonel added.

Jenny had a few choice words for the officer rolling around in her head, but she left it to the Americans to defend their agent in a more civil manner. They did not, and she seethed internally.

The British contingent departed, and the Americans walked her to a waiting car. The man to her right was an unassuming fellow, with jam from his breakfast staining his tie. His demeanor was mild, no hint of importance or authority, but when he leaned on the car door instead of opening it for her, that all changed. "Nice performance," he said. "When can we expect the contents of that case?"

Jenny's eyes flicked from him to the taller one, who, in the movies, is known as *the heavy*, always shown casually filing his nails before beating the hell out of the victim. "I don't know what you're talking about," she said.

"We know all about you, Miss Ryan," Mr. Authority said. "We know who your father was, what he was working on, what you've been doing for the last seven months, what you've been learning and why. I'm fairly confident the contents of that briefcase are still in your possession."

Jenny glared at them, but her heart was pounding. "Like I said, I don't know what you're talking about." The two men looked at each other, and Jenny knew it was time to go. "Thanks for the lift, boys, but I think I can make my own way back." She tried to walk away, but the heavy grabbed her arm.

"Things can get very difficult for your friend," he said. "The word *treason* has come up frequently. It doesn't have to be that way."

She yanked her arm away. "Who are you?"

"Friends," Mr. Authority assured her.

"I doubt it."

"We share your distrust of the government. Ours *and* theirs. Your father intended his work to benefit mankind, not destroy it. We won't force you to do anything. We want to earn your trust, and then we can all move forward."

"You want to earn my trust? By threatening my friend?"

"That is not a threat," said the heavy. "It is a certainty unless we intervene on her behalf."

"Who are you?"

Mr. Authority smiled. "We told you. Friends. Now ... about that case."

The first day of the rest of Kathryn's life was a blur of intermittent consciousness and the merciful bliss of really good pain medication. She wished the second day was more like the first. Either her body had adjusted to the morphine or they had backed off on the dosage. Either way, she just wanted to curl into a ball and make the waking world and everyone in it go away.

She felt almost human on the third day. She was in pain but willing to tolerate the people around her, especially the nurse who brought a syringe of relief every time she saw her, it seemed.

"This is QA Sister Vivienne Barclay," Smitty said, formally introducing them at last. "She's been taking good care of you." He paused and looked at the redhead affectionately. "She's been taking good care of all of us."

"Thank you," Kathryn said.

The Sister smiled. "My pleasure." She looked at Smitty's goofy grin. "Well, except for him. He's a pain in the arse."

Kathryn chuckled and then winced, the action hurting everything from her stitched split lip to her fractured ribs. Despite the pain, she still had the wherewithal to tease Smitty about his obvious attraction. "She's got your number, Smitty."

"Hey—" He held up his hands. "Anyone who saves your life is a friend of mine."

"I hardly saved her life," the Sister said.

Kathryn took Smitty's hand. "That's usually you."

"I'm just glad you're awake," he said, and kissed her hand.

The Sister excused herself and left the room.

Kathryn watched her leave and then looked at Smitty, wondering what the dynamic between them was.

Smitty pointed his finger at her, clearly noting the woman was just her type. "Don't get any ideas."

Kathryn feigned innocence. "What?"

"Tall, beautiful, redhead? Yeah, what's to like?"

Kathryn managed a crooked smile without pulling on her stitches. "I'm out for a few days and you've already lined up a new girl."

Smitty smiled, but it was tinged with the exhaustive pain of the last week. "I'm just grateful. She was really great to us, above and beyond, and I'm afraid I really was a pain in the ass."

"Shock," Kathryn said with a grin that soon turned solemn.

She was thinking of Jenny. She'd been away for days, and Smitty would know she was worried.

"She's okay, honey. I promise."

Kathryn nodded. The Sister had given her a note, and it was definitely from Jenny, who had drawn a rather poor representation of the slipper shell she had given her at the shore and written, *Stuck. Remember? I love you, and I'll see you soon.*

Kathryn suffered more from a sense of dread at Jenny's return than a fear of her well-being while she was away. What would she say when she saw her again? Past *hello*, what could she say? Even *I love you* seemed hollow, considering the way she left Jenny. And what of her relationship with Bouchaule? She had trouble accepting her surrender to him … how could Jenny possibly understand? She was glad for the few days to get her thoughts in order.

Jenny would be glad to see her, of course, but soon, the past months would sober her to the reality of their disparate paths and crush whatever fondness lingered from their time together.

. . .

Smitty watched Kathryn carefully, not sure of her mindset. This wasn't like the last time she'd survived the Nazis. She was restless, irritable, and nervous then. She couldn't sleep without violent nightmares, and she needed constant activity around her to occupy her mind and keep the horrible memories at bay. Now she was calm. Eerily so. She slept soundly, and if not for her physical wounds, you'd never know anything had happened to her.

She didn't say much, didn't ask questions, and although she spoke when spoken to, she never elaborated beyond a simple answer. Not even the liberation of Paris, which had happened the day before she woke up, elicited much of a response beyond a reverent "Thank God."

"What are you thinking?" he finally asked into one of the lingering silences.

He was sure she was thinking she wished she were alone with no one asking her what she was thinking or how she was feeling, but she valiantly shrugged and said, "Nothing in particular. Just a lot to process."

He nodded. "How are you feeling?"

She smiled pleasantly, but he could tell she felt awful. "Drugs are good."

He pressed on with small talk that purposely didn't require participation beyond a smile or a grunt of acknowledgment. They hadn't seen each other in almost a year, so there was plenty of material for him to draw on. He eventually got around to his training work with the SOE, hoping that would pique her interest, but it didn't. That part of her life was over. Bouchaule was dead, Jenny was safe, and she was out of the spy business for good.

She thanked him for staying by her side, and he assured her he wouldn't be anywhere else. He went on doing his best to fill the stillness in the room with chatter, hoping to distract her from the horrors she'd faced.

When Vivienne arrived on her rounds, he was relieved to have someone else to talk to.

. . .

Vivienne eyed Kathryn carefully as she took her blood pressure. She could tell her patience with John was flagging.

"I'm tired, Smitty."

"Okay, honey, you just close your eyes and I'll be here when you wake up."

Vivienne glanced at Kathryn's face as she pressed her stethoscope to the brachial artery in the bend of her arm and listened for the sharp thumping sounds of her systolic pressure.

"You don't have to stay, Smitty. You've spent more than enough time hanging around here."

He smiled. "I don't mind. Where else do I need to be?"

Kathryn didn't say anything, but Vivienne could see her sinking further into the bed in defeat.

"John, why don't you go have some lunch?" she said.

"I'm not hungry."

Vivienne narrowed her eyes, and he got the picture.

He straightened and patted his stomach. "Come to think of it … good idea." He kissed Kathryn on the head, told her he'd see her later, and offered a wink to Vivienne as he turned to leave.

After he had gone, Vivienne studied Kathryn's reaction, which seemed to be an uneasy balance of relief and guilt for being relieved.

"Would you like me to keep him out of here?"

"As if you could," Kathryn said with a poor attempt at a grin.

"I'm serious."

"No. Why?"

"Your blood pressure escalates whenever he's here." She'd seen it occur on two separate occasions.

"Does it?"

Vivienne raised her brow, letting her know she wasn't fooled.

"He's a great guy … the best."

"But?"

Kathryn paused before answering. "He cares a little too much."

"I see."

"We've been through a lot together. It's just a little overwhelming right now."

"I see."

She said it more definitively this time, letting Kathryn know she understood.

"Are you really tired, or would you fancy a proper bath for a change?"

Kathryn's eyes lit up at the prospect. "Have I mentioned you're my favorite person right now?"

A real bath sounded like a good idea at the time, but the physical reality of the pain and effort involved in moving from the bed to a wheelchair to a bathtub in a room down the hall and back again, with fractured ribs, made the whole experience a test of fortitude.

Kathryn didn't do very well the first time, requiring both Sister Barclay and another nurse to help her. Once she got back to bed, she passed out, exhausted. Every day she was a little stronger, and for her second bath, she maneuvered with just a steadying hand from Sister Barclay. It took forever as she plotted her moves around her aches and pains, and she was still exhausted at the end, but it was worth it, as she looked forward to the few moments when she was left alone to soak in peace and quiet.

She was enjoying one such moment when Sister Barclay returned with the razor and cup of shaving soap she'd promised. Kathryn didn't bother moving or even opening her eyes as she relaxed with her head against the back of the tub and her arms on either side, careful to keep her wrapped splint out of the water. The Sister was very efficient at her job. She didn't believe in idle chatter, and when she did have something to say, it was direct and to the point.

When asked how Jenny was, Sister Barclay had said, "She's holding it together for now. When she gets back and talks with you, the shield of worry will give way, and everything will sink in. You'll know better then."

The Sister's candor surprised her. "Sounds like you have some experience with this."

"Not a lot but enough to know how it goes."

"And how will it go for me?"

The Sister's pragmatic expression melted into one of a sympathetic friend.

"I think you know how it will go."

Kathryn did know. The only question was whether Jenny would go through it with her.

The clank of the tray and the rustle of the Sister's gray ward dress as she kneeled beside the tub pulled her out of her thoughts. She heard her wring out the sponge and felt her paint long, deliberate strokes the length of her arm—the arm she'd already washed before she left.

Kathryn opened her eyes and found Jenny staring back at her. She froze for a disbelieving moment, and then, in a stroke of idiocy, asked, "Where's Sister Barclay?"

"She got called away," Jenny said, as she continued gently bathing her arm. "You're stuck with me."

Kathryn sat up with a wince and a groan and took the sponge from Jenny's hand. "I can do that."

She felt vulnerable and inexplicably ashamed. When she shrank into herself like a turtle ducking into its shell to escape a predator, Jenny obviously didn't appreciate it.

"You let a perfect stranger bathe you, but you won't even let me look at you? I'm insulted. Give me that—" She snatched the sponge back.

Kathryn closed her eyes and bowed her head. Jenny's tone was light, but Kathryn was afraid to look at her. After all they'd been through, her reaction was absurd, but she felt like Jenny could see right through her and would see nothing but disgust for the woman she'd become.

Jenny stared at Kathryn and wanted to cry.

The moment she heard Kathryn was awake, she couldn't wait to look into her beautiful blue eyes and tell her she loved her and that everything was going to be okay now. When she got to the tub, she thought she was prepared for what she'd find, but the sight of Kathryn's thin, nude, battered, and bruised frame languishing beneath the water like a mottled stone on the bottom of a riverbed made her clamp her hand to her mouth to suppress a shocked gasp. She gathered her strength and her nerve, set down the tray, and kneeled beside her.

She didn't expect Kathryn's self-conscious reaction, but then again, she had no idea what she was thinking or feeling. Now that she was awake and had time to process everything, she could be furious at her for getting mixed up with Bouchaule after all she had done to keep her safe. Or for breaking her promise and letting the Germans take her. Or because she came back for her. Maybe she was upset that she wasn't there when she woke up. The list was endless. For all she knew, she could be the last person Kathryn wanted to see.

She put the sponge down and stood. "I'm sorry, Kathryn. Do you want me to go?"

"No," Kathryn said quickly and reached out with a trembling hand.

Jenny took it, and Kathryn held on tight, as if she were afraid Jenny would change her mind and leave. Her eyes remained down-turned, and she didn't relax. She just held on. Several beats passed before she spoke. "I don't know what to say."

Jenny kneeled beside her again. She'd never heard Kathryn sound so defeated. "Look at me, Kat."

It took a moment, but Kathryn reluctantly lifted her eyes.

The despondency Jenny found there broke her heart, but she remained calm and smiled. "Hi."

The corner of Kathryn's mouth tried twisting into a smile, but it didn't quite make it. "Hi."

Jenny squeezed her hand. "You don't have to say anything, okay?"

"Okay," Kathryn said quietly.

Be patient with her, Vivienne had said, and Jenny would be just that.

She reached for the cup of shaving soap and its brush. "Come on. Let's get this done before the water turns cold."

She watched Kathryn grimace as she leaned back and tried to get comfortable.

Jenny put her hand behind her shoulder and helped ease her back. "Take it slow."

"My new middle name," Kathryn joked.

"Beats Ethelyn."

Kathryn laughed and then winced in pain.

"Sorry. I'll try not to be so charming."

"Good luck with that."

They both grinned at each other as Kathryn relaxed, and Jenny took the long leg extended to her.

The exchange was a glimpse into their past, when things were relatively easy and carefree, and it was with a tinge of sadness that Jenny wondered if they would ever find that place again. She concentrated on her task, trying not to dwell on what was or what would be, but as she carefully cut a path through the lather on Kathryn's shin with the razor, she couldn't help but remember the first time she'd done that.

It had been a rainy Monday, and her touch had made Kathryn confess her attraction on the day they'd met in the ladies' room at The Grotto. She'd lost one of her best suits to the bathwater that day, thanks to Kathryn's devilish streak, but the lovemaking that followed had made it more than worth it.

Jenny saw the same memory in Kathryn's melancholy grin.

"Seems like a lifetime ago," Kathryn said.

Jenny suddenly found nothing but sadness in the memory. So much time had been wasted trying to pretend their devotion to duty hadn't poisoned every part of their love and vice versa. "It was."

Who were they now? Were bittersweet memories all they had? Were those memories enough to build a future on? There was a moment—that kiss, just before Kathryn was captured—that transcended everything that had gone before it. It was pure grace, and their love flowed from it, unfettered by the past. This was the love

Jenny knew would bring them together and heal them going forward.

She finished the shave in silence and noticed Kathryn's vacant stare through slightly squinted eyes. Jenny recognized that look.

"Do you have a headache?"

"A little."

"Do you want me to get you something? Sister Barclay is right—"

"Doesn't help."

Kathryn had grown sullen, and Jenny didn't know what to say or do, but she had to start somewhere. "I'm sorry I wasn't here when you woke up."

"Don't be silly." She held out her hand. "Help me out of here. The water's gone cold."

Just like their reunion, Jenny thought.

As she helped Kathryn from the tub, she could see the entire torture map written on her body. Her torso was marked with a boot mark here and here, a baton there, there, and there … even a few fists, with the knuckles clearly outlined on her pallid skin. She tried to hide her discomfort behind a stoic mask, but Jenny could tell every movement hurt like hell. Kathryn looked weak and exhausted as she steadied herself on the back of the wicker wheelchair. She was trying so hard to be strong. Jenny didn't know if it was pride, shame, or another emotion she couldn't even comprehend, but she knew it was because she was there. She wanted to wrap her arms around her and tell her to just let it all go and that she would be strong for both of them now. But clearly, Kathryn wasn't ready for that yet.

Jenny wrapped a towel around her instead and tried as gently as possible to dry her. Kathryn flinched a few times at her touch and finally took the towel from her. "I'll do it."

"Sorry."

"It's okay. I just know where it hurts."

Everywhere, Jenny imagined.

Kathryn moved slowly, even joking that Jenny might have time for lunch before she finished. Soon she was dry and wrapped comfortably in a soft cotton robe. She hugged a small pillow against her fractured ribs as she sat in the wheelchair and let Jenny towel her hair and comb it out.

Jenny wheeled her into the hallway, where Vivienne stood beside the door.

"Everything all right?" she asked.

"I think we managed," Jenny said brightly.

Kathryn concurred with a nod and a halfhearted grin. "Fine."

Vivienne pressed her lips into a forced smile, and Jenny knew she wasn't buying her cheery act.

Once back in the room, Jenny could tell Kathryn's headache was worse, but she again refused to take anything. She barely had enough strength to get out of the wheelchair and back into bed. The stoic mask finally broke, and she grimaced in pain with every move. By the time she relaxed against the raised head of the bed, she'd gone pale and sweat glistened on her knitted brow. She squeezed her eyes shut and let out ragged but measured breaths, as if every exhale carried pieces of the pain away.

Jenny rubbed her shoulder, and Kathryn moaned softly in appreciation. "I'll be okay in a minute," she said after a few breaths. "So ridiculous. It's just a bath."

"Give it time. You'll get stronger every day."

"Thanks for your help."

Jenny nodded, but guilt had her straightening the bedding to take her mind off Kathryn's condition. She made sure the wounded hand rested on a pillow to keep it elevated and tenderly kissed her brow. "Rest now."

Kathryn's eyes opened. "Will you be back later?"

"I'll stay if you'd like."

"I'd like."

"You got it."

Kathryn drifted off minutes later.

CHAPTER SEVENTEEN

Jenny sat in the chair beside the bed and watched Kathryn sleep. After spending days staring at her unconscious form, silently pleading for her to wake up, she had to remind herself Kathryn was only resting this time. She'd spent much of her vigil trying to stay positive by planning their future and imagining how it would be when they were free to be themselves, with no secrets, no hidden agendas, and no external plots working against them. She imagined it would be like the morning at the beach on Dominic's private island, when the fog had separated them from the rest of the world and nothing but their love existed. They would be happy. They deserved to be happy.

But now that Kathryn had come back to them, Jenny found she couldn't think of anything but the past, and all she found there was a miserable barrage of missed opportunities and missteps. She didn't think they would just ride off into the sunset when the war was over, but she didn't expect the anger she felt simmering just below the surface.

Happy memories pulled painful ones in their wake like a shadow, smothering their moments of joy with all that came after. Jenny fought against the melancholic wave and cast her mind back to that rainy Monday so long ago, determined to find comfort in it.

They had been happy that day and had made love for hours. How could everything have gone so wrong after that? She closed her eyes and exhaled her exasperation, then opened them when she remembered that day with a clarity she'd abandoned to the rose-colored filter of time. She wasn't happy that day. She was floundering after discovering the secrets surrounding her and her family.

They had made love for hours because she was trying to find something in their love that would make her feel whole again. She hoped Kathryn would give that to her. She didn't. She couldn't. And afterwards, Jenny had pressed her for information about the whereabouts of her mother's belongings, hoping that would help her find herself. Kathryn offered what comfort she could, but there were no shortcuts on the road to self-discovery, and they both knew it.

She eventually got her mother's belongings back, but they provided no more comfort than Kathryn's arms that day. It wasn't until she'd read her father's journal and discovered the truth vindicating her family that she finally understood her importance and saw her purpose clearly.

The secrets and lies that had controlled both their lives since the moment they met were gone now. The void they left quickly filled with anger when she thought of Kathryn's long road to recovery. The anger wasn't directed at Kathryn. It stemmed from everything and everyone that had brought them to this: the cursed war, the governments, the shadows of the past.

She got up and started pacing the room—that damn claustrophobic clinical room. The hours she'd spent there, staring, crying, regretting, hoping, planning. Her heart ached with it all. She wanted to grab Kathryn and run. Anywhere. Just run. As long as they were together. Fuck everything else.

That's what she longed for, but it was a childish dream. There was so much left to do. The war raged on, and there was no telling how long she'd be away from Kathryn. Could she do it? Go back to the war? Leave her like this? Now, when she was so broken and needed her? When they needed each other to heal?

Jenny stood at the open window and wanted to scream in frustration. She took a deep breath, and then another, and then another, fighting the urge to expel her rage. It was her turn to protect Kathryn. Those men had threatened her with treason, which was punishable by death. The charges were bullshit, but Jenny had no doubt they could make it happen. The threat lit a fire in her. She had something they wanted, and she would use it to protect Kathryn and the project so many had died for.

A slow, final exhale brought her back to her center. They had this time together, and she would make the most of it. When Kathryn opened her eyes and was up for it, she'd wheel her into the garden. It was a beautiful late summer day, and what better surroundings to heal the soul and begin the long road home?

There was something about the decision that cleared her dark mood. The room no longer pressed in, and she could breathe freely again. Kathryn looked peaceful, and Jenny was glad for that, however temporary the reprieve. She returned to the bedside chair and caught sight of something she hadn't noticed before. On the nightstand was a small manila envelope marked *Hammond, Kathryn Rm 14C*, with a wristwatch and a simple gold wedding band peeking out from its open mouth.

Her chest tightened. The ring drew her to it like a commoner reaching for the robe of a royal as they passed—the object awe-inspiring and forbidden, all at the same time. She picked it up and cautiously dipped the tip of her ring finger into the band's golden halo, daring herself to try it on. An avalanche of emotions threatened to bury her, and she couldn't do it. She felt schizophrenic. One minute she was high, one minute low, the next minute angry, and the next minute sad.

Engraved inside the ring were the words *better together*. The reminder of Bouchaule disgusted her. *Better together.* "Fuck you, you son of a bitch," she ground out under her breath. *Better together.* As if he could even touch the love they had.

Kathryn stirred, and Jenny quickly put the ring back where she found it.

"Hi," she said with a deceptive smile when Kathryn opened her eyes.

"Hey."

"Feel better?"

"Much. Thanks for sticking around." Kathryn glanced at her wristwatch. "I'm sorry. I didn't mean to keep you here so long."

No matter how stir crazy being cooped up in that room made her, Jenny didn't want to be anywhere but by Kathryn's side. She had no idea why Kathryn thought otherwise.

"Yeah, you know," she began sarcastically, "I was going to get my hair done, maybe a manicure, but"—she tapped her wristwatch and shrugged regretfully—"shop's closed now, so …"

"All right, all right, I get it."

"About time," Jenny grumbled playfully.

Kathryn offered her hand and Jenny took it. All the emotional turmoil melted away with her touch. This was all she needed right now. Kathryn was awake. She would be fine. Everything else could wait.

With a grimace, Kathryn shifted away from her and pulled her toward the small space she'd vacated on the bed.

"Kat, I don't think—"

"You look exhausted. Lie down. Just for a few minutes. No one will be back to check on me for hours."

"But … I don't want to hurt you."

"Come here."

Her voice was gentle, and it soothed her like an intimate caress. Jenny carefully nestled into Kathryn's side and rested her head beside hers on the pillow.

"Is this okay?"

Kathryn pulled Jenny's thigh over hers and entwined their fingers. "Perfect."

They didn't speak, and Jenny found the contemplative silence a welcome reprieve from the whirlwind of emotions.

As Kathryn drifted in and out of sleep, a wave of exhaustion washed over Jenny. The images that had stalked her dreams—Kathryn's beaten and bloody face, the slow motion horror of her flying off the back of the truck with her arms reaching out for safety that was no longer there, the look of helplessness and terror in her eyes as she fell away from her and tumbled into the street—all disappeared when Kathryn took her hand and their bodies became one.

She slept peacefully for the first time since she'd bid Kathryn goodbye in her father's lab seven months ago.

Vivienne found John napping in an uncomfortable wooden chair outside Kathryn Hammond's room when she arrived for her evening rounds. She would have sidestepped him if he weren't parked in the middle of the doorway. She stared at his whisker-stubbled face and smiled at his dimples, visible even when he wasn't smiling. The dark circles under his eyes sobered her, and a strange ache in her heart stopped her from waking him. What was she doing? She had rounds to finish.

She touched his knee. "John?"

He started and nearly fell off the chair. "You can't go in there," he blurted out as he got to his feet.

"Why ever not?"

"Uh, she's sleeping."

"Okay," Vivienne said and reached for the doorknob. John stopped her.

"Jenny is with her. They're sleeping."

He seemed flustered. "I see. I'll try not to wake them."

"No—" He reached out again to stop her, but she brushed by him and opened the door.

Kathryn was sleeping, turned slightly to the side, and Jenny slept spooning her from behind, their bodies filling the small bed.

"It's not what you think," John said, a little flustered.

Vivienne assured him with a kind smile that she knew exactly what it was, and it was fine with her. Others may not be so welcoming, so she warned him they should all be careful.

He agreed, and she shut the door and let them sleep.

CHAPTER EIGHTEEN

Kathryn had to admit, the sun felt good on her face as Jenny wheeled her down the winding path through colorful blooms of unkempt sweet peas, lavender, and rose bushes in the hospital garden. It almost made her forget the dull headache throbbing behind her eyes. As usual, the oral pain meds only went so far. She preferred to keep a clear head, especially with important conversations looming on the horizon, but she definitely needed the drugs today for the bumpy journey through the grounds in a wheel-chair and was glad she took them.

They were in the shade of a large linden tree now, on the far end of the garden, away from the bustle of the main building. The solitude of the place, with its sweet scents and birdsong, offered a surreal respite from the horrors beyond the walled estate, and she turned to Jenny to comment on it but was stopped by the dour expression on her face.

Jenny was sitting beside her on a wooden bench, twirling a heart-shaped leaf between her fingers while staring at the ground between her feet.

She'd been unusually quiet the whole day, and Kathryn sensed that the time for one of those heavy conversations was upon them.

"Penny for your thoughts?"

Jenny put on a practiced smile. "Just enjoying the beautiful day. How are you doing with all the jostling this morning?"

"Fine. What is it?"

Jenny stared at the ground again. "There's so much to say. So much we need to talk about, but I'm not sure this is the time."

If Kathryn could run forever and never have one of those conversations, she would. But that was the old her. She wasn't running anymore. Part of healing was facing her past. All of it. Even the parts she had rationalized away in the name of duty. Especially those parts. She had wounded Jenny in unforgivable ways. That she was still by her side was a grace she never expected. Yes, they had a lot to talk about, but Jenny couldn't stay with her much longer. The outside world still had a claim on her. Every minute that passed brought more dying men on the front lines, more bombs falling from the sky, and more innocent lives snuffed out in a fight against an evil ideology. Her war was over, but Jenny still had her part to play.

"We're going to run out of time soon."

Jenny met her eyes, and a flash of panic quickly turned into determination. "I'm not leaving this place until you do. And wherever you go after that, I'm going."

Kathryn took the leaf, now crushed in Jenny's hand. "I want that too."

"All right then."

"But we can't have that yet."

Jenny opened her mouth to protest, but Kathryn took her hand and squeezed it. "I love you. I love that you want to be here for me. But I know you can't."

"Watch me."

"You're being obstinate, which I also love, because your heart's in the right place. But our hearts can't stop this war. And until it's over …"

Jenny stood and stepped away with a curse.

Her disposition told Kathryn she was hiding something. Jenny had met with someone from the agencies, and she'd never said what they talked about. Knowing the agencies, Kathryn didn't have to stretch too far to guess what they'd said. "They threatened you with my prosecution if you didn't cooperate, didn't they. What was it? Desertion? Dereliction of duty?"

"Treason."

Kathryn raised her brow. "Well. They're not messing around."

"It's blackmail. I won't let them get away with it."

"It probably came from the top. You've no recourse."

Jenny raised her chin. "*I'm* the recourse. They want my cooperation? They'll bow at my feet now. I'll leave here when I'm damn good and ready."

Kathryn looked her up and down, admiring her confidence. "This may be the drugs talking … but, uh, that was pretty hot."

Jenny broke out laughing and came back to her side. "Hurry up and get well so I can make love to you all day in a field of wildflowers somewhere."

Kathryn laughed and regretted it when all her wounded parts complained.

Jenny winced. "Sorry." After a few soft chuckles and an extended moment of silence, she spoke again, but this time, emotion choked her voice. "Can you forgive me?"

The agonizing guilt peering out from Jenny's red-rimmed green eyes was unmistakable. Kathryn had seen it reflected in her own for years, and she would do anything to ease Jenny of that burden.

"There's nothing to forgive, honey. None of this was your fault." Jenny tried to pull away, but Kathryn held tightly to her, and when she felt she would stay put, she tenderly cupped her cheek. "Please don't blame yourself."

"This from the woman who has spent the last few years beating herself up over the deaths of those boys."

"Not anymore."

"Really?" Jenny said skeptically.

"Really."

Kathryn had been thinking a lot about the men who had valiantly tried to rescue her from her first bout with the Nazis. She was in their shoes this time, and while she couldn't say she'd absolved herself of guilt in their deaths, seeing Jenny about to embark down the same dark path certainly helped her find peace with it.

"Considering how it turned out for them, I can't say those boys would do it again, but at the time, in their hearts, they were willing to risk their lives for what they thought was right." She paused, still humbled by their sacrifice. "I have to accept that it was worth it to them. As for guilt over their deaths … I'll take responsibility for my part, but I can no more take responsibility for their choices than you can for mine."

"You turned your whole life upside down because of me. You left with Bouchaule and were nearly beaten to death because of me. Of course this is my fault."

"I left with Bouchaule because I had to make sure he was stopped. You came out of hiding for the same reason. He was a monster. There's no denying that. That's not your fault, and it's not mine. We both wanted the same thing, and you said it yourself … we chose our own paths. Can you honestly say you wouldn't do it again when you think you have the best chance to accomplish what needs to be done?"

Jenny shook her head, obviously not ready to forgive herself. "I never should have let you walk away from me that day in my father's lab. You were one extended hand away from falling into my arms, and I should have let you."

Kathryn pursed her lips, acknowledging how close she came to veering from her plan. "That would have been a mistake."

"I never would have let you go, and none of this would have happened."

"It would have been a mistake, and you know it."

Jenny didn't say anything, but a glimmer of acceptance twitched in her grim face, and Kathryn knew the seed of healing had taken root. There was truth in what Jenny had said though. Everything she did was to protect her. It was her Achilles heel, and her espionage career was doomed from the moment she fell for her.

Had she truly focused on what needed to be done, she would have killed Bouchaule the moment he handed her the Walther P.38 for protection before she left Paris.

But fate, ever the truth-sayer, reminded her that had she done that, Bouchaule wouldn't have been there to stop her interrogation, and she would be dead. Jenny would be in the hands of the enemy, and it all would have been for nothing.

Tears spilled from Jenny's eyes, and before Kathryn could absolve her again, an unexpected confession fell from her quivering lips.

"I tried to kill you."

Kathryn had no idea what she was talking about.

"When you fell off the truck, I grabbed your gun and unloaded the magazine at you."

Kathryn didn't know what to say. Her eyes drifted to a delicate purple peony growing in a bed of flowers beside them. Its beauty was a stark contrast to the horrific choice Jenny was forced to make—to the horrific choices being made all around them—and she wasn't sure she could have pulled the trigger if their roles were reversed.

"You always were a lousy shot," she joked, trying to rein in the empathy she felt and show there were no hard feelings.

Jenny faced her, anguish contorting her brow. "If we hadn't hit a pothole, you'd be dead right now."

Kathryn regretted her flippant remark. "I can't imagine what it took to do that. I know it must have been hard. Thank you for trying."

"*Thank you?*" Jenny turned away again to muffle a sob.

"You did the right thing, Jenny."

"Fuck that," she said as she stood and stepped away again, wiping her nose with the back of her hand. "And the worst part ... it wasn't hard at all. I just did it. I didn't even think of leaping from the truck to help you ... I just grabbed the gun and started firing."

Secretly, Kathryn was impressed her training was so ingrained, but she knew Jenny wouldn't appreciate the compliment. She'd lost part of her humanity in that moment, and Kathryn knew it was terrifying.

"You did the right thing, staying on that truck."

"Then I did the wrong thing and went back for you."

"You couldn't know the boy had been compromised."

"*Don't ever go back, people.* Isn't that what you taught us?"

"Jenny—"

"And then that Nazi? Look what he did to you, all because I wouldn't talk. What is there to forgive? My God, where do I begin?"

Kathryn reached out to Jenny's animated hand and tried to calm her. "Jenny, that Nazi was a sadistic bastard who would have beaten the hell out of me whether you were there or not. The fact that you were there to witness it and he was able to make you feel guilty about it was a bonus for him. Don't let him get away with that. I don't blame you, I blame *him*, and so should you."

Jenny wiped the tears from her cheek, and Kathryn tugged her back to the bench. When she sat and their eyes met, Kathryn smiled and kissed her hand. "I know I'm pretty pathetic looking right now, but I'm going to be fine. I promise."

Jenny nodded. "I know you will."

"Well then?"

"I almost killed you."

"But you didn't."

"It haunts me. I don't know how to let that go."

"You have to."

Jenny didn't need to ask how. "One day at a time, until it no longer tears your heart out."

"That's it."

Jenny nodded again, but Kathryn knew there was little comfort there.

"You're stronger than I ever was, Jenny. I admire the hell out of you for what you did. I'm just sorry you were in that position."

Jenny smiled despite her emotional beating. "Well, safe to say, you did everything in your power to prevent it."

Kathryn raised her brow. That comforted her. "True."

Jenny leaned forward and put her elbows on her knees and her head in her hands. Apparently, guilt hadn't released its stranglehold yet. "I broke your beautiful record."

Kathryn rubbed her back. She understood the anger, frustration, and doubt that led to the disc's destruction, but she brought it on herself. How could she blame Jenny for that?

"And I broke your heart."

Jenny leaned back and exhaled. "What a pair of assholes."

Kathryn couldn't help but laugh.

Jenny sat on the wide sill of the open window in Kathryn's room and leaned her back against the frame. Kathryn had tired quickly after their visit to the garden, and she was resting. Time wasn't on their side. When was it ever? She'd gotten a message when they returned that a driver would be there to pick her up in two days.

She talked a good game, but if they ordered her to go, she had to go. Kathryn knew it too. Jenny was still an OSS agent, and there was still a war to win, but she would go on pretending she could stay until walking out of Kathryn's room for the last time ripped her heart from her chest.

The unbearable ache of that inevitable moment caught in her throat, and she swallowed it down before it made her cry.

From across the room, she heard whispering in French. She couldn't make out the words, but they quickly crescendoed into anxious chatter and then exploded in a terrified cry, which Jenny was sure was a shapeless articulation of Bouchaule's first name. Kathryn was having a nightmare and had jolted awake by the time Jenny got to her side and took her trembling hand.

"You're okay. I'm here. You're okay."

Kathryn cursed through obviously painful gasps of air, and with wide eyes, begged Jenny not to let go. Her grip was surprisingly strong, considering, and Jenny had no intention of letting go. That settled it. There was no way she was leaving. They would have to remove her bodily and arrest her to keep her away. Kathryn needed her, and she wouldn't let her down.

When Kathryn's breathing evened out and she loosened her grip, Jenny wet a cloth with cool water from the pitcher on the nightstand

and gently placed it on Kathryn's sweaty brow and then on her warm cheeks. "Better?"

Kathryn nodded and closed her eyes. "I should have killed him."

Jenny's one regret about the day they were rescued was that *she* didn't kill Bouchaule. "You were second in line. He put the hit on my father and killed countless others. He was mine to kill. I'm only sorry someone got to him before I did."

Kathryn was quiet for a few moments.

"How did it happen? How did he die?"

Jenny hesitated.

"I want to know everything."

Jenny recognized the need for closure and relayed the details of Bouchaule's demise, starting from the moment he brought her to his car. When she got to his despicable plans to impregnate her, hoping to study her offspring for any trace of the unique qualities in her blood, Kathryn finally met her gaze with shock and then fury. Jenny skipped the part where he expressed remorse for ordering her murder. After all the people he had sent to their deaths, she didn't think him capable of remorse, only psychological games.

"He said you couldn't have children. Is that true?" she asked, wondering if Kathryn had come up with some scheme to avoid that particular ordeal with him. One look at Kathryn's tense jaw gave her the answer.

"It's true."

"I'm so sorry. I didn't know."

"Neither did I."

Jenny was at a loss for words, but Kathryn rescued her.

"Then what happened?"

There wasn't much else to tell. Jenny recounted the abduction and execution in the woods, which Kathryn took without a hint of emotion.

She stared at the ceiling, and Jenny wondered if she was imagining Bouchaule's body discarded in the underbrush on the side of the road while wild animals devoured his carcass and creatures of the earth gorged on his rotting flesh. That's what she would do until his memory disappeared from her mind.

"He can't hurt you anymore, Kathryn."

"He never hurt me."

"No, he only ordered your death," she said sarcastically.

Kathryn looked at her as if she couldn't understand why she was so upset. Jenny raised her brow, waiting for some sort of response.

"Right … that."

"Yes, *that*," Jenny said, but Kathryn's gaze drifted to a faraway place. "Are you sure you're all right?"

Kathryn blinked as if she wondered why she asked. "Fine."

Jenny knew that was a lie, but she wasn't sure Kathryn knew it. *"Sometimes they get lost in their legend,"* Holmes had said to her once, and suddenly Kathryn's strange behavior made sense. She nearly choked on the question but had to ask. "Did you love him?" She heard jealousy in her tone and regretted asking the minute the words passed her lips. "Never mind. Doesn't matter now. He's dead, and no one's going to shed a tear for that fucker."

She looked to Kathryn for the expected *amen, sister*, but Kathryn just frowned for a confused beat and then looked her in the eyes, wholly present. "It's complicated."

The reply pushed Jenny back. "I see." She didn't know what else to say and had to get out from under Kathryn's expectant stare. She stood and took a few steps toward the window but was stopped by the specter of Kathryn's wedding ring taunting her from the bedside table. *Better together.* The room was too small again, and she felt sick.

Kathryn followed her line of sight and saw it too. She pursed her lips regretfully and held out her hand.

Jenny didn't go to her. She needed a minute.

"It's complicated, Jenny," Kathryn repeated. "It was nothing like—"

"Us?" Jenny snapped reflexively, feeling that anger clawing its way up her spine again. "Nothing like what we had?"

"It wasn't," Kathryn said softly.

Jenny knew it in her head, but all the frustration she'd been harboring from the moment she realized the scene with Marcella was a ruse wanted to unleash its bile into the room. She took a cleansing breath. That fury had no place in their lives now, and she let the anger pass through her, where its chaos could dissipate in the dark void of their past.

Kathryn's relationship with Bouchaule had nothing to do with her or their love. She just got lost in her legend, like Holmes had said. How else could she have endured her life with him? She had to lose herself in it. Complicated didn't scratch the surface.

She returned to Kathryn's side. "I know it wasn't. I'm just sorry for you … for all that happened." It pained her that things had gone so far, and she took in Kathryn's broken body—the new crop of scars on her face, the damaged hand that probably meant she'd never play the piano again—and wondered how she could ever make it up to her.

Kathryn must have mistaken her regret for discontent because she had that faraway look in her eyes again.

"What is it?" Jenny asked.

"I'm sorry I hurt you."

Jenny stiffened. The memory of Marcella in Kathryn's bed still cut like a knife in her heart.

"We don't have to talk about that. It doesn't matter now."

"It will matter later. And I want there to be a later."

Jenny understood that they'd both been through something traumatic and that the sting of past transgressions was only temporarily subdued. Still, she didn't think now was the time to stir up those emotions.

"There will be a later, so I think we should just—"

"You were right when you said I ended things in the shittiest way possible."

So, they were doing this. Jenny hesitated, because piling on Kathryn now, in her condition, seemed callous, but if Kathryn wanted to talk about it, Jenny certainly had a few things to say. In the months since that horrible day, she'd come to terms with what Kathryn had done. She understood why she did it, but she agonized over *how* she did it, which led her to questioning how someone who loved her—and she didn't doubt that Kathryn loved her—could do something so heartless. And how could she still love and trust that person? Nothing had made sense until she'd found out why she did it, and then the how had just hurt more because it was so unnecessary.

"You once told me you didn't know how to love. That turned out to be true in a way I never would've imagined. I thought, everyone knows how to love. It's like breathing. It just happens and you know how to do it instinctually. Except you don't. You may think what you did was out of love … but it wasn't. It was cruel. And I know you were trying to protect me from the truth, but I'd rather have looked over my shoulder for the rest of my life than endure the heartbreak you put me through."

"You're right, and I'll regret that choice until my dying day."

Jenny believed her. Any lingering doubts about love or devotion vanished when Kathryn threw herself into a den of Nazis to protect her from Bouchaule. That didn't change the way she left her though. She still needed to understand why.

"Why didn't you just tell me I had to go under? I would have done whatever you asked. Why make me think we were a lie? And then twisting the knife with *Marcella*? God, Kat. Why? I begged you, *begged* you to tell me the truth."

Shame and remorse filled Kathryn's eyes, but her gaze never wavered.

"Because I had to let you go, and I couldn't. I tried. So many times. You may not believe me, but I loved you so much that it physically hurt knowing I'd never see you again. I just … I couldn't do it. I needed you to do it for me because I was weak, and for that, I'm truly sorry. I know it's unforgivable, but here I am, asking for forgiveness."

Jenny hated the explanation, but it was just so damn Kat. Only she could turn the greatest love she'd ever known into a self-inflicted train wreck. Kathryn loved her too much. Jenny almost laughed because it reminded her of the first time she tried to seduce Kathryn on her couch and Kathryn had pushed her away, saying she liked her too much to get involved with her. Jenny asked her if she could like her a little less? Say, for an hour? Maybe two? And they had both thought it was funny. She didn't understand what Kathryn had meant then, but she understood it now.

"I'm still here, aren't I?"

"I'm so thankful for that, but honestly, after everything I've done, I don't know why you are."

No matter how hard Jenny tried to fight against it, her love for Kathryn never left her. Despite Kathryn's method and the pain she'd endured because of it, she'd forgiven her long ago. "After everything you've done? You just saved my life. I think I'm obligated to stick around after that."

Thankfully, Kathryn got the intended humor and reluctantly smiled. "Cal, or whoever he was, saved your life. All I did was get caught."

She said it lightly, but it hit Jenny in a soft spot.

"You saved my life the minute I met you."

The moment of fond remembrance provided a welcome respite from the painful conversation, and Kathryn smiled.

"It took a little longer, but you saved my life too."

Jenny thought of how close Kathryn came to losing her life because of her.

Kathryn saw the flash of guilt in her eyes again, and she admonished her for it with a squeeze of her hand.

Jenny promised she'd work on it with a squeeze back.

"So you forgive me and we still have a chance?" Kathryn asked lightly, but Jenny saw the fear in her eyes.

"Only if you stop doing dumb, irrational things."

Kathryn took back her hand and raised it in an oath. "I swear."

They both grinned, but Kathryn's quickly faded, as if she were afraid the answer was no. Jenny put her out of her misery.

"As infuriating and heartbreaking as it was, I forgive you."

"Thank you. I'm so sorry. And thank you for not hating me."

Jenny remembered hurling that little dagger at Kathryn on the day they parted in her father's lab and regretted it.

"I don't hate you, Kathryn. I hate what you did to me, to us, but I could never hate you, and believe me, I've tried. I love you beyond reason, apparently, which is why I just want to put all this behind us and move on. We'll get you home, get you well, we'll sort out whatever needs sorting, and we can finally start our lives on a level playing field." She reclaimed Kathryn's hand and brought it to her lips. "Yes, we finally have a real chance."

CHAPTER NINETEEN

Kathryn sat on an uncomfortable concrete bench under the shade of a copper beech tree growing beside the garden wall while she waited for Jenny to retrieve a wheelchair. Her ribs hurt like hell, and her plan to appear strong for Jenny on their last full day together backfired spectacularly when a short walk was too much for her and she nearly passed out from the pain. Jenny saw right through her tough act, and Kathryn wondered why she bothered trying to deceive her. Before she left, Jenny had given her a stern reprimand for overdoing it, and when she returned, Kathryn would swallow what was left of her pride and agree it wasn't one of her better ideas. She couldn't hide her physical condition, but she could attempt to conceal the rest.

Jenny was so damn optimistic that Kathryn hadn't the heart to tell her how badly she was struggling. When she was with Jenny, she was hopeful too, but when she was alone, she'd never felt darker or less worthy of … anything. The feeling wasn't new, but even she didn't recognize the woman she'd become. Jenny didn't see it yet. She hoped she never would.

Sister Barclay was in tow when Jenny showed up with the wheelchair and didn't waste any time admonishing her as well. "When I said walk around a bit, I meant in your room. Not down a flight of stairs and then the length of the building. How do you feel now?"

"Better now that I'm not moving."

"Tell her if you're hurting, Kat. You're not helping yourself by being stoic right now."

Kathryn shot Jenny an accusatory glare for tattling on her. "I'm fine now. I promise."

Sister Barclay eyed her skeptically but relented without a further scolding and addressed Jenny. "I'll get two orderlies to help get her upstairs."

Kathryn did her best to suppress her discomfort as she transferred herself from the bench into the wheelchair, but two disapproving stares told her she wasn't fooling anyone. "I'd like to stay here a bit longer," she said, once she caught her breath.

Sister Barclay produced a small bottle from her apron pocket. "Would you like your pain pill now?"

"No."

The Sister arched a brow and addressed Jenny before walking away. "Orderlies when you're ready."

Jenny sat beside Kathryn on the bench. "Why didn't you take your pill, and why are you being so stubborn?"

"This is our last full day together. I'm not spending it drugged out of my mind."

Jenny took her hand and exhaled. "You don't have to prove anything to me. I know you're strong, and I know you're going to be okay."

Kathryn nodded, but when she looked at Jenny, she was eyeing her suspiciously.

"What aren't you telling me?"

Too many things. *Hold out. Don't say anything. Be strong.* Those instincts had gotten her through the worst moments in her life. They had also caused the worst moments in her life. A lie was always the next step. *I'm fine. What do you mean? I'm just tired.* So many lies. Which would she choose? One by one, they stalked her—past and present— filling her head with excuses and consequences until she couldn't see.

She realized she'd closed her eyes and was swaying. Her fragile facade was cracking. Darkness was rising. *Breathe.*

Jenny touched her shoulder. "Kat?"

Kathryn looked into Jenny's concerned eyes. She wanted to cling to her, sob in her arms, and beg her to stay. Please save her. Please fix her. But Jenny couldn't do either. This broken part of her, this thing that poisoned so much of her life since childhood, was hers to face and conquer. In her current state, it felt insurmountable. In the past, she would have succumbed to the hopelessness of it all. She would have steeled herself, let Jenny walk away unaware, and when they met again, she would keep her darkness at bay with skills honed over a lifetime, until she destroyed everything again. And she would.

The thought of it exhausted her, and for the first time since her ordeal, a tear spilled down her cheek. That wasn't her future. That was her past. Her future was in the hand holding hers. Jenny believed in her. Wanted her. Loved her. Jenny, who never shied away from the darkness. Jenny, who forgave her. It was inconceivable to Kathryn how Jenny could ever trust her again. How her promises of love and devotion could ever mean anything when she had hurt her so deeply, but Jenny was here, holding her hand.

Through tears, she looked into Jenny's open gaze and saw her last chance. Jenny would try to fix everything, because it was the only weapon against the helplessness of watching a loved one flounder, but Jenny would understand she couldn't. This was up to her now. She'd hidden so much of herself for so long that she didn't know where she ended and the lies began. This confession of the soul would be as painful to hear as it was to admit.

"I've spent my life molding myself into whatever, whomever, I needed to be to survive."

Jenny nodded solemnly, no doubt because she'd been a victim of it firsthand.

"I don't know who I am. I don't think I ever have. I'm trying to reconcile the things I've done in my life ... to you, in my relationship with Bouchaule ..."

"I know who you are, baby. I know why you did what you did to me. As for Bouchaule—"

"You asked me if I loved him," Kathryn interrupted. Jenny probably didn't want to hear what she had to say, but if there was a time for all cards on the table, this was it. "I did, in a way, but deep down … I knew evil lurked in him, but I refused to believe it. I rationalized the things he did to make him the man I wanted him to be. Does that sound like the woman you know?"

Jenny was silent for a few beats. "As you said, you molded yourself into who you needed to be to get the job done. You just got a little lost."

Kathryn shook her head. "You don't understand."

"Then help me."

Kathryn barely understood it herself.

"Help me understand, Kat."

She hesitated but then gave in to Jenny's pleading eyes. "We were the same. We deserved each other."

"You are nothing like him," Jenny said, her hatred of the man steeling her voice. "He was sick, and whatever twisted psychological games he played to get you to—"

"Stop." Kathryn squeezed her hand. "Have you conjured up some scenario in your head where I was trapped in an assignment, had no choice, and, therefore, I'm forgiven because I was only playing the hand I was dealt? I stayed with him willingly. I married him. And yes, having a child briefly crossed my mind. I was asleep at the wheel and willing to accept that life because I was dirty, and ugly, and it was what I deserved. I didn't want to wake up. Do I still rate forgiveness? Is there some rationale to be had, because I'm not quite there yet. You want to know how fucked up I am? Let's start there."

Jenny stared at her with a stone mask she'd never seen before. *This is the moment*, Kathryn thought. *This is the moment she sees me clearly and we're done.*

"I'm not here to judge you. I never have and I never will. You know that."

Tears welled in Kathryn's eyes again. How did she find this person who loved her, faults and all?

"Let me help you," Jenny said.

Kathryn closed her eyes again. Jenny's presence made her despise herself, but it also gave her hope that the person Jenny saw and loved did exist. Kathryn felt her once, but she crushed her when she crushed Jenny's heart. Her path since childhood had primed her to find solace in the dark shadows. She could never find peace with someone like Jenny until she faced that about herself.

"It seems every choice I've made in my life has been the wrong one. The only thing I ever did right was fall in love with you, and even that was the wrong thing to do."

"That was the best thing you ever did, Kathryn Hammond. I know you feel like you're drowning in the past, but you can't change any of that."

Kathryn reluctantly nodded.

"I know who you are, Kathryn. I've always known who you are, but you keep slipping away from me because you won't let me in."

"I am forever grateful for your grace, Jenny, truly. But you know who you want me to be … who you thought I was. That's not who I am."

Jenny leaned back and exhaled a groan to the sky.

"*I* don't know who I am, honey, and you, of all people, know you can't give that to me." It was the one thing she could say that Jenny would understand and accept, because she had gone through her own identity crisis over the truth about her family, but the grim set of Jenny's mouth made her sorry she'd said anything. "I didn't want to burden you with any of this because it's not something you can fix."

"You're right. I can't fix it, but I can't help you if I don't know what you're going through. You're not a burden. It breaks my heart that I can't be by your side through this, but please know that I do see you, *all* of you, and it's not through the eyes of some lovestruck innocent. Believe me."

Kathryn clutched Jenny's hand to her chest. "I know. You are the best thing that's ever happened to me, and I'll hold you close to my heart every day until I see you again." Jenny's smile was pained, and Kathryn could tell she was trying to keep it together so she wouldn't fall apart in front of her. She squeezed her hand and gave her an out. "I think I'm ready for those orderlies now."

Jenny nodded and rose quickly. As she headed toward the main entrance, she brought a hand to her mouth to muffle a sob.

As Jenny watched the orderlies carry Kathryn up the stairs in the wheelchair, she knew resting in bed would be Kathryn's agenda for the rest of the day. The morning had taken a lot out of her, and Jenny had to admit, it had taken a lot out of her as well.

She arranged Kathryn's pillows and sat beside her.

The weight of Kathryn's arm across her thighs and her hand resting possessively on her hip comforted her. Exhausted blue eyes traced her face like they were memorizing everything about her, and Jenny could almost hear an invisible clock ticking down the moments until their separation.

Kathryn must have sensed her anxiety because she squeezed her hip and pressed her lips into a half-smile. "I'm sorry I upset you earlier."

Jenny shook her head. "This whole situation upsets me. I should be by your side."

"You will be. It's just going to take time."

Jenny groaned. "Fucking time. You need me now."

"I won't be alone, I'll have—"

"Knock, knock," Smitty said, sticking his head in the open door. "Am I interrupting?"

Simultaneously, Kathryn said "No" while Jenny said "Yes."

Smitty hesitated, and Kathryn motioned him in.

He took one look at their tired faces and voiced his concern. "Say, what's—"

"Here she is, gentlemen," an orderly said from the hallway as he ushered in a uniformed American officer and a man in a dark double-breasted suit.

Jenny was on her feet in an instant, ready to fight for every precious minute with Kathryn. "I have until tomorrow, and if you think—"

"We're not here for you. We're here for Miss Hammond."

It only took one shocked beat before she and Smitty objected in unison. "This woman is in no condition—"

The uniformed man lifted his hand. "We're just here to talk."

"It's okay," Kathryn said.

Jenny didn't like it, and she feared it had something to do with the threat of treason suggested by her recent Allied interrogators. Perhaps a reminder of the deal she'd made with them. She eyed them with suspicion, and Smitty did the same as they exited the room.

The man in the suit closed the door behind them.

Jenny muttered curses as she paced in a small circle at the end of the hall.

Smitty calmly leaned against the wall with his arms crossed. "She can handle herself."

"The deck is stacked against her, Smitty."

"What does that mean?"

Silence was also part of her deal. Smitty couldn't do anything about it even if he wanted to, so the agitated and worried lover routine would cover nicely.

"Look at her"—she gestured toward Kathryn's room—"she doesn't need this noise. She needs rest, not an interrogation by baby Ike and Hoover Jr. in there."

"You know Kat. She's strong. She's a fighter, and she's going to be fine. Look how far she's come already."

Jenny wanted to think that her presence had something to do with that, but she worried about how Kathryn would fare after. "I'm leaving tomorrow."

That sobered Smitty. "So soon?"

Jenny nodded.

"That's tough, kid. I'm sorry."

His use of the word *kid* had gone from a term of derision when they had first met to one of affection now, and she would miss him too when she left.

She embraced him. "Thanks, Johnny."

He gave her an extra squeeze. "I'll look after her for as long as I can. Everything's going to be okay."

"I know."

Kathryn had barely bid the Americans goodbye before Jenny burst into the room and rushed to her side.

"Are you okay? What did they want?"

"Everything's fine."

Jenny sat beside her with a relieved sigh.

The uniformed man was a stern representative of the OSS, demanding a full accounting of her time with Bouchaule at her earliest convenience. The man in the suit was not introduced, nor did he speak. Kathryn assumed he was a lawyer. She didn't know for whom. Both looked at her with disdain, but no one mentioned treason.

Jenny had *I have questions* written all over her face, so Kathryn put her out of her misery.

"Evidently, a very important briefcase went down in a plane."

"Gosh, that's a shame."

"Isn't it?"

Kathryn eyed the open door, and Jenny got the hint to close it.

She waited until Jenny settled back onto the bed beside her. "There's more to that story, isn't there?"

"Do you really want to know?"

"I need to know if this is truly over." If everything she did was worth it.

Jenny hesitated. Never a good sign. Kathryn's heart raced with the drawn out silence. Having honed protection of your loved one to a fine art, she understood Jenny's reticence, but she needed to know. "Please, tell me."

"I had the briefcase."

"Had?"

"I turned it over to the Americans who pulled me aside after my debriefing."

Kathryn closed her eyes. She imagined it was part of a deal to spare her from prosecution. "They have everything then."

Jenny cast a glance at the closed door and then lowered her voice to a whisper. "Everything except certain papers from a certain secret compartment."

"Oh, thank God."

"They're safe, and they'll never see the light of day again."

"Will you destroy them?"

Jenny hesitated again but then raised her chin. "They're mine. They're about me. It's the closest I've come to understanding what I am."

"You're not a *thing*, Jenny."

"To some I am. Was. I don't think I have to explain how heavily a body count weighs on your soul."

It was unimaginable in Jenny's case, and Kathryn tightened her hold on Jenny's hip.

"What of your father's coded books?"

"They won't see the light of day again either."

Smitty had mentioned a whispered rumor about Holmes obtaining Daniel Ryan's coded books, and they could only have come from Jenny.

"What did you give Holmes?"

Jenny smiled the mischievous smile Kathryn loved so well and explained how she took a plain volume of one of her father's books from the shelf in the lab, copied the key code onto its page corners from one of the coded books Kathryn had given her, and then purposely burned the edges of that forged book, allowing enough of the code to remain, proving it was indeed one of the keys but not enough to make it useful. She presented it to Holmes and claimed she found it, along with the ashes of the two other coded volumes, in the incinerator of her father's newly discovered lab. They found the charred remains of two plain volumes Jenny had tossed in there to confirm her story, and they believed the keys were lost, rendering their cache of coded documents useless. Daniel Ryan's case was closed.

Kathryn raised her brow. "Why didn't I think of that?"

Jenny laughed.

Kathryn didn't. "No, seriously. Why didn't I think of that?"

"Because you're such a lousy agent," Jenny joked, getting her back for the "lousy shot" remark.

Bouchaule had also called her a bad agent. It was too close to the truth to be funny. "Does anyone else know about you?"

"As far as I know, that knowledge died with Bouchaule."

"And as far as I know, he didn't share it with the Nazis."

The realization that the threat against Jenny was over lifted a burden that Kathryn had carried since the day they'd met. Its absence almost made her giddy with relief.

She pulled Jenny to her and tucked her safely into the crook of her shoulder. "It's over. Now all we have to do is win the war."

"Piece of cake," Jenny said, and they both gave in to exhausted snickering.

Jenny stared at the far wall, lost in her thoughts, while Kathryn napped beside her. She felt Kathryn shift and turn her head toward the door.

"Where's Smitty?"

"I told him I'm leaving tomorrow, so he's giving us some time."

"That's very thoughtful."

"That's Smitty all over."

Kathryn chuckled. "Have you seen him around Sister Barclay?"

"Yeah. I think he's got a crush."

"Who wouldn't?"

Jenny lifted her head and gave Kathryn the stink eye. "I'm not sure that's funny just yet."

Kathryn pulled her back down and kissed her head. "Sorry." After a few beats, she said, "I want him to find someone like that."

"Are you playing matchmaker?"

Kathryn paused too long for a lighthearted conversation, and Jenny could see Kathryn's complicated history with Smitty playing out in her knitted brow.

"I've thought about letting him go so many times. It's all too much sometimes."

Jenny knew what she meant. The horrors she and Smitty had faced together would haunt them forever. Jenny didn't know if their constant interaction was a comfort because of their love for one another or a painful reminder of the past. A little of both, she supposed. Just like she'd feel every time she saw Kathryn's scars. But Smitty's love for Kathryn was an enchanted prison. She could never give him what he wanted, and Kathryn wanted more for him. Letting him go would extinguish the glimmer of hope that always lingered in the echo of unrequited love, but that wasn't the answer. Jenny had been on the wrong end of that heartbreak, and she would fight to spare Smitty that pain. She sat up to protest, but Kathryn cupped her cheek.

"But I've learned you don't treat people that way. Especially the people you love the most. For any reason."

The aching sadness in Kathryn's eyes for what she'd done to them broke her heart. Jenny had no answer for it, and she knew Kathryn wasn't looking for one. She kissed Kathryn's palm, cupping her cheek, and settled back into her one-armed embrace.

"Maybe things will be different now. Smitty just needs—"

"A girlfriend. Obviously," Kathryn said dryly.

Jenny laughed. "Obviously."

She knew Kathryn and Smitty shared a bond that would never break. Theirs wouldn't break again either, she was sure, but Kathryn was losing her support system just when she needed it most. In her fragile state of mind and her propensity for self-loathing, there was no telling where she might end up. It scared her.

Kathryn tightened her arm around her. "You just tensed up. What is it?"

"I'm okay."

Kathryn was quiet, but it was an *I'll just wait until you tell me the truth* kind of quiet, and Jenny gave in.

"Where will you go?"

After another beat of silence, Kathryn exhaled to the ceiling. "I'm going to contact my brother. See if I can salvage anything there."

Jenny was instantly relieved. "That's good."

Kathryn answered with a hum of agreement, but Jenny sensed some apprehension about approaching her brother after their disastrous parting.

"He loves you, Kathryn. It'll be fine."

"I'm counting on it."

Jenny would do everything in her power to guarantee Clayton would step up.

"You know, you can stay at the house."

Kathryn shook her head. "It would be too hard without you there. Clay will find me a place."

"Well, if he doesn't … I'll make him. I can be very pushy, you know."

Kathryn laughed and pulled her in. "Kiss me."

Jenny eyed her wounded lip. The stitches were gone, but it looked tender as hell. She kissed her gently, then again, and once more before settling back into the crook of her shoulder. Kathryn squeezed her and released a sound somewhere between a sigh and mild frustration.

"I'm going to dream of wildflowers."

Jenny chuckled. "I'm going to dream of a cold shower."

The rest of the day slipped by while they drifted in and out of a contented slumber. The heartbreak of the new dawn would come soon enough.

CHAPTER TWENTY

When Kathryn awoke in the morning, Jenny was gone. "You wouldn't," were the first words out of her mouth. She wouldn't leave without saying goodbye. Kathryn clutched at the rumpled sheets beside her as if she'd find Jenny hiding in there.

Kathryn recognized the stealthy goodbye as something she would do, and all the awful things Jenny had endured from her came back to kick her in her already burning gut. God, she'd been horrid. She teetered on the edge of a familiar dark well of regret and self-hate, but she stepped back. The pull of the darkness was torturously familiar, but it wasn't her home anymore. Her home was ahead of her. With Jenny … who loved her and couldn't bear to say goodbye.

It was probably for the best. If there was no goodbye, it would be easier to pretend she'd see her later. That way, the physical and emotional breakdown would come in stages as time went by and she slowly accepted her absence. Yes. That's how it would go.

Before her brain could call her logical bluff and drag her straight into the breakdown phase, she gently eased her feet to the floor and saw a note in Jenny's handwriting on the small stand beside the bed.

There's a call for me downstairs. Be right back with breakfast. You look beautiful this morning.

Kathryn nearly cried in relief. She went through her morning routine and dressed, crafting the strong image she hoped to leave in Jenny's mind.

She was standing at the open window in her room, staring off into a light summer rain, when a hand touched her back and startled her.

Jenny kissed her on the cheek. "Good morning. Breakfast has arrived." She set a small paper bag and a green Thermos on the table. "No coffee, of course, but Vivienne got us some tea."

Kathryn enveloped her in a tight hug—the pain be damned—and tried not to cry.

Jenny backed away, searching her eyes. "Did you get my note?"

"I did."

"But you panicked a little at first, didn't you?"

"I did."

Jenny hugged her again. "I'm sorry."

Kathryn shook her head. "I've been an absolute nightmare for you since the day we met. Thank you for loving me anyway."

Jenny backed off again. "Say, that must have been quite the few minutes you had there."

"I mean it. There aren't enough apologies in the world."

"Yes, well … you are a challenge."

"I'm going to spend the rest of my life showing you how grateful I am."

"I look forward to that. I've earned it."

Kathryn hugged her again.

"Are you okay?"

Kathryn nodded, but she wasn't okay. All the tricks she usually employed to get herself through emotionally fraught situations weren't working. She tried to pretend she'd see Jenny in a few days, but even that was too long. At that moment, even an hour was too long. She had to be strong, but her pep talks weren't working. Her stomach felt like it was eating itself, and she couldn't still her trembling hands.

"When will they arrive?" she asked.

"Soon."

Her limbs felt numb.

Jenny took her arm. "Do you need to sit?"

"No, I'd rather stand." A few deep breaths and one wave of light-headedness later, she changed her mind. "I'm going to sit."

Jenny led her to the chair beside the window and kneeled at her feet. "Do I need to call—"

"No, I'll be all right in a minute."

Jenny's concerned face was worn and so much older than the face that had gazed up at her in seductive innocence from this position when they first met. Kathryn ran her fingers through Jenny's blonde hair, dusted with a fine mist of water droplets from her dash in the rain, and longed for the day this would all be over and they could be together.

"The next time you're on your knees in front of me, mine are going to be spread wide, and I won't be wearing any clothes."

Jenny raised her brow and swallowed a whimper. "Jesus."

"And that's all the sexy flirty I've got today, because, honestly, I feel a little sick." She looked around for somewhere to throw up.

Jenny got up and grabbed a small tin garbage pail from across the room and set it beside her before gently rubbing her back. "Just breathe."

Kathryn's heart hammered in her chest and sweat gathered on her brow. She was having an anxiety attack and cursed her lack of control over her body. Not now. Not yet.

"Breathe," Jenny said again.

Kathryn closed her eyes and focused on her breathing, trying to block out her body's betrayal.

"That's it. Breathe."

Jenny's voice was soothing, and Kathryn wished it would always ring so clearly in her mind. But no one knew how long the war would last or how long they would be apart. Eventually, the sound of her voice would fade, as would the details of her beautiful face and the smell of the cleansing summer rain on her skin. All these things would drift into a hallowed place in her soul, where precious memories lived a half-life of warm remembrance.

Before long, her heart rate slowed and the nausea passed. Jenny retrieved a wet washcloth for her brow and pulled up a chair to face her.

"I don't suppose you can manage breakfast. It's just toast and jam."

"No, I don't think I can."

"I can't either."

Kathryn wiped her face and tossed the washcloth on the table with a weary sigh. They hadn't even started saying goodbye and already she was falling apart. "This is not how I wanted this to go. Sorry."

"There's no good way for this to go, Kathryn, so I'm going to be strong for both of us until you're in my arms again."

Kathryn was ashamed by her weakness. She put her head in her hands but misjudged the splint on her left hand and smacked herself in the eye. "Shit. Ow. God, I'm pathetic."

Jenny bit her lip, on the verge of laughter.

Kathryn gave in to the absurdity of it and laughed too.

"Kathryn, this"—Jenny made a small circle in the air at her—"what you think is pathetic … is strength. You're facing life head on and shouldering through the brick wall falling on your head. It hurts, it's messy, and you think it's going to crush you. It won't. You keep shouldering. And when you stumble … you get up. And when you feel like all the life has drained out of you … the sun rises on another day and you push the bricks aside and crawl until you can walk."

Kathryn recognized the voice of experience and her part in it. She opened her mouth to speak, but Jenny put words in it.

"If you say *sorry*, so help me. It's bright and sunny where we're going, so just put on a pair of sunglasses and look forward."

There was no arguing with that, and she reminded herself to take one day at a time. She could do this. Her cleansing exhale held too much fear in it, and Jenny placed a comforting hand on her thigh.

"Smitty will be here for a few more days."

"It might be easier if he weren't."

"Rip your heart out all at once, hm?"

"Something like that."

"And when we're both gone, you'll fall apart?"

Kathryn covered Jenny's hand with her own. "Yes. And then I'll pick myself off the ground, find my footing, and rebuild my life, because you'll be back in my arms before I know it, and we're going to be disgustingly happy together for the rest of our lives."

Jenny smiled. "You heard me when you were out."

In her unconscious state, Jenny's voice had an ethereal quality that had made Kathryn wonder if she was still part of this earthly realm, but her words had made their way into her heart and nestled there until she could come back to her. "I did. And I'm going to do everything I can to see that it comes true."

"That makes two of us. We can't lose."

Time stopped for a moment, and they were lost in each other's loving gaze until someone rapped on the door and broke the spell. "They're at the gates, Miss Ryan."

"Damn it," she muttered, and then called out, "Thank you. I'll be down in a minute."

Kathryn's heart rate picked up, and whatever measure of calm she'd managed went with it. Minutes. They only had minutes. *Breathe.* She had to hold it together. Just until Jenny was out of the room. *The bricks aren't falling. They're not falling.* The mantra wasn't convincing. She stood, feeling like she had to move or panic. Jenny took her in her arms, stilling her racing mind.

"You're okay."

"I know." Kathryn focused on Jenny's arms around her and slowed her breathing. This couldn't be easy for Jenny either. "You're okay too."

Jenny chuckled into her chest. "Sweetheart, I've survived loving you for this long ... this next part is a mere inconvenience."

Kathryn held her tighter. "Write to me. Send it to Clay. He'll know where to find me."

"Of course I will. You too. As soon as I land somewhere, I'll cable him my address."

They rocked wordlessly in each other's arms until Kathryn sought Jenny's eyes. She tucked a lock of blonde hair behind Jenny's ear and cupped her cheek. "Kiss me. Kiss me like you don't know when you'll see me again."

Jenny's breathing caught and her eyes darkened. "But your lip—"

"They can fucking stitch it back up."

"Hi, dollface," Smitty said cheerfully as he entered Kathryn's room.

Kathryn welcomed him with a smile from her chair by the window. "Hi, handsome." Just like the old days.

The rain had tapered to a drizzle, and the sun was trying to come out. She willed it to break through the clouds, hoping to cling to it like a good omen. A surprising calm had settled over her, or maybe she was just emotionally exhausted.

Smitty sat before her in the chair Jenny once occupied, and she recognized him mentally gauging her mood. She looked at him in a way she hadn't in years—the way she used to look at him when they were kids—like she was genuinely glad to see him. It brought instant worry to his face.

He took her hand. "How are you?"

"I'll be fine."

He nodded. "I ran into Jenny on my way up. I know you'll miss her and you're worried about her, but she seemed okay. A little emotional, as you'd expect, but okay. She's developed a fine imitation of a stiff upper lip." He looked her up and down. "It seems you have too. Are you sure you're all right?"

"I am."

He lovingly clasped her hand between both of his and gazed at her expectantly. She hoped he would understand what she was about to say.

"We've been through a lot together, Smitty."

"Hm. I don't like this already."

She squeezed his hand. "I love you. You've seen me through the unimaginable with unflinching bravery and devotion. I can never thank you enough for that. I know I haven't always been—"

"I love you too, Kathryn," he interrupted, letting her know that anything she was about to say was unnecessary. "I'd do anything for you. You know that. What's all this about?"

"I know you're leaving in a few days."

"I can try to stay longer. I'll be here for as long as you need."

She pressed her lips into a smile. It was so like him. "You've got a job to do, Smitty, and I've got one too. You can't help me this time. No one can."

He hated that. She could see it in his eyes, but she also saw understanding. She'd ignored too much for too long, until it buried her under an avalanche of dysfunction, and her loved ones had paid the price. She would do things the right way for a change.

"It's not that I don't want to spend these last few days together. I just …" She didn't know how to explain it without hurting his feelings.

Smitty bowed his head. "You have a lot to process and you can't do that with me hovering over you like a mother hen." He said it kindly, as only a selfless man who loved her unconditionally could.

"I'm absolutely terrified of time to myself, but I need it. Can you understand?"

When he raised his eyes, they were swimming with emotion. She didn't know if his tears were for their imminent parting, for the long overdue first step in her recovery, or because he was terrified too.

"Of course," he said and quickly swiped a tear from his cheek as if she wouldn't see it.

Kathryn stood and took him into her arms. He hated showing his emotions, but he was losing control of them now. His shoulders shook, and she held him tighter. "Are you all right?"

He laughed through his tears. "Aren't I always?"

"You pretend to be, but your wounds are as deep as mine. Deeper, maybe." He released a sob, and she felt him cover his face with his hand. She didn't let him go. He wouldn't want her to see him like this. After a few muttered curses over his breakdown, he calmed. She still held him.

He cleared his throat and sniffled, regaining control. "You'll contact Clay?"

"Yes."

"You'll get through this. You know that, right?"

"I do."

He nodded, and they stood in the silence of their embrace until Smitty had gathered himself. "I'll see you when this godforsaken war is over, yeah?"

"Not if I see you first."

Their usual chuckle was absent, and they ignored the fear surrounding his unknown future.

Smitty gave her a final squeeze. "Look out the window, wouldja?"

She released him and turned away. "Yep."

The gentle rustling of his clothes as he crossed the room and opened the door signaled their last few moments together.

"Love you, dollface."

"Love you too, handsome."

She closed her eyes as the door snicked shut.

Vivienne was down the hall in the storage room, where she was gathering supplies for her rounds, when strange sounds she couldn't place came from the hallway. She'd set down her bin and stuck her head out the door. John Smith was leaning against the wall outside Kathryn's room with his head buried in his hands, sobbing.

Vivienne quickly pulled back, torn between comforting him and giving him privacy. His footsteps descending the stairs made her decision for her, but she stood motionless in the small room for moments after, her heart beating wildly. She clutched her chest at the ache she felt for him. He wasn't the first emotionally distraught man she'd ever seen. She saw them so often that she'd become numb to it. But not this man's pain.

She shook her head and rolled her eyes at herself. They would all be out of her life soon, and mooning over a stranger was childish, ridiculous, and wholly unprofessional.

With a dismissive lift of her chin, she put it all aside and added Kathryn's pain medication to her cart. She didn't know what had happened to put John in such a state, but with Jenny's departure just before his arrival, it was safe to say Kathryn would be in quite a state of her own.

She was sitting in the chair by the window when Vivienne entered her room, massaging the spot on the back of her neck that Vivienne knew signaled the beginning of a migraine.

"How're you feeling?"

"I've had better days."

"Would you like your pain meds now?"

"Yes, please."

She handed Kathryn the pills and a glass of water, which she swallowed in one gulp before handing her the empty glass. "You'll probably find him at the nearest bar for the next twenty-four hours," she said.

"Who?"

"John."

Vivienne was oddly pleased that Kathryn had noticed her preference for his given name rather than the disrespectful slang of his surname. She hadn't realized she'd thought it disrespectful until that moment. *"Everyone calls me Smitty,"* he'd once told her. She didn't want to be everyone. What an odd thing.

She straightened her apron. "He's a big boy." Her professional mask was slipping, and she must have overcompensated, because her reply dripped with disdain.

"You don't approve?"

"I'd never deny a man a good stiff drink when he needs one. Or ten."

Kathryn chuckled.

Vivienne had thought about going after him, but Kathryn was her priority. Men are funny about emotions, and she didn't know John well enough to know whether her presence would be appreciated. In any case, he needed time to absorb whatever had happened and accept it on his own.

"We've a complicated relationship," Kathryn said without prompting. "I told him I needed this time to myself. He took it hard, I fear. He might need a friend."

Vivienne eyed her curiously. Was she setting them up? She admired the woman for having the courage to face the future alone. No matter who wants to help, in the end, there's only one face in the mirror. Most people in her situation desperately cling to the familiar, trying to hold on to what they've lost in themselves. Kathryn was different. Maybe she'd tried it the other way and knew its pitfalls. Whatever the reason, she certainly didn't seem the type to play love match games. "Do you think John and I are friends?"

"I know you care about him, and I know he cares about you. He's hurting, and I apologize if I've overstepped."

Vivienne didn't know what to say. Americans were so straightforward. "Don't apologize. You may be right."

"I just worry about him. He's a good man. He doesn't deserve any of it."

"You're all good people. None of you do."

The sun burst through the clouds and hit Kathryn in the eyes, resulting in a drawn-out groan.

"You should lie down for a while. Let those pills work."

Kathryn agreed and gingerly made her way to the bed.

Vivienne untied the blackout curtains and let them fall into place, plunging the room into a comfortable twilight. She eyed her patient and couldn't imagine what was going through her mind. In her experience, solitude would bring her no comfort as she came to terms with her losses, her demons, and her long road to physical and mental recovery. She hoped she had someone, somewhere, to lean on.

"May I ask a favor?"

Kathryn's voice was soft, and Vivienne didn't know if it was from pain or exhaustion. She went to her side. "Certainly."

"At your convenience, could you bring me some stationery and a pen?"

"Yes."

"And if the hammering in my brain doesn't kill me first, I may have a complete breakdown later. Fair warning."

Vivienne put her hand on her shoulder. "I'll be here."

"Thank you."

CHAPTER TWENTY-ONE

$\mathcal{V}$ivienne walked into the local pub and acknowledged the wave of Billy Regan, the friendly bartender, with a lift of her chin. She wasn't exactly a barfly and preferred a good book to a stiff drink, but she could hold her own with the chaps when the daily grind of the war needed to be put in its place—or when she was worried about a certain bloke who'd had an emotional breakdown that afternoon. There was no reason John would still be around, not after Kathryn asked him to go, but Vivienne hoped to at least say goodbye to him.

There was no such thing as a twenty-four hour bar in England, and it took searching three pubs before she finally found him, but they were well within the evening's alcohol service hours, and by John's bleary-eyed appearance, he'd started as soon as service started. Through the thin veil of smoke hovering just below the low ceiling of the dark-paneled watering hole, she'd spotted him at the end of the L-shaped bar with his head bowed over a drink.

Vivienne straightened her uniform jacket over her hips and approached the bar unnoticed. She didn't know what to say to him, and she felt a little silly for being so forward, but she trusted Kathryn knew what she was talking about.

She slid onto the stool beside him and called to the bartender, "Whiskey, Billy. And none of that watered down swill."

John cast a bleary glare her way and then turned to Billy. "And I'll have two more of what she's having."

Billy raised a questioning brow at Vivienne, since it seemed she'd be babysitting for the evening, and she nodded. He poured three shots of whiskey and lined them up in front of the pair.

"Did you know?" John asked accusingly.

Vivienne threw back her shot and shuddered. "Know what?" Her voice was rough from the burn.

"That she wanted me gone. Did you know?"

"I don't think it's as simple as that."

"She wants me gone."

Smitty was in no condition to listen to reason, but she tried anyway. "It's not that simple, but I think you know that."

John turned back to his drink and mumbled, "Traitor."

Vivienne couldn't help but smile. The man was pitiful but adorable in his resolute defeat. He was indeed hurting, but Kathryn's absence in his life for the duration was not something the bottom of a bottle would cure.

"Would you like a glass of water?"

He looked at her like she was insane.

"Right," she said, and tapped on the bar. "Billy?"

He poured her another shot and eyed Smitty as if he were glad he didn't order another one. Or two.

"You don't understand," Smitty said.

"About?" Vivienne asked before downing half her drink.

"She's had a rough ride. A lot of it is my fault."

Vivienne finished the rest of her whiskey and clanked the glass on the bar. "Billy?"

Billy eyed her, and then Smitty, who stared at Vivienne with a raised brow.

"It's one of those nights, Billy."

"There are rules—"

"One of those nights," she reiterated, and he poured her another.

Smitty turned and stared at her. It didn't make her uncomfortable, even when his eyes drifted slowly up and down her uniformed figure.

"You're pretty," he said, the alcohol obviously having its way with him.

Vivienne shook her head and smiled into her drink.

"Jenny said you look like Greer Garson. I never saw it, but in this light, with your hair that way and four shots in me … yeah, Greer Garson, but prettier."

"Well …" Vivienne said, feeling heat rise to her face. Or was that the whiskey?

"Just stating a fact," Smitty said, turning back to the bar. "Don't read anything into it."

"Wouldn't dream of it."

They ended up shoulder to shoulder on a bench seat in the corner booth of the pub, and Vivienne listened patiently—albeit in an alcohol haze, not used to hard drinking—to John's protracted dissertation on "dames" and their wicked power over men. He finally quit complaining, and she hoped the venting made him feel better. She turned her head to ask, only to find him staring at her again.

"You look tired," he said, with no hint of the frustration he'd exhibited for the last hour.

"Chasing after you isn't easy."

"Who's running?" He leaned in and kissed her soundly on the mouth.

She just barely withheld a reflective slap as she jerked away. "What the devil are you doing?"

John blinked at her, his mouth agape.

Vivienne was about to storm out of the booth when she decided the kiss wasn't that bad. In fact, it was pretty good, and her humming body was something she hadn't felt in a long time.

She sensed John was about to apologize, so she silenced him by planting her own kiss on his lips. It wasn't timid or demur. It was hungry and desperate, decorum be damned, and he welcomed her into his arms as the kiss intensified.

"Hoy!" Billy shouted from behind the bar.

They both followed the booming voice.

Billy pointed at a sign above his head that read *No kissing! No spitting! No fighting!* "Get a room!" he said with a good-natured wink.

Vivienne looked at John, and it took exactly two ragged breaths for them both to agree it was a splendid idea.

Vivienne had been billeted to a small room in a two-story boarding house close by, and fortunately, was between roommates, so she had the place to herself. The kissing and heavy petting turned into groping before they were even in the door. She hadn't had sex with anyone since her husband, and she was long overdue. John's hands were all over her as she fumbled with the lock, and as they tumbled into the room, she felt like an adolescent, unable to control her hormones as she hastily pulled her shirt from her skirt and began unbuttoning her blouse.

John kicked off his shoes and stumbled backwards onto the bed. Vivienne could see he was ready for her. This accentuated the ache between her thighs, and she popped the last button from her blouse as she tore it from her shoulders and then released her breasts from her bra.

"You are breathtaking," John said as he fumbled blindly with his belt.

Vivienne dropped her skirt and panties and then helped him with his pants. She yanked them down and had one knee on the bed, ready to straddle him, when she stopped. "Bugger me."

"Okay," John said with a hand on her breast.

"Have you got a condom?"

"A wha—"

"A condom, a condom!" she snapped, wanting him inside her already.

"Uh, no."

Vivienne stood, frustration getting the better of her. "Bloody hell." She snatched her robe from the back of the closet door.

John raised himself on his elbows. "Where are you—"

"Don't move. And don't do anything with that 'til I get back!" She pointed at his arousal.

John held up his hands in surrender.

Vivienne ducked down the hall to a room belonging to a woman she was almost certain was a prostitute, with her endless parade of men coming and going—literally. She got several condoms, just in case, and rushed back to her room.

She fanned them out like a handful of cards and opened the door. "You're in for it now, Mr. Smith," she said with a seductive grin that quickly faded.

John was sound asleep and lightly snoring.

"Bugger me," she said again and leaned against the door in defeat. She made a not-so-subtle production of undressing him fully and tucking him in, and when he didn't awaken or even stir, she knew he was passed out rather than sleeping. She stared at him for a moment with her hands on her hips. Just as well. He was drunk, and she would have been taking advantage of him in a vulnerable state. Who was she kidding? She was drunk too. They both would have hated themselves in the morning. But then again, she would be leaving in a few days and they would never see each other again, so would it really have been so bad?

She shed her robe, crawled into bed beside him, and stared at his handsome, boyish face. No, it wouldn't have been so bad at all. She curled around him, enjoying the comfort of another human being pressed against her naked skin for the first time in years.

———

Vivienne counted to three, trying very hard not to snap at the young nurse's aide who had just broken a sterilized glass syringe taking it out of the autoclave. She had been in a foul mood all day, and it had very little to do with the hangover she was battling. John was gone when she awoke in the morning ... no note, no nothing. Just gone. On the one hand, she was thankful. It would have been awkward. On the other hand, the only thing worse than not having seen him was almost having a one-night stand with him after getting drunk and throwing her naked self at him, and then having him so embarrassed over the whole incident that he skulked off in the morning, never to be heard from again.

She cringed as she remembered ripping her clothes off—how humiliating. Never in her life had she been so forward, drunk or otherwise, and she couldn't imagine what he thought of her. It pained her to think his last memory of her was as some passed out trollop in rumpled sheets. She closed her eyes and exhaled.

"I'm sorry, Sister Barclay," the aide said, assuming the frustrated exhale was for her.

Vivienne lifted her chin, trying to get her head back into her work. "Just be more careful, for heaven's sake."

The rest of Vivienne's day was spent at the army encampment in the field adjacent to the hospital taking care of non-critical patients, and although she knew John wouldn't be there, she couldn't help but look for him in the sea of faces. She didn't know why. If she saw him again, she would probably die of embarrassment. She'd wasted her small window of opportunity on drunken debauchery and now looked forward to her new post so she wouldn't be reminded of it every time she stepped foot in the hospital.

Smitty sat on the stone bench in the garden behind the hospital, waiting for Vivienne to return from her day with the British army. He had to admit to a little jealousy, wishing he could have her all to himself for his last days in Bedfordshire. He had to duck out of her room early in the morning to report in and finalize his travel plans. He would leave for Scotland at his earliest convenience and resume his training duties there.

He twirled a flower in his hands and smiled, remembering the vision that greeted him that morning. The sun had filtered through a crack in the blackout curtain covering the window and illuminated Vivienne's perfect profile. One arm was thrown over her head, framing her beautiful face, and the invitation of her parted lips was rivaled only by her bare breasts and the possessive hand on his hip. He touched her hand and she rolled away from him, toward the window. Faced with her beautiful back, he pressed himself to her, finding the warmth of her against him too much to enjoy alone. He kissed her shoulder and then her neck to small mews of pleasure, and then he caught sight of the clock on the nightstand, putting an abrupt stop to his advances.

Shit! He was late for his meeting. He weighed the fallout of a quickie versus standing up his superiors, and he decided he wanted nothing about making love to Vivienne Barclay to be quick. He froze like a thief on a creaking floorboard, hoping his advances hadn't roused her from her sleep. When she resumed the heavy rhythm of her breathing, he carefully extricated himself from her bed and got dressed. He chuckled when he saw the handful of condoms on the nightstand—they must have had quite an evening. If he had any say in it, they would pick up where they left off when he got back.

Her belongings were neatly folded and stacked on the dresser. She didn't have much. All her clothes were uniforms. The only personal items he saw were a lipstick, a hairbrush, and a small collection of books atop a small, well-loved suitcase.

He couldn't find a pen or pencil to leave a note, and he didn't want to wake her, so he slipped out quietly, knowing he wouldn't be long. She was gone when he returned and was told she was working at the field hospital, so he was waiting patiently in the garden for her to return.

He caught his first glimpse of her as she crossed the wooden footbridge over the creek separating the hospital grounds from the field housing the army encampment. He watched her approach with a widening grin. Even the battledress uniform couldn't mask the graceful curves of her body, making her stand out from the two nurses walking beside her. They were engaged in conversation, and Vivienne didn't notice him until she got closer. She slowed to a halt, looked like she needed some place to hide, and then sent her companions on their way with knowing smiles and quiet whispers.

Smitty stood with a broad grin and held out the flower in his hand. "Hi, gorgeous."

"Hello," Vivienne said, plucking the flower from his fingers. She stared at him expectantly.

Smitty was unsure of her mood, so he figured an apology would be a good place to start. "Listen, about last night … I didn't mean to run out on you this morning, but—"

"Do you want to apologize for last night or this morning?"

"Well, I—" He paused. What the hell did he do last night that required an apology? He remembered the pub, remembered kissing—oh, how he remembered kissing—and he remembered her room at the boarding house and her clothes hitting the floor. Whatever followed, though foggy in his mind, couldn't have been all that bad. "I thought last night was pretty grand."

Vivienne raised her hand. "It's all right. Nothing happened."

"What do you mean, nothing happened?" He distinctly remembered voluptuous milky white breasts and a very erect nipple between his fingers. His eyes drifted to the scene of the crime.

"Hey—" She snapped her fingers near her face. "Up here."

He obeyed.

"You passed out, stud. But don't worry about it. We were drunk … one of us more than the other, evidently … we were lonely, and we had a moment. It happens. No one need be embarrassed about it."

Smitty suppressed a grin and took in the beautiful woman before him. She wasn't angry, going by the playful glint in her eyes. In fact, she was awfully understanding for someone deserted in the throes of passion. *What an idiot.* He watched the sun disperse its light into her red hair, making it redder than he thought naturally possible. He'd never really seen her outside the confines of Kathryn's unflattering pale green hospital room, or a poorly lit pub, which suppressed the finer points of her lightly freckled porcelain-like skin.

He had a lot to make up for, and he stepped closer, tucking an errant strand of hair behind her ear. "I'm not embarrassed, and I'm not drunk, and at the moment, I'm not the least bit lonely." He leaned in and gently kissed her. "May I see you tonight?"

"I'm leaving in two days."

"May I see you tonight?"

Vivienne hesitated. She glanced at the hospital and then quickly around them.

Smitty hoped she was about to engage in behavior unbecoming the uniform. He wasn't disappointed.

She kissed him hard before backing off. "My place, sixteen hundred hours." She hurried away, waving the flower over her shoulder.

Smitty grinned, knowing it was going to be the best two days of his life.

Vivienne counted the heartbeats under her fingers as she rested her arm across John's chest and placed her fingers on the pulse point of his neck. It was an occupational habit, but this time, every beat brought them closer to parting, and she couldn't believe she'd set herself up for the painful goodbye.

It had been a marvelous two days. She knew John wasn't in love with her—he was hopelessly in love with Kathryn. It shouldn't matter, anyway. They were sharing a moment, one that would pass quickly but remain as a fond memory. That's what she tried to tell herself, but she knew she had fallen in love with a man she couldn't have. Expressing her feelings would only bring her heartache.

They'd spent every moment that she wasn't working together, mostly in her room, and mostly undressed, as they were now, sharing not only intimate physical moments but emotional ones as well. They were strangers not so long ago, but now she felt they'd known each other for years. John agreed. It was the war, Vivienne reasoned. It had a way of making life urgent, a way of cutting through the boundaries and defenses until all that was left was the raw need to be close to someone, to prove life goes on, no matter the horrible circumstances around them.

She stared at the small battered suitcase on the dresser. Inside was her favorite prewar evening gown, with its matching shoes and veiled hat. It was silly to drag it around with her—she wasn't allowed to wear anything but a uniform or ward dress, not even off duty—but it was a reminder that she was still a beautiful, sensual woman. Her dreams for the future had left her long ago, but one day this brutal war would be over, and she would reclaim all she had lost of herself and the life she had let slip away without protest.

"Healthy male?" John asked.

"Very healthy male." She couldn't hide the sadness in her voice.

"Hey—" He lifted his head and shifted to his side. "What's this?"

Vivienne tried to be brave. Tears were not something she let fall easily, but she was having a hard time holding them back.

John kissed her. "We still have all night. No tears until tomorrow. Okay?"

She cleared her throat along with her tears. "Who says I'm going to cry over you tomorrow?"

He laughed. "Who's talking about you?"

She laughed too, but he was right. There would be time enough for tears after they parted. They should enjoy the time they had left. She kissed him, then stroked his cheek, knowing she would need his help to let him go.

"Listen," she began, "I've got to look after a few things early in the morning, and I'm not very keen on goodbyes, so when I return to gather my kit, I don't want you to be here."

John furrowed his brow.

"Don't be dashing and leave a note or a flower or any sort of keepsake."

"Viv—"

She put her fingers to his lips, sensing he was going to say what she had been feeling for the past few days, but he wouldn't mean it. His heart was elsewhere, and a few idyllic days with a stranger was a distraction, not an epiphany.

"Just go straight away in the morning, would you?"

"What if I said no?"

She smiled, finding his defiance endearing. "I would say please."

"What if I said no?"

He was serious, and Vivienne didn't know why she was surprised after witnessing his devotion to Kathryn. She didn't know what he was playing at. There certainly wasn't a future for them, but he was acting like it was the start of something.

"I'm going away tomorrow. We're never going to see each other again. And that's that."

"Only we determine that."

Vivienne laughed out loud. "I know you're not that naïve. There's a war out there that I'm sure has other plans. These last few days were marvelous, and I'll never forget you, but it was just a fleeting moment, like everything has to be these days. To pretend it means anything beyond that would be asking for something that's out of our hands."

He had a look in his eyes, one she'd seen once before. It was the look her husband had the moment before he threw logic and caution to the wind and asked her to marry him. At the risk of making the same mistake twice, she sat up and decided to head him off. "Do you think you love me, John?"

"Yes."

"Well, you don't. It's not real. It's the war. It tricks you, and these things happen."

John sat up too. "Not to me."

Not to her either, but the situation was what it was, and they would part to very different worlds in the morning, with little chance of seeing each other for the remainder of the war, however long that might be. She knew he wasn't going to give up though—she'd learned that from her patient. She just had to get him to see it was hopeless for them.

"Do you love Kathryn?"

"Of course. What's that got to do with anything?"

Vivienne realized that what started as an attempt to get him to accept their fate came out sounding like a jealous lover's accusation, and to her horror, she realized it just might have been.

"Nothing," she said, turning away in embarrassment. She couldn't believe she brought up Kathryn. Feeling exposed, she got out of bed and put on her robe.

"What do you care what I feel for her, or what I feel for you, for that matter? We're never going to see each other again, right?"

Vivienne glared at him, seeing the perfect way out. "Right. In fact, why don't you just go right now."

"*Dames!*" John threw back the covers and got out of bed. He collected his clothes and got dressed.

Vivienne crossed her arms.

He put his hand on the doorknob and paused. "Do you really want me to leave?"

Her head screamed go but her heart screamed stay, and in the end, neither had a say when her body found its way into his arms. She stayed in his arms all night and slipped out early in the morning. When she returned, he was gone. There was no note, no flower, no keepsake of any kind.

CHAPTER TWENTY-TWO

*J*enny exhaled a defeated breath as she slumped in the back seat of the sedan taking her into the English countryside. She'd spent two days in London severing ties with the OSS and the SOE, against her will.

A folder of instructions had greeted her when she entered the car that took her away from the hospital in Bedfordshire. It was from her blackmailing American "friends," who, at this point, she wasn't even sure were OSS. Their credentials looked legitimate, and they were inside OSS headquarters when she first met them, but with platitudes like *You'll understand soon* and *We're here to protect you*, she didn't know what to think. Protect her from what? She was an agent of the Office of Strategic Services, and she had a duty to serve her country for the duration. She couldn't wait to meet their bosses and give them an earful.

Her indignation slipped away like sand through her fingers when she met with officials from both agencies and they informed her she was out. It didn't make any sense. She was a field agent. There was a war to win. She'd trained for months and never even stepped foot in Bouchaule's lab. His death had ended the one and only mission of her OSS career. She expected to resume some role in the organization, a desk job at the very least, but they handed her forms to fill out in triplicate, and it was all over. The reason was already filled in: mental distress due to enemy incarceration.

She eyed the men around her. They all knew this was bullshit, and they were letting it happen anyway. This had the blackmailing Americans written all over it, and they stood by mutely while she seethed. She was on the verge of an outburst about coercion, blackmail, secret organizations, and anything else she could think of when she realized that would play right into their narrative. She signed the documents with a disgusted scratch of a pen, and just like that, her OSS career was gone. She'd already turned in her identity card before she left the States, and although that was protocol for an agent heading overseas, it made everything feel like one big conspiracy. Like they knew she'd never use it again.

"I know you're upset, Miss Ryan," the taller American said as he escorted her to a waiting car, "but a whole new world of opportunity is about to open up to you. All you have to do is take it."

"What is that supposed to mean?"

He opened the back seat door for her. "Get in and find out."

"And if I don't?"

"I promise, you'll regret it."

"Is that another threat?"

"Not at all. In fact, you're a free woman. Say the word and the driver will take you wherever you want to go. But ... a lot of people have gone through a lot of trouble to arrange your next meeting, and I encourage you to attend. I know it sounds trite, but your future does depend on it."

The subtle manipulation was astounding. They present things like she has a choice and then stand by while she chooses what they want. He must have seen her disdain because he tried another tack.

"Look at it this way ... we will win this war. And no offense to your skills as an agent, but we will win it without your help in the field. You feel like you're skirting your duty, but I promise you, you're not. This won't make sense yet, but it will."

Jenny opened her mouth to speak, but he held up his hand.

"I know you have some choice words for us, and maybe you want to stick it to us by joining some resistance group and getting yourself killed. Maybe you're smarter than that and you just want to return to your friend. I understand completely, but you should think of your future. Say you return home. Then what? Return to your uncle's newspaper? Knit socks for the Red Cross? You have the opportunity for a career in which you can make a real difference in the world, and based on your exemplary work in Toronto, one you are uniquely qualified for. All you have to do is get in the car and attend one meeting."

She felt like he'd gone through her file and run its high points through Morale Operations to get the most effective propaganda speech to use on her. He was wrong about the resistance, but he was right about returning to Kathryn's side. She wanted to forget her responsibilities, forget the war, and ignore the future and the past. The slightly raised brow above the man's expectant stare showed how predictable she was.

She cursed under her breath and got in the car.

"Enjoy the ride. It's lovely."

"You're not coming?"

"You'll be in better hands than mine where you're going. I wish you all the best, Miss Ryan."

He shut the door and stepped back on the curb.

They may work for the OSS, but they were working with someone else as well. Who was this group that had the power to burn her at two intelligence agencies in desperate need of agents during wartime?

Whatever they wanted from her, she'd refuse until they got her reinstated and stopped holding Kathryn's freedom over her head. The OSS had the briefcase, and they couldn't possibly know about Bouchaule's secret papers ... could they? No. This was about something else, and whatever it was would not stand between her and Kathryn. She ignored the sinking feeling that it would.

Kathryn was out of the spy game—the root of all her deceptions and lies—and so, apparently, was she. Freedom wasn't a word she used lightly, but walls that once seemed insurmountable were crumbling, and their relationship would no longer be sacrificed on the altar of anyone else's agenda.

Her life had been one manipulation after another since her father's death, and she was sick of it, but not even anger could hone her focus. She was so damn tired and emotionally wrung out that she didn't have the energy to fight anyone today, let alone make sense of what was happening.

She'd fallen apart in her hotel room on the first night in London and didn't get any sleep. So many emotions tore at her, and she allowed them all. Hate for the choices Kathryn had made and the way things played out made an appearance, but they were ugly memories that just wanted their say before they slinked off into the past, where they belonged. Love watched them go, and Jenny let guilt run after them to keep them company. There was a time when she thought she'd never trust Kathryn again, but she had to admit, her own insecurities played a part in allowing her head to overrule her heart. That wouldn't happen again.

Kathryn was so transparent to her now. She'd been drowning since the day they met, and not even their love could save her. That was the heartbreaking part. Whether they were together or apart, Kathryn had to save herself. She had stopped running, and Jenny had just started.

The droning of the car and the blur of the green countryside as she stared out the side window made her drowsy. She scrubbed her face with her hands, trying to stay alert.

"Don't worry," the driver said. "You're perfectly safe."

"I'm too exhausted to be worried," she said, resting her head against the back of the seat. It wasn't a lie, but she felt for the L-pill tucked into her pocket, ever vigilant against an unknown threat. What a cruel irony that would be. A life with Kathryn was in her grasp, and she was fondling a capsule that could end it all. She shook her head and pushed it out of her mind.

The driver eyed her in the rearview mirror. "You just relax. We'll be there before you know it."

Jenny didn't know if she'd ever relax again. She now understood what Kathryn meant when she'd said that she kept her demons one hundred yards behind her sprinting body at all times. Jenny's mind tortured her with things she'd never forget. A brutalized Kathryn. The dead boy and his friends. The muzzle flash of Bouchaule's execution. Blood. Gunshots. Cries of pain. Tears. Fear.

How did Kathryn live with her torments? How did Smitty live with his? How many times had Smitty protected Kathryn? Or Kathryn protected her?

God, the lengths Kathryn had gone to. She remembered the desperation in Kathryn's eyes when she stood in her destroyed living room and begged her to follow her to safety.

"What the hell have you done?" Jenny had shouted instead, blaming Kathryn for everything from the upended room to the war itself. Kathryn tried to make her see the truth. Instead, Jenny threw Kathryn's gift of love to the floor, shattering the shellac disc and the only recording of Kathryn's beautiful voice before it was changed forever. She hadn't meant to, but it was the only weapon she had that would wound Kathryn as deeply as she had wounded her. It didn't feel good. It felt awful, and she regretted it immediately. Kathryn looked as if she'd impaled her with a broadsword, but she recovered quickly and kept trying to save her. Because she loved her.

Jenny closed her eyes, allowing the regret for everything that had happened that day, and everything after, to pass through her without adding another thorn to her crown. Hindsight would make her drown in regret if she let it, but she was moving forward now, and the only part it would play was to ensure she wouldn't make the same mistakes again.

A violent shudder of the sedan hitting a pothole woke Jenny from some much needed rest. Fields of wildflowers lined the road on both sides. Was it a dream? No. Because if it were, she'd be lying in that field with her head resting on Kathryn's chest, and they'd both be relaxed and sated after an afternoon of lovemaking. The sky would be a clear deep blue, to rival Kathryn's eyes, and they would have flowers in their hair. She would crack a joke, and Kathryn's warm laughter would rumble beneath her ear. She loved her laugh. They would be blissfully happy.

It seemed like ages since either was so carefree. Maybe Kathryn never was. Jenny would do all in her power to remedy that.

Before she left the hospital, Vivienne had told her Kathryn would be transferred to another facility soon, and when she regained her strength, she would be released. She didn't know where, and she would be leaving for her next post in a day or so. Jenny thanked her for her kindness and excellent care, and after exchanging best wishes and pleas to stay safe, she hugged her goodbye.

Kathryn's journey home was about to begin. She would rest safely in her family's care soon—Jenny had cabled Clay to make sure of it— and once this bit of business was over and this group got her reinstated, she would help win this war and return home to join her. She gazed at the blur of colors passing by and drifted off again, hoping Kathryn was dreaming of wildflowers too.

"Almost there, Miss," the driver said, loud enough to rouse her.

Jenny rubbed her eyes as they passed under an arched entry made of stone. She didn't know how far they'd traveled from London, but after several minutes on the slow, winding drive, a country estate rose before her. Its grandeur was in the expanse of its property, not the modest structure, which, in the kindest of descriptions, could only be called a square stone box with windows. Subtle Georgian influences around the window and door casings were lost amid the stark mediocrity of its design, and the grounds were covered with sparse clumps of knee-high weeds and overgrown berry bushes. Not to be outdone by the ground's neglected state, the building's sandstone exterior was strangled with clinging vines and seeping cracks that drew carpets of moss, clambering to the fissures like settlers to a riverbed.

The driver stayed in the car while she climbed the steps to the wide landing and stepped through the building's open front door. The interior was typical upper-crust English country, with its well-worn Victorian parlor furniture—hand-me-downs from another era—and Persian rugs, reflecting the Empire's dalliance there. Dotting the dark dadoed paneling were fox and hound pictures of their beloved hunts, accompanied by the always charming oil paintings of dead birds and ghastly mounted heads of conquered wild beasts.

Six men stood and greeted her when she entered the drawing room. She was offered tea, which she politely refused, preferring the stiff drink everyone appeared to be nursing, along with their pipes, cigarettes, and cigars.

The air in the room was stifling in the August heat, and not even the open full-length casement windows helped dissipate the foul cacophony of tobacco, body odor, and a room infused with the stale redolence of its infrequent use.

She took the tumbler of scotch handed to her but didn't drink it, waiting instead for someone to say something.

"Thank you for coming, Miss Ryan."

"I didn't really have a choice, did I?" she said, alluding to the veiled threat against Kathryn.

"There's always a choice," the man countered, deflecting Jenny's accusation with a fatherly smile. He was a bespectacled older gentleman, American, who had shed his expensive suit jacket in deference to the heat. "I am Arthur Wheaton, from the Wheaton-Rhoades Institute." He then presented the man standing beside him. "This is William Rhoades."

Rhoades held out his hand. "Hello."

Jenny didn't accept his greeting.

He smiled, as did most of the men in the room. "Fair enough," he said, the words rolling genially off his upper-class British tongue.

"Why don't you just tell me what this is about?" Jenny said impatiently. "I gave your boys the briefcase … I assume they're your boys, OSS or not … and in return, you had me tossed out of the intelligence services. Which, by the way, you're going to rectify before we go any further."

Wheaton raised his brow, just like the rest of the men in the room. "Miss Ryan, they won't have you. None of them will."

"You have no right to do that, and if you want me to—"

"I'm afraid you managed that all by yourself."

She stared at him as if she had no idea what he was talking about. But she did. "The briefcase."

"You lied to them about it. Then you turned it over under the threat of blackmail. They had no choice but to find you untrustworthy after that and, therefore, useless to them."

A surge of anger was muted by a distant memory of Kathryn calling her untrustworthy when they'd first met at The Grotto. The thought of Kathryn and how beautiful she looked that night nearly brought her to tears. It was one of her last innocent hours, and she hardly recognized herself now.

"You set me up."

Wheaton lifted his hands. "I fear we're getting off on the wrong foot. These have been exceptionally trying times for you, and—"

"Why? Why are you doing this to me? What do you want?"

Rhoades stepped forward. "Miss Ryan, we've waited many years to meet you. The timing and circumstances are unfortunate, but we are glad you're here now, and when you're ready, we can talk about your future. For now, we just want to introduce ourselves and build some trust between us."

Jenny exhaled a bitter laugh. "And why should I trust you?"

"Because your father did," Rhoades said.

She set her drink on the black marble-topped table beside her hip with a clank. "That worked out well for him."

The mood in the room shifted, as the specter of Daniel Ryan reminded them all of the fragile line they walked.

"Every man in this room knew your father," Rhoades said solemnly, "and we mourn his loss. He was more than a colleague … he was a friend. Unfortunately, the best laid plans often fail to yield their desired results. Our plans didn't protect your father, Kathryn Hammond's plans didn't protect you, and your plans won't let you keep your secret forever."

"I don't know what you're talking about."

Wheaton smiled, with no affection in it. "Truth and honesty, Miss Ryan, that's how you establish trust."

Jenny scoffed. "I'm sorry, but invoking my father's memory and calling him a friend does not earn you my trust."

Wheaton handed her a tin security box from the table and opened it, exposing employment records and pay stubs documenting her family's cooperation all the way back to her grandfather.

"Who do you think equipped the lab in your home?" he said.

Jenny looked up from the paperwork in her hand, shocked they knew about the lab.

"Who do you think cleaned up after he was gone?"

Jenny was torn. She wanted to believe him, if for no other reason than she wouldn't be alone with her secret, with no clue where to begin unraveling its riddle, but it was too dangerous to trust the wrong people, and she couldn't allow herself to fall into the wrong hands.

Wheaton must have sensed she wanted to sway their way, and he looked to Rhoades, who nodded.

"Gentlemen?"

One by one, like a wave of falling dominoes, everyone reached into their respective briefcases and set their copies of her father's coded volumes on the table before them.

Jenny eyed them suspiciously, then picked up the closest volume to her. She thumbed through it and saw that it had the key penciled in the upper corner of each page, just like the volumes Kathryn had given her. It gave her pause, and the urge to trust them, but not for long. There were many clean copies of her father's volumes in the lab. If they had access to the lab, they had access to the books. She had no way of validating the key at that moment. For all she knew, these were just random numbers scribbled on the pages, designed to lull her into dropping her guard. She tossed the book on the table.

"So you have copies of my father's books and you know how to use a pencil. Doesn't prove anything to me."

"This is madness!" said a tall American with a Boston accent, who was standing beside the spacious fireplace. "How many more are going to die while we wait for you to open your eyes?"

"Robert!" Rhoades shouted.

"What more does she need, Bill?"

Jenny glared at him. "And you are?" When the man turned to answer her, she could see the cold disdain in his eyes.

"I am Dr. Robert Hall. You met my brother, Stewart, when you stepped over his dead body in your study."

Jenny recalled the blank eyes of the murdered man in the study, and guilt, which didn't need any more fuel, branded another life taken on her soul. "I'm sorry for your loss."

Hall slammed his drink on the mantle. "You think I want your pity? What is it going to take for you to wake up and see what's happening around you? *Because* of you!"

His attitude made her furious. After all she'd been through, she had every right to her reservations about the group. Hall, of all people, having lost someone, should appreciate her cautious approach, which gave her one more reason to doubt the man's intentions.

"Look, I'm awfully sorry about your brother, but I didn't ask for any of this, and I'll not be bullied into making a decision!"

Hall coughed a disparaging laugh. "Your friends and loved ones are being maimed and murdered all around you, but God forbid we bully you into doing the right thing!"

"That's enough, Hall!" Wheaton shouted. "Take a walk until you cool off."

Hall gave one more acerbic glare to Jenny and stalked past her without a second look, slamming the heavy wooden front door as he exited the building.

"We're terribly sorry, Miss Ryan," Rhoades said. "That was uncalled for."

Jenny pursed her lips and swallowed the lump in her throat before speaking. Hall may have made her angry, and he may or may not be trustworthy, but he had a point. "He's right."

They stared at her hopefully.

"But I stand by what I said. I won't join you just to assuage my guilt. I don't trust you. I don't trust anyone."

"And rightly so," Wheaton said. "No one is forcing you to do anything. We told you we would earn your trust."

"And how do you propose to do that?"

"We'll start by reiterating that your father trusted us."

"I'm sorry, I won't take your word for that, and those books"—she pointed at them—"easily forged."

Rhoades smiled. "We know you're special, Miss Ryan. Your physiology is unique, and I know you know what I'm talking about."

On the off chance he was bluffing, she said, "Humor me."

He went into detail about the unusual characteristics of her blood, things she'd read in her father's journal and seen in his decoded papers, but instead of the exposition convincing her the men were friends, she was struck with panic that she was in a room full of strangers who knew her secret. In an instant, she had gone from having the upper hand—a choice to join them or walk away—to feeling like dinner in a cage of hungry lions. All eyes were on her, and every gaze seemed sinister. Time slowed to a crawl, and a sickening, helpless feeling of déjà vu gripped her. She had escaped the frying pan only to walk into the fire.

Her idyllic dream of returning to Kathryn disappeared on a panicked exhale. These men knew everything, and while Bouchaule had ambition and an idea of her potential, this group was an organized network that knew exactly her worth and how to extract it. They had spun their web using Kathryn's freedom as bait and her father's memory to mask their true intentions. There were too many of them, and Jenny knew what she had to do to make sure they'd get no return on their carefully plotted deceit. She couldn't think of Kathryn. This was bigger than either of them.

She instinctively stepped backwards, only to bump into Hall's chest as he returned to the room. He placed his hands on her shoulders to steady her as she stumbled over his foot, but she jerked away, reaching for the L-pill in her pocket. One of the other men quickly grabbed her from behind, and another grabbed her wrist before she could bring the capsule to her mouth.

"Drop it!" Hall shouted.

"Let go of me!"

"We won't hurt you, you little fool!" Hall pried the L-pill from her clenched fist.

The seated men were frozen in shock, while the man at her back had a death grip on her arms. He guarded himself against flying elbows and was doing a good job of keeping his toes away from her violently mashing heel, the only defense left to her.

"Stop! Stop!" Wheaton shouted. "Jenny, stop! Harold, let her go."

Jenny stopped struggling when Wheaton approached, but Harold didn't release her.

"Let go," Wheaton commanded sternly.

Jenny jerked away from his relaxed grip and rubbed her arms as she backed toward the door. No one tried to stop her.

"We understand, Miss Ryan," Wheaton began with his hands raised. "Your courage and vigilance are admirable, but we are not the enemy. We won't hurt you, and you are free to leave at any time."

Hall set the L-pill next to her drink and stepped away.

Jenny eyed the group warily. They all looked as if she had a loaded gun pointed at them, all except Wheaton and Rhoades, who stared at her with steely determination.

"Truth and honesty," Wheaton assured her.

Jenny had little choice but to take him at his word. "If I leave right now, you'll keep your end of the bargain? Kathryn gets a pass at her review?"

"It's already done," Rhoades promised.

There was no way of knowing, Jenny lamented. No way of knowing anything. She had a decision to make, and the men in the room slowly settled back into their seats to wait for it. Wheaton and Rhoades remained standing.

"Your father protected you his whole life, and we are determined to do the same," Rhoades said.

Jenny thought of everything she'd gone through and chuckled. "I don't think you're up to the task."

"Stewart Hall was in your house to protect you. We were about to bring you in because Bouchaule had discovered your secret."

Jenny flicked her eyes to Stewart's brother, Robert, whose dark glare told her it was the truth.

"And how was he going to convince me to go with him?"

"He was going to show you the lab."

That would have done it, she had to admit. It had worked for Kathryn.

"Unfortunately, someone else got there first. Then Miss Hammond showed up with what we have to admit was a good plan to keep you safe."

"Until I blew it up."

Wheaton smiled. "You know how important you are. It's not in your makeup to sit on your hands and let your gift go to waste. That's why we're approaching you … because you know the good you can do."

"I know the harm I can do if I fall into the wrong hands."

"That's why we won't let that happen."

"Best laid plans, gentlemen. You may not be able to stop it."

"But we know you are not afraid to." He looked at the L-pill on the table. "One day, your unique physiology will be revealed. And when it is—not *if*, but *when*—you can face the enemy alone or we can stand with you to fight them."

Jenny looked at the grim faces staring back at her and knew he was right. The truth would come out, it always did somehow, and she wouldn't stand a chance on her own. She might not even get the opportunity to end it before it was too late, as would have been the case here had they really been set on doing her harm.

Whichever way she turned had its own set of negative consequences, but there was still a war to win. She'd start there.

"Call the OSS in London. If you're so almighty powerful, get me reinstated."

"Miss Ryan—"

"Truth and honesty, Mr. Wheaton. Earn it."

She picked up the lethal capsule from the table and headed for the door.

———

Jenny sat in the back seat of the idling car while the driver looked at her expectantly in the rearview mirror.

"Where to?"

She didn't know. Home to New York and Kathryn? Knit socks for the Red Cross? Back to London, hoping Wheaton would sort things with the OSS? Or stay and go back inside? This group knew too much about her and was obviously powerful. Could she trust them? Should she? Her father did, and he was dead.

She fondled the small rubber-coated glass capsule and closed her eyes. She was so tired. Now that the initial shock of the situation was over, the weight of her responsibility to those who had sacrificed so much for her survival pressed in. Her beautiful life with Kathryn was moving further out of her reach with every revelation, and she clenched the pill in her fist in frustration. No. She was in control. There was a war to win, and Kathryn would be waiting for her at the end of it.

"London."

As the car rolled along the gravel drive, Jenny took one last look at the odd building on the hill, noticing absentmindedly that the three-stack chimney had lost half a stack before a large oak tree obscured her view. The image brought back a memory.

"Stop the car."

"Miss?"

"Stop, stop, stop!" She bolted out of the car while it was still rolling. She ran back along the drive until the scene before her matched the image of a photograph in her memory. Her parents, sitting under an oak tree, smiling at the camera. In the background stood a building with a three-stack chimney.

"Son of a bitch," she whispered under her breath. The photograph in the study was taken right from where she was standing.

CHAPTER TWENTY-THREE

When Jenny burst through the front door, the six men brooding in the parlor got to their feet.

"Why were my parents here?" she asked out of breath.

Wheaton and Rhoades looked at each other, obviously surprised she didn't know.

"They met here," Rhoades said. "You were born here."

Which meant … "She died here."

"Yes."

"She was English?"

"Irish."

"Irish," Jenny said in a reverent whisper. Her gaze drifted away as she tried to form a revised image of her mother. That she was anything but American had never crossed her mind. "Did you know her?"

"Yes. Bill and I did."

A strange sense of relief washed over her. She'd found not just one person who knew her mother but two. An unexpected wave of emotion closed her throat, and before it could bring tears to her eyes, she lifted her chin and swallowed it down. "What was she like?"

Rhoades smiled, and Jenny could see the warm memory of her mother come back to him.

"Smart. Courageous. Stubborn as hell." He looked at Jenny affectionately. "You're the spitting image, right down to her age. It's a little unnerving, frankly."

Wheaton raised his brow and nodded in agreement.

Jenny tentatively sat on the sofa "Tell me her story."

The men looked at each other with what could only be described as the somber discomfort of the woman's tragic end, and all except Wheaton and Rhoades excused themselves from the room and filed outside.

The elderly men sat, putting her between them. "It was September 1918 when your mother came here, very ill with influenza," Arthur Wheaton began without ceremony, as if he'd been waiting his whole life to tell the story. "It was the second wave of the pandemic. The mortality rate was dismal among young adults and especially high for expectant mothers. She was three months along in her pregnancy, so we were all very concerned, as you can imagine. Truth be told, we didn't hold out much hope for her survival or yours."

"Why here?" Jenny asked. "How did she wind up here?"

"We took part in a government study on the effects of the virus on pregnant women and their offspring," Rhoades explained. "Collaborating with local hospitals, patients we deemed suitable were transferred to our main medical facility here on the property."

Jenny remembered reading about the study in her father's papers as well as his adamant protests against it. "My father had a strong opinion about that."

"As did we," Wheaton said. "It got"—he glanced at Rhoades—"shall we say, out of hand."

"It caused a fissure in the group," Rhoades said. "It went beyond mere study and into manipulation, which we all found reprehensible."

Jenny was surprised at his candor, and she didn't try to hide it.

"Truth and honesty," Wheaton said.

Jenny nodded. "Go on."

"Your mother survived her bout with the virus, and she agreed to stay on to help us in our research."

Jenny glared at them. "You took advantage of her."

"It was all strictly voluntary and above board," Rhoades assured her. "Observation only. If anything, we had to forbid her from volunteering for risky procedures that could have endangered her life and yours. She just wanted to help in any way she could. The influenza was devastating populations around the world, including her family, of which she was the only survivor. It was a desperate time for us all."

"And amid all that death," Jenny began bitterly, "some evil genius realized if the virus could be controlled, they would have the perfect biological weapon."

"There *was* a war on," Rhoades said.

Jenny shook her head, finding man's appetite for self-annihilation astounding. "And then?"

"During this time, Daniel and your mother became quite close, inseparable, really." Wheaton paused and smiled. "Your mother was utterly charming. Your father never stood a chance, I'm afraid. They married a month before you were born."

That concluded their recollection, leaving the tragic ending to Jenny's imagination. "And then she died when I was born."

Wheaton's lips pressed into a somber line. "She fought so very hard," he said. His statement was more matter-of-fact than an attempt at funereal compassion. "She survived the initial illness, but she was never really well again. The virus devastated her immune system, weakened her heart, and well, the strain of a pregnancy, the trauma of birth—"

Rhoades glared at Wheaton.

Jenny wiped a tear away as her mother's loss hit her like never before. Bess Ryan was real now, not some storybook notion of what a mother should mean to a child. This woman carried her to term against the odds, and the rigors of that gestation slowly sapped the life from her until, finally, in the ultimate sacrifice, she gave the last of her strength so that she might live.

Wheaton rested a gentle hand on her knee. "She was so happy

when they placed you in her arms. She loved you very much. Her last act on earth was kissing your brow."

Jenny closed her eyes, imagining her mother's arms around her and her warm lips on her forehead. A flood of emotion rose from the ache in her heart and spilled over in a cascade of tears. "I'm sorry." She put her hand over her mouth and hurried from the room.

Jenny ran past the men milling on the landing and continued down the steps and across the gravel drive until she collapsed to her knees in the grass under the shade of the vast oak tree's canopy. Tears she'd waited her entire life to shed poured out of her. She didn't know how she could miss someone she never knew, but imagining her mother cradling her gently in her arms moments before cruel fate stole her life away opened a floodgate of regret for moments never lived and tore at her heart as if she had known the woman her entire life and just now realized she would never see her again.

She felt a chill, despite the warm summer day, and wrapped her arms around herself as if she'd just emerged from the warm womb into the cold abyss of the waiting world. The universe expected her to do something, be something. People had suffered and died to make sure of it.

The weight of the past and the expectations of the future made crying feel like a childish indulgence, but Jenny sat back on her heels and put her hands on her thighs, allowing herself to be that mourning child. She wept for her father's pain, for her mother's tragic life, and for the hole in her heart that would always ache for their presence.

The emotional breakdown was all-consuming but short-lived. She wiped her nose on the back of her hand and attributed her sudden loss of composure to the necessary cleansing of an old wound. When the tears subsided and her vision cleared, she looked out over the rolling hills of the estate spread before her. This was the view her parents saw the day of their picnic. The great oak had grown until its thick branches sagged to the ground with the weight of its years, and the neglected building behind her saw its manicured pride succumb to a cocoon of green flora, but this was the spot where they had sat. Her parents had been happy here. She closed her eyes to conjure up the smiling faces from the photograph. It filled her heart with love instead of loss. "Wake up and see what's happening around you," Hall had said, and she did.

She was born here. Her mother died here. She'd come full circle, and her eyes were wide open.

Jenny extended her legs and settled her back against the rugged bark of the old oak tree. The sun filtered through the dense canopy, creating an intricate dance of shadow and light on the ground, like a film projector casting a dream. It was peaceful here, and she was oddly calm. She didn't believe in ghosts, but she swore her parents were close. This is where she was supposed to be. All the fighting against this path, the teenage defiance, the almost obsessive need to do something important … it all led her here.

The gentle breeze picked up, drawing her attention to the rustling leaves above her. A sign of approval from her parents? She smiled. No —that was silly—just the wind. She closed her eyes and took a deep breath, filled with the scent of shaded green earth and sun-warmed stone.

Footsteps crunching on gravel alerted her to someone approaching from the house. Arthur Wheaton was heading her way.

"May I join you?"

She nodded.

Wheaton grunted and groaned his way down, mirroring her position against the tree. "I may have been too blunt earlier," he began. "I'm sorry."

"Truth and honesty, Mr. Wheaton."

He smiled. "If you have any questions, I'd be more than happy to answer them."

Jenny pulled a long blade of grass through her fingers and was silent for a few moments. These men had the key to her past, and she suddenly felt small and vulnerable. She pulled her knees up to her chest and wrapped her arms around them.

"Do you know anything about my mother's family or my biological father?"

"Not a lot. Your mother's only family, her mother and a younger brother, had died in the pandemic, and when asked about the father of her child, she just shook her head. No one broached the subject again, to my knowledge."

And that was that. At least she didn't have to wonder if there was someone out there to find. The news may have had more of an impact at one time, but she had all the family she needed now, and her path was clear. If only so much time hadn't been wasted.

"So my father and your group did what, altered my records to hide me from the evil geniuses?"

"Yes. Then he took you away from all this to keep you safe."

Jenny couldn't help her wry laugh at winding up right back where she'd literally started.

Wheaton stiffened, as if he were offended. "He wanted to protect you. We all did."

"I know. I just wish … he should have brought me in, made me a part of this instead of hiding it from me. We could have tackled it together."

"He wanted to, but …"

Wheaton stared at her, and she heard every word he wasn't saying. Her father had tried steering her toward a career in science, but rebellious teens being what they are, she went in the exact opposite direction.

She bowed her head. "But I wasn't ready."

"Everyone finds their own path, in their own time."

Jenny shook her head. Unless a war comes along and throws them face-first into their destiny. "Now that my father is gone, who leads the project?"

"Robert Hall."

She raised her brow. He was obviously no fan of hers. "Silly question, but do you trust him?"

Wheaton eyed her sternly. "Nothing is more important to us than your safety. He is the right man for the job."

Jenny imagined standing toe to toe with the unyielding forces against her, and it terrified her. Like her father, she was prepared to do anything to protect the work and the potential harm it could do in the wrong hands, which included taking her own life if the situation warranted it. She thought of Kathryn and her grief should that happen. The urge to protect her from all this was strong. Six people knew about her other than Kathryn. Six. Jenny couldn't imagine what her life would be like now. Whatever it was, Kathryn didn't sign up for a lifetime of looking over their shoulders. She had so much to deal with already. Wild ideas about how to spare her from that fate swirled briefly in her head, and she understood why Kathryn gave in to her protective instincts.

"Hall took over for my father?"

"Yes."

Hall was definitely more interested in the project than her feelings, and the fact that he had taken the bold step to send someone out of the shadows to bring her into their secret world showed something of his mettle, but the core of their organization was still questionable to her, including the actions under her father's watch.

"Bouchaule was once part of your group, wasn't he?"

"He worked closely with your father."

"Until he betrayed him and had him killed."

Wheaton pressed his lips into a grim line. "Thierry Bouchaule was a brilliant man who had his eye on the right goal, but he was impatient, and his methods were devoid of any ethics or morals whatsoever. We removed him from our organization."

Jenny shook her head. "And right into the arms of the Nazis."

"We should have eliminated him," Wheaton said. "We recognized our mistake and sorted it. It took longer to arrange than we would have liked, but it was taken care of."

Jenny looked at the man, surprised he openly admitted to murder. She thought back to the people who had fallen around her and wondered how far Wheaton and Rhoades had gone to protect her.

"Who else have you *taken care of?*"

"We do what we must."

That didn't answer her question, but it told her there were many. Mysteries with no answers began to click into place like tumblers in a lock. "Cal, or whoever he is … that was you?" Before Wheaton could answer, another tumbler fell. "He killed LaPaglia at the bar the night of my birthday."

Jenny imagined him climbing out the bathroom window, doing the dastardly deed, and crawling back in the same way. Bernie had found him disrobing in the bathroom. Cal claimed someone spilled a drink on his sleeve, but Jenny pictured him washing LaPaglia's blood out of his shirt.

Wheaton stared into the distance. "Bouchaule set LaPaglia on you. We couldn't risk what his intentions were. We didn't want you to wind up like your father."

Bouchaule again. "What drew him to me in the first place?"

"Kathryn Hammond. She was connected to Forrester, and then she suddenly became interested in you. That made Bouchaule look in your direction. When he discovered you were Daniel's daughter, his curiosity did the rest."

Kathryn. Another tumbler clicked. "The accident! The men who shot at us and ran us off the road … you?"

"She was taking you to Forrester."

Jenny uttered a curse under her breath. "You're nothing but a murderous cabal."

"These are not good people, Miss Ryan."

"Kathryn is a good person! You nearly killed her … *and* me."

He bowed his head. "A mistake."

"No more killing."

"I think you underestimate your importance."

"No. More. Killing. I'll not be party to that or any other under-handed tricks you've got up your sleeve in the name of *protection*."

"You're being naïve, if you don't mind my saying so. We're at war."

"I have a feeling you were at this long before the war started."

"We are always at war."

Jenny understood he didn't mean this war. From here on out she would be at perpetual war against those who would harm her or use her physiology to harm others. A war had swirled around her since the day she was born. She just didn't know it.

An unbearable weight settled on her shoulders. She didn't know how to be a part of this world. No one could, or should, control life and death. "You're mad. You've no right to play God."

"It's not as difficult as it seems," he said too calmly for comfort. "Personnel placement is the key to success. Find someone with an ax to grind, put them in position to use it, and they will. You don't even have to convince them or let them know they're doing you a favor."

The larger picture unfurled like an oversized map in a command center. The people around her were pawns in a deadly game, and they had no idea. How far had they gone to control her?

"What about Kathryn? Was she part of your grand scheme from the beginning?"

Wheaton cocked his head like someone disbelieving of his luck. "She was just in the right place at the right time ... depending on how you look at it."

Cruel fate, Jenny decided. She didn't buy that Wheaton-Rhoades hadn't tried to use her as an instrument in their endgame though. "I would think she was in the perfect position to facilitate your plan to rid the world of Thierry Bouchaule."

Wheaton raised his brow. "You would think."

He needn't say more. The unspoken reminder of Kathryn's fall into her legend said it all. Jenny focused on something else. It didn't seem to matter whether she joined the group. Wheaton-Rhoades would be lurking in the background, pulling their own not so ethical strings.

"This will always hang over my head. I'll never be safe." And as long as Kathryn was with her, *she* would never be safe either.

"I assure you, you will be."

"How can you say that? Hall's brother was killed in my house. *In my house!* Those men are still out there."

"Those men were Colin Donnelly's paid thugs. Now that he is dead, they pose no threat to you."

"How can you be so sure?"

"Miss Ryan, we don't have the luxury of *pretty sure* or *fairly certain.* If we weren't positive it was safe, I wouldn't say so."

That didn't sound very comforting. "Were you positive my father would be safe?"

Wheaton stared at her for a beat, but then she saw his failings come back to haunt him. His gaze fell to the ground. "Your father stepped outside our protective circle. I'm afraid it cost him his life."

"Why would he do that?"

The man shifted uncomfortably, and Jenny sensed he wanted to say *he did it for you* but thought better of it. "He did it to protect the organization. The fallout from Bouchaule's betrayal exposed his work, which attracted every unsavory character imaginable. The cascade of unfortunate events was unstoppable after that ... even for us."

Bouchaule again, Jenny seethed internally.

Wheaton concurred with everything she wasn't saying.

"I was arrogant enough to think Bouchaule would never be able to continue the work without us. I let him walk away, and your father is dead now because of it. That is something I cannot change or ever make up to you, but I can promise I will protect you with my life, as will any of the men here, and we will help you and support you in any way we can. This is your work now, Miss Ryan. Your legacy."

Jenny closed her eyes. The last thing she needed was more lives sacrificed on her behalf. The sentiment was nice, but all the dedicated strangers in the world couldn't replace her father.

"I don't want anyone killing or dying to protect me, Mr. Wheaton. I can hardly live with the ones who already have."

He nodded in understanding, but she wasn't sure her words made any difference to him.

"You belong with us. We'll provide your education. Help you build a career."

"I can do that without you."

Wheaton grinned like he wanted to say *oh, you poor misguided child*, but he went on without derision. "No one understands your unique situation like we do. No one will do more to protect you."

Kathryn would, Jenny wanted to say. But Kathryn was stitching her own life together now.

"No one can take the place of your father, but we will guide you and support you as if you were our own. We will make sure you have anything you need to maximize your potential. Be realistic. It would take you decades to reach the heights we can provide with a very specific targeting of your skills."

"My skills or my physiology?" she asked. "My potential or your bank accounts?"

"I assure you, this is not about money."

"When isn't it?"

"When discovering our physiological secrets can alter the course of human history."

She thought his remark heavy-handed, but he appeared serious, and the implication was sobering. "No pressure."

He smiled. "No pressure."

It all sounded too good to be true, and if that was the case, it usually was.

"What is your hesitation?" Wheaton asked.

"There's a war on, in case you've forgotten," she said.

"And you're a proud American ready to do her bit."

"Are you mocking me?"

"I admire your devotion, but people have died—"

"You don't have to remind me how many have died because of me. What is my hesitation? That more people will die. That my loved ones will be harmed. That I'll be harmed. That my physiology will be used *against* mankind. You can't stop any of that, no matter your intentions. Tell me I'm wrong."

"Unfortunately, that is correct."

"Then?"

"It will be a lot harder without us by your side. You know this. You want to make a difference in the world? Here's your chance. Let us help you."

"We're still at war. I'm not turning my back on that."

"You have a responsibility to—"

"I know damn well what my responsibilities are."

Wheaton smiled kindly. "You may not want to hear this, but there is nothing we can do or say to reinstate you in the intelligence services, and I won't say I'm sorry for that. We lost track of you once, and it nearly cost you your life."

"Who are you? Do you work for the government?"

"We work for mankind."

Jenny nearly laughed. "That's ridiculous. Everyone works for someone."

A serious face stared back at her.

"I don't know anything about this work."

"We'll see to your continued education and make sure you learn everything you need to know."

"I'll have to think about it."

"No, you don't. You know this is where you belong and this is what you were meant to do."

She looked out over the rolling hills and knew he was right. Her future was set. Never again would she wonder which path to take. She didn't trust the members of the Wheaton-Rhodes Institute yet, but she had a feeling that she would, and she should.

"Just because I'm safe from Donnelly's men doesn't mean I'm safe. Surely, you know that."

Wheaton pursed his lips. "It's true, we are not all seeing, but the known external forces working against us have been eliminated. And just to be sure, we will provide security—unobtrusively, of course—to ensure your safety."

A life of looking over her shoulder. Just as Kathryn had feared. "How many know about me?"

"Only the men you met today … and Miss Hammond, of course."

She nodded. "Thank you for taking care of things regarding her."

"There was nothing to take care of. Hazards of the trade. No one in the services condemns her for her actions."

Jenny glared at him for planting the notion that they had.

"She did everything she could to protect you. We owe her a debt of gratitude." He paused. "I'm sure we could find a place for her."

Adrenaline straightened Jenny's spine. "You stay away from her."

"She's special now, like you."

"My father already went down that road. So did Bouchaule. Exposure once removed doesn't have the same properties. It's a dead end, and you know it. You leave her out of this."

Wheaton smiled. "That sentimental detachment isn't easy, is it?"

"Leave her out of it. She's suffered enough because of me."

"What she did, she did of her own free will."

"Just—" Jenny stalled his attempt to ease her guilt. "Just leave her alone. I want your word. And that extends to Hall or anyone else who gets any funny ideas."

Wheaton raised his hands in surrender. "My word."

They were both silent until Wheaton cleared his throat. "In the spirit of truth and honesty, we know you have Bouchaule's secret papers."

Jenny feigned confusion, but she could see he wasn't buying it.

"And it's fine that you want to keep them to yourself. They're useless right now anyway. As you've pointed out, the science isn't there yet. But when it is, and when you're ready, you'll know what to do with them, and we will be here to help you if you so choose."

Jenny was feeling manipulated again.

"And what if I just want to walk away from all this?"

Wheaton inhaled and then exhaled sharply, the way one does before a scolding. "Miss Ryan, walking away is your prerogative. I think you know that we will always be here when you change your mind. Please note I said *when* and not *if*."

"Arrogant and condescending, but noted."

"And at the risk of adding misogynistic to your list, you are a woman. Opportunities are scarce in the sciences, and you would have to work twice as hard as a man half as smart to get ahead. You know this is true."

She did, and she hated that he was making perfect sense and making her feel like she'd be a fool to refuse. "What are you proposing?"

"Two things. I know you want to help the war effort. We have a division of WRI in need of the skills you learned in Toronto. We have one of the few labs in Europe with an electron microscope and no technician to keep it running. Interested?"

"Only if you have nothing to do with biological weapons."

"I promise you, this is a civilian war effort operation that pertains only to medicine, materials science, and non-weaponized biology."

"And where is this lab?"

"Switzerland."

"And the second?"

"When the war is over, we will continue your education and set up a lab anywhere in the world tailored specifically to your work, which you will oversee."

"That's—" Before she could say "insane," raised voices from the men gathered in front of the house drew their attention.

Hall waved a folded newspaper in the air and was clearly the more agitated of the group.

"Excuse me," Wheaton said as he slowly got to his feet.

Jenny watched him join the others. When Hall handed him the newspaper, he read something below the fold and immediately looked at her. They all did. Then the arguing began again. It was time to see what she was getting into. When she got within earshot, she overheard Hall say, "We kill him. Why is this even a discussion?"

More killing. The group went silent when she stepped into their circle.

"What's going on?"

Everyone looked at Wheaton, then Rhoades, but no one said anything.

Jenny snatched the newspaper from Wheaton's hand as he attempted to conceal it behind his back.

"Miss Ryan—"

Celebrated French Doctor Escapes Nazi Clutches, the headline read.

Jenny couldn't breathe. Bouchaule. Alive. In London. Her fists clenched with barely contained rage, and she shook the crushed paper at them. "Was this you? Did you do this? Did you lure me here just to turn me over to *him?*"

All the men protested, but Wheaton's voice boomed above the rest. "Absolutely not! We were told he was dead."

"Bloody government," someone muttered in the background.

Jenny pointed at the driver, who was milling among the men and obviously the source of the newspaper. "Take me to London. Now."

Rhoades stilled the driver with a shake of his head when the man eyed him for permission.

Jenny headed for the car.

Wheaton called after her. "Miss Ryan, stop. We'll take care of it,"

Jenny turned. "Clearly, you're not capable. He's mine."

CHAPTER TWENTY-FOUR

Vivienne ran along the crowded train platform frantically searching for John. This was the last place he could be. The train would pull out in a few minutes, and he would be gone forever.

She'd nearly run the length of the platform when she saw him lined up to board.

"John!" she called out.

He turned around, along with three other men, but then caught sight of her and headed toward her with a broad grin. "Hey, gorgeous. Miss me already?"

She grabbed his biceps before he could embrace her. "She's gone. Kathryn. She's gone."

"What do you mean? You said she wasn't transferring until tomorrow."

"Right, but she's disappeared." She handed him the newspaper she'd found beside a broken teacup on the floor in Kathryn's room when she went in to say goodbye at the end of her last shift. "I'm not sure if this means anything?"

John stared in disbelief at the headline. "This can't be." He quickly skimmed the article.

From what Vivienne gathered, some French hero, a doctor named Bouchaule, had been liberated from the clutches of the Nazis. A celebration in his honor was happening at The Westwood, in London, at seven that evening.

John looked at his watch. "I pray Jenny doesn't see this. When did Kathryn leave?"

"I don't know, but she took my case."

"She what?"

"I stowed my kit in the supply room while I finished my rounds. When I came back, the bag was open and my small suitcase was gone. It contains a lovely evening ensemble, which is probably just her size, and a bottle of pain medication and some wrapping for her ribs is missing from the supply shelf."

"Damn it, Kat," he cursed under his breath.

Vivienne gathered this all had something to do with what happened to Kathryn in France, but she didn't see how this would end well for anyone. "I don't know what she thinks she's going to do, but she's not in any condition to even get to London, let alone do whatever she has in mind. The Westwood is an exclusive private club. I don't care how spectacular she looks in my marvelous frock, she won't get in the door without a membership or invitation."

John frowned. "She's very resourceful, and I assure you, whoever the gatekeeper is won't stand a chance, no matter what condition she's in." He looked at his watch again. "I'll never get to London in time."

Vivienne didn't know whether she was impressed or jealous, but there was no time for either. She took his arm and pulled him along. "Here, we have a ride."

He resisted. "What do you mean *we*? You're not going."

She stopped and put a hand on her hip. "Do you know London? Do you know where The Westwood is?"

He stared blankly at her.

"I didn't think so. Kathryn may need medical attention after this little adventure, and I've got to rescue my one and only dress and favorite lipstick. Come on, you're wasting time."

He didn't argue.

Kathryn leaned against a Doric pillar in the portico just outside the heavy wooden entry doors of The Westwood. Without the pillar, she would crumble to the ground, and without an invitation inside, her plan ended here.

Seeing the article about Bouchaule at breakfast that morning made her on-the-fly plan to get to his location frantic and chaotic, two characteristics that should never form the basis of a mission. But she needed to right a wrong. Bouchaule had to die, and every life taken or led to suffer at his hand from this point on was on her head for failing to kill him when she had the chance.

He would come for Jenny again. Hell, he would come for her again as well once he found out she was alive. Someone went out of their way to make Jenny think he was dead. Kathryn didn't put it past Bouchaule to arrange it himself. The tide was turning, and Bouchaule would gravitate to the next group who would fund his work. Presenting himself as a beleaguered hero fighting Nazi treachery from the inside was exactly how he presented himself to her. She bought it. The British would too. She could see it all so clearly now, and this was the last time he'd get away with it.

Borrowing, well, stealing, Sister Barclay's elegant evening apparel was not her finest moment, especially after all she'd done for her, but she had the bottle of pain medication from the supply closet in her hand, and at her feet was the Sister's canvas kit bag. She had to get into that club, and this would do. She had intended to liberate a uniform and feign some medical emergency to get in, but she'd discovered a small case in the kit bag, and the contents were perfect: an aquamarine long-sleeved column gown, veiled hat, shoes, scarf, purse, and makeup. When this was all over, she would definitely owe Sister Barclay something bigger than an apology.

The visiting British Red Cross provided her with clothes for her journey to London, and a sob story about her husband arriving in the city from France bought her a ride with a sympathetic driver heading her way.

It was a long, hard day, one in which the pills were numbing everything but the pain. Her head was pounding, her limbs felt like they were abandoning her, and she was running out of energy fast. Just a little longer, she kept telling herself, and that thought carried her until she finally arrived. Bouchaule was inside, only yards away. God, if only the pain would stop so she could think.

Not knowing the layout of the club, she was making things up as she went along, which she hated.

A stag middle-aged man in white tie and tails approached the door, pulling his invitation from his pocket. Kathryn steeled herself for her performance and stepped forward, hoping her legs would hold her up.

She rummaged through her small purse and purposely dropped a slim lighter at the man's feet. "Blast it," she said with a refined British accent while crushing an unlit cigarette between her fingers.

As planned, he retrieved the lighter for her. "Here," he said, as he sparked it to life and cupped the light of the flame with his hand, ever vigilant of the blackout.

She couldn't hold the damned cigarette still for the flame.

The man eyed her shaking hand. "May I?"

She nodded, and he guided her hand with his to the lighter, where she lit her cigarette and blew out an exasperated exhale to the sky.

"Are you all right?"

She shook her head and huffed, getting into character. "I'm afraid I've had a row with my scoundrel husband, who has left me here on the doorstep while he's off to spend the evening with his mistress."

The man raised his brow, appropriately shocked. "The cad."

"And good riddance, I say, but the public humiliation ... again, is just ... I'm sorry." She waved away her complaint and took another irritated drag. "Christ, I need a drink."

His gaze drifted from the chiffon scarf draped strategically around her splinted hand to her makeup-covered bruises and damaged lip. By the indignant straightening of his spine, he must have assumed she was a battered woman.

That would do.

"My dear, shall I hail you a taxi, or shall we go inside and get that drink?" He lifted his bent elbow to her, which she took with a smile.

She was in.

Knife to the side. Hammer to the head. Knife to the side. Hammer to the head. That's what every step felt like. The shoes were a half-size too small, which didn't help either, but her feet were mostly numb to it now. The pain pills were a balancing act, and she feared she'd already taken too many. She was operating on sheer force of will. Killing Bouchaule was all that mattered. That and escaping unnoticed. Not long ago, that wouldn't have mattered, but she had Jenny to consider now. Thank heavens she found out about Bouchaule before Jenny did. She didn't want blood on Jenny's hands.

Pain, drugs, and exhaustion were all working against her, but she couldn't stop now. *Breathe*, she told herself. *Forget the pain. Breathe.* Her vision was fuzzy around the edges. *Focus. Find Bouchaule and focus.*

Her escort brought her a coupe of champagne, which she took but didn't drink, and she thanked him. He questioned her condition, but she assured him she was fine, and he gravitated toward friends and went on his way. She set down the glass and pulled an ice pick from the block of ice at the bar as she passed, concealing it beneath her scarf. One quick stab in the right place and Bouchaule's murderous reign would be over.

After climbing two steps of the grand stairway to get a better view over the bobbing heads, she found him at the head of the drawing room. The crowd gravitated to him in turn, and every time someone new approached, they raised a glass to him. He reciprocated with a sip of champagne from his coupe, which he kept on the table beside his hip.

Kathryn had to isolate him, get him out of the crowd. She eyed the mezzanine and found it nearly empty. If she could get his attention from afar, he would certainly follow her up there. All she had to do was make it to the top of the stairs without passing out, which, at this point, was questionable.

Another greeting, another toast, and to Kathryn's horror, a familiar blonde in a beautiful sleeveless green dress appeared behind Bouchaule, heading straight for him. She blinked. Was she hallucinating? No. It was really Jenny. What was she doing? Kathryn wanted to scream, *No!* Would Jenny kill him on the spot with all those people watching? She had wanted justice for her father from the moment they'd met, and now the man was standing before her, laughing and charming his new benefactors. Jenny's determined face told her everything she needed to know.

Just before Jenny reached Bouchaule, she scanned the room one more time. They locked gazes.

Kathryn shook her head, pleading with her not to do it.

Jenny smiled and disappeared behind his back.

Adrenaline propelled Kathryn forward. The crowd around Bouchaule laughed as he made a speech. People pressed in, trying to hear. The room was too warm. Bodies too close. The wrap on her ribs tightened with every breath it seemed. Elbows became spears to her side, and her head throbbed with every heartbeat. *Breathe.* God, she couldn't. The air was stagnant. Perfumes. Body odor. Foul breath. Alcohol. The room was growing dark around the edges. Not now. *Breathe.* Ice pick. Bouchaule. Someone gripped her elbow. The ice pick fell from her hand.

"Come on, let's enjoy the show."

It was Jenny, leading her back toward the staircase.

Kathryn's head was swimming. She didn't know how she was still standing. "I don't think I can make it."

"You have to, or it's going to get messy. We can't afford that."

Jenny plucked a coupe of champagne from a passing server's tray as they climbed two steps and faced the room.

Kathryn clutched the railing with a trembling hand. "What's happening?"

Across the room, Bouchaule raised his glass and bellowed, "To victory!"

The crowd cheered and echoed his toast.

Jenny lifted hers and whispered, "To justice."

Kathryn eyed her as she drank along with everyone else, and then followed Jenny's gaze to Bouchaule.

He saw them just as he swallowed the last of his champagne. It only took a beat for comprehension, in the form of shock, to register on his face.

Jenny tipped her glass to him. "Rot in hell, fucker."

He looked at his empty coupe, then, wide-eyed, back to them. His face turned dark red, and the glass fell from his hand. He clutched at his throat before sinking into a sea of black tails and festive frocks.

Kathryn gasped but quickly schooled her expression.

Jenny took her by the elbow again. "Time to go. Can you make it?"

Kathryn nodded as the room erupted in panicked shouts and screams.

Some of the crowd rushed in while the rest moved quickly to the exit. They streamed out along with them.

A harried Smitty battled against the fleeing masses and intercepted them. "Oh, thank God," he said, out of breath when he reached them.

A Vauxhall came to an abrupt stop at the curb behind him with Vivienne behind the wheel. "Get in!"

Through the growing fog in her head, Kathryn heard Jenny say, "Perfect timing. We need some help here."

That was the last thing she remembered before everything went dark.

Jenny cradled Kathryn's head on her shoulder as they rode in the back seat and Vivienne calmly drove through the darkened London streets. She would prefer that Kathryn lie down, but the car was too small for that. In the chaos outside the club, no one had seemed to notice Smitty scooping a fading Kathryn into his arms and into the car. By the time they got underway, Kathryn was coming around.

"Thanks for saving me in there," she said weakly. "I never would have made it without you."

"You always land on your feet."

"I think I may have run out of lives."

Jenny exhaled and kissed her temple. "What am I going to do with you?"

Kathryn looked up pitifully. "Did that count as dumb and irrational?"

"In your condition? Probably."

Smitty chuckled from the front seat and then turned, eyeing them seriously. "Sorry I was late."

Jenny wasn't. "He was mine."

Smitty nodded. "Mission accomplished?"

"Yes."

"Clean?"

"Spotless."

"Atta girl."

Vivienne glanced in the rearview mirror and then turned down the next street, which dead-ended into a pile of debris from a bombed-out building. She entered an alley and pulled over. She was all business when she opened Kathryn's door, medical bag in hand, and kneeled on the running board. "Hold this torch, love," she said to Smitty, handing him a flashlight.

Jenny raised her brow to Smitty at the absentminded term of endearment, but he didn't seem fazed.

"How are we doing here?" Vivienne asked Kathryn rhetorically as she donned her stethoscope and checked her blood pressure. Her brow creased when she felt Kathryn's forehead and checked her pupils. "How much fluid intake have you had today?"

"Cup of tea at breakfast."

Vivienne pulled a large jar of clear fluid and a length of small diameter red rubber hose from her bag. "The same cup that was spilled all over the floor in your room?"

"Okay, a sip of tea."

"I assume food intake was about the same?"

"I didn't think I could keep it down."

They all glared at Kathryn.

As Vivienne prepared an IV, her movements were curt. "You're dehydrated, among other things. How many pills did you take?"

"I lost count."

Vivienne's disapproving glare turned into a creased brow again.

"Not that many," Kathryn said. "It's been a few hours. I'm fine."

Vivienne had to take Kathryn's word for it, but Jenny could tell from the impatient swipe on Kathryn's forearm with a sterile pad soaked in alcohol that she wasn't happy about it.

When she approached with the IV needle, Kathryn said, "Sorry about the dress."

Vivienne paused and looked her up and down. "Keep it. It looks better on you than it ever did on me."

Kathryn deployed what Jenny recognized as her most charming smile. "I doubt that."

Jenny and Smitty looked at each other, then back to Kathryn. "We're right here," they said in unison.

Kathryn and Vivienne chuckled, relieving the tension.

Vivienne got on with her task. "This may sting a bit."

Kathryn took the needle's insertion without a reaction.

"Thank you," she said. "All of you."

Smitty looked at Jenny. "Do you have a plan?"

Jenny did, and he was probably driving around the city trying to find her. Wheaton-Rhoades arranged her entry to the club, her clothing, and a man assigned to protect her. She agreed to all of it but made it clear Bouchaule was hers. She'd left the man somewhere in the crowded club. Wheaton-Rhoades wouldn't be happy, but after tonight, her life would never be the same. Until morning, she would spend every moment she could with Kathryn.

Before she could answer Smitty, Vivienne spoke up. "I have a flat in Islington. Well, it's not mine. There's a group of us …" She waved off the explanation. "It's empty right now. You're welcome to it."

Jenny's eyes lit up. "That would be—"

Smitty shut off the light. "Shh."

They froze as an engine purred close by and road debris crunched under slow-moving tires. Jenny heard Smitty move for the ever-present gun under his jacket.

A car crept into view, and as it passed the opening to the alley, it stopped, centering the driver. No one breathed in the darkness. Jenny hoped the car would just back up when it realized the street was a dead end, but then she recognized the silhouette of the Jaguar that brought her to London. Her protection would be behind the wheel. A spotlight from the car briefly lit up the alley and then went out.

She touched Smitty's shoulder. "It's all right."

"Part of your plan?"

"Unfortunately."

"Tell me what you need."

"You can stand down." She turned to Vivienne. "We'll take that flat."

Vivienne took a small notepad from her uniform pocket and scribbled on it. "It's all yours. Here's the address. The key is under the ceramic planter beside the door on the right."

Kathryn stopped Jenny with a hand to her forearm when she tried to get out of the car. "Are you sure?"

"Yes. It's okay, honey."

Smitty moved with her. "I'm coming with you."

"It's fine, Sm—"

"I'm coming with you."

The concerned expressions told her everyone would be more comfortable if he went with her.

"Okay, but stay behind me."

Smitty balked at that.

"Behind me. Trust me. Please … just do as I ask."

Kathryn tried to get out of the car, but Vivienne's hand on her shoulder prevented it. She acquiesced and settled on an uncomfortable twist to look out the back window at Jenny's exchange with the man standing beside his car at the end of the alley.

From what she could see, a reasonable exchange quickly turned into a lot of head shaking by both parties and then brusque arm movements by Jenny, who clearly wasn't happy.

Smitty stood close by but wasn't part of the conversation. He kept his hands behind his back, like a soldier at ease, but Kathryn knew he had a gun in his hand and wouldn't hesitate to use it.

After the terse exchange, Jenny started giving orders, if the emphatic hand movements were any indication. When she was done, she put her hands on her hips, appeared to issue one more command with a sweeping arm movement, and returned the way she came, with Smitty dutifully following behind.

The man hesitated as he watched them walk away, but he got into his car and pulled into the alley behind them.

Kathryn eyed him warily as he joined them.

Jenny lifted her hand in introduction. "This is Mr. Andrews ... my bodyguard."

Smitty watched the Jaguar's taillights disappear around the corner, taking Kathryn out of his life. For the first time, he didn't have the urge to follow. She had Jenny, who had come so far since he'd first met her. No longer rash and reactive, Jenny had matured into someone more measured, and he had every confidence she'd do anything to keep Kathryn safe.

He didn't know who this new group was, but Jenny seemed to have the situation well in hand. She knew he was only a phone call away if she ever needed him. He prayed she never would, and that when this war was over, their lives would be filled with peace and happiness. It's all he ever wanted for Kathryn, and now he wanted it for Jenny too.

"Are you worried?" Vivienne asked, slipping her arms around his waist.

His body relaxed at her touch. She made him feel like the weight of the world was off his shoulders. "I'll always worry about the people I love." He tightened his arms around her and cocked his head toward the end of the alley. "They have each other now, and that group will have their hands full with Jenny. She trusts them, or she wouldn't let them near Kathryn, so I'm less worried today than I was yesterday."

Vivienne rested her head against his chest. It felt like it belonged there, always.

"Do I even want to know where you got that car?" he asked.

She tilted her head up and smiled. "You do not."

He raised a brow. "You've got a little wild in you, don't you?"

"Not usually, but something tells me you like a little wild."

"I could be ready for a little less wild, to be honest."

She snuggled closer in his arms. "I might know a girl."

Smitty laughed but didn't say anything. He didn't move either. Vivienne followed suit, then she sniffed and shook her head like she was casting off raindrops. She stepped back, still holding his hands, and smiled.

"So, here we are, then," she said lightly. "Off to the next adventure."

Smitty cupped her face. He didn't want to let her go. "I'm going to find you after the war, and I'm going to buy you a fancy dress in Paris."

Tears filled Vivienne's eyes and her smile grew pained. "I don't care about any of that. Just find me." She kissed him and then hastily pulled a slip of paper from her pocket and slipped it into his hand. "My mam's address. Write me. It'll get to me eventually. She will be delighted I've got a man. I have got a man, haven't I?"

He kissed her passionately, leaving no doubt in her mind he would move heaven and earth to find her again.

CHAPTER TWENTY-FIVE

*J*enny stood in the dark at the open terrace door of Vivienne's flat, overlooking Arundel Square Garden, clutching a thin cotton robe around her shoulders. Past the chimney-potted rooftops, barrage balloons swayed in silhouette against the moonlit sky like tethered sentinels, ready to do their duty to protect the city from low-flying bombers. Even inanimate objects were doing their bit for the war. Tomorrow she would do hers. It wasn't in the way she expected, but somehow it seemed fitting.

Her path forward was clear now. Everything Wheaton said was true. She didn't stand a chance alone if things went sideways, and the opportunities WRI could afford her would be a dream come true. Perfect, except she'd be far from Kathryn for the remainder of the war. They'd both expected that because of her service in the OSS, but in their wildest imaginations, they couldn't have predicted Wheaton-Rhoades and their part in their lives—past, present, and future.

She despised their questionable morals, but she was like them now. A murderer. She felt no remorse for Bouchaule's death. He had her father killed and had ordered Kathryn's death. And yet he wouldn't have been prosecuted for either. Maybe an international tribunal would have found him guilty of crimes against humanity after the war for his work with the Nazis, but she wouldn't chance him getting away with it because someone thought him a valuable scientific asset. She understood what Wheaton meant when he said, *"Find someone with an ax to grind, put them in position to use it, and they will."* And she had.

Did Wheaton-Rhoades plant the newspaper story about Bouchaule on purpose, knowing what she or Kathryn would do? She didn't know, but the efficiency of a group who could arrange such things and then manage the fallout to their advantage was frightening. One minute she was on her way back to London to plan a murder, and one detour later she was dressed to the nines and escorted to the private club on the arm of a man she knew was there for her protection and to finish the job if she couldn't. She hadn't needed either. A covert emptying of her L-pill's contents into Bouchaule's coupe of champagne signaled the end of one part of her life and the beginning of another. What would Kathryn think of that life? The question had her on edge.

Closing her eyes, she rolled the tension from her shoulders and released a slow exhale to the ceiling. She sensed Kathryn at her back before she felt her lips on the side of her neck and her arms slipping around her waist.

"Restless?" Kathryn said, her voice heavy with sleep.

Jenny relaxed into the security of Kathryn's warm body pressed against her. How could she live without this for the duration of the war? "You should be in bed. How do you feel?"

"Much better. It's amazing what fluids, food, and sleep will do for you. How about you? What's keeping you up?"

Jenny thought about lying, letting Kathryn go home without knowing about Wheaton-Rhoades. What good would telling her do? She could break the news to her gradually, explain things and show her that Wheaton-Rhoades only had her best interests in mind. It sounded reasonable for all of a minute. God, how did she get to this place?

Yesterday, she thought her secret was safe—they were safe. And now? Now, she ... *they* ... were at the mercy of strangers. Jenny had never given

Kathryn a reason to trust her judgment, but now their future depended on it. She couldn't imagine Kathryn blindly accepting those terms. She was a fighter and a survivor. She nearly died protecting her. Kathryn deserved a quiet life. She needed to go home, bond with her family, find herself, and find peace. Jenny couldn't offer her that anymore.

For as long as she could remember, she'd wanted to make a difference in the world. Well, she got what she wanted, but at what cost? Would she lose Kathryn because of it? She wanted one last unspoiled night before she faced that fear. Wheaton-Rhoades had backed off, but she knew they were close by—watching … waiting for her call. They would always be close by. This is what Kathryn tried so hard to save her from, and if they stayed together, Kathryn would be looking over her shoulder too. How could she ask her to live that way? But after everything they'd been through, how could she not?

"We can talk about it tomorrow." The last word fell from her lips like a whispered death knell.

Kathryn sought her eyes as she leaned around her.

Jenny turned into her embrace to hide her tears. "We came so close," she whispered into Kathryn's chest. Only when Kathryn answered did she realize she'd said it aloud.

"That sounds ominous. What is it? Did you get an assignment already? Please tell me you're not going back into France."

"No, baby, nothing like that."

Kathryn relaxed in her arms. "Whew. You scared me for a minute."

Jenny dried her tears with her sleeve. The unspoiled night she longed for had already slipped away. "It involves our future."

Kathryn smiled. "The disgustingly happy one?"

That seemed like a distant dream now. Jenny dropped her gaze so she wouldn't see that dream die in Kathryn's eyes.

It took one beat for Kathryn to gauge the gravity of the situation. She stepped back to get a better view. "What's going on? Was that man tonight from the OSS or the SOE?"

Jenny lifted her chin. "Neither. I'm out at the agencies." Before Kathryn could ask why, she added, "The briefcase."

"Oh, Jenny. You lied about that for me. I'm so sorry."

"I'd do it again. This is bigger than that."

"Bigger than a world war?"

"Yes."

Kathryn eyed her warily. "Should I sit down for this?"

Jenny handed her a robe from the back of a chair. "Yes."

"Seated and clothed … this must be serious," Kathryn joked, but Jenny could hear the fear in her voice.

Once Kathryn settled, Jenny stood before her and crossed her arms. "Do you trust me?"

"With my life."

That caught Jenny off guard, but it was what she was asking of Kathryn. "There's an organization of scientists. My father was a founding member. In that organization, six men know about me."

Kathryn blinked in disbelief. "*Six?*"

Jenny nodded.

Kathryn stood with a wince and a hand to her ribs. "Shit. Okay." Her gaze darted around the room, looking for an answer. "We go under. We can—"

"No."

"Jenny—"

Jenny touched her shoulder, easing her back down. "I've already panicked enough for the both of us, believe me. Just listen."

Kathryn exhaled a shaky breath and nodded.

Jenny methodically laid out everything that had happened since she left her at the hospital. After making it through her parents' story without crying, she explained her war job in Switzerland and Wheaton-Rhoades's postwar plans for her. When she was through, she held her breath, waiting for Kathryn's reaction.

To Jenny's relief, she stood again and gathered her in her arms. "I hardly know what to say." She leaned back and turned her toward the open terrace door to see her eyes. "You trust them?"

"They're no angels, but they certainly don't mean me any harm."

Kathryn accepted her judgement with a nod, but her brow creased with concern. "Are you okay? All this and then Bouchaule … you must be overwhelmed."

"I was. Until last night. Now I see what I have to do. What I was meant to do."

Kathryn searched her face, and Jenny wondered if she was looking for that naïve girl she used to know. That girl was gone forever, replaced by someone who was just beginning to realize her potential. She hoped Kathryn would love her too.

"I know being part of this isn't the life you hoped for, and I'll understand if—"

"Jenny …" Kathryn waited until she looked at her. "My life is with you. If this is the best way forward for you, it's the best way forward for *us*. Whatever that looks like. I'm not going anywhere. Okay? It's you and me. For better or worse, from now on."

Tears filled Jenny's eyes as Kathryn's faith in her filled her heart. "Is this the part where I say I do?"

"Oh, would that we could," Kathryn said and kissed her.

The nagging fear in Jenny's gut uncoiled, and she melted in Kathryn's arms. "I love you. Thank you."

"I love you too, but I have one request …"

Jenny leaned back, some of the tension returning.

"I want to meet them."

Jenny's mouth opened and shut. She wanted to keep Kathryn far away from Wheaton-Rhoades, but there were no secrets between them now, and Kathryn had a right to judge the situation for herself.

"I'll arrange it."

"You seem pensive."

"They wanted me to bring you in because you're special too. I told them absolutely not. You are not their lab rat."

"Bring me in. They won't find anything. We all know the science isn't there yet."

"Kat—"

"There's nothing more intriguing than the unknown. Give them what they want before they do something stupid to get it."

Jenny stared at her. Who was this woman? "You're being awfully agreeable."

"From what you've told me, this group has been looking out for you since you were born, and they will not stop. That means we have three options. We walk away, which is fighting against them, we join them, or we go under and disappear."

"I would never take you away from your family."

"My family has lived without me for most of their lives, and while I love them and I'd miss them terribly, you are my family. If we need to run, we'll run. Say the word."

"No." She settled back in Kathryn's arms. "I'll join their war effort, get a feel for the organization, and we'll go from there. I'm only sorry we'll be apart."

"Our time will come. You've got a lot of hard work ahead of you, and so do I." Kathryn looked her up and down. "And I don't need all this … this … green-eyed sexy distracting me while I'm trying to find myself."

Jenny laughed, but Kathryn was right. She was a distraction. Like going after Bouchaule had been. Like tonight was from everything that lay before them. They couldn't be together right now, and it broke her heart, but she couldn't help Kathryn, and Kathryn couldn't help her. At least this parting would be filled with love. "You'll be with me every day."

Kathryn cupped her cheek and became serious. "I don't want to be without you, Jenny. Ever. Whatever comes next, whether we're near or far, we're in it together. And I know you don't trust me with your heart yet, but—"

Jenny kissed her. "I trust you with everything that I am." She kissed her again and again, until Kathryn took her into her mouth, filling the room with sounds of their longing. Their bodies pressed together in a desperate thrumming of desire. Hands clutched and positions shifted as their kiss intensified. Jenny broke it off in a panic when she realized she wasn't sure if Kathryn's moans were of pain or pleasure. "I'm sorry," she said breathlessly. "That was … I'm so sorry … am I hurting you?"

Kathryn carefully pulled her down onto the bed. "Not yet."

"Kat—"

"I'll tell you if we need to stop."

Kathryn didn't need to tell Jenny to stop. Her touch was gentle, slow, and maddeningly sensual, as her fingers traced familiar paths across her skin on the way to her most intimate places. Kathryn was no help, as she awkwardly navigated positions one-handed while trying to get comfortable. They both wound up laughing at her hopeless attempts at the upper hand until she finally surrendered and let Jenny take her.

The familiar intimacy of their joined bodies erased the oppressive weight of the future from her mind. Jenny became her world, as warm, wet, hard, soft, sweet, salty, breathy, insistent, timid, and desperate overwhelmed her senses. Murmured promises of love and devotion passed between them in whispers and gasps, as Jenny's soft lips brushed and nipped their way up the heated skin of her inner thigh. Moments later, she came in Jenny's mouth, crying out in pain and pleasure. Jenny faltered, afraid she'd hurt her, but the pain was fleeting, and she reached for Jenny, who slid her way up her body until she could touch her.

Jenny was wet and ready when Kathryn entered her to throaty moans and curses of encouragement. They moved together in an escalating rhythm, but the position was uncomfortable in her condition, and she could tell Jenny needed more. She guided Jenny to her mouth.

With one hand clutching the headboard and the other in Kathryn's hair, Jenny took what she needed, repeating her favorite curse word over and over as her hips undulated and her thighs quivered. It was enough to bring Kathryn to the brink again, and she reached between her legs in time to join Jenny's shuddering release.

Whatever doubts Kathryn had about Jenny's faith in her vanished in the aftermath of Jenny's raw emotion. Tears led to more kisses, and more kisses led to reassurances that their connection would always lead them home to each other's arms.

. . .

A dog barked in the square below the terrace as the rising sun painted its rays across their entwined, exhausted bodies. The stillness of the room echoed their unspoken understanding that this parting was a beginning, not an end. Kathryn etched these moments into her heart. She'd need them in the days, months, and maybe years to come. Time and distance had met its match in their love, and this time, they would overcome them both.

CHAPTER TWENTY-SIX

March 1946: New York City

Kathryn stepped out of the taxi at The Grotto's front door while the doorman retrieved a large dress box and two shopping bags from the trunk. She hadn't seen the club in the daylight for ages, and she noticed the awning above the door was on its last season. It took her a minute to remember it didn't matter. The Grotto wouldn't see another season.

"Luc?" she called out into the empty club as she pulled off her gloves and set them beside her purse.

The door to Dominic's office on the third tier opened, and Luc burst out. "You're here!"

"Where is everyone?" she asked, as he weaved his way toward her through tables with upturned chairs on them.

He took her hands and they exchanged kisses on the cheek. "I don't know. I just got here myself. You're early."

"I just wanted to drop—"

"Is that the dress?" Luc broke in excitedly. "Let's see it, let's see it!"

Kathryn laughed at his boyish excitement. She hadn't seen that light in his eyes in a long time.

"Let's see it," he repeated with a little hop.

"You can't see it until this evening."

His pout was so comically pathetic, she couldn't stand it.

"Oh for—" She opened the box and carefully pulled back the tissue paper to reveal a pewter-colored satin gown.

Luc gasped. "It's perfect." He stared at the dress for a few moments and then looked at her with tears in his eyes. "I wish he could be here."

She knew he meant Dominic, and she tried hard to hold back her own tears.

"I'm sorry about Jenny as well," he said.

That nearly pushed her tears over the edge, and she bowed her head. "Me too."

"You know she would be here if she could."

Kathryn raised her chin and stuffed down her emotions. Tears would come later, at the end of the evening. "I know."

Luc smiled sympathetically and held out his hand. "I have something for you. Come with me."

He led her up the stairs to the office and retrieved a light gray velvet box from the large safe in the corner. Nestled inside was a pear-shaped sky blue topaz surrounded by a ring of small diamonds and matching earrings. "They were my mother's. I want you to have them."

"Oh, Luc. I couldn't."

"Nonsense. Dad would have wanted you to have them. You were the daughter he never had."

"Luc …"

"No argument. They're yours, and they'll look perfect with that dress. Here. Turn around." He lifted the sparkling necklace from its velvet pillow and draped it around her neck from behind. She dropped her chin out of habit so he could join the clasp without it getting caught up in her hair, but she needn't have. She'd cut it shorter last year, when she found the complicated hairstyles too hard to manage with her weak hand.

Luc faced her. "So beautiful."

Kathryn hugged him, and they both held back tears. "Thank you."

He drew back and wiped his eyes. "Sorry. I don't mean to slobber all over you."

She chuckled. "We're even. Listen, you keep this here until tonight" —she unclasped the necklace and handed it back to him—"I've got some running around to do."

"Me too. See you at seven?"

"I'll be here at six."

They hugged again, and Kathryn left before the emotional weight of the day spoiled what should be a celebration.

Six months ago, the joy of V-J Day brought a sorrow none of them expected. On the eve of Luc's return to the States, his father died unexpectedly. Dominic Vignelli was found alone at his desk at The Grotto, slumped over the night's receipts, with an untouched glass of port and an unlit cigar beside his hand, as if the end of the war had ushered in the end of an era and the end of his life.

He had died quickly, of an aneurysm, they said consolingly, as if the swiftness of his demise would lessen the sting of his loss. Luc had told her his father's death had hit him like a sucker punch after the bell. The war was over. No more loved ones were supposed to die. He vowed to hold on to the club to honor his father, but his interests lay elsewhere. He knew planes, and that's where his focus remained after he left the service. He hired people to run the club, and then he started a small charter service out of Roosevelt Field on Long Island.

An outrageous sum offered for the property housing the club pitted sentiment against practicality, and he told her he knew it was time to close The Grotto's doors and leave the father he loved to his heart, where Dominic would live on, with or without his beloved nightclub as a physical reminder.

Jenny stepped into the microscopy lab at the Switzerland branch of the Wheaton-Rhoades Institute in Basel and greeted Beatrix for the last time. Emotions were close to the surface, which surprised Jenny after all the curse-laden sessions they'd had together. Beatrix, Bea for short, was the reason she wasn't with Kathryn. She should hate her, and maybe deep down she did, but it wasn't Bea's fault she was so damn popular. Men, and a few women, flocked around her like butterflies to nectar, and Jenny's attention to detail and efficiency made it all possible. Bea filled a need that had been lacking for too long among the scientific set at the lab, and Jenny understood the attraction completely. She had to admit, she was a little smitten herself.

Bea was taller than her by about a foot and weighed over a ton, which might have intimidated some, but Jenny felt like she'd known her forever from the moment she laid eyes on her.

She'd seen artist's renderings of these behemoth electron microscopes in scientific magazines—commercial models wrapped in beautiful dark wood art deco cabinets with chromium accents. Bea, named after her model name, was not one of them. She was like the machine Jenny had trained on in Toronto. No fancy cabinets, just shiny cylinders, heavy copper piping, valves, pumps, fans, switches, and dials contained in a hastily constructed wooden base that Jenny swore was part of the crate the instrument arrived in. Bea wasn't pretty, but she was all hers. Now she was someone else's.

She'd longed for this day. Kathryn was waiting with extraordinary patience for her. Jenny had let her down so many times since the war had ended. Cables with a date, promising she was coming home. Cables with heartfelt apologies when something delayed her departure. This happened often enough that she feared if it went on much longer, Kathryn wouldn't open them anymore. If Kathryn's pain was anything like the knife in her heart with every delay, she wouldn't blame her. Jenny decided not to send another one until she was about to board her flight home—and she made sure Wheaton-Rhoades paid for transatlantic passage by air, not sea. She was not staying away from Kathryn one moment longer than necessary. She would go insane on a ship's crossing.

"Bittersweet, hm, kitten?" Miriam Reynolds asked from the doorway.

Miriam was the only other American at the lab, and her first friend when she arrived a year and a half ago.

"I didn't think I'd miss her, but I will."

Miriam came to her side and put her arm around her shoulder. "You single-handedly put this lab on the map, Jenny Ryan."

Jenny scoffed. "Bea did that."

Miriam became serious, which was unusual. "Don't do that. Don't diminish your importance to this community."

Jenny had to admit, the Switzerland branch of the Wheaton-Rhoades Institute had no community when she arrived. The electron microscope was new but untested and nonfunctioning when she found it, due to the absence of a technician to service it. She battled misogyny, endless gawking, and unrelenting pressure to get the instrument working, and once she had, the lab became the most popular spot in town.

Thanks to Miriam, Jenny became popular too. Despite her usual outgoing personality, Jenny focused only on Beatrix, and then, as the scientists flocked to the instrument, she learned as much as she could from them about the fields that interested her most, much like she did in Toronto. Miriam forced her to socialize—group hikes in the mountains and drinks with the lab gang at the local watering hole. Jenny appreciated all of it, but she preferred working. It was all-consuming. There was no room for error there. She focused on her task until the heartbreaking longing she had for Kathryn became a dull ache in her mind and her heart. Socializing just made her melancholy. She wanted to share the beautiful mountain view with Kathryn. Hold her hand under the table at a bar. Watch her charm the socially inept scientists with just a smile and then beam with pride that Kathryn was hers. She wanted to feel her again, taste her again, make love to her again, and make up for every damn lost second stolen from them.

"I'll miss you," Miriam was saying.

Jenny turned and hugged her. "I'll miss you too." She released her and looked her up and down. "Listen, I may have a position for you in New York City. Interested?"

Miriam blinked in surprise. "What, leave this mountainous

paradise of snow, chocolate, cheese, and Edelweiss for the dirty, noisy, claustrophobic chaos of the Big Apple? *Yes, please!*"

Jenny laughed and hugged her again. "I'll be in touch."

She gave Bea one more self-satisfying look and began her journey home.

CHAPTER TWENTY-SEVEN

*E*merging from the Pelham Parkway Station on her way home, Kathryn felt as old as the wooden El car that had just carried her up the Dyre Avenue shuttle line. She had enjoyed the nostalgic ride up the Third Avenue El as she escaped Midtown—anything to avoid the overcrowded Lexington Avenue subway—but today, the jostle and bustle verged on overwhelming. Between seeing Luc again, receiving his gift, mourning Dominic, and missing Jenny, she felt emotionally untethered for the first time in a long time.

Stepping through the French doors of Clay's guesthouse, the place she'd called home for the last eighteen months, she was surrounded by memories of a happy childhood before everything went horribly wrong. Old family photographs, familiar furniture from their home, and the knowledge that her father had spent his last years here, comforted her in a way she'd never thought those memories could. It didn't always feel that way.

When Clay met her at the pier when she returned home to New York City, he was kind and worried. She was defensive and wary. He was supposed to find her a place to live where she could privately fall apart and then, little by little, reintroduce herself to her family as she pulled herself together. On their drive home, his insistence that she stay in the guesthouse behind his house had sent her reeling. She was going to fall apart during her recovery—probably more than once. But how could she under his watchful eye? Or Nan's? Or, God forbid, Stephanie's? He'd never let her near his family again.

As if on cue, the inevitable became a self-fulfilling prophecy. His kindness felt suffocating, the car too small, and her thundering heart left her gasping for breath. Her panic attack forced Clay down an exit ramp and to the side of the road. She'd burst from the car and run blindly under the cathedral of steel girders supporting the elevated West Side Highway, trying to hide what she'd become. Clay caught up to her and was appropriately shocked by what he saw, but he didn't shrink from it. He soothed her until she calmed and wanted to know everything when she felt ready. She told him right then and there. There was no place for instability like hers in his home, and she waited for the realization to hit him. He took her in his arms instead and whispered promises of support and comfort. For the first time since her mother's death, family meant grace and forgiveness.

A light tapping on a glass pane in the door drew her attention back to the present. It was Nan, with a covered plate in her hand. She motioned for her to come in with a wave and a smile.

"Big night tonight," Nan said, "so I brought you a late lunch, early dinner. I know you don't like to eat too soon before a show, so I'm giving you plenty of time."

"Thank you, Nan. You didn't have to do that."

Nan put the plate in the refrigerator. "I know, but you've been … not yourself." She eyed the yellow cable from Jenny on the coffee table, still sealed in its envelope.

Kathryn eyed it too. She'd received it yesterday but hadn't had the strength to read it.

Nan sat beside her on the couch. "You haven't opened it."

Cables only came when Jenny needed to send a timely message;

otherwise, they relied on letters, which were maddeningly slow to arrive. International phone calls were outrageously expensive, if you could get a line, and usually of poor quality. They'd given up on those early on. After the war, the cables were only about Jenny's return home. The first was an apology that she would be stuck in the Switzerland lab until a replacement technician could be found. *Shouldn't take long,* she promised. And true to her word, another cable arrived with a departure date. It was finally over. They would be together. A year of longing and loneliness and the fear of their uncertain future rushed out of Kathryn like a held breath, extinguishing the torch she'd been carrying. She didn't need it anymore. Jenny was coming home. Elation, mixed with tears of joy and relief, nearly brought her to her knees. Nan was there to hold her up. Nan was there to hold her up again when the next cable came, bearing a simple, agonizing apology.

HOMECOMING DELAYED. SO SORRY. I M CRUSHED TOO.
LETTER ON ITS WAY. LOVE YOU SO MUCH=
J

This whiplash of emotions happened three times over the last six months. If the pattern held, the cable before her would carry disappointment, but with all the emotions of the day, it would feel like devastation.

"I can't, Nan. Not today. I'll read it tomorrow."

Nan took her hand. "I'm so sorry, darling."

And then Nan didn't say anymore about it. Kathryn loved this about her. She never would have expected it from their rocky beginning, but Nan's love and determination had become a crucial part of her recovery.

Nan patted her thigh and stood. "Come on, I'll sit with you while you eat."

"Thanks, but I'm not hungry."

Nan sank back into the couch and stared at her. "You didn't eat much breakfast. Did you eat while you were out?"

"No."

"Don't make yourself sick, Kath."

"I won't."

"Please, Kathryn."

Kathryn recognized a familiar panic in Nan's eyes. She placed her hand on her knee. "I won't, Nan. I promise," she said, reassuring her there would not be a repeat of the events that nearly doomed their fragile family before it even got started.

Nan and Clay's second child, Jackson Hammond II, was two months old when Kathryn had first felt the stirrings of discontent. She'd been home six months and was losing her grasp on whatever progress she'd made since she'd rejoined her family. She couldn't say it was the introduction of the child—Jackie, they called him—because he was an angel, and she adored him, but she'd started to feel like an outsider, a kindly voyeur observing a life that would never be hers. This was Clay's family—his children, wife, and happy home. The stark difference between their full lives and her wounded shell magnified her inadequacies, and she began to resent their happiness, then herself, for feeling that way. She even began to resent her home, as once comforting objects taunted her and became fuel for her bitter revolt of emotions. What a cruel charade she endured, all in the name of family.

It was an ungrateful attitude awash in self-pity, and she knew it, but she had to let it come and go. The routine was to wallow in it for a day or so and then it would pass, just as it always did. She drew the window shades, a signal to the family she needed time alone, and waited. But self-pity wrapped in anger continued to swell in her until it burst like a rain-sodden cloud, exposing the dark roots of its poison. The facade of progress she'd created washed away, and she was back in the mire where she started. Demons she'd thought conquered found their tongues. Undeserving. Weak. Toxic. The hollow ache of unbearable loneliness and lost hope washed over her, pulling her under in a torrent of despair. Her longing for Jenny left no room to ride out the pain until it let her go. It would never let her go. She was still clinging to Jenny as a savior. The brutal truth was that in the end, she'd only drown her too.

"Save Jenny," the demons whispered. "*Save* her. Let her go."

That sounded right. Save her. When Kathryn loosened her hold on Jenny, she sank beneath the barrage of torment and watched their future slip beyond her reach. The void welcomed her, and the light above her grew dim. Panic gripped her. No. This was wrong.

"That's it," the demons cooed to the contrary.

No. Jenny. Their beautiful life. She promised to fight. She clawed for the light, for their love, for their future, but it was gone.

The rest of her sins took that opportunity to pronounce her situation as hopeless, and they wrapped themselves around her ankles like sand-filled sacs pulling her down, down, down.

Darkness came, and with it, debilitating fear. Her heart raced and she couldn't move. *Breathe*, she kept telling herself, but it only prolonged the torture. Voices tried to fool her into trusting them, but she knew better. Hands reached for her and held her down. It was all too familiar. The voices became angry, and a syringe came at her. She was helpless to resist and swore Bouchaule had come back to finish the job. She cried out and struggled with all her might. "You're dead!" she screamed. "You're dead!" But he merely smiled as he injected her, and then the world faded away with lies of comfort and reassurance drifting down to her ears.

Nan had stayed by her side that terrible night and all the next day, pushing through the awkward silence with the same haughty indignation she applied to any situation that made her uncomfortable.

Kathryn had just wanted the woman standing vigil over her to leave so she could suffer her humiliation in private.

"You can go home now, Nan," she had said the next morning, huddled in the corner of the sofa, looking like the wrong end of a night of hard drinking. "I'm okay."

Nan looked her up and down. "I think not."

"Please, I just want to be alone."

Nan crossed her arms. "Being alone is what got you into this state."

Kathryn looked away. Nan meant well, but she couldn't possibly understand what she was going through. If she wouldn't leave when asked nicely, Kathryn was certainly capable of driving her away with rudeness. "You don't know what you're talking about."

"You're right. I have no idea what brought this on, but I'll not let it happen again."

Kathryn shook her head. "Believe it or not, Nan, it's not up to you. Please just leave."

Tears welled in Nan's eyes, and Kathryn thought she'd turn on her heel and go, but then Nan did something unexpected. She grabbed her by the shoulders, and with more desperation than she'd ever seen or expected from the woman, she shouted, "The doctor wanted to take you away from us, Kathryn! To commit you!"

"Then maybe you should have let him," Kathryn had snapped defensively, feeling like an ant burning in the sun under Nan's intense glare. She didn't belong here. How many episodes like last night's would they tolerate? What if Stephanie had seen her that way? The family experiment wasn't working, and now they knew they couldn't trust her. It was time to get her own place, just like she wanted from the beginning.

Her response twisted Nan's face into a grimace of pained emotion. She put her hand over her mouth as she straightened and turned away. Kathryn saw her swiping tears from her cheeks and regretted putting them there, but why did the woman care so much? Nan quickly composed herself and turned around wielding determined fury and an accusing finger. "You begged me not to let them take you last night."

"I was out of my head. I didn't know what I was saying."

"I think you knew exactly what you were saying."

Kathryn knew she couldn't thwart a determined Nan on the warpath, but she wouldn't become the woman's next pet project, falling in line with the endless parade of charities she made time for in between raising two children and running a household.

"I am not discussing this," Kathryn had said. "I'm begging you to leave me alone until I choose to have company, and if you cannot respect my wishes, I'm leaving, and I mean immediately."

Nan raised her chin and called her bluff. "You leave now and I will have you committed myself."

"Don't threaten me!" Kathryn shouted, as her panic, masquerading as anger, propelled her to her feet.

"Oh, it's not a threat," Nan warned. "It will be a necessity if you leave us in your current state, and you know it."

Kathryn tried to maintain her incensed posturing, but the truth wouldn't let her.

"What if we hadn't been here?" Nan went on, her voice rising in pitch and volume. "What if you had hurt yourself, or someone else? What then, Kathryn? What? What if you were living alone in some godforsaken hole in the wall where nobody gives a damn about you? What would have happened then?"

Nothing good, Kathryn had to admit. The room became unbearably small, and every word out of Nan's mouth stole more air from it.

"They would have found you dead in a corner, rotting in your own filth because you pushed away everyone who loved you or cared about you. Is that how you want this to end? Is it?"

Kathryn found it hard to breathe as Nan's prophetic description of her ignoble death etched itself into her brain like a forgone conclusion.

"What about Jenny?" Nan continued. "If you won't do it for yourself, do it for her."

"Jenny can't fix it, Nan. You can't fix it. Only I can, and I'm failing miserably. Don't you see?" Of course she couldn't see. Nan barely knew her, and what she did know would hardly endear her to her.

Nan shrugged awkwardly into the sudden silence between them, resettling her flowered dress on her shoulders as if her outburst had tarnished the shine on her fine breeding. "I'm sorry, Kathryn," she said in clipped tones, clasping her trembling hands at her midsection. "I know you're frustrated, and I don't mean to raise my voice, but I must insist you stay and let us help you."

Kathryn might have found Nan's attempt to restore her lofty disdain comical if her world weren't crashing down around her. She'd done everything right since she'd arrived. She'd faced her demons head on, mended fences with her brother, and waited patiently for the day she would be well enough to stand on her own. Instead, she was still a broken woman chasing a flickering light in a constantly twisting maze. There was no escape. She knew she should fight. For herself. For Jenny. For their beautiful life. But despair had sapped the last ounce of determination from her, and she slowly sank to the edge of the sofa.

Nan sat beside her, and Kathryn leaned into her, numbly drawn to her strength like she was the last way station before the end of the world. She barely held back her tears.

"I don't think I'm going to make it, Nan."

Nan swallowed, and when she spoke, her voice was wavering but full of love and kindness. "But do you want to, Kath?"

It was a simple question, but her answer meant everything. Once you give up hope, she had taught her trainees, you are truly doomed. As a young girl, Kathryn had been devastated by the actions of her father and the subsequent abandonment by her brother, and now, years later, here was Nan, of all people, throwing the proverbial cape over the mud patch so she could cross unsullied to the other side. It felt like a trick. It made no sense that the woman cared so much. Sure, she was Clay's wife. Sure, technically, they were family. And, as expected, Nan played the part flawlessly. But surely, her sister-in-law was merely tolerating her presence for Clay's and Stephanie's sakes … just like she was merely biding her time until she was well enough to get on with her life.

That's what she told herself to make her dependence on them safe, but when Nan reached out and put her arms around her, she remembered what it was like to feel truly safe, to trust. Jenny had taught her that, and her voice filled her head and heart. *"Please let them help you,"* Jenny had said before they parted in England. She would, but first she had to square things with Nan.

"I know my being here isn't ideal. I promise I'm doing my best to get out of your hair."

Nan didn't say anything, and Kathryn thought she'd hurt her feelings, but after a beat, she straightened and cleared her throat.

"I had a free-spirited older sister. When I was young, my austere parents tossed her out of the house, sure she would quickly come to her senses and return. She did not. She died of a drug overdose four months later, alone and on the streets, at the age of eighteen."

Kathryn sat up. "Oh, Nan."

"That was the end of our family. My parents divorced. I lived with my mother. My brother lived with my father. When I met Clay and learned he had a sister, I was delighted. Then we met. You hated me. Do you remember?"

The memory, long buried, came back to her, and she cringed internally at the actions of her twelve-year-old jealous self. "I do. You took him away from me."

Nan exhaled a chuckle and squeezed her. "You were horrid about it."

Kathryn recalled a summer filled with temper tantrums and pouting. She covered her eyes. "Could this day get any more embarrassing?"

"You are my family, Kathryn, and I love you. I will always be here for you, and this home is yours for as long as you want or need it. Please stay."

She didn't want to leave, she didn't want to bide her time, and she didn't want to be merely tolerated by her family. As much as she wanted to be left alone to lick her wounds, she didn't want to fight alone—she couldn't. She had a family and Jenny, and she was loved. All she had to do was let them.

Kathryn sank back into Nan's arms, surrendering her pride, her fear, and the painful memories of the past that had rendered family an emotional liability. It felt right. She was safe.

"I'll stay. I want to make it. I have to."

"That's all I need to know, darling," Nan said, holding her tightly. "That's all I need to know."

CHAPTER TWENTY-EIGHT

enny settled into the roomy seat on the American Overseas Airlines DC-4 that would carry her over the Atlantic and back into Kathryn's arms. It was 3 a.m., and she'd had a day of travel from Switzerland behind her already. She was on the longest leg of her journey now, after refueling in Shannon, Ireland. Ten hours over the open waters of the Atlantic to their next refueling stop in Gander, Newfoundland, and then a five-hour flight home after that.

She'd waited until she was at Hurn Airport in England to cable Kathryn with the flight information and the long-awaited good news that she was really coming home this time. After passing through several time zones, she should arrive at LaGuardia at 2 p.m. on Saturday. She'd call Kathryn and tell her to meet her at the house. Those first few moments would be private and not in a busy airport or at Kathryn's place, where her family would be respectful but a looming presence just the same. No, they would be utterly alone. They'd run into each other's arms, kiss savagely, and then separate to arm's length as they tried to take each other in. Tears would blur their vision, and they'd laugh as they came together again in an embrace that neither would relinquish. Jenny could almost feel Kathryn's warm body pressed against hers and her voice, heavy with emotion, whispering, "I've missed you so. I can't believe you're finally in my arms again."

Jenny's pounding heart joined her humming body, and all the longing she'd held in check since they parted threatened to burst from her in a sob.

"Are you all right?" the stewardess asked over the constant drone of the piston-powered engines in the unpressurized cabin.

Jenny blinked and wiped a tear from her cheek. "I'm fine. Thank you. Just returning home after too long an absence. I'm a little emotional."

The stewardess, the picture of professionalism in her blue tailored AOA skirt suit and side hat expressed just the right balance of kindness and concern when she placed her hand on Jenny's shoulder and smiled in understanding. "We'll have you home in no time." She eyed the small case that Jenny had set on its side in the unoccupied seat beside her. "Would you like me to put that up?"

Jenny glanced at the shelf holding a blanket and pillow above her and shook her head. "I'd like to keep it with me, thanks."

When the stewardess moved on to the next passenger, Jenny reached for the case as if she were reaching for Kathryn's hand. It might as well have been. Inside was a journal she'd kept of her time in Switzerland and eighteen months' worth of letters, V-mails, cables, drawings, photographs—anything Kathryn had sent while they were apart. When days were long and loneliness seeped in, these pieces of Kathryn's heart and soul carried her love across the miles and bridged the distance between them.

With every soft rustle of paper in her hand and every faint trace of Kathryn's scent on the page, Jenny imagined her sitting beside her, their fingers entwined, sharing their troubles and their dreams.

As promised, Kathryn had been brutally honest about her struggles with her recovery. Those letters brought tears, and Jenny felt helpless, knowing the events had happened weeks before. Often, another letter would quickly follow, assuring her she was fine. Kathryn adopted this habit early after Jenny overreacted to Kathryn's first cable announcing her arrival home.

. . .

Jenny had been having a frustrating day in the lab, which was not unusual in those first few weeks at WRI's Switzerland facility. Beatrix needed extensive testing and calibration. Adding to that pressure, Jenny was incessantly worried about Kathryn. She should have arrived home in New York City by now, but Jenny had heard nothing. It was driving her mad. She avoided newspapers, because if she read of a torpedoed transport ship, she would fear the worst and might lose her mind. Fucking war. When her concern became overwhelming, which was often, she would take a deep breath, or a stiff drink, and repeat as needed, day after day.

Bea was almost ready for action, but a preliminary check of the instrument's vacuum system showed a leak. It was a small one, just outside the acceptable range, but it wasn't safe for operation.

Jenny let out a groan and tossed the service manual to her desk. "Dammit."

Miriam came into the room waving a yellow Western Union envelope. "Cable for you, Ryan. Hope it cheers you up."

Jenny met her in two strides and snatched it from her hand. Miriam offered a knowing glance over her shoulder as she left the room.

```
DEAREST. HOME SAFE AND SOUND. YOUR THREAT
WORKED. CLAY TAKING ME IN. JOKE. HE S BEEN
GRAND. LETTER ON ITS WAY. MISS YOU. LOVE YOU=
K
```

Relief pushed tears from her eyes, and she blinked them away as she read the cable again and again. Relief quickly gave way to concern. Kathryn didn't say she was fine. Safe and sound is not fine. Is it? She looked on the back of the cable as if she'd find more words there. Her heart raced with worry. *Miss you. Love you. Home safe and sound.* Jenny closed her eyes, trying not to overthink it. She's fine. *Home safe and sound. Letter on its way.* She'd tell her everything in the letter. The thought of communicating through letters made her heart hurt. Between the war and the Office of Censorship, a letter could take weeks, months even, to arrive. It was like gazing into the distant past of a starlit sky. Jenny hated it, but this was their life now.

It had been easier in Toronto, where she'd put Kathryn out of her mind completely and focused solely on her work. She was trying to do the same here, but it wasn't the same. Kathryn was hers now. She worried about her constantly. How was she doing? What was she doing? Was she being kind to herself or beating herself up? Jenny had no control over any of it. She had to trust in Kathryn's strength and the people around her. Her family was with her. They would look after her. Kathryn would be fine. Please let her be fine. To ease her mind, she sent a slightly panicked cable to make sure. Kathryn's reply was encouraging.

```
I M FINE. PROMISE. STOP WORRYING. PLEASE DON T
READ BETWEEN THE LINES. IT WILL ONLY ADD UNDUE
ANGUISH TO AN ALREADY ANGUISHED SEPARATION.
GOOD NEWS. LATE BLOOMING WILDFLOWERS IN THE
NEIGHBOR S GARDEN. I MAY LIBERATE SOME. DON T
TELL ANYONE. DREAMING OF YOU. LOVE=
K
```

Jenny smiled at the memory. Kathryn had sent a pressed wildflower in her letters when in season and painted small ones in watercolor on the upper right-hand corner of the thin stationary when out of season. Jenny carefully saved each flower in its envelope, intending to frame them when she came home.

What a long journey they'd had, but that half-life was over. Kathryn would be in her arms soon.

The afternoon sun seeped into Kathryn's living room and brought out the beautiful reds in her mother's mahogany Steinway baby grand.

She sat at the bench and lifted the fallboard to the sweet subtle scent of aged wood and polish, a smell that always brought back thoughts of her mother and the hours they'd spent at the keyboard together. Sadness tinged the edges of her memories when she remembered she might never regain her ability to play the way she used to. She'd learned to compensate for the weakness in her hand by adjusting her movement and alignment. Power came from the arm, after all, not the fingers, but she still stumbled over keys when muscle memory took over and her physical limitations betrayed her. Progress would only come through exercise and repetition, so each day, she pushed through the nagging ache and stiffness until her fingers were limber enough to play. It was frustrating, but the instrument itself always brought her comfort.

She was glad for that today because, as the hours passed, the sense of unease that had plagued her all day grew heavier. She'd let the buildup to the evening's performance overwhelm her. Besides the finality of it all, it was three years, almost to the day, that she had met Jenny at The Grotto. Her absence on this night of all nights felt ominous, like the disconcerting stillness before a storm. She convinced herself it was just nerves.

The closing of the nightclub represented not only a farewell to Dominic's dream but also her career onstage and the golden swing era. Music was changing, and she could change too, but she had grown away from that scene. While she hadn't performed for an audience since Paris, occasional jam sessions with some of the old gang assured her she was perfectly capable of returning to the stage should she wish to. But she didn't. Not as a career. That life was over for her. Everything about it that she'd thrived on—freedom, purpose, emotional connection, escape—she'd now found in other aspects of her life. Saying goodbye to that part of her past was bittersweet. Once, it had defined her, but beyond it was a new start that had begun in the most unlikely way.

When she'd first come home, she'd struggled with loneliness, even though her family was all around her. Nan had sensed that the isolation of idle recovery was doing more harm than good, so she introduced her to the War Orphans Relocation committee chair, hoping a few hours a day devoted to something other than internal dissection would help her move forward. The organization needed French speaking volunteers to help transition the displaced children into their new families in a strange country. Kathryn jumped at the opportunity to finally be useful and found working with the children rewarding in a way she hadn't expected. Their resiliency was inspiring. These lost little souls, stripped of family, friends, and the only home they'd ever known, were transported across the sea from Europe to America, where well-meaning strangers speaking a foreign language expected them to trust and behave and be thankful for the kindness shown them.

Some were quick to adjust, others were not. Kathryn understood well their fear and anger and gravitated toward that troubled group. Those children spent more than the customary six weeks with the organization, sometimes as long as three months before they were placed, and watching them slowly come back to life and begin to thrive in their new surroundings made Kathryn feel like their progress was her progress. She began looking forward to seeing them each day. Children in general were amazing creatures, but these kids had endured traumas and tragedies that would bring adults to their knees, yet they still retained their sense of wonder amidst their lost innocence.

She was hired by some of the families to tutor the children in English because of her great rapport with them, which she was happy to do. That led to offers for full-time positions, which inspired her to finish her abandoned teaching degree. Now she had a job at a local private school teaching art on Mondays and Fridays, music on Tuesdays and Thursdays, and French to the older kids on Wednesdays. Never in a million years did she imagine this as her life, but she cherished the normality of it. She felt like she belonged and was helping instead of hurting for a change. The routine grounded her, and it was a welcome change from the chaos of her former life. All she needed was Jenny by her side.

She worried Jenny would find her and her domestic life dull

compared to the woman she'd first met and fallen in love with. Elegant gowns and high heels had given way to sensible dresses and comfortable flats, and instead of plotting missions and deciphering codes, she was planning lessons and shaping young lives. She usually consigned these fears to a journal she'd kept since she returned home, but she confessed this fear to Jenny, who eased her mind in her next letter.

I want you to be happy, Kathryn. That's all I want. And if that means I don't have to fend off strangers ensnared by your beauty in some smoky club or worry myself to death because you're off on some mission to save the world, well, I'll make that sacrifice every day and twice on Sunday. I love you. You're amazing. You're everything I want and need, and I can't wait to come home to you.

Kathryn couldn't wait either, but she would have to. She took Jenny's cable out of her pocket, where she'd put it to feel closer to her, despite the looming fear of disappointment, and held it to her heart. "I miss you."

She closed the fallboard without playing a note and exhaled. She had to pull herself together and prepare for her show. It was time to eat something, shower, and put everything out of her mind except her upcoming performance. She offered one more glance at the cable and then reverently leaned it against the piano's solid mahogany music desk. She'd be stronger tomorrow.

Her path to the kitchen was interrupted by the ringing telephone. She glanced at her watch, wondering who would call at 2 p.m.?

"Hello?"

CHAPTER TWENTY-NINE

D earest J,

I won't say that I count the days until I hear from you again, because I promised you no more lies. The truth is, I count the minutes. I miss you so, I can't stand it sometimes. You sound like you're making a place for yourself there. They need only look beyond their inflated egos to see how brilliant you are. I'm so proud of you. Thank you for the picture of you in your lab coat standing beside Bea. She's lucky to have you, and I'm not beyond admitting I'm jealous. I may need my pump valves serviced when you return home.

Jenny smiled as she folded up one of her favorite letters from Kathryn and tucked it safely back into its envelope. It was her first microscopy-induced double entendre, but it wasn't the last, especially during the war, when all their communications were censored. Kathryn used at least two per letter and one that was actually censored. She'd have to ask her to act that one out when she saw her. A glance at her wristwatch told her they'd be landing in Gander soon. With a generous refueling estimate, she would be in Kathryn's arms in six hours. It seemed like a dream. She realized she was grinning like an idiot and looked around the plane, wondering if anyone noticed.

The cabin lights were low, and most of the passengers were sleeping. Jenny had been awake almost twenty-four hours, and she should be sleeping too, but she couldn't turn off her mind. She stared out the window into the dawning new day, and the smile left her as she caught sight of her reflection. She looked older, and it wasn't because of the lack of sleep.

She leaned back against the headrest, taking stock of the last few years of her life. Europe and all that had happened there was behind her, but the scars would always remain. She'd once asked Kathryn, "How do you know if you'll be able to kill someone?"

After trying to explain the unexplainable, Kathryn had simply said, "It's different over there. It all makes sense somehow when you're there." And it had.

Jenny briefly thought of Bouchaule. She'd had a year and a half to think about what she'd done. Was she sorry? No. Would his death haunt her? No. Did it change her? Yes. The whole war had. She was no longer the ingenue Kathryn had fallen in love with. Sometimes she worried that she'd changed too much. What if that's what Kathryn loved about her? What would happen now that that woman didn't exist anymore?

She didn't think that way often, but six hours away from facing that possible reality, she did what she always did when insecurity and doubt seeped in: she reached for Kathryn. She opened her box of letters again and pulled out a well-worn envelope containing a letter and a recent picture of Kathryn with a note written on the back.

Bernie was in town last week. I'm sure you know he's started his own photog studio out in L.A. while Robert is trying to break into Hollywood. We had a lovely afternoon together, and we both thought you would love this. I would say I love you more than you'll ever know, but you must know. Mustn't you?

Forever yours,

K

. . .

The black-and-white photograph—burnished with B. Roth Photography in gold in the lower corner—was a close-up portrait of Kathryn, with her head resting on the back of a chair Jenny didn't recognize. Her face was tilted toward the camera, lips parted slightly, and love and longing filled her eyes in the soft light coming from a source to the far side. Kathryn's beauty and vulnerability both broke her heart and filled it with love.

Nerves were understandable, she kept telling herself, but questioning Kathryn's love after everything they'd been through was ridiculous. Yes, she had changed, and a heavy burden now rested on her shoulders, but Kathryn had changed too. Through letters filled with both tears and laughter, Kathryn had chronicled her struggles and triumphs. Jenny had watched her raw vulnerability gradually transform into purpose and drive as Kathryn found solace in her family, her teaching, and the gentle cadence of everyday life. It was all Jenny ever wanted for her.

She put the photo in her suit jacket pocket, close to her heart. She had the feeling she'd need it to calm her nerves again before the trip home was over.

Jenny peeked out the window as the plane began its descent and the coast of Newfoundland slid into view. She smiled and mentally checked the last refueling stop off her list of things standing between her and Kathryn. The captain's voice crackled over the intercom, announcing their approach to Gander airport.

"We'll have you on the ground in a few minutes, folks. Unfortunately, we may have an extended stay with our friends here in Gander due to some equipment issues with a fuel storage pump."

Groans went around the cabin.

"Sorry folks, I know," the captain said, as if he could hear the discontent all the way up in the cockpit. "It could take a while, but rest assured, we'll get you back on your way as soon as possible. In the meantime ..."

Jenny didn't hear the rest as she slumped back in her seat and watched her carefully planned reunion with Kathryn at the house vanish into thin air. The weight of exhaustion, unchecked emotions, and disappointment came together in a frustrated exhale. "You have got to be fucking kidding me."

Framed by soft lights, Kathryn leaned into the vanity mirror in a dressing room down the hall from The Grotto's stage and touched up her makeup. The anxiety she'd felt earlier in the day had run its course. It helped that Stephanie had called and asked if she wanted to go for a walk in the park. That wasn't unusual for a Saturday, but she had a sneaking suspicion that Nan might have nudged her into it this time. Nan was worried about her and knew she could get lost in her own head sometimes.

Kathryn tried not to distract herself when that happened, opting instead to take a hard look at whatever upset her so that she could face it honestly and work through it. But today, she didn't mind. The crisp March air did her good, and an afternoon with her effervescent niece was always good for her soul.

Her soul now stared back at her from the mirror, and she was no longer afraid to face it. The scars of her past remained, but she didn't run from them anymore. The war and everything she'd done in service to it had revealed the darkest parts of herself. She had surrendered to them, deeming herself unworthy of love or kindness. She never expected to fall in love with Jenny—Jenny, who saw through her pain and self-loathing and recognized she was more than the sum of her tragic past. Jenny, who had seen and experienced the worst of her and loved her anyway.

Kathryn rationalized her darkness, blaming it on circumstances— the war and losing her mother and family at such a young age—

because that's how the mind makes sense of trauma, but the darkness was still a part of her. She'd come to understand that's all it was though, just a part. Goodness lived in her too. Jenny saw it, and so did her family. And staring at the settled woman in the mirror, she finally saw it too. Emotion welled in her. Grace, acceptance, and forgiveness had pushed her demons aside, leaving them muttering in the dark while she stepped into the light. In this quiet moment of self-reflection, with her eyes shining with unshed tears, every flaw melded seamlessly with every victory, and the shadows of her past became distant echoes of a complex life that had led her to this place of calm and clarity.

"I know who you are, baby," Jenny had said more than once.

Kathryn was just beginning to know that woman too.

She eyed Jenny's cable, which she'd tucked into the mirror's frame. It was moments like this that Kathryn missed Jenny the most. She closed her eyes and imagined her arms around her. Jenny would kiss her and whisper, "I'm so proud of you." A tear slid down Kathryn's cheek, and she uttered a quiet curse as she plucked a tissue from its box to save what she could of her makeup.

Two sharp knocks on the dressing room door startled her. "Ten minutes, Miss Hammond."

"Thank you," she called out, and reached for her compact.

She'd just finished applying her powder when a gentler knock came.

"Kat?"

She smiled. "Come in."

"Are you ready?" Luc asked, leaning on the open door handle.

"As I'll ever be."

She didn't try to hide her emotions, and it only took a beat for him to notice. He quickly stepped in, shutting the door behind him, and went to her side. "What is it?"

"I'm fine. Honestly. Just an emotional day."

His gaze shifted to Jenny's cable, and he gave her shoulder a reassuring squeeze. "You don't have to perform tonight if you're not up to it."

"Are you kidding? This is my swan song. I wouldn't miss it for the world."

His expression soured. In the last month since they'd reconnected over the club's closing, they'd had many discussions about her decision to leave the stage. He had tried to sell her on part-time gigs during the summer, when she wasn't teaching, but smoky clubs and early morning hours had lost their appeal. Every discussion about it ended with Luc wearing his *oh, the crying shame of it all* face. It was comical now. She couldn't say she'd never perform on a stage again, but she didn't want the pressure of that expectation. When she was ready, her performance, like tonight's, would be for pleasure, not obligation.

She put her hand on his. "I'm where I belong. I'm happy."

"I know. Can't blame a guy for trying to put beautiful music into the world."

The muffled notes of a trumpet dancing around a walking bassline seeped into the silence between them. Kathryn smiled as the band onstage played a classic swing tune that was nearly unrecognizable under the asymmetrical phrasing of its bebop arrangement.

"Speaking of beautiful music," she said, cocking her head toward the sound, "your dad would have hated this."

Luc laughed. "I know, but the crowd loves it."

Kathryn put the finishing touches on her face and noticed Luc had grown serious as he watched her in the mirror.

"You look stunning," he said reverently, his soft voice carrying more weight than his words.

She turned to face him and saw the sorrow of the day swimming in his eyes. She rose and embraced him in a silent farewell. To the club. To Dominic. To each other.

Luc stepped back. "Don't be a stranger after this, okay?"

Kathryn promised she wouldn't, but they had said the same after Dominic's funeral, and neither had kept in touch. The war had brought them together, and peacetime would watch them drift apart, but they would always hold a special place in each other's hearts.

A flurry of improvisational scatting came from the musicians on stage, and Luc raised his brow. "Whoops, we missed our cue."

They laughed and dashed toward the stage.

Unbridled excitement had turned into a case of nerves by the time Jenny exited the cab from LaGuardia and dropped off her luggage, coat, and hat with the checkroom girl at The Grotto. She followed Kathryn's distant voice as if it were a siren's song coming through the double doors leading to the club. She'd made it as far as the hostess when the woman held out her hand expectantly.

"Invitation?"

Jenny pulled herself away from Kathryn's song. "What?"

"This is a private event. Invitation only. Without one, I'll have to ask you to leave."

Jenny's exhale was part laughter, part disbelief. She'd flown halfway around the world to get here. Her first glimpse of Kathryn in eighteen months was one bar length away, and nothing was going to stop her now.

"May I speak with Luc Vignelli, please?"

"I'm sorry, Mr. Vignelli is very busy tonight." She gestured toward the entrance. "Please, if you don't have an invitation …"

Jenny searched the bar over the hostess's shoulder for Bobby, Kathryn's favorite bartender. He would vouch for her. He wasn't there, so she leaned in, remaining as calm as she could. "I don't want to cause a scene, but I am this far away"—she held her thumb and forefinger barely apart—"from turning this place upside down to get into that room."

Before she really got going, she heard a familiar voice. "Jenny?"

She looked up to see Luc rounding the corner into the bar, and she wilted in relief.

"Oh, thank God."

She'd barely had the last word out of her mouth when Luc bounded the space between them and wrapped her in a hug.

"I can't believe you're here," he said, releasing his hold and stepping back to look at her. "This is the best surprise ever. She's going to lose her mind."

He hugged her again.

Jenny frowned. "Surprise? I'm late, but Kat knows I'm coming."

Luc released her and glanced toward the main room. "I don't think she does."

Jenny closed her eyes. *Oh, Kat.* "She didn't read the cable."

"Who cares," Luc said enthusiastically, "You're here now. Come on. She just started." He took her hand.

The Grotto's enigmatic elegance hadn't changed. Moody dark corners formed by walls draped in gold-trimmed burgundy velvet surrounded a room of dimly lit tables under crystal-laden chandeliers. Kaleidoscopes of light glinted through the thick curls of cigarette smoke, painting muted spectral hues on the walls and ceiling.

The room opened up to the stage, where a spotlight illuminated Kathryn in a shimmering pewter gown, an ethereal vision that left Jenny breathless. In an instant, the guilt for not being with her, all the miles, the letters, and the endless waiting, evaporated. She marveled at Kathryn for a few frozen moments while she listened to the lyrics of "Bésame Mucho" roll off her tongue in Spanish as if she'd spoken the language her whole life. Mercy.

Luc leaned in. "Isn't she magnificent? Here, I'll take you backstage."

"No, I just … I just want to watch from out here."

"Nan and Clay are here. Would you like to join them?"

"No." She eyed the room and found the table she was looking for in the exclusive third tier wing. It was empty. "There."

Luc smiled. "Perfect. Kat reserved it for the evening, and I think we both know why."

It was their table, and Jenny loved that Kathryn couldn't bear anyone else sitting there tonight.

"Scotch neat?" Luc asked as they passed the bar.

"Club soda with lime, please." She wanted to be absolutely sober for this reunion.

Luc relayed the order and table number to the bartender and

escorted her to her seat. After another hug, he left her alone with the woman she loved.

Kathryn's powerful vocals during "The Song Is You" were a revelation. She'd never heard Kathryn sound more relaxed. Her eyes were closed more often than not, which told Jenny she was singing for herself rather than for the audience, something she had never done on Dominic's watch. Music critic Lionel Sinclair had always referred to Kathryn as "Sing It as Written" Hammond, a knock Jenny never understood, but tonight's vocal interpretations of songs she'd heard Kathryn sing many times proved Sinclair right about her former style —or nonstyle, as was the complaint. The songs were personalized now, alive, and Kathryn was the focus of the room, not background noise for late-night dinners and business meetings.

Jenny couldn't take her eyes off her. Gone was the fragile Kathryn she'd left in England. There was a new strength in her that was both mesmerizing and reassuring. She looked healthier than she'd ever seen her. The silk satin material of her gown created highlights in all the right places, as the strapless bodice converged with a supporting twist between her breasts and lifted a heavenly pillow of soft flesh to cradle the sparkling jewels around her neck. Her shoulder-length hair, styled into a wave and parted at the side, made her look younger, or maybe it was her triumphant demeanor. The room was hers.

The crowd's thunderous applause at the end of the song made Jenny beam with pride. Kathryn's broad smile was infectious, and when she lifted her white-gloved hand to the audience in a gesture of thanks, Jenny just barely resisted stepping forward to command her attention with a furious wave back. She fell back in line with the rest of the applauding crowd, content to let her heart and soul fill with a warm rush of memories that washed the years away.

All her nervous anxiety had disappeared, and it was like 1943 again. They were in love and it was just another night on the town. They would stay for a drink or two after the set and let the anticipation of what was to come peak their desire until their longing for each other urged them to take action. The memory of lustful looks and discreet caresses made for delightful torture, and Jenny smiled as she remembered the insufferable train rides to her house and the scandalous cab rides to Kathryn's place, as nosy cabbies adjusted their rearview mirrors to get a glimpse of the action in the back seat. Kathryn was notorious for arousing her in public just to watch her try to maintain some semblance of decorum, and tonight was no different, except this time, Kathryn wasn't even trying.

The telltale heat of arousal spread across Jenny's chest, and she was glad she was wearing a blouse and jacket instead of the spaghetti-strap gown she would have chosen had she made it to her house before the show. Instead, she'd made a mad dash in a taxi directly from the airport, stopping only to wash her face and brush her teeth in the ladies' room after she got off the plane. Not exactly the romantic reunion she'd imagined, but they would have years together to make romantic moments.

———

Kathryn stood in the wings, her heart racing as Luc introduced her onstage. She took in a deep breath and let it out slowly. She had no boss to please, no demons to exorcise, no persona to hide behind. She was just Kathryn, who taught art, music, and French to kids at the local private school.

The woman who had once lived on the edge, shrouded in half-truths and danger, seemed like a stranger now. She felt like an alcoholic going onstage sober for the first time. It felt new and liberating. A hush of anticipation rippled through the audience when Luc extended his hand to her. She raised her chin and donned a genuine full-faced grin when she stepped into the light to thunderous applause.

She was surprised by the audience's enthusiastic greeting, and a familiar adrenaline rush carried her to Luc's side.

"Tell me again how you don't miss this," Luc said in her ear before heading offstage.

She smirked at his departing back as the band leader kicked off the set with "Bésame Mucho." The Latin beat pulsed through the floor and rumbled in her chest while the sharp notes plucked from the steel guitar sent tingles up her spine. When the low hum of the male background singers joined in, the vibrant tapestry of sound enveloped her in a welcoming embrace. The energy of the room and the musicians around her sent her body thrumming.

Luc was right. She hadn't realized how much she'd missed the stage until this moment.

As the night went on, her performance was everything she could have hoped for, considering her prolonged absence. The players were tight and professional, but they all took liberties with their parts and infused the sets with a jam session atmosphere.

In the middle of her second set, she addressed the audience.

"I would like to take a moment to thank Luc for inviting me to participate in this very special occasion. It's bittersweet, of course, knowing this grand party is the last this club will ever see, but I will never forget the time I spent here or the generosity and love of Dominic Vignelli."

Murmurs of agreement went around the room.

"Dominic had very specific rules for music and how it was performed in his club, and I'm pretty sure we've broken every one of those rules tonight."

There was a smattering of laughter from the musicians and the audience.

"But in the spirit of the evening, I hope we'll be forgiven."

Luc arrived at the microphone with two coupes of champagne and handed her one. "You're forgiven."

Kathryn smiled and lifted her glass. "To Dominic and The Grotto. May they both live forever in our fondest memories."

A rumble of "*Salute!*" floated above the audience's raised glasses.

Kathryn shielded her eyes from the bright stage lights and acknowledged table thirty-six, in the fourth row behind the dance floor, with a nod and a smile, thanking them for their song request. The final set had been chosen by the audience from a list on their tables when they were seated. After the instrumental bridge, she went back to the microphone and finished her vocals.

As her evening onstage neared its end, she had mixed feelings about it. She loved being in front of a crowd again with her old bandmates, but she knew it was only sentiment calling her back to that life. The music scene and the solace she'd found there had been replaced by a fuller life than she'd ever imagined.

She took note of the final song and set the audience request list back on the piano. The band began "I've Never Forgotten," and, as per the other requests, Kathryn sang until the instrumental bridge and then wandered back to the list on the piano to note the table to thank. She paused in disbelief when she saw it was *their* table in the exclusive third tier. For a beat, she was perturbed that someone was at her reserved table, but the sentiment of the song and the source of the request couldn't be a coincidence. Her heartbeat raced as she anxiously turned and lifted a hand to block the spotlight. She couldn't believe her eyes. Jenny was there, raising a glass in her direction.

Kathryn gasped. "Jenny." She brought her hand to her mouth and then slid it to the base of her throat, afraid her thundering heart would beat out of her chest. She glanced toward the stairs and resisted the urge to run from the stage mid-song. She barely recovered in time to finish her vocals.

The last few measures were a blur, and she had no idea how she sounded, but the crowd gave her a standing ovation as she took her final bow and waved her thanks.

Luc met her as she hurried offstage, and she grabbed his arms. "She's here! Did you see her?"

"Sure. I gave her the keys to my office. She'll meet you there. Enjoy the champagne."

She hugged him. "Thank you."

Jenny stood on the third tier balcony in front of Luc's office, applauding with the rest of the crowd. Kathryn greeted Luc briefly on her way off the stage before gathering her gown and making her way down the steps. Despite her exhaustion, Jenny was buzzing with anticipation. She wanted to run to Kathryn, but patrons were intercepting her as she crossed the dance floor. Kathryn politely shook hands and accepted their well-wishes and remembrances, but Jenny recognized her determined tight-lipped smile as masked impatience. Kathryn raised desperate eyes to her before moving on to the next extended hand, and then the next. Jenny slipped into the office before she shouted at the crowd to make way.

Kathryn burst in a few minutes later like a cartoon character skidding to a stop. Her long gown was gathered in her fist, and she was breathing heavily from the climb up the stairs to the office. She was already crying.

No words were exchanged when they fell into each other's arms. Kathryn had played this scene in her mind a hundred times. In it, she wasn't laugh-sobbing uncontrollably in Jenny's arms, but here she was.

Jenny held on to her and let out a few laugh-sobs of her own.

"God, I've missed you," Kathryn finally managed when the sobbing subsided.

"I've missed you too."

"I want to look at you, but I can't let go."

Jenny squeezed her tighter. "I couldn't tear my eyes away from you tonight. You were incredible."

Kathryn finally released her, cursing under her breath when she couldn't see through her tears. She dabbed at her eyes with a gloved knuckle, trying to clear her vision. "I should have read your cable. I wouldn't be such a god-awful mess if I had."

Jenny held her at arm's length. "You are absolutely gorgeous, and I'm glad you didn't read it because—"

Kathryn got her first good look at Jenny in eighteen months. She was glorious. Obviously tired as hell, but so beautiful. She was explaining something in rapid-fire oratory, but her words drifted into the background. It was as if Kathryn couldn't look and listen at the same time.

"I had everything planned—" Jenny went on, her gaze darting around the room as her hands orchestrated the story.

Kathryn focused on Jenny's moving lips. God, those lips.

"I'd meet you at the house with champagne—"

Kathryn stepped closer.

"Candles and enough food to—"

She moved even closer.

Jenny's hands stilled. Her words faltered and became breathy. "—last a week, because that's how long I'm going to keep you in my—"

Kathryn cupped her face and gazed deeply into her eyes.

"Bed."

Their foreheads pressed together. Their breath mingled.

"But then we got delayed—"

Their lips brushed ever so slightly.

"I tried to send a—"

"Why are you still talking?"

"Clearly, I'm delirious."

"Would it help if I kissed you?"

"Let me check." Jenny took Kathryn back into her arms, into her mouth, and into her life again.

EPILOGUE

June 1949: Beach Haven, New Jersey

The early morning sun cast its golden glow through the sheer curtains of the bedroom at the beach house. Kathryn rested on her side, her head propped up by her elbow, lost in thought as she watched Jenny sleeping on her back beside her. The soft cotton sheets lay tangled at their waists, giving her a magnificent view of Jenny's body.

It was the end of a blissful week alone together at the shore. Her summer teaching break had just started, and Jenny's busy travel season was winding down with a trip to Chicago later in the day.

She wanted to reach out and touch her, but Jenny needed her sleep, especially after last night, when they had made love until way past midnight and then again just before dawn. The memory warmed her in all the right places and did nothing to help her keep her hands to herself.

Kathryn treasured weeks like this. They didn't get enough of them, but any time apart felt too long, so they both compromised when they could.

Jenny worked as if she was making up for lost time. She'd formed a bad habit during her time in Switzerland of spending all night at the lab. Kathryn didn't demand much, but she quickly broke her of that with support from Jenny's colleague, Miriam Reynolds, who agreed it was counterproductive. "Science moves at its own pace, kitten," Miriam had said, "and you burning your candle at both ends will not make it speed up." Apparently, she'd been telling Jenny that since they'd started working together, but Jenny was relentless in her quest for knowledge and answers about her blood's unique properties. The needle hadn't moved on that, which Kathryn knew was a point of frustration for Jenny, but she had a stellar group of scientists around her who she trusted, and she seemed happy, frustrations aside.

Kathryn had met the WRI group before she left England and was satisfied they only had Jenny's best interests in mind. They certainly could protect her better than she could at this point. A bodyguard discretely accompanied Jenny on her trips, and one was always nearby, but Kathryn put the urge to seek them out behind her long ago. After all this time, she rarely thought of them at all. True to its word, WRI had given Jenny everything they promised, and Jenny was flourishing in the environment they created. She was so proud of her. Jenny had always wanted to make a difference in the world, and her work was making that dream come true.

"You're staring at me while I sleep again," Jenny said groggily.

"I'm admiring you, and thank heavens you're awake, because I've been wanting to do *this* for the past hour."

Kathryn traced a soft circle on Jenny's breast.

"We don't have time for that again, Kat. I've got to head back to the city. I mean it this time."

Kathryn leaned over and took Jenny's erect nipple into her mouth, first sucking gently to approving mews, then harder, ending in a sharp nip.

"Fuck," Jenny gasped as her hands fisted in the sheets.

"Do you want me to stop?"

"Yes."

Kathryn drew back and looked her in the eyes. Jenny's heart raced under her hand, and her darkening eyes and writhing body did not signal stop.

"Dammit," Jenny muttered after a beat and gave in. She kissed Kathryn and pulled her on top of her, letting her thigh settle between her legs with a pleasurable moan. Kathryn started a rhythm with her hips, and Jenny clutched at her back, her moans escalating with every thrust against her core.

Kathryn eased her hand between them and slowly slipped inside her. Jenny broke the kiss with a guttural gasp. "You'd better make this fast and hard, Hammond. We cannot spend all day in bed today."

"Oh, yes, that would be just awful," Kathryn said between her own gasps, then did exactly what she was told.

Packed and ready to go, Jenny stood before the mirror and clipped on her earrings. Kathryn, wrapped in a silky peach colored robe, came up from behind her and wrapped her arms around her waist. Jenny looked at their reflection and nearly teared up. She'd dreamed of this life—of excelling in her field, running her own lab, and sharing her life with the woman she loved. Kathryn was everything she dreamed she could be and more. They'd both feared that the changes they'd gone through while they were apart would alter their relationship. It wasn't all smooth sailing when she arrived home. They both harbored insecurities that seemed ridiculous now, but they were open and honest with each other, and the more they rediscovered each other the deeper they fell in love. Looking at their happy reflection now, it seemed silly that they'd wondered if what they'd had was real or just a product of extraordinary circumstances, but they both feared that when they were first reunited. They hesitantly exchanged the journals they had kept for each other, questioning if what had happened during their separation mattered anymore. But they had read them together most evenings, periodically adding more context when needed. Sometimes Kathryn would mutter curses in solidarity with

Jenny's frustrations at work, and Jenny would shed silent tears at Kathryn's struggles. Sometimes they would just reach for the other's hand—no words necessary—when things they couldn't write in censored letters appeared. This intimate emotional exchange spanned the ache of lost time and brought them closer than ever as a couple.

She had to admit, she was the unstable element in their relationship. As Arthur Wheaton had predicted, she had to work twice as hard as a man half as smart to get ahead. Not at WRI but in the greater field, where respect was hard to come by. Kathryn listened patiently to her frustrations and never complained when plans changed last minute or a trip came up out of the blue. Kathryn had her own busy schedule, working with her school kids, volunteering with veterans groups, and performing at small clubs when the opportunity or mood struck her.

Jenny felt there was never enough time together, and she took the blame for it, but Kathryn made sure they always had time away from everything, like this past week, where they could focus on each other.

Jenny checked in with Kathryn often to make sure they were all right. Kathryn always said it was unnecessary, but Jenny felt it was better safe than sorry.

As Kathryn planted a path of gentle kisses below her ear and to her collarbone, Jenny entwined their fingers. "I'm sorry I've been away so much lately."

"'Tis the season for brainy science things," Kathryn mumbled into her neck.

"I mean it."

Kathryn turned her in her arms until they were facing each other. "Is everything okay?"

"This week together at the beach has been wonderful. Heading back to the real world is … well, I know I work a lot, and there's a lot of travel, and I don't want—"

"Jenny?" Kathryn brought Jenny's left hand to her lips and kissed the wildflower engraved gold band on her ring finger. "Yours," she said, reiterating the word engraved inside.

Jenny smiled. For better or worse, they had promised each other.

She kissed the matching band on Kathryn's ring finger, reiterating the inscription inside hers. "Mine."

Kathryn loved reminding Jenny that nothing would tear them apart again. She grinned remembering the day two years ago when they exchanged rings on the deserted beach of Dominic's island. The island was a state park now, but it would forever be the sacred place where their love was found and then sealed in a sunset ceremony between just the two of them. Their union had no legal standing, but their closest family and friends knew what it meant. Strangers assumed they had husbands, and that worked in their favor too.

Kathryn enjoyed watching Jenny from across the room at events where she interacted with her colleagues. She had a habit of twisting her ring when her patience was wearing thin with the conversation or if she was just biding her time until she could set someone straight.

Jenny broke her reverie as she stared at her from the mirror. "What's that ridiculous smile about?"

"You. How much I love you."

Jenny grew serious. "I hate going away."

"It's only ten days this time, and then I'll have you for two whole months. I'll come to London with you later this summer. We'll visit Smitty and Viv again."

"I'd love that, and I know they will too. I can't wait to see how much Kathy has grown."

Kathryn wasn't surprised when Smitty stayed in England and married Vivienne after the war or that they had a child soon after that, but she was shocked when they named her Kathy and asked if she'd be her godmother. She agreed, of course, but worried it might be awkward when they all got together. Her fears were unfounded, and she adored seeing Smitty happily in love. Vivienne was the ideal match for him, and their little girl was the perfect blend of her red hair and his dimples.

"I think she's going to be a hellion."

Jenny snorted. "Well, namesake and all, you may be right."

Kathryn tickled her ribs. "Why, I'm as docile as a sleeping kitten."

"Yes, but it took you thirty-three years to get there."

"Well, I'm here now."

"Yes, you are." Jenny was serious again. "Are you happy?"

"Happier than I've ever been."

"Me too."

Kathryn smiled. "Kiss me, Mrs. Hammond."

"My pleasure, Mrs. Ryan."

After their kiss, Kathryn gently stroked Jenny's cheek. "I'll miss you."

"I wish you were coming with me."

"And what would I do while you're attending your incredibly fascinating lectures and the wildly entertaining cocktail parties after?"

Jenny chuckled, noting Kathryn's sarcasm. "Are you saying I'm stuffy and boring?"

"Darling, you are a bright light in the dark halls of science. Cellular biology will never be the same."

"Sweet talker. What are you going to do while I'm away?"

Kathryn swept a lilting hand dramatically across her forehead. "Pine, pine, pine."

Jenny pinched her backside. "Besides that."

"Grocery shopping today. Nan and the kids will be here for the rest of the week."

"I'll love Nan forever for teaching you to cook."

Kathryn laughed. "Then I've got that gig at The Blue Angel in the city this weekend."

"I'm sorry I'll miss that."

"You saw a rehearsal. You won't miss a thing."

"If by a *thing* you mean you dolled up in that gorgeous black and silver number, I beg to differ."

Kathryn grinned. "I think you've got the best view in the house right here."

Jenny parted Kathryn's robe and kissed each breast, leaving traces of lipstick and goosebumps in her wake. "I agree."

"I know what you're doing, and you won't win."

Jenny slipped her hand lower. "Won't I?"

Kathryn closed her eyes with a deep-throated moan at her touch.

Leaving the other in a state of arousal had become a pre-trip tradition in their household, and while Jenny rarely had the last advance, she did get lucky sometimes.

A car horn sounded from the street. Jenny pulled back and tied Kathryn's robe closed with a triumphant grin. "I win."

Kathryn put her arm around her and walked her to the front door. They exchanged I-love-yous and a quick kiss and embrace before Jenny stepped onto the front porch.

"Hey, honey?" Kathryn said through the screened door.

Jenny turned. "Yeah?"

"You know what I'm going to do as soon as you get into that car?"

Jenny stared wide-eyed as Kathryn untied her robe and slipped her hand between her legs.

"I'll be thinking of you every minute. Safe trip." She closed the front door.

Jenny bit her lip and let out an involuntary whimper. "You're going to pay for that when I get home," she called out when she found her voice.

"Can't wait," came Kathryn's muffled sing-song reply through the closed door.

Jenny laughed, but the reminder of Kathryn's steadfast love for her unleashed a profound sense of gratitude and intense devotion. Jenny steadied herself on the handrail. Even after all these years, Kathryn still had the power to leave her breathless. She was her heart. Her home. *Mine.* She fondled the ring on her finger. *Yours.* She was Kathryn's heart and home too. Every stolen glance and lingering touch whispered promises of forever. They'd met in a world on fire, battled both a war and the worst parts of themselves, but their love had emerged triumphant, strengthening them at every turn until they felt unbreakable.

Two quick taps on the bay window beside her revealed Kathryn peering out at her—her robe securely fastened, thank goodness—with her head at an inquisitive tilt.

Jenny's face brightened at the sight of her, as joy quickly replaced everything else. Kathryn winked at her and smiled that smile that always made her melt.

As Jenny pressed her hand to the window, the sun glinted off her ring like a lighthouse beacon showing her the way home. Kathryn did the same from the other side, mirroring the silent pact of their enduring love.

Finis

Thank you, lovely reader, for taking this wild ride with me. I'm so grateful for your support.

If you enjoyed this story, please consider leaving a review. It doesn't have to be long. Even a few words can enhance a book's visibility and help other readers find their next great read. Thank you from the bottom of my little indie author heart.

For updates on my upcoming projects and more, connect with me through the socials or sign up for my newsletter at jeleak.com. Scan the QR code below with your phone's camera app to reach my site.

Psst … there's an exciting announcement on the Also by page!

ACKNOWLEDGMENTS

The end of a series is bittersweet. It's a time to celebrate an accomplishment, but it's also time to say goodbye to characters, who, let's be honest, have been to hell and back. Sometimes writing feels that way too, but thanks to the amazing people around me, I always feel supported and loved.

My first thanks goes to my wife. Thank you, love, for your patience and belief in my story. Your unwavering support is the reason that this series exists. You allow me the space to dream and create, and I can't thank you enough for your sacrifices and understanding. I love you to the moon and back. You mean everything to me.

To Pam Greer, my editor and bestie, I love you dearly. I am forever grateful for your friendship and your willingness to pour over my words ad infinitum with the same enthusiasm as the first day you read them. You were here at the beginning of this journey, and your love, input, encouragement, and tolerance as I whined about "my vision" made me better at my craft. I've learned so much from you, and I would look like an idiot without you. You're aces, doll.

To my dearest friends—my TRIBE—you are all magnificent. You've listened to me blather on about the never-ending "writing project" with nary a complaint and cheered with relief when it was finally done (amen). You've helped me in so many ways and never failed to lift me up when I doubted myself. Thank you from the bottom of my heart. I love you all.

To my extraordinary beta team, your insight and expertise not only make me a better writer, but you made this a better book. To

Ellen, Mayra, Jo, Charlotte, Meichelle, Alaina, Callie, and Jeannie … your input was invaluable. I send you my heartfelt thanks. All of you went above and beyond my expectations and have left an indelible mark on these pages. You can critique me anytime.

To my wonderful ARC readers, thank you for reading, and thank you for your reviews. The success of an indie author depends so much on reviews and word of mouth, and your support means the world to me.

I am blessed with some incredible author friends, and I want to extend a special shout out to my fellow author and pal Jo Havens. Perhaps it's hyperbole to say I couldn't have done this last book without you, but it sure felt that way at times. Thanks for the hours of plot mooching, hand-holding, confidence boosting, and babysitting as I worked my way through the challenging finale. Hugs times infinity.

And last, but certainly not least, I want to thank you, dear reader, for trusting me with your time and your heart. It's not easy to read a series book by book with so much time in between, but you stuck with me through the rollercoaster of emotions and continued to believe in the world I've created. Your patience, enthusiasm, and love for the characters have filled me with joy and inspiration. Your support is everything, and I am grateful for this journey we've shared together. I hope you'll join me in the adventures to come!

ABOUT THE AUTHOR

J.E. Leak was born in Washington, DC, and grew up on the beautiful South Jersey shores of Long Beach Island. An antiques conservator by trade, she has always been fascinated by history and the stories objects could tell if they could speak. When she isn't bingeing 1940s noir films, she's writing or photographing nature on the spring-fed azure rivers of Central Florida. She has an Associate of Science degree in graphic design and is a devoted night owl.

In the Shadow of Victory is the fourth and final novel in the noir inspired Shadow series.

facebook.com/JELeakAuthor
x.com/J_E_Leak
instagram.com/j.e.leak

ALSO BY J.E. LEAK

In the Shadow of the Past (Shadow Series Book 1)
In the Shadow of Love (Shadow Series Book 2)
In the Shadow of Truth (Shadow Series Book 3)

Coming up is an exciting collaboration with award winning author Jo Havens! This novel promises a riveting blend of suspense, romance, and the supernatural.

Teaser

In a ghostly tale set between the roar of the sea and the whisper of the wind, two women breathe life into an old lighthouse and unwittingly find themselves entwined in a timeless curse. When their hearts promise freedom but their passion threatens doom, can they trust their love to save them?

Visit jeleak.com to sign up for my newsletter and receive updates on new releases, works in progress, blog posts, giveaways, and more! Discover Jo Havens at johavens.com.